A BREAKING OF WILLS

By Daniel Fansler

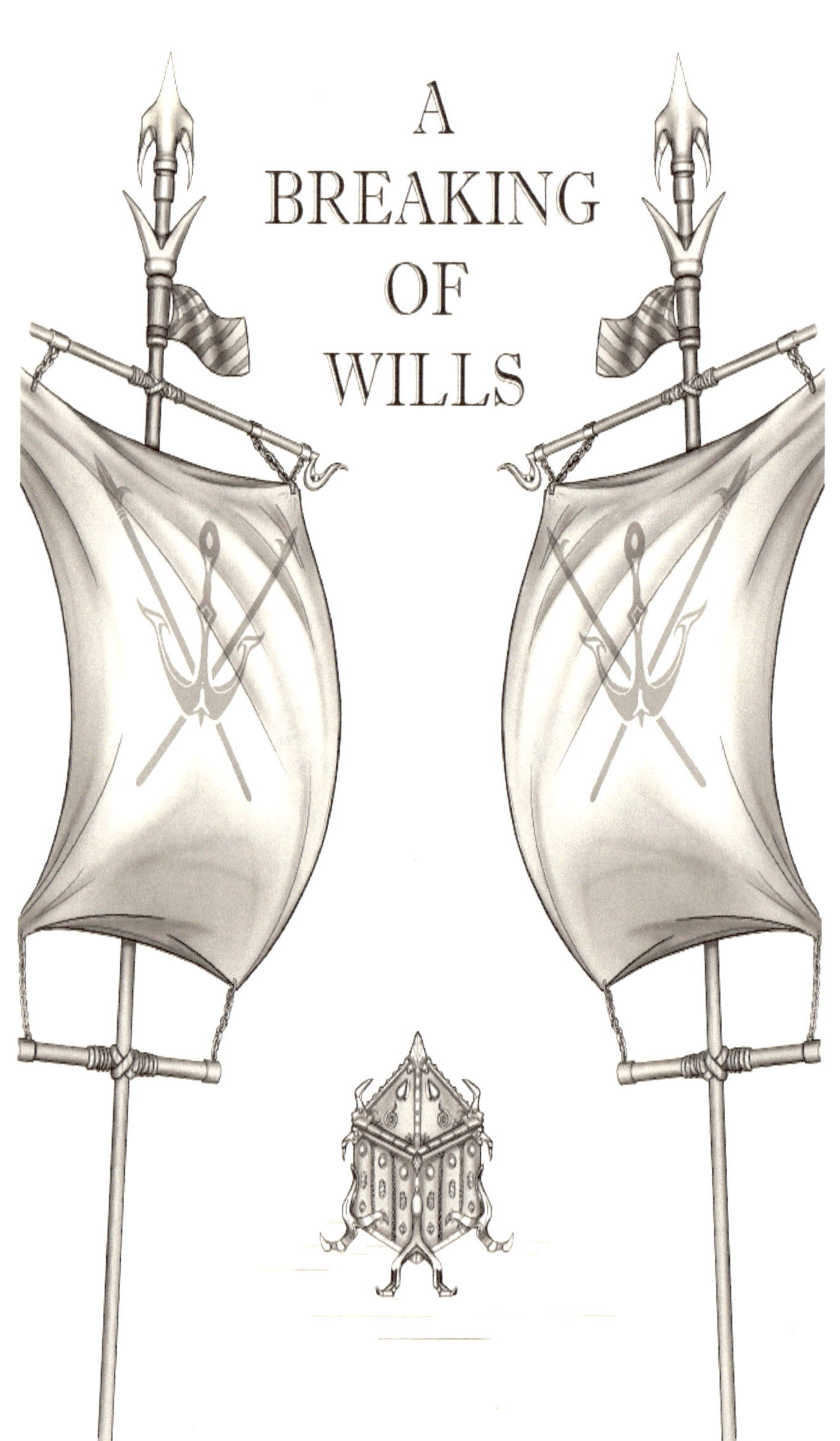
A
BREAKING
OF
WILLS

First Paperback Edition, May 2026

ISBN 979-8-9946183-0-1

Map by Daniel Fansler

Title Page illustration by k_olser

Book Design by Bobooks

Follow me on Instagram and Tiktok
Instagram: @danielfansler.writer
TikTok: @daniel_saurus_rex

For Lauren, my friend, who encouraged me to never stop writing.

Thank you for buying this book, dear reader! As an indie author, I appreciate each and every one of you for supporting me. The best way to support an indie author, aside from buying and reading their book, is by leaving a review on Amazon and/or Goodreads! If you like this book, I would appreciate it so much if you took the time to do so. Thanks!

TABLE OF CONTENTS

ACKNOWLEDGEMENTS

This book almost didn't happen.

Sometime in 2020 I had every chapter in this book outlined and ready to begin writing. But then I got a new phone. Like the boomer I sometimes am, I had written out each chapter's outline in my phone's Notes app, just because that's how I'd always done it. When I changed phones the notes transferred, but they remained unbacked up. Usually, because I don't understand the cloud and, frankly, don't like it, I will just email myself each chapter outline to have as a backup in case I lose or destroy my phone. Well, I didn't do it for this book for some reason and just kept putting it off.

Fast Forward to sometime in 2021 and this new phone I have completely dies. Black screen of death. I try all sorts of troubleshooting, but nothing works and eventually I have to send it to Samsung, who basically resets the phone to get it working again. All my apps and profiles were saved thankfully, but when I went into my Notes app, all of the chapter outlines I had made for Book 4 were gone. Every. Single. One.

Needless to say, at that point, I was ready to throw in the towel. In my mind, those outlines had been perfect. 38 chapters of excellent plot, twists, and character development. And now it was all gone and there was no way I could replicate it. So I went on an unannounced hiatus, which is why there was such a gap between Books 2 and 3. I didn't write, didn't plan, didn't do anything with this story for a full 2-3 years.

Then, thankfully, early in 2024 I decided to go ahead and publish Book 3 (since it had basically been sitting and ready this whole time, anyway) and that renewed the creative spirit I had lost. I promptly remade Book 4's outlines (backing them up this time, as well) and ended up with two extra chapters!

To this day, I know that this version of the book is not the same as the one I had originally planned for in 2020. But, in the end, I think it turned out better. And I hope you enjoy it.

Now, for thanks I want to thank my wife for always supporting me. It's not easy being married to an indie author who has to do all the leg work of this industry by himself; form making Tik Toks (marketing) to spending hours at the computer writing and formatting and editing. It's a lot. Especially with two young children. I am extremely thankful to her for always giving me the time and silence I need to work on these books. I love you, booboo.

Special thanks also goes to my mom, who read the first iteration—the roughest of rough drafts—for this book. As writers, we don't always have those people we can send our first drafts too just because they are so rough and sometimes unreadable. I am thankful to have that someone.

Thanks also goes to my mother-in-law, Marian, and her sister, Aunt Phyllis, who are two of my biggest hype women.

Thank you to Lauren Jeter, my friend, who told me it was okay to take a break after losing all of Book 4's outlines, so long as I came back and continued writing.

Finally, thank you to all of you who follow me and interact with me on TikTok. Pulling the trigger and creating a community on that app has been a crazy experience and I've met so many other indie authors who are undergoing the same struggles I do. It's nice to know I'm not alone.

Anyway, welcome back to the world of Azar!

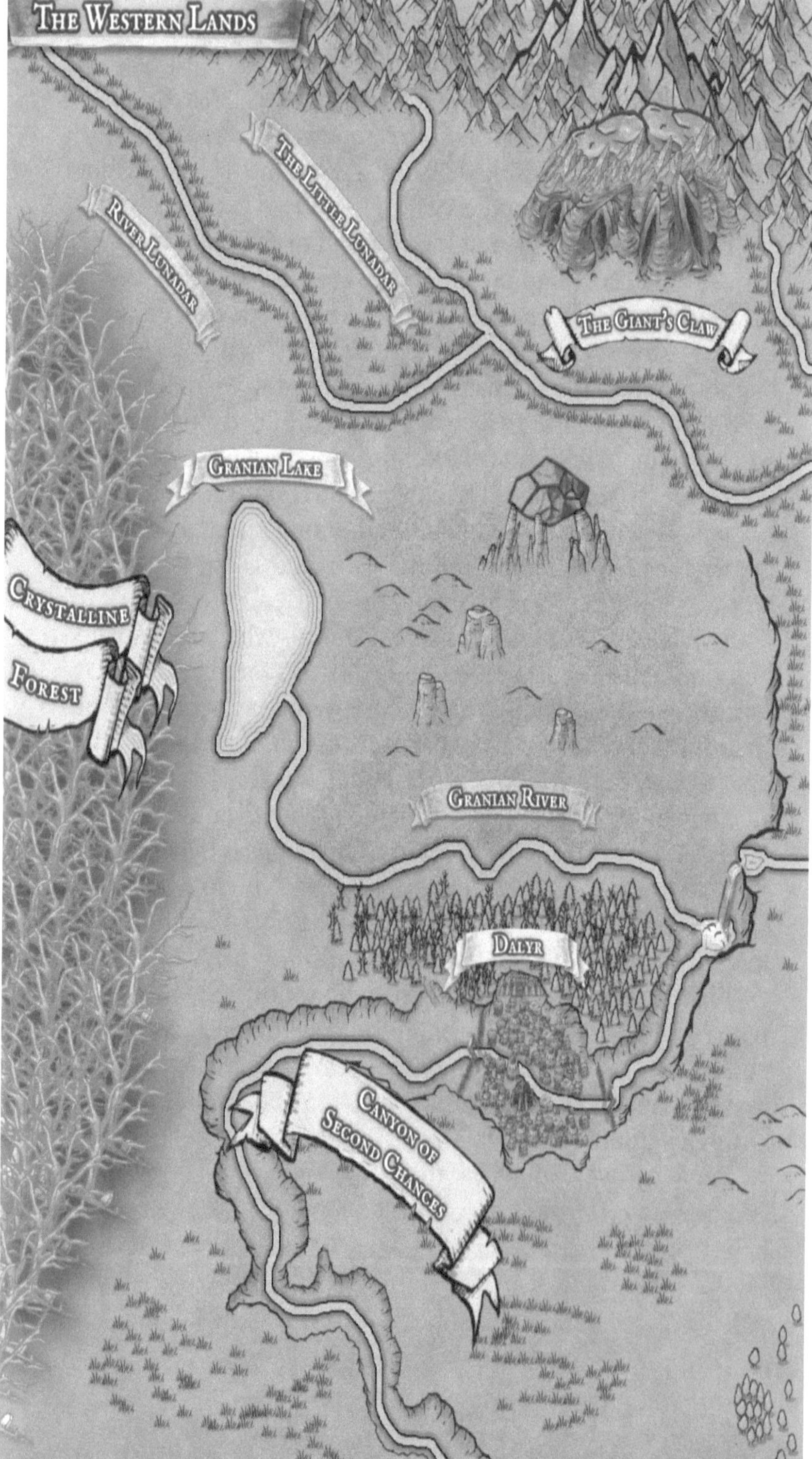
THE WESTERN LANDS
RIVER LUNADAR
THE LITTLE LUNADAR
THE GIANT'S CLAW
GRANIAN LAKE
CRYSTALLINE
FOREST
GRANIAN RIVER
DALYR
CANYON OF
SECOND CHANCES

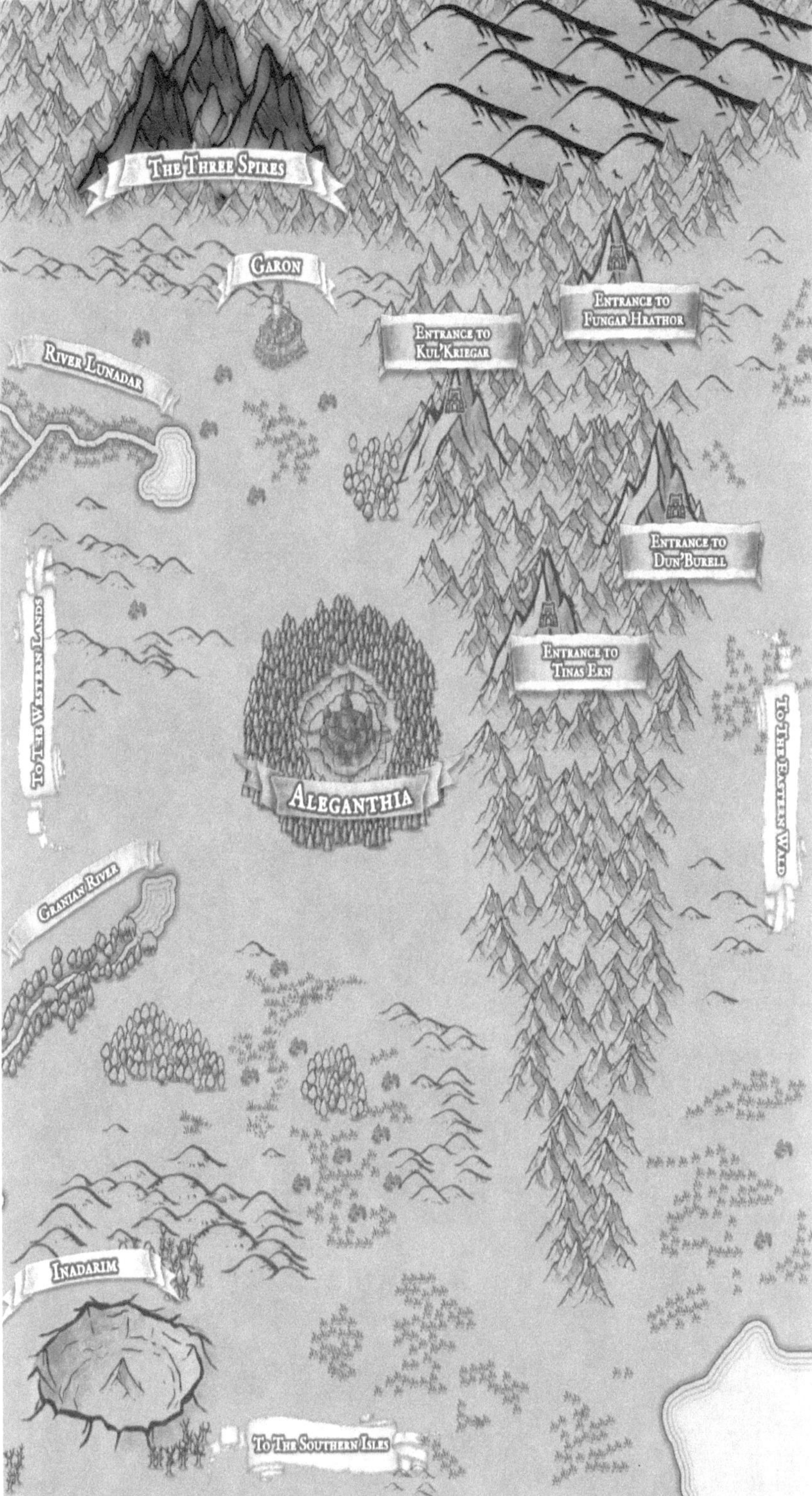
The Three Spires
Garon
River Lunadar
Entrance to Kul'Kriegar
Entrance to Fungar Hrathor
Entrance to Dun'Burell
Entrance to Tinas Ern
To The Western Lands
Aleganthia
To The Eastern Wald
Granian River
Inadarim
To The Southern Isles

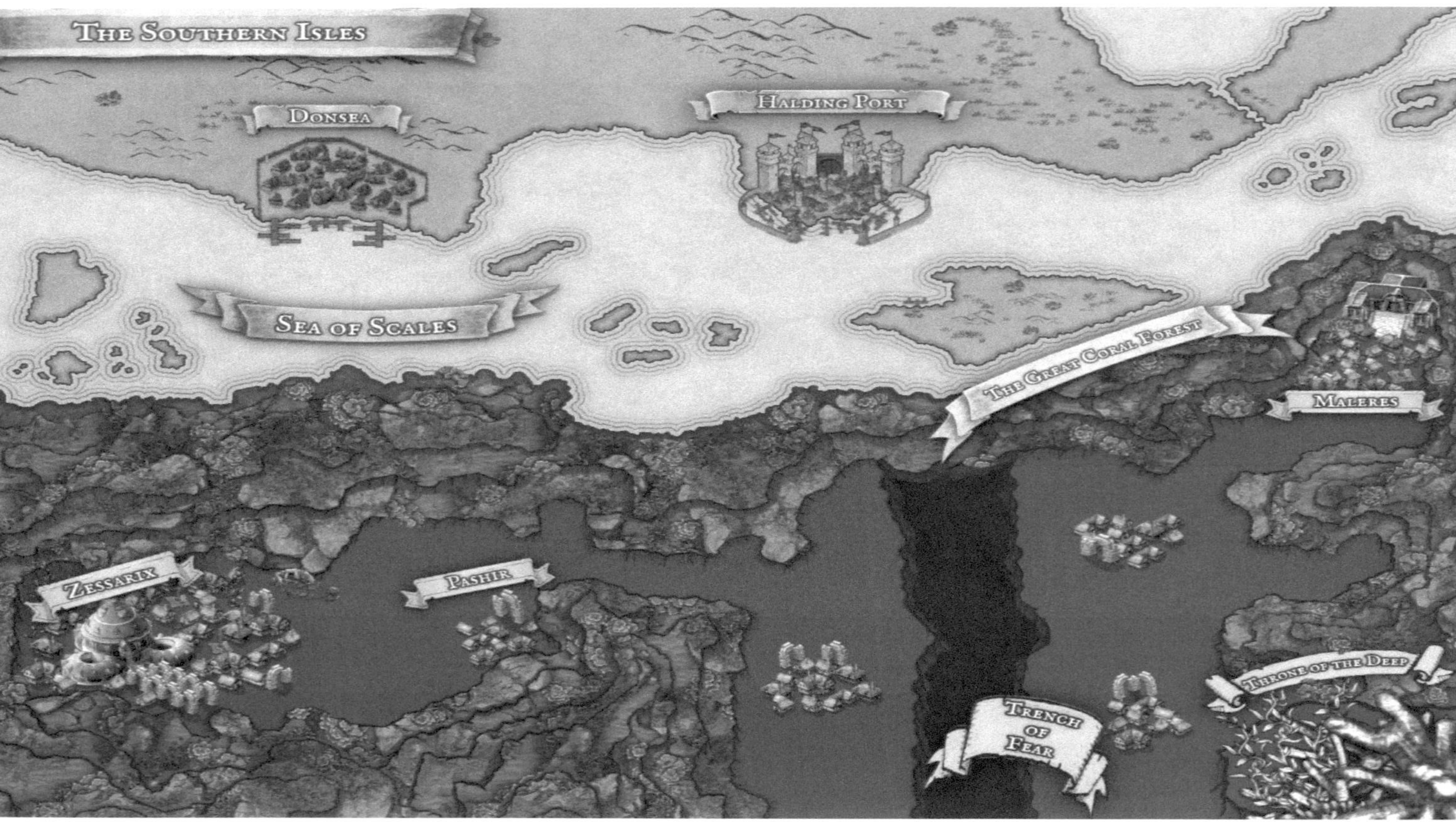
THE SOUTHERN ISLES
DONSEA
HALDING PORT
SEA OF SCALES
THE GREAT CORAL FOREST
MALERES
ZESSARIX
PASHIR
TRENCH OF FEAR
THRONE OF THE DEEP

READ WHAT PEOPLE HAVE BEEN SAYING ABOUT *THE LOST KING*

"Daniel Fansler's debut novel is a sprawling adventure in the Tolkien tradition with satisfying new twists to keep the journey fresh. . . readers will want to follow this band of warriors for pages to come."
– John McDermott, Author of *The Last Spirits of Manhattan*

"In *The Lost King*, Fansler takes the trope of the hero's journey and turns it on its head . . . Fans of worldbuilding will delight."
--Lauren Jeter, author of "Lizard Light," *2020 Crab Creek Review Poetry Prize* semifinalist

LIFTING THE SIEGE

"In this sequel to *The Lost King*, Fansler reminds us of his ability to flawlessly weave together war and wonder. He. . . promis[es] to leave reader again awestruck by the beauty of his world even when all hope seems lost."
--Lauren Jeter, author of "Lizard Light"

"*Lifting the Siege* keeps you guessing—and reading!"
--Kelly Schorn, author of *Year 01*

"Reminds me of the fiction books I loved when I was younger."
--Austin Reichert, Amazon customer

"Never a dull moment."
--Ganonslayer, Amazon customer

ACOLYTES

"It kept me on the edge of my seat and I couldn't put it down."
--Cindy V, Amazon customer

"This third book in the series is the most intense yet . . . Fantasy elements are excellent."
--Michael, Amazon customer

"Everything was extremely interesting and I cannot wait for the next book."
--Jordan Encee, Author of *Devil's Spider*

"This installment of The Chronicles of the First Gods is my favorite so far . . . something for everyone – intrigue, relationship development, action, and lots [of] lore and world building."
--Susan S, Amazon customer

OTHER WORKS BY DANIEL FANSLER

THE LOST KING (BOOK 1)

LIFTING THE SIEGE (BOOK 2)

ACOLYTES (BOOK 3)

A LONGSHIP EULOGY

CHAPTER ONE

A lone, hooded figure peered over the edge of a rocky outcrop extending out past the mountain face. Far below, lines upon lines of tents spread out along the foothills of the Northern Mountains. From their vantage point, the figure could even make out movement within the camp. And there was a lot of it. Lines of warriors of various races gathered together, preparing to move out.

A battle was coming, and the crows knew it. Layers of the black avians circled lazily overhead like a dark cloud, patiently waiting for their chance to gorge.

The figure shuffled back from the edge, pushing themselves back to their feet and making their way back up the mountain path where a staggered line of similarly clad companions waited.

"What did you see, Victria?"

Victria Bloodletter pulled back her hood, if only to let the cold mountain air cool her face for a moment from the thick, stuffy cowl she'd been wearing. She regarded the one who had called out to her with cool, blood-red eyes and a mischievous smirk, revealing sharp fangs as a breeze played with her long, silver hair; tell-tale signs that she was one of the viatari.

"I thought we weren't using names here, Tera."

Tera pulled back her own hood, revealing a voluminous mess of curly, blonde hair and a teasing smile. "We aren't supposed to show our faces here either, dear, now are we?"

Victria shrugged but conceded the point. "Our forces are preparing to move out. We'll have our distraction."

"Hopefully it will be enough."

"Enough of thisss banter," another figure hissed. By the emphasis of his speech, it was obvious this was one of the vashi, a race whose origin was of the Southern Seas, far from the mountains they now traversed. "Our ssscaled bodiesss are not accustomed to being outside of water for sssuch long periodsss of time. We must find thisss rumored lake asss sssoon asss possible. I don't know how much more of thisss we can endure."

A chorus of approving hisses came from the other vashi in the party.

Tera conceded the point. "Right you are, Cotovas. Let's move on."

The line of hooded figures continued making their way up the mountain. Lightning flashed in the distance.

Adjacent to their current path loomed the Three Spires. These three peaks were well-known among dwarves as the tallest and most perilous in Azar. On a cloudless day, the peaks reached impossibly high, scraping into the blue sky. Now, however, their immense size was well-covered by a thick blanket of rolling black clouds. The sight alone was enough to make the dwarves in the party shiver. They had heard horror stories of this place since they were mewling for their mother's breast.

"Why are we here again?" One of the dwarves, an Enurg'en, muttered. "It's mad enough that Felix wishes ta assault this place, but ta send out a small raiding party ta try and infiltrate these peaks because of a burrower rumor—"

"No rumor," another member grunted, his hunched back prominent even under his cloak. "Burrowers live here once. We know of waters within Three Spires through stories told from father to son for long time. Same way we know of hot springs on mountain. We will find."

"So ye say."

"Quiet," another dwarf spoke with a note of finality. Despite his cowled head, a thick, gray beard, separated into three separate braids with golden bands looped around each one, spilled out. Thuradin Stonebeard stroked one of these braids. He understood the Enurg'en's trepidation, but it did no good to voice such sentiments and spook the others. Not when they were in the middle of such an important task.

"The burrowers clearly know more about this place than we do. King Dunkell and Felix were convinced enough ta approve this expedition. That should be enough for ye."

"I dunno, Thuradin," another dwarf spoke up, one Thuradin certainly didn't care for. "Who cares if there's wa'er in the Three Spires and an 'ot spring on this'n. How is this helpin' our side? Personally, I'd rather get me blades wet. Much simpler that way."

"I have no doubt of that, assassin," Thuradin sighed. "Were ye nae listening at the briefing?"

Morteth Shadowmeld shrugged. Thuradin could imagine the smug look on his face from under his hood. "I may 'ave 'ad other thoughts on me mind."

Thuradin rolled his eyes. "Ta make it simple for ye, then.

The vashi have the ability ta move from one body of water ta another instantly. We find the hot springs, we *liquefact* inta the Three Spires, we find The First One's lost brother, we get out, mission complete."

"Incredible! A plan so simple, even a burrower could do it. I'm sure we'll nae run inta any enemy forces while we prance 'round their 'eadquarters." Morteth clapped his hands, "No offense ta ye, friend," he added when one of the burrowers glared back at him.

"Enough chatter," Natiari Lunglow, another viatari, called out from the front. "We need to focus on the task at hand."

Felix had given them three days to find the hot springs and already two had been spent searching with no result. On this third day, Felix intended to march forth and engage The Turned One's and Creature's forces on the presumption that their infiltration of the Three Spires was underway. Already, as Victria had reported, the army was on the move. Thuradin was glad for the action. It had been three months since the siege began and the days had gone by slowly as each one had been filled almost exclusively with mundane tasks to maintain their camp. And the whole time, The First One's brother had been held under the corrupting powers of his fallen siblings. There was no telling how far the acolyte's mental state and will had deteriorated during his captivity. They couldn't even be sure he was still trying to resist.

Time was not their friend.

And so, they trudged on.

The path they were on was not overly difficult to traverse. The mountain was barren of any vegetation. The only obstacles in their path proved to be loose rocks and boulders, as well as the ever-present fear of a rockslide. Thuradin had expected to run into some grattles, giant lizards that typically lived on the mountains, but the size of their party appeared to be enough to dissuade any potential attack from the predators.

Layers of mist slowly rose ahead of them. A burrower in their group named Brap sniffed the air. He threw back his hood and turned to face them, his cracked lips curving into a gloating smile.

"We arrive."

As they crested the next rise in the land they saw a vale below with numerous pockets of water spread throughout. Steam continuously rose from them, slowly mixing together to create a thin blanket of mist over the land. Vegetation remained sparse, but moss at least grew on the wet stones that encircled each pool, making the trail slippery as they all carefully made their way toward the largest one at the center of the vale.

The dwarves and burrowers in the party split up and formed a perimeter around the spring, their eyes scanning the surrounding peaks, weapons in hand. If anyone dared approach, they would encounter a stiff resistance.

Meanwhile, within the perimeter, eleven members of the party prepared for an impossible but vital mission: to retrieve the acolyte of the Eastern Wald.

Seven months ago several parties were sent out from the viatari city of Aleganthia to go and retrieve three brothers of The First One. These acolytes, like The First One, were beings of ancient origin, handcrafted by the First Gods themselves. There were six total, scattered across Azar, with the sole purpose of maintaining order in the world when the First Gods departed. For a time, each acolyte, located in a different wonder of the world, worked in harmony to accomplish this task. But as time went on, corruption seeped into the consciousness of one, and then another.

The Turned One and Go'al, who later became known as the Creature, betrayed their brethren and their purpose, choosing instead to steer Azar toward a path of chaos and ultimate destruction. The First One, along with his remaining brothers, fought the two fallen acolytes into a deep slumber that lasted millennia. And as the acolytes slept and their existence faded even from legend, the remaining denizens of Azar flourished.

But the acolytes did not sleep forever. And when they awoke, their war resumed.

Gathering all the remaining acolytes together had been Felix's goal. With their combined strength, these ancient beings presented the best chance for ending this war and destroying the corrupted acolytes. But while they had managed to collect two of The First One's brothers, the party they had sent into the Eastern Wald had fallen to The Turned One's forces and the acolyte there was captured by the enemy.

But now, with the enemy about to be preoccupied defending their hold on the Spires, an opportunity existed for them to rescue the captured acolyte. This was their chance to snatch back hope from the jaws of defeat. This was their chance to save the world.

After all, if they failed here, it would only be a matter of time before Veliris, too, fell to his sister's corruption. Then, all hope would be lost. There would be no second chance for victory. Azar would fall into chaos.

Thuradin looked at each and every member who was about to join him on this critical task. They all understood the importance. Determination was chiseled into their faces. They each removed their cloaks and stepped into the hot spring, the vashi leading the way and sighing with relief as water lapped against their scaled bodies. They moved toward the center of the pool, waiting for their companions to join them.

The others followed, trudging through the shallow water and splitting into pairs of four. Thuradin, Morteth, an Enurg'en named Erdeth Steinhew, and Tera grabbed hold of one of the waterseers known as Meri. Victria, Natiari, Madira Starglow, and Tessa Shadoweaver gathered around Cotovas and did the same. The remaining waterseer, a vashi named Varaxir, stood alone. But that was for the better. His job would be to liquefact with the acolyte, once they retrieved him. There was no need to burden him with anyone else.

Each of them shared a final glance, steeling themselves for what was to come. Thuradin locked eyes with Cotovas and nodded.

"Hold on tight everyone," the vashi warned. "Meri, Varaxir, and I will clear the cavern if necessary while you recover from the liquefaction. But let usss hope there isss no one waiting for usss."

One moment, half of Thuradin's body was submerged in hot water that nonetheless felt soothing. Then, his breath caught. His body felt loose, separated, as if it could be thrown against a wall and splatter into a million pieces. A strange pulling sensation came from his stomach. The next second, his body was back to normal, though his lower half now stood in frigid water. His heart raced.

He let go of Meri not by choice but because his limbs failed him. His face went under, which helped reenergize him as cold needles pricked every inch of exposed skin. He pushed up, bringing his face back above the surface, and sputtered. Groaning, he forced himself onto his feet and tried to catch his breath. He gripped his knees firmly, leaning into them to keep himself balanced.

Finally, his head stopped spinning and he could stand upright. He waded his way out of the underground pool. And they were certainly underground; though, by ensconced torches attached to several stalagmites scattered throughout the cavern, they weren't alone here.

Thuradin looked over his shoulder and saw that the others were having just as difficult a time recovering from the vashi method of travel as he did, even the viatari who had gone through it before.

"That feeling never gets better," Victria gulped in a huge breath.

They made their way out of the pool and onto a small stone strand. Ahead of them was a gaping tunnel, a stairway carved out of the stone leading upwards.

Once everyone had shaken off their disorientation, they began to climb the steps, weapons in hand, making sure to keep their footfalls light and silent. The vashi remained in the pools to ensure the cavern stayed under their control so that when it came time to make their escape, there would be little issue.

The stairway was short and led into a wide three-way junction of tunnel that wound and curved away from them deeper into the mountain on either side. Torches lined the walls, allowing for some visibility, but also creating dancing shadows everywhere. This was good. There would be no shortage of places for them to keep a low profile.

Tera, who led them, made a few small gestures with her hand once she poked out of the stairway to see if they should expect any problems. She pointed to the right and led them forward.

They traveled silently from shadow to shadow. No words were said, as their voices would surely echo and carry through the whole tunnel system. Instead, Tera continued to communicate with her hands, and while Thuradin and the others weren't too familiar with what each gesture meant, they knew enough to get the gist of what she wanted.

As they continued through the tunnel, they passed minor depressions along the wall, doorways carved into the stone. Unsure of where the lost acolyte might be hidden, they decided to check each one. They barged through, silently, but with enough ferocity to catch any potential enemies off guard.

But they met no one.

That was as it should be, too, Thuradin thought. If anything, they should only have to deal with a few minor patrols as they made their way deeper into the mountains. The majority of The Turned One's forces would have emptied out of the Three Spires to do battle with Felix.

While there were no enemies in these rooms, they didn't find the captured acolyte either. Instead, they discovered a number of storerooms, many empty, but some still filled with racks of lethally sharp spears, swords, cudgels, axes, and many other kinds of weaponry. A mixture of human and burrower craftsmanship reflected off the steel.

A few rooms held empty rows of beds and straw mats. Another was for storage and held a vast array of foodstuffs. Thuradin thought they should burn these supplies, which would devastate the enemy's ability to withstand a long siege, but that was not their main objective, and they couldn't risk being discovered before finding The First One's brother.

Perhaps on the way back, then.

They discovered more storage rooms as they continued on. Most held the same items as before, though more rooms were now also laden with treasures. One in particular caught Thuradin's eye. Inside were shelves upon shelves of gems, both cut and uncut, bars of precious metals, some strange items made of wood or straw or dried grass whose purpose Thuradin couldn't identify and a strange scepter with a round, red orb held at one end by a metal claw shaped like that of an eagle's.

He couldn't spend too much time inspecting the strange scepter, however, as his companions quickly cleared the room. Tera motioned for them to move on.

Within their second hour of searching, they found a side passage that dug deeply into the tunnel wall. It was just wide enough for them to pass through one by one. There was no telling what was on the other side, but Tera thought it was inconspicuous enough to warrant a search, and so she motioned for them to follow her through.

The walls weren't so close together that they hugged Thuradin as he moved along, but there was certainly not enough space for him to move as freely as he would have liked in the event of a fight. Still, he thought, such a disadvantage would apply to their enemies as well.

It didn't take long for them all to reach the other side. A sizeable cavern spread out before them with a high-reaching ceiling. Small stalactites grew in bunches high above, barely visible by the few torches that were placed around the cavern's perimeter. The light was dim, but there was still enough to make out a triangular chest sitting in the middle of the space.

They approached cautiously. This chest *could* be the artifact of The First One's brother, but there was only one way to know for sure.

Now close enough for a better look, Thuradin saw that the chest was made of jade, the sickly green hue of the stone unmistakable. Lines of colorful gems decorated the edges of each triangular face in repeating patterns of jasper, citrine, and carnelian. The colors were muted under the dim torchlight, but the dwarf was sure that if the chest were presented to him under the sun, his breath would be taken away by its beauty.

Though they were close enough to touch it now, no reaction came from within. With other acolytes, they had a tendency to show off their flare by releasing colorful, transparent tendrils, leaving all those around them awestruck. If this was the acolyte they were meant to find, he didn't seem to have the same style.

"Veliris?" Tera whispered. "Veliris, is that you? You must tell us, if so. We've come to rescue you. Your brother, The First One, sent us."

Slowly, like a chick coming out of its egg, a single blue tendril poked out of the chest and regarded each member of their party.

"I sense truthfulness in your words, human," the acolyte said. His voice was ancient, just like his brothers, but there was a layer of pain mixed with every word he spoke. No doubt, his siblings' attempts to break him during his captivity had not been lighthearted. "If my brother has sent you as you claim, you must take me from this cursed place. And quickly!"

Victria and Natiari unfurled a litter upon which they could place Veliris, making it easier to carry him. Erdeth dug his hands into the stone floor and muttered in Ancient Dwarvish, using his powers as an Enurg'en to detect any hidden wards or unseen traps that might keep them from moving the acolyte from his platform. If there were any, he would be able to nullify them.

"Don't worry," Tera whispered encouragingly, "You won't have to be here much longer."

"You do not understand," Veliris groaned, more tendrils poking out of his chest. Their ethereal blue glow brightened the cavern slightly, lighting their faces. "My sister knows you are here. She is nearby. She wanted you to come. I have been shielding your presence from her. But my strength wanes. We must leave this place immediately, or none of us will escape these mountains alive."

CHAPTER TWO

As Tera and the viatari busied themselves with moving Veliris onto the litter they had brought and securing him with leather straps, Thuradin took some time to further inspect the cavern. There didn't appear to be anything special about this place on its surface. Veliris seemed to think they were in imminent danger, that they would soon be dis-covered. But as far as he could tell, there was only the one passage they had taken leading into this cavern. And they could defend that easily enough if they had to.

He walked along the walls, brushing his fingers against the stone, wondering if there was some manner of trap door or hidden groove where enemies could pour in from. He had inspected nearly half the circumference of the cavern when he stopped, his heart skipping a beat. But he quickly relaxed. Before him, hidden in the shadows between torches, was a small tunnel—a crack in the wall, really. Barely perceptible. If not for his trained dwarven eyes, he would have missed it entirely.

He drew closer. The passage appeared wide and tall enough

to allow him through with ease, but not much else. If he had to guess, this was part of the mountain's ventilation system, much like what the dwarves had in their own kingdom, to keep fresh air from the outside world constantly moving between caverns and tunnels. Which meant, if he was right, this hole could lead him into another delve.

Thuradin glanced behind him. The viatari were still busy tying down Veliris. There was enough time for him to take a quick jaunt through to see what was on the other side without anyone ever knowing he was gone.

"Well, are ye goin' in or wha'?"

Thuradin jumped back in alarm. Leaning up against the wall right next to the passage was Morteth. His arms were crossed, a knowing glint in his dark eyes.

"I know curiosi'y is burnin' inside ye, commander. Shall we take a quick peek?"

"I'd rather go alone," Thuradin replied stiffly.

"Nonsense!" Morteth waved his hands in an exaggerated manner. "Ye should always 'ave somebody ta watch yer back when explorin' new places." With that, the assassin entered the passage, melting into the darkness.

Thuradin hesitated, but Morteth was right. Something inside him was urging him to go through, as if he *had* to know what was on the other side.

He went in.

The passage was as dark as expected. He made his way forward slowly, moving his hands along the walls on either side and ahead of him so he wouldn't be rudely surprised by any low-hanging rocks.

Before long, a faint light appeared ahead. The single speck flickered, as if coming from a flame. The silhouette of a small figure sat crouched, still as stone, just before the exit. Thuradin crouched beside the dwarven assassin.

The two dwarves kept silent as they observed their new surroundings. Thuradin's heart hammered mercilessly. He was sure it was audible to anyone nearby. The cavern they had stumbled upon was immense. It went on for as far as the eye could see. Torches with dancing purple flames lined the wall. Individually, their light was dim, but there were so many here that a steady purple glow filled the whole area.

Yet it wasn't these strange torches that made Thuradin catch his breath. It was what was transpiring inside, only a stone's throw from where he and Morteth sat hidden.

Two rectangular chests sat on a multi-tiered, elevated stone platform: one the color of bronze, and the other black as night. An oppressive aura emanated from both as tendrils of purple and black swayed calmly, intertwining with each other. The Creature and The Turned One together. The sight sent a violent shiver down the old dwarf's spine. Cold sweat formed on his brow.

Standing before the two corrupted acolytes were four figures. Two humans, one a vashi, and the last was of an unfamiliar race.

Despite only having met the vashi recently himself, Thuradin recognized the one here from Victria's tales of her time in the Sea of Scales. He had been a thorn in her side, trying to covertly bring the vashi into the corrupted acolytes' fold. In the end, he had failed, but had managed to escape before Victria could capture or kill him. And now, here he was. The unique set of black scales that made up the vashi's whole body along with his flowing green hair left little doubt that this was Koranam, cousin to the Supreme Overseer.

The two humans were unfamiliar and looked as different from each other as night and day. One was tall and well-built, with long black hair that was tied back in a ponytail. A long scimitar hung from his hip. He looked like he knew war, perhaps reveled in it.

The other wore a long silk robe the color of the sky on a sunny day. A cloak of magenta and white wrapped around his shoulders with a large hood that was, at the moment, pulled back. Thuradin couldn't see any weapons but noticed that he carried a long staff with a large, glowing red orb attached to the end. His face and head were bare of hair save for some wispy blonde strands hanging from his scalp. A strange violet glow seemed to come from his eyes.

The two men stepped forward and knelt before the acolytes. Their voices carried in the stone room, reaching the dwarves' ears with ease.

"Esteemed acolytes," the man with the scimitar said. "I am Drake and have come here as you bid me in my dreams. I have considered all that you offered me and, while the rewards are tempting, it is reward enough for me to lead your armies and help usher this world into its next inevitable era. I would love nothing more than to see your vision become reality."

A sweet voice, soft yet laced with poison, came from The Turned One's artifact. "It has become clear to me that I lack the tactical ability to lead mortals in the field of battle—perhaps my only shortcoming. I happily accept you as my servant and am eager to watch your performance on the field."

Drake cracked a smile. "Worry not, my master. Already I have set numerous traps and surprises for our viatari friends. They will find themselves hard-pressed to break through our defenses. The cost for this blatant attack on our headquarters will be severe."

"Very good."

Now the robed man spoke, his voice meek and monotone

as if he were in a trance.

"Acolytes, your cause is noble. Know that for many years, I, Jorgon, traveled the entirety of the Northern Mountains and the lands that lie beyond. During my travels, I encountered a spirit of pure energy which allowed me to wield the energies around us in a way that, up until now, was unheard of. The spirit merged with my body and, during that process, granted me a vision. Of all the energies in Azar, the most powerful and natural is chaos. I have since dedicated my life to having this be the sole source of energy in the world. In this, I believe I can aid you in your goals, though my powers are meager compared to yours."

The black tendrils of The Turned One shot out, enveloping Jorgon in a cocoon. The man didn't flinch.

"I find myself intrigued by these powers you speak of. Their source feels . . . familiar. I gladly accept your help as well."

Her tendrils returned to their previous state and the energy-wielder bowed. The humans stepped back, allowing for the third figure among them to step forward—or rather, slither forward.

This unfamiliar being was similar to the vashi in that their bodies were scaled but that was where any similarities ended. While the being's white torso was humanoid, around the hip is where it transformed to more resemble a snake. Two lines of bony spikes protruded along the length of the being's spine. Thuradin thought he could see a cluster of slender tentacles hanging from the chin. By the being's figure, he deduced that this was a female, though if what he saw here was any standard of beauty, he shuddered to think what the males might look like.

She was followed by a large crab-like creature the size of a dwarf. Sharp spines protruded from its joints and various spots around its thick exoskeleton. It moved with an alarming agility that belied its size. Koranam also stepped forward, though he kept his distance from the stranger's pet.

The female bowed as her tail coiled up beneath her. When she spoke, it was with the same hiss the vashi had. Her voice was light yet with a clear sense of malice and authority. This was someone who was accustomed to being obeyed.

"I am Enishar, leader of the darinsha. We have heard your whispersss from our lonely watersss in the Northern Seasss and have decided asss a people to join you, if you would have usss. We understand our cousinsss, the vashi, have joined with your enemiesss. It would be our pleasure to bring war to their watersss, asss we did centuriesss ago, to weaken their resolve. I only ask, onccce the war isss won, that dominion of the Sea of Scalesss be given to my people, that we may rule the entirety of the ocean asss Oceausss alwaysss intended."

"I object to this," Koranam seethed. "The Sea of Scales was already promised to me for my services."

Enishar struck the vashi with the back of her bony hand. Despite her slender figure, it was clear she had an abundance of strength.

"How dare you ssspeak out of turn, whelp. I should ssset my kush on you for sssuch an outburst."

The kush clacked its spiny claws in gleeful anticipation. Koranam hissed and drew two blades from the sheathes strapped to his back. The blades curved in a crescent shape, running from his knuckles to his elbow.

A soft chuckle came from The Turned One, bringing everyone's attention back to her.

"It is true I promised you the Sea of Scales, Koranam, but the services you offered remain unfulfilled. Did you not fail to turn your people to our cause? Were you not forced to escape them and come to us for our protection instead?"

"Yes, but I—"

"You will hold your tongue. The only reason you draw breath now is because I still have some need of you. Sadly, Enishar, because of that, I will have to ask you not to kill this poor fool. His knowledge of the vashi's defenses and capabilities will no doubt be invaluable when you launch your invasion against them."

Enishar's bloodshot eyes widened hungrily, "Then. . ."

"Yes," The Turned One purred. "I accept your people's allegiance and shall grant them my blessing. You may proceed with your preparations. Those fish-men have proven to be more of an annoyance than they're worth. In fact, as I understand it, your plans fit perfectly with Jorgon's project as well, is this not so?"

"Indeed," Jorgan mused. "Once the humans fall into line, the seas will be open for the taking."

"Sister, . . ." the Creature's ancient voice reverberated through the cavern. "Do you not sense them?"

Black and purple tendrils converged and there was silence. Whatever was being discussed was only for the corrupted acolytes to know. Thuradin and Morteth shared a look, their faces ashen. What they had stumbled upon was a treasure trove of information. Felix had to know about this. Everyone had to know about this. But if they didn't escape from here, no one would ever know until it was too late.

The Turned One's sweet voice once more filled the dark space.

"My brother has been more attentive than I have, it would seem. We have guests."

Thuradin's breath caught as he looked back into the cavern

and saw four pairs of eyes staring straight back at him.

"Time ta go," Morteth huffed as he scurried back the way they came. Thuradin was right behind him and not a moment too soon. Enishar uncoiled herself and slithered over to where they had been hiding with alarming speed. Thankfully, the passage proved too narrow for her. She reached for them with a clawed hand but could fit nothing else inside. Her claws fell short. She pulled back, glaring at the two dwarves as they disappeared.

Thuradin and Morteth hurried back to the previous cavern. By the time they returned, the viatari had finally finished securing Veliris to the litter and were now lifting him, ready to depart.

Victria saw them running back to join them. "Where have you two been?"

"No time," Thuradin said breathlessly, his mind still spinning from what he had witnessed. "Trouble coming. We need ta leave *now.*"

"The dwarf is correct," Veliris strained to say. "I am no longer able to cloak your presence. My siblings know you are here. They are coming."

"To hell with the shadows, then," Tera said urgently. "Weapons out. We move quickly and stick together. With any luck, we'll reach the pools before they can gather a large enough force to stop us."

"What about the supply stores we saw on the way here?" Natiari asked. "We need to destroy them."

"There's no time," Tera drew two curved daggers from her boots and twirled them expertly between her fingers. "We can't be caught here. We'll have to leave them untouched. Our main objective right now is to escape and nothing else. Understood?"

Everyone nodded.

"Good, then let's go."

Tera led them back to the passage they had entered from. It was a small struggle to force Veliris through the narrow gap on a litter but with everyone's help they managed it.

Once the last of them had made their exit, they ran back through the tunnels making for the pools. The rooms they had so meticulously searched before now passed by in a blur as they ran out in the open. A single temptation that Thuradin should take a torch to at least one storeroom passed through his mind briefly, but he shook it off. Now was not the time for heroics.

Ahead of them, humanoid shadows stretched out against the curvature of the wall. As soon as they rounded the corner they came upon a small patrol of corrupted humans and burrowers. The patrol, surprised by their sudden appearance, could do nothing as Tera slid her blades first through one burrower, then the other. Victria took care of the humans, bashing their heads in against the tunnel wall with a startling ferocity.

They continued on for a while longer but stopped suddenly when a chorus of voices reached their ears.

They listened, their chests heaving. Cheering reverberated along the stone walls, a constant holler of excitement for the hunt. The Turned One had unleashed her forces. Thuradin had a feeling whoever was after them now would be led by none other than Drake, as well. The man had seemed so confident in his abilities, despite being only human. He didn't want to stick around to see if that confidence was warranted.

"They're only behind us," Tera surmised. "The way ahead should still be clear. They shouldn't be able to catch up, but we can waste no more time. Keep running."

Again they were off. As they ran, Thuradin occasionally glanced over his shoulder. He expected to see a horde of The Turned One's corrupted warriors emerge from the shadows behind them any second. Perhaps a few darimun would be among them. So far, there was no sign of their pursuers, except that their yelling was getting louder.

Finally, they reached the tunnel junction and the stairway that led to the underground pools. They hurried down them, bringing Veliris to the front so that he could be de-livered to Varaxir for immediate liquefaction.

As they sprinted from the last stone step into the cavern, the vashi poked their heads out from the water and swam to shore.

"The enemy is coming. We need to go," Tessa explained as she and Madira brought Veliris forward, setting him down by the water. They quickly undid the leather straps securing him and then let the waterseer grab hold. Varaxir dragged the artifact a few inches into the water so that at least a quarter of it was submerged, then, within the blink of an eye, he and Veliris were gone.

Success.

A triumphant laugh sprang from Thuradin. They had accomplished what few had believed was even possible. And they had suffered no casualties. Now all they had to do was escape themselves, make their way back to camp, and it would all be behind them.

Thuradin heard a clash of steel coming from the stairs. Turning, he saw Victria and Natiari guarding the cavern entrance. Already, a few burrowers and humans were making their way down only to be felled by the viatari's sharp blades. They were the quicker ones, Thuradin guessed, and if they were already here, the main force couldn't be far behind.

"Let's go!" Tera shouted.

She, Thuradin, Erdath, and Morteth waded into the water and grabbed hold of Meri. Once his grip was secure, Thuradin looked one last time back at the cavern entrance. Victria and her viatari companions disengaged and rushed for the water. A growing number of enemies poured in from the stairway and gave chase.

Behind them, stepping calmly down the stone steps came a man with a long scimitar in hand. Thuradin recognized him immediately. Drake. The human who had sworn fealty to the corrupted acolytes, not out of some desire for reward or from coercion, but by his own will. A crooked smile lined his fair features as he pulled his free arm back and shot it out as if reaching for them.

There was a flash of metal. Thuradin felt the air shift around him as something flew past. A sickening squelch came from behind. A grunt and a long, drawn-out sigh. The water around them turned murky and red.

Victria's voice called out in distress. "Cotovas!"

Then, Thuradin blinked. And he was back in the hot springs. His feet touched solid ground. Hot water lapped at his waist, washing stains of red from his armor.

The temperature of the springs may have been hot, but Thuradin felt cold. That was all he felt. Not even the effects of liquefaction could distract him enough as it slowly dawned on him what had just happened. He looked over his shoulder, hoping to see Victria and the others appear suddenly in the water.

But no one came and the spring remained still.

CHAPTER THREE

Victria stared ahead in disbelief as she tried to process what just happened.

She and Natiari had been guarding the cavern entrance, a mound of corpses piling up at their feet. A glance over her shoulder told them that Veliris had been successfully rescued from the Three Spires and now it was their turn to leave. Already, Tessa and Madira were clutching onto Cotovas, who was now waiting for her and Natiari to get to him so he could liquefact them all out. The rest hung onto Meri.

"Let's go," she had said to Natiari. The two viatari kicked back their current opponents with force, knocking them into their own reinforcements. Then, they turned and ran.

It was a short distance from the stone steps to the water's edge. Within a minute they would be clutching onto Cotovas and making their escape. But then everything had gone wrong.

Something flew over Victria's shoulder, making her flinch and stop in her tracks. It was only a brief pause, but before she could get moving again, a horrifying picture unfolded before her. Cotovas, eyes wide and in shock, stared down at his chest where the short hilt of a dagger stuck out. He gasped and stumbled, gripping the hilt as if to pull it out, but that was all he could do. A sigh escaped his lips and his eyes rolled back as he fell into the pool and floated in place, streams of red mixing in with the water.

It was at this point that Victria's mind had turned numb.

"Cotovas!" She cried.

She was aware enough to recognize that Meri had escaped with her charges, leaving the viatari without a means to do the same.

Natiari pulled on her arm, bringing her back to the present.

"Come on, Victria, we have to hide!"

But there was no hiding. The enemy had already seen them. They would come for them, surround them, kill them, butcher them. There was no escape. They were trapped here, vastly outnumbered and alone.

Tessa and Madira splashed through the pool, heading for one of the stone pillars that formed from the ceiling and reached into the water. Natiari pulled Victria along to do the same.

Laughter rang out behind them.

The water was shallow enough for them to stand behind the column. Once they were all gathered, they turned to each other, the heavy question of what they should do hanging in the air.

"Come now, ladies," a soft-spoken but confident voice called out to them. "I know where you're hiding, there's no use playing this game. We can either come to you and kill you on the spot, or you can come out yourselves, throw down your weapons, and surrender."

Victria didn't know who this was, but clearly he had some authority if he was making offers like this. He wasn't like the other corrupted humans within The Turned One's ranks. This one wasn't a mindless servant. That was dangerous.

"Who are you?" she called back, trying to sound braver than she felt. "Why should we believe that you would spare us?"

"I don't think you are in any position to be asking questions," was the reply. "Decide now. Live, or die."

"It's a trap," Tessa whispered. "There's no way they would lure us out just to take us alive."

"They don't need to lure us out," Natiari chuckled scornfully. "They know where we are and it's not exactly a defensible position. They could easily rush in and overwhelm us."

"Then what do we do?" Madira quivered. "Even if they spare our lives, we'd be their prisoners. I hate to think what that could mean for us."

"Madira's right," Natiari frowned, the grip on her weapon tightened, turning her knuckles white. "There's no way out of here and I'd rather not become a prisoner."

Tessa scoffed. "So, what? You'll die fighting? How honorable of you, how very *dwarvish.*"

"I'm sorry, do you have some magical way to escape?"

"We can't escape," Victria said flatly. She'd been thinking while her companions bickered. She agreed with Natiari and Madira that to become a prisoner would be risking a fate worse than death, so logically, the only option they had left was to fight—which would inevitably lead to their deaths. But the longer she considered the idea, the more she couldn't bring herself to follow through with it. She didn't want to die. Felix's face lingered on the edge of her mind. She still hadn't had the opportunity to tell him how she felt about him. He would never know, and she would never get the future she had been yearning for since she realized the truth. Her heart ached with regret.

But as she thought of him, a faint hope churned within her.

Felix never failed in any task he set his mind to, she knew. Once he learned that she and her companions had been captured, he would surely launch every effort to come and rescue them. To rescue her. And he would succeed. It wouldn't be done in the next day, perhaps not even the next week. But it would be done. The real question, then, was how long would it take him to accomplish this? How long could she and her friends hold out against whatever horrors The Turned One had in store for them?

It was a gamble. A huge one. But her mind was made up. She wanted to see Felix again, desperately. If there was even the slightest chance of that happening with this path, she would take that risk.

"We can't escape," she said again, "but I think we have a chance to be rescued if we can hold out long enough to give Felix the opportunity."

Natiari's eyes bulged as they turned to her. "You can't be serious. You're going to surrender? You think he'll be able to come for us? We were lucky enough as it is to sneak into this place while using everything at our disposal to distract The Turned One's forces. No one is going to be able to do this again."

Victria shivered. She wrapped her arms around herself but there was little warmth to be had. Natiari had a point, but she was determined to see this through. She had to trust that Felix could overcome all odds. She had to give him that chance before completely giving up. Otherwise. . . .

"All the same," she said, trying to sound more confident than she really was. "I'm going to do it. If we die here, we accomplish nothing. We die alone in the dark, forgotten. Who knows what happens with our corpses afterwards."

She stared into the eyes of each of her friends. They were scared, just like she was. Uncertain, just like she was. But deep in her heart, she knew this was the better option.

"I need you to trust me."

There was a pause, then one by one they began to nod. Natiari looked like she had more to say, like she wanted to sway them away from what was surely a path of pain and horror. But she couldn't summon the words. The very thought of convincing her friends to end their lives with her was revolting, and when she compared it to the hope—however faint it was—that Victria offered. . . .

"We're with you, Victria, wherever it may lead."

"Well?" the voice called out again. "My patience wears thin. What is your answer?"

Victria stood, and, with arms raised over her head, walked out from behind the stone column and made her way to the waterline where a horde of enemies stood waiting. Tessa, Natiari, and Madira were right behind her. Once they reached the strand, they threw down their weapons, staring defiantly into the vivid green eyes of the human in charge.

He wore a complete suit of dark, leather armor. His chest-piece was entirely black, with four blood-red rubies embedded in a diamond formation in the center. His voice dripped with malice despite the light tone he maintained as he spoke.

"I must say, I had expected you to fight. I find myself . . . disappointed."

A few burrowers moved behind the viatari and knocked them to their knees, tying their hands together behind their backs with a heavy cord of rope. Victria grunted at the rough treatment but continued to leer at the man. A cold smile crept onto his face.

"It is certainly a first for my master to take on any sort of prisoners. The fact that you and your companions were offered this luxury is a great honor. That you chose it, however, tells me that you must have some delusion of escape in your mind. Allow me to bring you back to reality."

He reached out and gripped Victria's hair, yanking it back so that her face was turned up to him. He leaned in close, so close that his cold eyes were all she could see. She winced as she instinctively recoiled.

"You will die here. You will be held so deep within these mountains that even I won't be able to find you. If you think the leader of your silly coalition, this Felix Draka, will come to your rescue, you are sorely mistaken. I will be there every step of the way to counter his every move. If any survivors remain after my master's plan comes to its head, they will whisper the name of Drake and know that it was I who helped bring about the world as we will come to know it. Remember that name, girl, and may it pass through your mind unbidden as you take your last breath."

He let go, and Victria fell back with a gasp, her heart racing, pushing an unfamiliar feeling through her veins. Fear, she realized.

"You see, The Turned One recognizes Felix's clever talents as a tactician. That is why I am now here." His hand twitched and, without meaning to, Victria shrank away. He chuckled. "I believe you understand your situation a little better. Cling to hope if you wish. I'm sure your caretaker will enjoy it if you do, as it will mean more fun for him when he breaks you."

With that, he jerked his head to the side and the burrowers grabbed the viatari by their bonds, pulling them up, and shoved them away toward the stone stairway.

"You three, darinsha," Drake pointed at a few strange beings Victria had never seen before, but which reminded her vaguely of the vashi. "Search the pools. I want to make sure we don't have any more vashi lurking about, waiting for a chance to strike."

The darinsha hissed approvingly and moved for the water. Another rough shove came from behind, forcing Victria to turn away from the scene and face her doom.

The stairway loomed threateningly before her. Her head dropped. Fear gripped her in earnest now, fueling her heart and making it continue its rapid cadence. She had never felt this way in all the centuries she had lived. But she'd made her choice. She would see this ordeal through to the bitter end and come through it alive. She would make sure her friends did as well. Despite Drake's words, she wouldn't let this glimmer of hope she felt in her chest wither away. Felix would come for her—for them. She was sure of it. He'd never failed her before.

Hours passed with Thuradin sitting by the edge of a hot spring, staring into it, willing for Victria to emerge from its shallow waters. Behind him, dwarves and burrowers bustled about getting everything gathered and prepared for a quick trek down the mountain. Veliris was again strapped to a litter, this time carried by six dwarves. His sky-blue tendrils waved freely in the misty air.

In truth, they had been ready to depart the vale for some time now, but they made a show of making preparations because they were waiting. They were all waiting, watching the same pool of water. Waiting for one more member to rejoin their ranks.

As soon as it became clear that Cotovas would not be bringing the viatari back from the underground pools, Meri had volunteered to go back to see if she could bring them back herself. Or, at least, to see what fate had befallen them.

She had been gone for an hour, and Thuradin worried that she too had been caught up in whatever situation Victria and her companions were in. But only minutes after having this thought, Meri emerged from the spring, alarm written across her face. She trudged out, steam coming off her scaled body as everyone gathered around, eager to hear the news.

Finally, she sighed. "Cotovasss isss dead. Victria and her friendsss yet live, but they have sssurrendered and have been taken prisoner."

Murmuring broke out all around.

"Prisoners?" Thuradin repeated. "I cannae believe it. That lass would never allow herself ta be captured. She'd sooner go down fighting."

"Believe what you will, dwarf," Meri shook her head tiredly. "I sssaw it with my own eyesss."

Thuradin's brows furrowed as he thought what this could mean. This was certainly not a path he ever thought Victria would take—unless she believed this was the best option for survival. And with that thought came realization.

"She expects Felix ta rescue her."

"Well, that's rather presumptuous of her," a nearby dwarf harrumphed.

"Or calculated," Thuradin shot back. "She knows if Felix hears that she's been taken prisoner, he'll put all his efforts inta taking the Three Spires because—believe me—he'll want ta rescue her more than anything else. If he were told she was dead however, he might lose all taste for this war, and we would be left leaderless."

"Whatever the cassse," Meri interjected. "It isss sssomething we must ssspeculate on at a later time. Before I left, their leader ordered a few darinsha into the waters. No doubt, with my liquefaction being so recent, they'll discover its origin point and traccce usss back here. We may be facing a battle we do not wish to fight on thessse mountainsss if we do not leave sssoon."

There was a murmur of agreement, and the gathered crowd broke up, picking up their gear so they could finally depart. But Thuradin didn't budge.

"Thuradin," Tera called out with a heavy voice. "We need to leave."

"Aye," Thuradin said, snapping out of his own thoughts. "But time is of the essence. We don't have the luxury of wasting three whole days climbing down these mountains. We must get ta Felix's tent immediately."

Tera was already shaking her head. "We don't have enough vashi to liquefact all of us back to camp."

"We don't need them."

Thuradin's gaze fell on the acolyte who had remained silent this whole time. Perhaps he was aloof to what was going on. Perhaps he was listening intently. Thuradin couldn't tell and, frankly, he didn't care. The fact of the matter was that Veliris owed them. He especially owed it to Victria and her companions to do anything within his power to help secure their own freedom. And what Thuradin had in mind was definitely within the acolyte's power.

"Veliris," Thuradin approached the acolyte. Blue tendrils turned in his direction. "Ye have the power ta teleport us all off this mountain, do you nae?"

"I could indeed, dwarf, but my captivity has left me weak. I cannot go far with so many in my care."

"Can ye bring us ta the foothills just below these peaks? Our main camp is there. It would save us a great deal of time. The faster we get down, the sooner we tell Felix the news, the quicker action can be taken."

Veliris considered for a moment. Then, his tendrils surrounded the dwarf, planting themselves directly onto his forehead.

I will do as you ask this time, dwarf, Veliris' voice rang out in his mind. *Though it shall be taxing for me to do so. I do it because I am indebted to you and your companions for freeing me, just as you perceived. I will honor my debts. But do not grow accustomed to this level of servitude. Now, bring into your mind the location you wish for me to take you all and I will have it done.*

Thuradin conjured an image of the command tent, thinking of everything within that he could remember. He tried to make it as detailed as he could, then waited. A moment later, he and everyone around him began to glow with light. The luminosity amplified, surrounding each member of the party until it became too much and Thuradin was forced to close his eyes.

He felt a pull on his stomach. There was a great *woosh* of sound like a rushing wind, and the next thing he knew, he felt weightless.

Felix Draka was tired and covered in sweat, dirt, and blood—very little of it his own. The day had been a taxing affair, a difficult battle. They had taken losses in the fighting, perhaps more than many had been anticipating, and had been forced to retreat.

But that had always been the plan. His attack was the distraction meant to lure out The Turned One's forces, emptying out the Three Spires. He had never been meant to win this battle in the field. Everything about the plan had been executed perfectly. However, that didn't make accepting the losses they had suffered today any easier.

Now, legions of dwarves, bands of viatari, humans, and some companies of vashi as well as burrowers trudged back to camp, just as tired as he was. By their downcast eyes, he could see their disappointment. They had set out as a grand army, had fought hard all day to the point of exhaustion. Many had lost friends. Yet, for the common soldier, all they were rewarded with was a return to the status quo. No progress had been made as far as they were concerned even as the sun bade them farewell with its final rays of light.

Felix grimaced. While he had yet to learn if their true goal had been accomplished himself, he could see the aftereffects of today's battle becoming an issue of morale. He made a mental note to have a word with the camp's cooks. He would have them throw a feast tonight. Nothing, he had learned, could liven up spirits as quickly as good food and good drink.

While everyone made their way back to their tents to take off their armor and collapse into their cots for an early night's rest, Felix made his way to the command tent. If there was any success today, he would find out there. And he was eager for the outcome.

Shaking off his own fatigue, he entered the large tent with his sister, Salevari Mistguide, her daughter, Serania, and Simon, a leading figure for the humans, following close behind. The viatari and dwarven guards outside saluted as they passed. Inside the tent stood a single wooden table with an assortment of maps piled on top and several weights holding down the corners. On them were a variety of weighted figures, meant to represent their forces as well as the enemy's.

The tent was well lit by small hanging braziers, so Felix had no trouble finding his way to the stone basin filled with water at the far end, despite the fading light from outside.

The elder viatari bent over and splashed his face several times, being sure to rub the cool liquid well along his neck and through his short, buzzed hair. Salevari and Serania did the same, wringing their hair until every last droplet had fallen back to the floor. Simon refrained from washing his own face, instead leaning over the table, his eyes studying the various maps carefully. Feeling refreshed, the viatari joined their human companion at the table, each one reflecting on their own recollection of the day's events.

They had set up their main camp in the foothills directly under the Three Spires with smaller outposts built and garrisoned in a line east and west curving toward the Northern Mountains. As far as Felix was concerned, The Turned One's forces were surrounded. They could not go farther north because, as far as he knew, all that lay beyond the Three Spires were more mountains, inhospitable and void of life. No, the enemy was contained. He was sure of it. All there was left to do now was to wait them out, no matter how long it took. And so long as their mission today was successful, with the power of four acolytes on their side, they would hopefully not have to wait too long.

Still, the enemy had proven stubborn in their fortifications. Their assault today had been incessantly harassed by traps, ambushes, and a number of well-timed flanking maneuvers that could have broken any lesser army. Either The Turned One had suddenly developed a mind for war, or someone else was now leading her forces. Someone formidable. Which meant any future battles would result in greater loss—for both sides.

The elder viatari was just about to open the discussion by sharing this thought when a sudden flash of light to their right captured his attention. He turned to see a large party of dwarves and burrowers suddenly in his command tent. A few of the dwarves carried a litter with a triangular chest strapped onto it. From it emerged several blue tendrils swaying tiredly.

A great weight lifted off Felix's shoulders. He stood a little straighter, all thoughts of a new adversary forgotten. They had done it. All four acolytes were now on their side and their chances for ultimate victory were within reach.

As he took this in, his eyes continued to shift from face to tired face, looking for one in particular. He saw Tera. He noticed Morteth, the dwarven assassin, slinking away. He saw two of the waterseers he had sent with them and realized one was missing. His wasn't the only missing face either.

Felix's grin faded, turning into a puzzled frown. How could *she* be missing? She had always been there. He *wanted* her to always be there. The thought of her ever being out of reach had never crossed his mind as a possibility.

His gaze fell to Thuradin with a dreadful question. One he dared not utter. What he received for an answer was a quick shake of the head. That was enough. And in that moment, the night felt darker to Felix, its crushing weight threatening to suffocate him where he stood.

CHAPTER FOUR

"How could this happen?"

Felix clenched his fists and slammed them on the table, producing a sizeable crack down the middle. Several leaflets and rolled up scrolls fell off the sides onto the floor from the sudden action. The elder viatari's ancient red eyes were swimming with a mixture of rage, disbelief, and grief as he repeated himself, this time, with more force.

"How could this *happen?*"

There hung a tense silence within the command tent as everyone watched Felix, ever calm, bellow in anger. Only once could Thuradin remember such a visceral reaction from him; the day Aleganthia had been sacked by the Creature and set aflame. So lost in his thoughts and emotions, Felix didn't register the majority of dwarves and burrowers shuffling out of the tent, eager to leave the scene and find their beds. A few had the wits to grab Veliris and take him with them so that he could be reunited with his brothers.

Finally, with great effort, Felix faced the remaining members of the raid party. His focus fell on Tera.

"Tell me what happened."

"It was a trap," Tera's shoulders drooped, her words laced with regret. "The Turned One knew we were coming to save Veliris and was ready for us. Veliris masked our presence for a time but once we were discovered we were quickly overwhelmed.

"After we extracted the acolyte, we tried to escape ourselves but before Victria and the others could reach Cotovas, he was struck. I didn't see who struck him or with what, but he died, stranding them. . . ."

Tera shuddered and dabbed at her eyes, raw with a deep sadness and exhaustion. Thuradin sympathized with her. It had been a long and difficult day for them, made all the more so by the loss of several of their companions. He knew from his own experience how hard it could be to lose those whose lives had been entrusted to you. Such was always the possibility in war, but it never dulled the sting when it happened. Especially when one of those lives had been that of a friend.

"And then what?" Felix demanded. "Surely you sent someone back to save them."

Tera took a steadying breath and answered, "Yes, Meri went back. But the cavern was already overrun by that point. Nothing could be done."

"Then," Felix faltered, almost choking on the words he had to force out. "Then, Victria . . . all of them are—"

"They yet live, Felix," Thuradin said gruffly. "They surrendered ta the enemy and have been taken prisoner, according ta Meri."

"They surrendered?" The elder viatari repeated in a soft voice. A faraway look took hold.

"Aye, they surrendered."

A jolt, and then new life and energy returned to Felix's

eyes. Flames appeared to burn behind them, tinged with a hint of madness as he spoke, "But then, they must believe they can be rescued."

"Aye, that was my own conclusion as well."

"Good, I see . . . good," a million thoughts flew at record speed through Felix's mind, but only one truly took hold. "Then our path forward is clear. We must do all we can to make this a reality." He turned his gaze back to the maps on the table, studying the region of the Three Spires and its foothills that they depicted. Silence followed.

Salevari took a tentative step forward, clearing her throat. "Brother, we can't rescue them."

Felix froze for a moment, but then scoffed and shook his head. "Of course we can rescue them. We have a whole host of skilled warriors just outside the enemy's doorstep."

"And those warriors are spread thin keeping The Turned One shut in as it is. We don't have the resources available to send out a rescue party. For one, we don't even know where Victria and the others are being held or if they'll even be kept alive."

"Exactly. Time is of the essence," Felix moved over and grabbed a different stack of leaflets, shifting through them absently as he continued to think and talk. "The Turned One and Creature's forces are not anything new to us. With Veliris now among us, we can take this mountain if we wanted to. If we take the Three Spires, we win. Is that not beneficial for all? Is that not why we are here in the first place?"

Salevari's eyes widened, she took half a step back in disbelief. "You would risk everything–our entire war effort, the fate of Azar–for one viatari? And let's be honest, brother, it is *just* for her. You would not be this crazed if anyone else had been captured.

The accusation hung in the air. Felix slowly looked up from the leaflets in his hands. His face said everything, but he wouldn't allow even an ounce of confusion or doubt to remain in anyone's mind.

"She is not *just* any viatari."

Salevari's shoulders fell and she shook her head in disappointment.

Worried glances passed between those still present. Thuradin wondered if perhaps a change of subject might help refocus Felix's perspective.

He cleared his throat, "Felix, there's more ye should know about our time in the Three Spires. While everyone was preparing Veliris for his escape, Morteth and I–"

Felix held up a hand, silencing the dwarf.

"Forgive me, my friend," he said. "Normally I would be interested to hear more, but I have heard enough. Now, I must plan. It will take everything we have to rescue our friends."

Felix returned his attention to the table and the many rolls of parchment spread out before him, ignoring the stares, ignoring the mutterings, ignoring everything.

With the discussion over, most of the remaining raid party began to file out one by one until the only ones left in the tent were Salevari, Serania, Simon, and Thuradin. Each one of them was deep in thought, trying to come up with some idea, anything, that might steer Felix away from his current path.

And as they thought, the water in the basin began to churn. What was once a flat surface of liquid slowly rose, taking shape, eventually forming into the visage of a vashi from the shoulders up.

Everyone, save Felix, turned to see their new visitor.

"Avmoshir!" Serania said in surprise. "What brings you–

or half of you—here?"

Avmoshir chuckled, a raspy sound muffled by the basin-water his body was currently composed of.

"I am not technically here. My body remains in Zessarix. Current events here require me to oversee them personally. Otherwise, I would be at the foot of the mountains with you all, leading the vashi myself."

Felix still did not acknowledge the vashi leader. Avmoshir noticed this and hissed softly, trying to gain his attention. With one final, frustrated scowl at her brother, Salevari made her way to the basin and addressed the young vashi directly.

"You'll have to excuse him," she said, "We have recently received some distressing news that he is taking some time to process."

"Distressing news seems to follow everyone these days," Avmoshir said. "What has happened to cause the ever-calm, ever-wise leader of the viatari I've heard so much about to falter? It must be truly monumental if it has brought you to this state. Victria always spoke so highly of you. I'd hate to learn her words were false."

Felix flinched.

"That's just it," Salevari grimaced. "Victria has been captured and taken prisoner by the enemy along with Tessa, Natiari, and Madira."

If Avmoshir had been there physically, he might have stumbled back from the shocking news. As it was, his water-image rippled like a pebble had been thrown into it. The young vashi's face fell.

"Ill newsss, indeed." He took a moment to compose himself so that when he spoke again, his speech was perfect once more. "But they are strong. They will break out themselves if you do not rescue them first. I believe that with all my heart."

Salevari nodded, checking over her shoulder to see if there was any acknowledgment from Felix. His position at the table remained unchanged. He still refused to look at Avmoshir, but he also wasn't mindlessly shuffling through papers anymore. He was still. He was listening. That was something.

She turned her attention back to the young vashi. "Thank you for the kind words; but in the meantime, I will speak on Felix's behalf. So, tell us. What news comes from the seas?"

The young vashi hissed, baring his sharp teeth as the reason for his presence returned to him.

"There are rumors—whispers—in the currents of a coming invasion of our waters. If these rumors are true, we believe the darinsha, an ancient enemy of ours, are planning to wage war against us. It is something that has not happened for many centuries, but the last time we fought, the seas boiled with blood. Generations were lost. It took everything we had, including the sacrifice of our Supreme Overseer at the time, to push them back into their ancestral home in the Northern Seas. If these rumors are true, I fear for the future of my people. I am requesting aid to help us push back against these . . . *sea serpents.*" Avmoshir said the last like it was a vulgarity.

"We cannot sacrifice our strength here just on the basis of rumors," Felix said before Salevari could get a word out. They all turned to look at him. Avmoshir frowned.

"The darinsha are a brutal enemy. If they are planning to invade our waters, and you refuse to send us aid, I will be forced to recall every vashi I have sent you to help bolster our own defenses. We will need every fighter we can get."

"If, if, if . . . ," Felix muttered. "Is there any proof the darinsha plan to invade, or did the waters simply speak to you?"

"You dare—"

"He speaks the truth," Thuradin interrupted before the situation could escalate. "These are no mere rumors. It's exactly what I wanted ta tell ye earlier, Felix. When we were rescuing the acolyte, Morteth and I stumbled upon a cavern holding The Turned One and the Creature."

Felix's lips formed a thin, neat line.

"As fascinating as that is—"

"The darinsha were there," Thuradin continued, unwilling to let Felix derail him again. This information was too important. "Their leader swore fealty ta The Turned One. She spoke plainly of her desire ta conquer the Southern Seas." The dwarf looked at Avmoshir's water-image adding, "yer cousin was there, too. Enishar, the darinsha's ruler, will use his knowledge of yer waters ta help invade yer home."

Avmoshir sighed sadly. "How far my cousin has fallen. To betray his own people like that. . . ."

"There's more," Thuradin grunted. He went on to tell Felix about the two humans who had also sworn fealty to the corrupted acolytes. He did his best to recollect everything he could about what was said, but so much had happened between then and now he was sure he was missing some details. Still, so long as he conveyed the nature of what had happened he felt he had fulfilled his duty.

"The robed man, if I remember correctly, said something about how once the humans fell inta line, the seas would be open for invasion. I can only imagine he was speaking of the humans on the coast. Whatever the case, this action he's taking is meant ta help give the darinsha an edge over the vashi."

They all mulled over Thuradin's report. It was a disturbing revelation. Their enemies were growing, multiplying, and seemingly without effort.

"We can't afford to lose the vashi's support," Salevari muttered.

"It's obvious what's happening, isn't it?"

All eyes turned to Simon, who had been silent and still as a statue this whole time, yet absorbing everything that was being said.

"What is so obvious?" Felix asked.

"This is a ploy by The Turned One to divide our forces and weaken us. We must not fall for it. If we weaken our position here, it will only be a matter of time before she and her brother break through our lines and begin spreading chaos wherever they will."

"It is no ploy," Avmoshir hissed. "By what this dwarf says, the threat of invasion is no longer rumor, but real and confirmed."

"The threat may be real," Simon countered, holding up a finger, a knowing grin on his face. "But it's still a ploy. There are two desired results from this sequence of events, which are to weaken our position here or destroy the vashi altogether. She wants us to think we can only prevent one of those things from happening by bolstering one front and sacrificing the other. In reality, I think we can prevent both."

Salevari's eyebrows raised. "Well, well, it seems you have given this some thought. Tell us, what is this solution that you see that we fail to grasp?"

The human chief sneered. "I'm surprised it hasn't come to you yet, Chancellor. We must acquire new allies to help aid the vashi in repelling the darinsha invasion."

"And what new allies–"

"The humans!" Serania jumped in, her one eye bright with excitement. "Halding Port is a powerful coastal town. They could send their fleet to counter the darinsha."

Simon nodded approvingly. "Exactly. And by what Thuradin

has said, it seems The Turned One already has some plot prepared for the coastal humans that I can only assume is not to their benefit. I'm sure the people there are wholly unaware of anything nefarious taking place amongst them as well. If we can uncover this scheme and eradicate any trace of The Turned One's forces hidden within Halding Port, we can show the leadership there that they are already in this war, whether they like it or not. Once they reach this conclusion themselves, they will have little choice but to join our cause."

"Hmm," Avmoshir stroked his scaly chin as he considered Simon's daring proposal. "Vashi and humans working together. While their fleet would add considerable strength to our defenses, it would be difficult to convince my people to accept their aid, if they would even give it in the first place."

"Your people seem to work well with ours as far as I'm concerned." Simon shrugged.

"We work with you humans because you are from the plains and we give you the benefit of the doubt," Avmoshir said. "The coastal humans are different. There is much bad blood between us."

"And us plainsmen hated the viatari," Simon countered. "Yet, here we are working together. I'm not saying the vashi and the coastal humans must become friends, but the darinsha pose just as much a threat to them as they do to you. Trust me, a common enemy creates a large amount of leverage when it comes to politics."

Avmoshir sighed but nodded in the end. "What you say is true, and our need is great. Very well, I will do what I can to convince the Assembly to move forward with this. But who will convince the humans? Right now, they would sooner spear us than speak with us."

"Leave that to me," Salevari said, taking a map from Felix's hand which depicted the southern coastline and the Sea of Scales beyond. "This is too important to leave to chance. I'll make sure whatever plot The Turned One has for Halding Port is thwarted and exposed and that the humans are forced to see reason."

"I will go as well," Simon stood next to the Dalyran Chancellor. "You will need someone with human expertise to help you pull this off. I already have an idea forming on how we can make our approach."

"What do you mean?"

"You can't just march into Halding Port as a viatari and demand to speak to their leader. We must be tactful, use our wits, until the time is right to reveal our true identities. To that end, I believe Tera should come along as well, since she has a better knowledge of coastal human culture and social norms than I do. I'm sure she will need little convincing to join. It will do her good to be away from these mountains for a time after today's events."

"Fair enough," Salevari agreed. "Then I will bring some viatari as well to accompany us. A little extra muscle will be to our benefit when the time comes to dismantle whatever plot The Turned One has manufactured."

"It seems this matter is settled, then." Avmoshir observed.

"Wait," Serania said in disbelief. "You can't just leave, mother. Without you . . . ," she cocked her head toward Felix, who had remained as he was this whole time.

Salevari nodded her understanding but smiled encouragingly. "I must go. And should Felix continue in this stupor, I trust you will lead our peoples down the right path."

"Me?" Serania laughed incredulously.

"I have every confidence in your ability to lead, my daughter. Your strength and wisdom will keep this siege from falling apart in my absence."

Serania looked like she wanted to argue, but bit her tongue and instead said, "I will not fail."

"I know you won't." With that, Salevari turned back to Avmoshir, all business. "We will need a few vashi to liquefact us to the shoreline outside of Halding Port. If we take horses we will be riding for weeks and we don't have that kind of time to waste."

"No, we do not," Avmoshir agreed. "My vashi are at your disposal. Thank you, Salevari. I look forward to hearing of your progress."

With those words, the water-image of the vashi leader broke down, sinking back into the basin until it was once again a flat surface.

"Come Simon, Serania," Salevari turned and briskly strode toward the tent's entrance flap. "We have provisions to prepare and a task to complete."

They followed her. As she passed Felix, she stopped, sympathy filling her eyes. She reached out and gripped his shoulder. He would not look at her.

"I know these are difficult times," she said gently. "But we need you to return to us. Not just for each individual warrior out there in our camp, but for the world. Victria made a sacrifice to ensure her task was successful, and for that she should be honored and remembered. But you waste her sacrifice and her memory if you forget our purpose here. Do not let yourself do that."

"She is not dead yet," Felix responded bitterly. His red eyes narrowed. "But you are speaking as if she is. I will do what must be done. You should go."

Salevari took back her hand and let it slump to her side. Without another word, the trio exited the command tent, leaving Felix and Thuradin alone. It was a difficult situation for them all, the dwarf thought. Salevari had made several good points in her attempts to refocus Felix, but objectivity wasn't the winning factor here.

The fact of the matter was this was *Victria.* Thuradin thought of their first encounter just outside of the forest surrounding Aleganthia. Admittedly, it was a fairly embarrassing episode for him, but it was what had started their deep-rooted friendship. Of all the viatari, he had always thought of her most fondly.

He moved to leave, his mind conflicted and still replaying the final images he had of her; running for the water, a horde of enemies giving chase. He shook his head, knots wrapping themselves around his heart and squeezing. That would *not* be his final picture of her. He couldn't let that happen.

And so, just as he reached the tent flap, he stopped and turned back. Felix gripped both sides of the table hard, his fingers turning white. His face was blank, his eyes empty as they perused the same map repeatedly.

"Felix," Thuradin called out firmly. The elder viatari jumped and looked at him. "If ye think of anything, any plan ta save her, no matter how small the chances are of success, know that I will be there by yer side ta make sure it gets carried out. I'll be waiting ta hear from ye."

The elder viatari blinked slowly. His lips twitched, a small reservoir of confidence returning.

"Thank you, Thuradin, I will not forget your kindness."

Nodding, the dwarf exited the dark interior of the command tent and stepped into the sun's light, just now peeking over the horizon. Warmth spread across his body even as he now began to feel the ache in his bones from the past day's events. With a new resolve, he marched his way into camp.

CHAPTER FIVE

The camp was just stirring as Thuradin strode through the dirt pathways laid out between the multiple lines of tents. The kitchens were a bustle of activity as human and dwarven cooks shuffled about within their block of pavilions, gathering and chopping vegetables, slaughtering livestock, and checking the contents of a plethora of variously sized pots. Already, a line was forming, snaking its way through the camp as people from every race waited their turn to be served breakfast. The dwarves grew particularly rowdy as they quickly moved from eating their food to having their first brew of the day, courtesy of the small brewery they had established next to the kitchens. It was there that a staggering number of barrels of ale were kept to keep the dwarves sated. Jovial singing filled the morning air. If anyone hadn't woken up yet, they would now.

Thuradin took his attention away from the goings-on of camp life and looked forward. A lone figure stood a few dozen paces ahead in the middle of a crossroads, arms crossed, observing the camp's activity herself. He approached her, standing by her side. Serania noticed his presence and nodded acknowledgement, her long silver hair flowing with the morning breeze, though the strands covering her right eye remained in place as always. He thought he could detect a shade of worry written on her features, not that he could blame her. The situation they found themselves in was dire, and a great responsibility had been thrust upon her without much of a choice.

"Good morning, Thuradin," she said far too casually.

"Morning, lass," he replied. "Quite a night, aye?"

A strained laugh left her lips. "That's an understatement if ever I heard one." She took a breath as if to say more, hesitated, then let her worries spill out. "What are your thoughts on Felix? Do you think he'll recover?"

Sighing heavily, Thuradin shrugged. "Lass, ye've known him longer than I have. Ye should tell me."

Serania thought for a moment, a deep frown forming. "That's the problem I think we all have. None of us have ever seen him like this before. And it couldn't have happened at a worse time. I fear if he remains like this, he will be incapable of leading us. And without him. . . ." Her voice trailed off, her fears now making themselves plain on her face for all to see.

"Give him some time," Thuradin said after a few minutes had passed in silence. "He's only just received the news and ye know how dear Victria is ta him—ta all of us. I cannae blame him for reacting this way. Anyone would. Even my heart aches at the thought of her fate."

"As does mine," Serania closed her eye. "But I still remember our purpose here, and I can't let her loss be the distraction that leads us to ruin."

Thuradin's gaze was drawn toward the three massive peaks to the north that made up the Three Spires, far larger than any of the surrounding mountains. They were a dark shade of black, even as the sun's light touched them. A sense of foreboding came from them that made the dwarf shudder. This place had long been known as a place of evil within his culture for as long as anyone could remember. None had ever ventured through its valleys and certainly not into the Three Spires themselves. And yet, here they were, besieging this nefarious place to fight The Turned One, to keep her trapped, to eventually defeat her for good. It seemed the fate of the world being under threat was reason enough for every dwarf here to push aside their inner misgivings. For Thuradin now, there was at least one more reason to brave those treacherous peaks.

"She's nae lost," Thuradin said confidently. "We can save her. I think she knew that. She would nae have surrendered only ta suffer a slow death. We must do what we can for her. I, for one, would do anything Felix tells me for a chance at getting them all back."

Serania turned to look at him. "That's the problem. We *all* need to remember our purpose here. We have to either take the Three Spires by force, a task that may be impossible with our current numbers, or we draw The Turned One's forces out of the mountains and defeat them in a pitched battle. And we must defeat them decisively. Anything less means the siege continues. We need every warrior we have for this. We can't afford reckless actions being taken, even by a few. My mother understands this. Simon understands this. Everyone in this camp should understand this. I believe Victria would have understood it too, if she were here."

Thuradin shook his head. "We disagree on that, lass. I don't think the two end results must be exclusive. We can still defeat our enemy and save Victria at the same time. We just need ta go about it the right way, and that's for Felix ta figure out. He's the one with the tactical mind, after all."

"So you would throw away Victria's sacrifice, which has

given us Veliris and a chance to truly end this war? You used to be a commander of dwarves, Thuradin, you should know better than to let emotion rule your decisions when it comes to these difficult situations."

Serania's words cut as sharp as her sword. Heat rose into the dwarf's face. An edge entered his voice as he said, "It's nae a sacrifice she must make. I will nae abandon hope when there's still a chance–and there *is* a chance–for us ta save her." With that, he stormed off. Anger bubbled within him and he did not wish to unleash it on Serania, even if she had been the cause of it. He felt her gaze pierce his back as he walked away, burrowing deeper into the rows of tents, heading for the one section of camp affectionately referred to as the "dwarven grid."

It wasn't long ago that Thuradin had once been a complete exile to dwarven society. His part in the death of King Ronorim Ironaxe, had sealed him to that fate. But his more recent adventures, which had kept the dwarven clans from warring against each other, gave the current monarch, Dunkell Ironaxe, the excuse he needed for a full pardon. Even so, Thuradin had remained in Aleganthia with the viatari. He may have been able to live within the Silent Mountains again now, but the events that had led to these hardships of his life were still too fresh. Perhaps in another century, if he made it that long, he would be able to return home for good.

For now, though, he was happy to pitch his tent with his own people. A few still glowered at him with disapproval, but there were many more now who chose to ignore him, and some would even incline their heads in acknowledgement. That was progress.

He made his way to his tent and called out to Borim Tomestone, his oldest friend, who had pitched his own right next door. Borim sat on a stool outside his tent, his white beard draped back over his shoulder as he worked diligently inspecting his armor and weapons. He looked up and broke out in a broad smile.

"I was wondering when I'd see yer pitiful face again."

The two dwarves shared a laugh as Thuradin removed his own armor and the long, black cloak that had hidden him so well in the mountains. He dragged them into his tent, tossing them onto his cot. He would deal with their maintenance later. For now, he needed some time to decompress. Any thought of sleep he may have had on his way here was long gone. His mind was far too busy to settle. Instead, he retrieved a short, wooden tankard that he kept on a nightstand next to his cot and filled it with a dark amber liquid from a personal barrel he had procured from the brewery. He took a sip, letting the sharp, bubbly drink wet his lips. He sighed contently and went back outside with the rest of his drink to sit next to Borim.

Borim was once more inspecting his steel breastplate, wiping away any blotches of blood or grime he found with a white rag.

"Word is the little raid ye took part in was a raging success," he said without looking up.

Thuradin took another sip before answering. "Has word spread so quickly?"

"Aye, the camp is simply buzzing with the news. The acolyte was seen being transported from the command tent. No keeping it secret after that."

"Aye, we got that blasted acolyte. But I don't agree with the raid being a great success." He shared Victria's fate with Borim, who slowly stopped polishing his armor and looked up in surprise.

"Captured? Her? Impossible."

"And yet, it's so. Felix is distraught. There's a great worry that he'll now be incapable of leading us all against The Turned One's forces, though I'm sure Salevari and Serania are going ta do all they can ta keep his state of mind a secret from the rest of the camp."

Borim shook his head. "It's terrible news. But if I know Felix, and I think I know him a little, he'll think of some way ta rescue her."

Thuradin nodded and downed what little remained in his tankard. "What about ye? How did it feel fighting knowing ye were nothing more than bait?"

Borim chuckled, but there was little mirth in it. "Ta be honest, my friend, that was a battle I'd sooner forget." He tossed his rag onto the ground and looked up, his gaze far away as he recalled yesterday's events. "The enemy is well and truly dug in on that blasted mountain. There's only one path leading up ta a tunnel entrance, which we, theoretically, were supposed ta take. But those mountains are so large and there were an endless number of switchbacks that we had to fight for control over. We suffered losses at every turn. The enemy had traps everywhere. If you were unlucky, ye were dead before ye even realized it."

The two dwarves shared a look. Borim continued. "I'm no brilliant commander like yerself, but I find it hard ta imagine any assault on that mountain being met with success. Their defenses are impregnable. There's no chance of victory for us if we have ta take them."

"Well," Thuradin mused. "That's why they made me the commander and ye were just a captain of the wall guard."

Borim's well-humored grin returned and he barked with laughter, shoving Thuradin playfully.

After a while he spoke again, his tone somber once more, "I think that battle shook everyone ta their core. Many lost friends in brutal ways. I think it was made worse because we knew we weren't meant ta truly win the day. We were nae defeated, but our spirits took a beating. So, it's good that ye were able ta bring back that acolyte, Thuradin, despite the cost. The sight of the bloody thing did much ta lift everyone's spirits. Made the sacrifices of the day worth it."

Thuradin dwelt on this for a moment. He supposed he was pleased with their success as a whole, but he still felt the vestiges of failure weighing down on him. He knew satisfaction wouldn't come until he corrected what went wrong.

"Agh," Borim fussed. "I wish the full might of our people were here. Same with the burrowers. If this is ta be our final effort in ridding the world of The Turned One, we should be approaching this challenge with full force. Perhaps then we'd have some chance of success."

Thuradin grunted dismissively. "Ye know why that's nae possible right now. Dunkell is already sacrificing much in security sending as many legions as he has. There's still much damage ta repair in our Kingdom after The Turned One's attack. Fungar Hrathor has ta be rebuilt from scratch, the mushroom fields regrown. The new tunnel the enemy dug out needs ta be sealed. Dunkell cannae simply empty out all of the Silent Mountains."

"I know that," Borim grumbled. "Doesn't keep me from wishing it, though. I suppose it's lucky we have dwarven farmers outside the mountains now or we'd be dealing with a famine on top of everything else." His gaze shifted, following some other dwarves returning to their tents after a night of sentry duty. They were exhausted, dropping their weapons and shields as they walked. They didn't even bother to take off their armor as they entered their tents, ready to succumb to the sweet comforts of sleep.

"I hear Dunkell intends ta pay us a visit in the coming weeks. Should boost morale."

Thuradin agreed. Much had changed within the Dwarven Kingdom since the clans nearly fell into civil war, not least of which was the image of the King himself improving substantially. Once an extremely controversial figure, Dunkell Ironaxe had proven to be the unifying force that kept the dwarven clans intact when The Turned One set her corrupted burrowers against them. He supposed it was because of that attack that the dwarves would come back stronger than ever, eager to have their revenge on the dark acolyte for what she had tried to do.

Another unexpected change was that the burrowers—the ones still untouched by corruption—were no longer the enemy. Having helped save the dwarves during the battles for Fungar Hrathor and Tinas Gran, this new relationship was the only natural path forward. According to reports Thuradin had read himself, burrowers were now aiding in the reconstruction of the dwarven cities. In exchange, the dwarves were helping the burrowers excavate a tunnel that would directly connect their capital city of Trek-ti with the outside world. It was a new partnership that, only a year ago, would have sounded like an impossible fairytale had someone tried to describe it. Now it was reality, and it gave Thuradin hope for the future.

The same ruminations seemed to be running through Borim's mind as he pointed at a small rise in the land that overlooked the dwarven grid and said, "I don't think I'll ever get used ta that sight."

On this rise was the camp's armory occupied by a legion of blacksmiths. Canopies stood scattered throughout, providing patches of shade. Forges were set up in neat lines with plenty of anvils nearby. Makeshift walls had been erected every few feet within the canopies, holding a number of tools that every blacksmith needed. Even from where he sat, Thuradin could feel a faint glow of heat coming from the many furnaces burning around the clock. But it wasn't this that Borim was referring to. It was who was working the forges, for it was not only dwarves manning them.

Burrowers worked there as well, mixed in with the dwarven smiths, drawing crowds around them as they uttered guttural chants to keep control of the multi-colored elementals they summoned from their fires. Thuradin remembered seeing this phenomenon himself for the first time during his stay in Trek-ti. The burrowers used these elementals in their smithing to enchant their armor and weapons to strengthen them. It was what had always given the burrowers an edge over the dwarves during their many battles, despite their simple weapons. It was an impressive display. Based on the size of the crowds the burrowers continued to draw in around their forges, everyone else was of the same opinion. Along with the dwarves and burrowers were several humans, hammering away at hot metal, sending sparks flying with each strike. It was an incredible sight. Each blacksmith appeared so different from their peers, but put them all next to a lit forge and anvil and give them some ore and they became as one, working together like a well-oiled machine.

As Thuradin watched them work, two dwarves crossed his vision, making their way down the rise toward the dwarven camp, one following the other. His eyes followed them. The two appeared to be fighting as they walked between tents. He might have thought nothing of it if they were anyone else, but he knew these two, and cared deeply for one of them.

Lyrie Swordmeist and her husband Hork Anvilgar were the two dwarves in question. Lyrie was an old friend of

Thuradin's. He had always admired her bravery, her honesty, her loyalty. Hork, too, he had once considered a friend, though those days were long dead. Now, ever since Thuradin had begun to suspect something was amiss in their relationship, something that erased the joy he was so used to seeing on Lyrie's face, that brought a disconcerting fear into her eyes, he had decided to keep his eyes on them.

Lyrie trudged into camp, her eyes downcast, her body slumped, tired. Hork followed in her wake, fiery and expressive as he spoke. Thuradin thought he might be yelling at her, though he was too far away to hear anything specific. He wasn't sure what could have elicited such a reaction from the bedraggled dwarf. The two certainly looked worn and dirty, like they had been out all night, most likely on sentry duty. It was easy for tempers to run hot from lack of sleep. Even so, he doubted this rage had any justification for being directed at Lyrie.

As the two dwarves neared their tent, situated at the end of the row directly opposite the one Borim and Thuradin were set up in, Hork suddenly raised his arm and brought it back down, shaking off his bracers. Lyrie flinched. Without breaking stride, Hork entered their tent. After some hesitation, she followed.

Anger boiled deep in Thuradin's stomach. He dreaded to think what might be happening behind those sheets of canvas, away from prying eyes. Everything in him was screaming that something was wrong with what he had seen. Another part reminded him that this was not his business. Lyrie was a married lass, and more than capable of handling herself.

And yet, with each passing day in camp, every time that he had observed them and noticed something that raised an alarm in his mind, the former thought had grown stronger.

The idea that he should do something, needed to do something, to help Lyrie was becoming overwhelming.

His thoughts were brought back to when The Turned One's burrowers had been defeated outside of Tinas Gran. He had watched Hork drag Lyrie away back to Kul'Kriegar, despite the injuries she had sustained from the battle. He remembered the offer Morteth Shadowmeld had given him. A permanent solution. It was an offer that had come back to haunt him numerous times since that day. Most times he didn't think of it. When it did make itself known, he was always able to shake it off, leaving him with a sense of guilt for having harbored the idea in the first place.

He was thinking of it now. Morteth's offer bounced about in his mind, his sweet, tempting words echoing. He lingered on them for a while longer before they slowly faded away back into the dark recesses of his memory. This time, however, there was no guilt to follow.

CHAPTER SIX

"Where are ye going?" Borim called out as Thuradin launched himself from his seat and marched over to the end of the tent line. The dwarven warrior quickly followed, still calling his name out.

Thuradin himself wasn't quite sure what he was doing. Was he finally going to confront Hork? What would he say? How would he respond when Hork inevitably told him that this was none of his business? He tried to calm down enough to visualize a few scenarios and mentally prepare but his anger was too hot. It was made even more so when he saw the tent flap pushed aside and Lyrie step out. He was close enough now to observe her puffy red eyes, her flushed cheeks. She'd been crying.

It wasn't long before she saw him coming. Something in his face must have given away his intentions. Her eyes widened and she rushed toward him, her hands up placatingly while she glanced over her shoulder as if to make sure she wasn't being watched.

"Thuradin," she whispered, trying to hold him back as the

two met in the middle of the path. He brushed past her and kept marching. She followed in his wake. "Please, leave it alone, Thuradin. Do nae rile him up. There's nothing here ye need ta concern yerself with."

"Oh, nothing, aye," Thuradin grunted. He was close enough now to call out his summons, which he did in a booming voice.

"Hork!"

Hork's glowering face poked out from the entrance, saw Thuradin, then shook with laughter. He stepped out in a dirty tunic, his lower half still armored with plate. He ambled lazily toward Thuradin, scratching his unkempt, black beard as he sized him up.

Thuradin glared. At one time this dwarf had been a friend. Many decades had passed since the last time they'd truly interacted with each other, and it was clear the years had not been kind to Hork. The wind played with his scraggly hair, or what was left of it. The stains on his shirt looked old. The stench of alcohol hung on his breath, and it wasn't from beer. No this was from something stronger. Much stronger.

"And what do I owe the pleasure of being summoned by the former commander of the royal guard–in the company of my own wife, no less?" Hork drawled.

"Don't be coy with me," Thuradin said sternly. He took a breath, checking himself. Now that he was confronting the dwarf, he realized a game was being played. Hork was keeping his wits about him. Instead of coming out of his tent blustering and raging for a fight, as Thuradin had been expecting, he came out amicably. He even pretended that being called out by Thuradin was some sort of honor. It was all tongue-in-cheek, he knew, which made it all the more impor-tant that he play the same game. He could not come into this encounter with axes raised high and a battle cry to follow.

"I've called on ye because I saw ye and yer wife come inta camp just now."

Hork yawned. "Aye, we did. We've had a long night on sentry duty and I'm looking forward ta a long, deep slumber. So, if ye don't mind?"

"Quite a night, was it?" Thuradin asked. "Ye came inta camp with such fire in yer step I would've thought ye'd just caught yer wife deserting. Did ye speak ta her with yer hand too while no one was looking?"

Hork's visage darkened.

"Thuradin, please," Lyrie begged in a strained voice. "Leave it alone."

Thuradin heard the tremor in her words. He hated to hear it. Hated that the source behind it was this pathetic dwarf standing before him like he hadn't a care in the world. This dwarf who didn't realize how lucky he was.

"Is it any of yer business how I speak ta my wife, commander? I know it's been said ye sometimes have difficulty understanding, so let me make it plain." He stuck out a fat finger at Lyrie, who took an involuntary step back. "She is *my* wife. And I'll thank ye ta keep yer large nose out of our business. I'll speak ta her how I please."

"I'm under no illusion ta whom Lyrie is married, as unbelievable as it may be, considering the pathetic specimen before my eyes," Thuradin growled. "I simply think it a waste ta take what ye have for granted considering the gem ye've acquired. Perhaps ye should spend some time polishing yer sapphires instead of dragging them through the mud."

Hork chuckled and shook his head. "Ah, Thuradin, Thuradin. If we're speaking of gems here, what happened ta yers? Ye let yer emerald sit on the shelf ta gather dust. What do ye know about polishing, commander? Yer gem cracked and shattered into a million pieces, only ta be swept away and tossed inta the scrapheap. And that, my friend, was yer own doing."

Thuradin's eyes bulged and he let out an incoherent roar as he shot a fist out, connecting with Hork's jaw. His blow hit so hard, Hork nearly completed a full spin in the air before landing on the floor. Thuradin instantly felt a pair of strong arms wrap around his torso.

"Easy now," Borim grunted into his ear. "Take a breath. Ye don't want ta create any more of a scene than ye already have. Calm down, Thuradin."

Lyrie rushed over to Hork's side, gingerly trying to pull him up. He brushed her off roughly, knocking her over. With a grunt, he rolled onto his back and leaned up on his elbows, staring daggers at Thuradin. He put a finger to his nose and pulled away with it stained red. He laughed.

The sound snapped Thuradin out of his blind rage. Fury remained, but now he had enough self-awareness to regret allowing himself to lose control. He had lost the game. Hork had gotten the better of him. He turned to Lyrie to apologize but she wouldn't look at him, keeping her eyes fixed on the ground as Hork continued to cackle, gasping for breath.

"Just go, Thuradin. Leave us be."

With a grimace, Thuradin turned and stormed back to his own tent, Borim following close behind. His hands shook. His mind was a whirlwind of thoughts and emotions, none of which he could focus on. He kept his eyes on the path ahead, ignoring curious stares from others who were peeking out of their tents to see what the commotion was about. Hork's laughter followed him with every step he took.

The two dwarves finally reached their tents. Thuradin sank into his stool and let his face fall into his hands. Borim sat down next to him. An uneasy look entered his eyes, but he gave his friend a sympathetic pat on the shoulder nevertheless.

"What in Nythirim's name is going through yer mind, my friend?"

Thuradin didn't lift his head. His breathing relaxed. His thoughts were no longer awhirl, nor were his emotions. They had finally settled and focused onto one singular thought. The contemptible leer of Morteth Shadowmeld loomed large in his mind's eye.

He sighed. "Nothing good."

It was noon when Felix finally awoke, slumped over the table sitting in the middle of the command tent. He had been there all night, numb to everything around him, determined to forego sleep until he could come up with some scheme that would lead to Victria's rescue. Eventually, with no such idea coming, his eyes had betrayed him, and he had entered the blissful world of dreams without realizing it.

Now awake, his memories returned. The severity of the situation was coming back. Victria and her friends were captured.

Victria.

His hands balled into fists, but he controlled himself. He would not let despair rule the day. He had to keep calm and collected if he was going to figure out how to free her.

As he thought that, he also recalled how unwilling everyone else was to help him. They already considered her lost. Dead. But she wasn't. And he would do all he could to ensure she didn't end up that way. But he needed more information, more help.

He left the command tent and brought his hand over his eyes, squinting. The sun was high in the sky and blinded him after having spent so much time in dim lighting. Once his eyes had adjusted, he made his way over to the only other tent as large as his own. It was a short walk. As he approached, the ring of guards surrounding it saluted and let him pass without question. He pushed the tent flaps back and entered.

Before him were the four acolytes who had vowed to defeat their corrupted siblings. Each one came in their own uniquely designed artifact, chests made of precious metals of varying sizes and shapes with different gemstones set into them in random patterns. Glyphs and runes decorated the sides, running their way all around.

The acolytes were set in a semi-circle facing the entrance. Each one's ethereal tendrils extended out of their respective artifacts and swayed softly like blades of multicolored grass. The First One's white mixed with Scorpus' green; green mixed in with Faenerus' yellow, creating a new and lighter shade of the color; Faenerus' tendrils intertwined with the blue of Veliris, creating a deep vibrant green that reminded Felix of the forest surrounding his home.

He still didn't understand what these tendrils were or what they were made of. Were they energy? Were they the physical bodies of the acolytes? He had no idea. He could, however, appreciate their wispish nature and thought they were pretty to look at. He took a minute to let the picture before him sink in, his worries temporarily forgotten. But it could not last.

He cleared his throat, as if the acolytes did not already know he was there.

"Ah, Felix," The First One said gently. "I expected you to come. Veliris has already told me of Victria's fate as well as the capture of her companions. I cannot say I understand how you feel, being who I am, but I am sorry such a sacrifice was necessary to free my brother from captivity."

"There will be no sacrifice."

Each individual tendril slowly turned to face the elder viatari. Light pulsed through the tent as The First One spoke, "Explain."

"I intend to rescue them," Felix said with some force in his voice. "Victria and her friends are prisoners. They are not dead yet, and I will not let their fate be one of torture and misery. I intend to rescue them with every means at my disposal. But first, I need information."

The acolytes hesitated. "I trust you have spoken with the others about this matter already?"

"I have spoken to some."

"What questions do you have?"

Felix took a moment to organize his thoughts. "First, I need to know what plans your sister might have for them. Why would she take them captive? What could she possibly gain?"

"I cannot speak for her," The First One answered thoughtfully. "She is not one to normally take prisoners, so I can only speculate. But Victria may be a prized capture because it gives her an opportunity to learn more about how the viatari body works in relation to her corruptive powers."

"You think she will try to bring them over to her side?"

"Victria would be a prized asset," the acolyte's tendrils nodded. "Not only would she be a detrimental emotional weapon to be used against you, but her strength and speed as a viatari would be enhanced in a corrupted state. She could prove a dangerous foe if my sister does indeed manage this."

Scorpus chuckled. "It would be like her, wouldn't it? Using emotion to defeat the leader of those who oppose her. Manipulation at its finest."

"Aren't the viatari already easily susceptible to her corruption?" Faenerus asked. "Did you not tell us, brother, of when this exact viatari before us drank from waters polluted by her essence and how easily she took over his systems?"

"Yes," The First One said. "But that is not the kind of corruption she seeks. Her essence nearly killed Felix because his body rejected the properties of its infectious nature and chose to die instead. What I think she will try to learn is how to corrupt the viatari without killing them, so that she may control them as she does the humans and burrowers. That being said, I doubt her disciples will shed a tear if one or two of their newly gained prisoners dies in the process."

"A dangerous prospect if realized," Veliris murmured.

"Indeed. Which is why, Felix," the acolytes returned their attention to the elder viatari. "If you plan on rescuing them, we will do what we can to assist you."

Felix felt a weight lift off his shoulders. He had come here primarily to ask for their aid when it came time to do battle. Instead, they had offered their services of their own volition without him having to convince them. This had gone better than he had anticipated. A good sign for the future.

"I am grateful for your aid, First One," Felix bowed his head in thanks. "It will be invaluable."

"We do this for the good of the cause," The First One responded. "You would do well to remember that." One of the acolyte's white tendrils slithered close to Felix's face, as if looking directly at him. "I can sense your thoughts, viatari. Yes, even you. Be sure you are doing this for the right reasons. Do not allow emotion to cloud your judgment, for that will only lead to our own destruction."

Salevari had said much the same thing. Felix swallowed back a retort he had prepared for the next time he heard such a sentiment. The acolytes could warn him all they liked, so long as they helped him accomplish his goal.

The First One continued, "I imagine you will launch a full assault on the Three Spires, this time with the intention of truly taking them. Am I correct?"

Felix nodded. "That is the only way forward that I can see. Though, I have yet to draw up a strategy for such an assault. I have more to consider before we move forward."

"Let it be a plan that is well thought out, then, for I warn you: though we voluntarily give our efforts, we cannot risk capture. If we sense that the battle goes ill, we will be forced to retreat. Even without your orders to do so."

Felix nodded his understanding. "I will do my best to ensure a strong plan of action, then."

"Don't think too long, viatari," Scorpus spoke up, his pale green tendrils joining The First One's. "You must be prudent but swift. If the whole point of this attack is to save your beloved, there will be no point in risking ourselves should our sister turn her before we can make our move."

Felix felt his cheeks flush. Scorpus had called Victria his beloved, and while he certainly felt that way—and now recognized his feelings for her—he was still surprised to learn how many others knew or suspected the truth.

"She is strong," he said. "I know she will fight The Turned One's corruption with every fiber of her being. She and the others will not fall easily. I have every confidence."

Scorpus retreated back to his artifact. "Very good."

"Then, if that is all, child of Arokun, you must leave us," Faenerus said. "While you make your plans, we acolytes must combine our might to break through our siblings' mental wards that they have surrounded themselves with. Once we accomplish this, we will better understand the full measure of their intentions and how we might counter them."

Felix began to walk out, but The First One's voice pulled

him back before he could leave.

"There is one other thing, Felix, that you must be aware of."

The elder viatari turned back and found a cluster of white tendrils hovering only inches from his face. It was a dazzling display of pulsing energy that might have blinded him had he not shielded his eyes in time.

"With us being so close to my sister, there are some risks that come with that. Yes, we can affect her and her forces when we need to with our powers, but she can do the same to us. Her corrupting influence can reach out from the mountains into this camp and affect those whose moods or thoughts are dark enough. This is something everyone must be aware of. Should anyone from our camp fall too deeply into despair or anger or doubt, with time, she will come to control their actions without them even realizing it."

The First One took a moment to let the thought sink in. "I tell you this because I sense your own despair. There is darkness within our camp. It hangs heavy like a fog. It would be wise for you to share my warning with everyone else. Have them practice discipline of the mind; control their emotions, their thoughts. My aura can counter my sister's to a point, as it has while we've been here. But my options are limited if someone willingly allows themselves to fall into darkness. Do we understand each other?"

Felix considered the acolyte's words. He didn't particularly feel any foreign presence around him. Yes, he felt despair, but who wouldn't after what had transpired? Still, he knew better than to allow it to control his thinking. This decision to assault the Three Spires was his and his alone. Still, this warning was not one to take lightly.

"I understand."

White tendrils returned to their golden artifact. "Then go and plan your attack. May the spirit of Arokun guide your hand."

Felix nodded and left the tent. He expected to step out into sunlight but found he had spent more time with the acolytes than he had realized. The sun had almost completely disappeared, replaced by the moon and a scattering of stars. The camp was settling down for the day. Sentry shifts were being changed. Campfires were lit. Laughter and the buzz of conversation rose from several parts of camp as those without sentry duty relaxed with their fellows around a fire.

Felix stayed where he was, taking it all in. He observed the camp as best he could from this hill where the acolytes' tent had been erected. He was deep in his own thoughts. His mind was a flurry of planning and imagined scenarios. He thought of their last assault on the mountains. Of course, it hadn't been a true attempt, but it had been a costly distraction. Traps had been laid out in various locations up the mountain path. If they made another assault, Felix had no doubt that at least some of those traps would be reset. Based on what Thuradin had reported, his opponent was not The Turned One herself anymore, but someone with a mind for war. Someone who knew what they were doing. Felix would have to tread carefully if he wanted to lead them all to victory.

He wished he could get more information about the Three Spires themselves, but he had already exhausted all the knowledge the dwarves and burrowers could offer. That left him with only a shallow understanding of what lay before and within the three threatening peaks. Sadly, that meant much was to be desired when it came to making preparations. No matter what he planned, no matter how much he prepared, if they managed to fight their way into the mountains, they would be charging into its tunnel systems blind.

Still, that wouldn't keep him from trying. An image of Victria leaning comfortably against one of the numerous arched windows that populated Aleganthia's keep, looking out at the white-stoned city, flashed through his head and filled him with a new sense of energy and resolve.

His gaze rose from the camp below him to the looming mountains in the distance. In the darkness of night, he couldn't make out many features, but the Three Spires themselves rose high above the other peaks, looking like they might topple over and crash into camp.

Within them was his beloved, as Scorpus had called her. And he had never told her. If—when—he rescued her, he would not fail again in that regard. He would not let their remaining moments in this world slip away with things unsaid. He just needed her to hold on and wait for him. Just a little longer.

"Please," he whispered, tearing his gaze away and forcing himself back into the command tent where he could think and plan undisturbed. "Please, just wait for me."

CHAPTER SEVEN

Salevari had never experienced liquefaction before. From what Serania had told her, she hadn't been missing much. After experiencing it for herself, she had to agree.

A second ago she had been standing just outside of their camp beneath the mountains with her other companions and two vashi. The next second, she heard a roar in her ears, felt a cold wetness seep through her leather armor and clothes. Salt stung her eyes, forcing them to remain shut as she felt herself jostled forward by some natural force. Her face fell beneath the waves as they knocked her over and she took in a mouthful of salt water. Feeling the sandy bottom beneath her feet, she kicked up with force and burst out of the ocean's grasp, gagging. She tried stepping forward but was quickly pulled under again. Her eyes still stung, but she opened them anyway to try and get an idea of what was going on. To either side of her, it seemed her companions were struggling just as much as she was to get out of the water.

One of the vashi grabbed her by the arm and pulled her the rest of the way. The waves kept coming, pushing against her back, but the vashi's strong hold helped steady her until she finally was on the sandy beach, out of the water's reach. The vashi withdrew his grip and Salevari collapsed onto her knees, breathing deeply. Sand clung to her wet body. She tried brushing it off as she stood and surveyed her surroundings, but the coarse grains stubbornly stuck to her until she eventually gave up.

To her east and west stretched out more beach. Ahead of her, the shore sloped gently upward. Tufts of grass and shrubs grew on it, fluttering with the coastal breeze. Behind her the waves continued to roar as wall after wall of water rose up, curled, and crashed in one motion, only to be drawn back so it could repeat its endless dance.

"Where are we?" she finally sputtered.

"On a remote beach between the townsss of Donsea and Halding Port," one of the vashi responded. "We thought it prudent that we not deposit you too clossse to either town, in cassse they sssee usss in your company."

The other vashi hissed in agreement. "It would be difficult to gain their trust if they sssaw usss with you."

Salevari nodded but frowned with some annoyance. "Still, it would have been nice to not have such a rude welcome. You could have warned us."

The two vashi bowed. "Our apologiesss, Chancellor. We forget sssometimesss how unaccustomed the other racesss are to the sssea."

Unaccustomed was one way of putting it. Now that her adrenaline from almost drowning was dying down, Salevari took in the majesty of the ocean for the first time. She had heard descriptions of it from Serania, had listened to all her stories of her time in this region with great interest. But she could never believe how vast it truly was. She couldn't fathom so much water existing in one place, nor that it could move on its own as it did. She beheld the clouds, which seemed fuller, larger, and more majestic here than they did in the Western Lands or even by the mountains. They floated lazily across, crossing from sea to land with an ease and speed that belied their size.

Next to her, Drathanar Sungard, Aniria Windryder, and Zael Windkeeper were on their backs, propped up by their elbows, taking it all in themselves. Drathanar's normally wild hair was soaked and stuck to his face as he stared dumbfounded at the scene before him. Aniria was wringing out her shoulder-length silver hair, just as stunned. Only Zael, with his ever-serious face, perfect in its appearance save for a crooked nose, seemed unfazed. He shook his long hair dry next to Aniria, drawing a reproachful look from her, then stood up and climbed the northern slope, no doubt to check for any dangers that may lay beyond. Tera and Simon simply lay where they were, taking in deep lungfuls of the salty sea air as they let the hot sun dry them off.

Salevari brought her attention back to the vashi who remained a few paces away, their feet still in the ocean.

"Thank you for bringing us here," she said with sincerity. "You saved us a lot of time, which in itself has helped us greatly with our task."

The two vashi bowed once again.

"We are happy to ssserve." One of them said.

The other added, "With your leave, we will return to our friendsss in the mountainsss. Should you need the aid of the vashi again, you will need to travel into our watersss to contact usss."

Salevari nodded. "I will remember that. Thank you."

Dismissed, the vashi slunk back into the ocean, their heads

disappearing underwater. Salevari followed their movements beneath the waves for a time, but when the two figures suddenly disappeared she knew they were alone.

They spent some time on the beach, following the humans' lead, and allowed the sun to dry them as they considered their next step. Salevari had studied the maps of this region intensely, committing them to memory. If the vashi dropped them off where they had said, Halding Port would be to their east and Donsea to their west.

"Come," Salevari finally said, feeling they had waited long enough. "We must make our way to Halding Port."

Tera perked up at that. "If I might ask, don't you think it would be wiser to go to Donsea first?"

The Dalyran Chancellor weighed her words, remembering what she could from Serania's tales. "I was under the impression Donsea was just a fishing village. Halding Port, as I've been told, is much more powerful. Their fleet would go a long way in meeting our needs, is this not so?"

"Yes, but–"

"Then we go to Halding Port first," Salevari decided with finality. "We do what we have to do to convince their leader of our cause. If we accomplish our task quickly enough, then we can visit Donsea and see what they might have to offer as well."

With that she turned and trekked eastward along the shoreline. The others followed.

Tera shrugged, muttering, "I wouldn't underestimate the people of Donsea. Then again, what do I know?" But she followed all the same.

There wasn't much for them to do as they walked. As far as Salevari was aware, there were no natural threats in this part of the coast and Zael had reported that the land to their north turned into swampy grasslands past the sandy slope. They were far enough away from human civilization that the viatari could travel in their natural forms, rather than donning their human illusions, without worry. She decided to make the most of this downtime by learning. She called Tera and Simon up to walk beside her as the others held back. Drathanar and Aniria continued to admire their surroundings, marching forward almost in a daze, often bumping into each other. Zael, on the other hand, remained focused, his watchful eyes surveying the land around them constantly.

"Tell me of Halding Port," Salevari said. "My daughter has already shared her experience there, but I wish to know more. Who is their leader? What's he like?"

"Tera," Simon offered. "That would be more your domain than mine. I have not had the pleasure of stepping foot in that city even during my wandering days."

Tera nodded and cleared her throat. "As I'm sure you know, Halding Port is a major city that specializes in the fishing industry. They have other manufacturing enterprises as well and excel in trade, but fishing is their priority. It is entirely because of this industry that they developed their fleet, which is unmatched in the Southern Seas. They are a militaristic people, very ordered. Rulebreakers are punished harshly, lawbreakers even more so. They run a very tight ship, if you'll excuse the pun."

Salevari absorbed this information, then asked, "And the people are all like this? Down to the lowliest beggar?"

"It is a culture that is bred into them," Tera nodded.

"And what of their leader?"

"He holds the title of 'Grand Admiral.' I believe his name is Fradrick, though I haven't had the pleasure of meeting him personally. There's also a class of elite socialites who think they run the city, though as long as they remain well-fed and well-dressed they don't really care how the city is run. From what I've heard about Fradrick, though, he is respectable. He runs Halding Port with a tight, orderly fist. If there is some plot within the city that we must unravel, I would be surprised if he is unaware of it. I hear he runs a vast intelligence network that gathers all sorts of information on every person who enters the city's walls. You can be sure that when we arrive, he'll know of it."

The viatari considered this. If Halding Port's intelligence was as formidable as Tera claimed, that could pose a problem when it came to offering the people there a solution for whatever problem The Turned One had brewing for them. If they had nothing to offer these humans, there would be little reason for them to join their alliance, much less help the vashi repel the coming darinsha invasion.

"Tell me of the history between these humans and the vashi."

Tera sighed, her head drooping. "It's a long story that everyone born in Halding Port knows by heart. It's drilled into them during their school days. I'll give you the short version.

"At one time, humans were primarily a nomadic race. Over time, we settled in various lands. The ones who settled on the coast quickly encountered the vashi. At first, the two were friendly, but cautious of each other. Problems quickly arose when humans learned how to fish, and how to do it well. At first, the vashi let them go about their business. The humans needed to eat, just like they did, so they allowed them to continue as they desired along the coastline. The fishing industry was so new and rudimentary that it had little effect on the natural populations within the sea.

"As the centuries went on, however, the human population

grew. Their expertise with fishing advanced in leaps and bounds. They learned first how to build ships, then bigger ones, eventually creating a vast trawler fleet with the sole purpose of setting out to the deeper parts of the sea where there were larger and more exotic fish. It increased how much they brought in as well. Along with feeding their own population, they used the excess to trade with other human settlements that did not have the resources they did, bringing in large profits. At this point, the industry became detrimental not just for survival, but also the thriving lifestyle its people began to enjoy.

"The vashi realized their mistake too late. The humans by this point were sailing far too deep into the ocean, harvesting fish by the netful, even ones that the vashi themselves wouldn't hunt for one reason or another. They realized the humans' inability to control their own growth would never end and so they took matters into their own hands and declared war on Halding Port; but really, it was war on any human who lived on the coast.

"It was a brutal, bloody, and long conflict. Many towns used to pocket this coast, but they were all destroyed. Only Halding Port, Donsea, and a few small villages survived the fighting. When the war started, humans had only begun investing in a navy, but what they had already put in turned out to be enough. Their large, sturdy ships could weather a vashi attack, even withstand the storms summoned by their waterseers. They brought devastation and death to the vashi waters, even laying siege to Zessarix at one point for a time.

"As the war dragged on, it became clear that the vashi were losing. They sued for peace. And though the humans had clearly won, and had every right to take what they wanted, they only took what they needed to maintain their fishing enterprise, having lost all taste for battle themselves. That is why the Sea of Scales is divided; the northern half for the humans, the southern half for the vashi. An agreement was made that no humans would venture past the line where the Great Coral Forest began. The vashi guard this border strictly to this day."

Salevari whistled. "Not to cut you off, Tera, but I thought you said you would give us the short version."

Tera raised an eyebrow and said soberly, "That was the short version. Needless to say, atrocities were committed by both sides. The war lasted so long and so many people died that it left a bitter taste. Because of that, hatred for the vashi runs through the veins of every human in Halding Port even now, three centuries after the war's end. And this goes both ways with the vashi."

This was a lot to take in. Salevari had known the animosity between the two races would have some kind of origin like this, but having heard the story herself, she could only hope the hatreds were not still so strong that they couldn't be reasoned against. Perhaps their hatreds could be redirected. If the darinsha were as bad as Avmoshir claimed, could she convince the humans to shift their focus onto a new target? She asked as much.

"Knowing how we humans work, they won't believe you that there is some greater threat than the vashi unless they see it themselves," was Tera's response.

"I have to agree," Simon said. "Not only that, but with how strong their fleet appears to be, they may believe they can take on the vashi *and* the darinsha alone."

"Then our only true option is not only to show Halding Port that they are already a part of this war, but also that they cannot fight it alone." The Dalyran Chancellor pursed her lips, thoughtful as she meandered down the sandy beach. "The

Turned One rarely uses brute force to accomplish her goals, however. She will have created some cunning plot that will require more than a powerful fleet to unravel."

"Probably so," Simon said. "That's assuming this intelligence network Tera mentioned isn't as good as she says they are and hasn't already handled the problem."

"Well," Salevari sighed. "Yes, that's true. Let's hope that isn't the case then or we will have nothing to bargain with and we'll have failed before we've even begun."

They stopped to rest after having walked for several hours. The scenery around them hadn't changed. Sandy beach stretched on for miles, curving inward along the water until it disappeared from sight. Behind them, Salevari could see the line of tracks they had left all the way to the horizon. With any luck, the tide would erase them eventually, though she had no way of knowing how high the waters here could rise.

While some of the party rested in the sand, absorbing the hot sun, Drathanar, Aniria, and Tera ventured into the ocean to cool off. At first, the two viatari nervously stood by the edge of the water, letting it rush to their feet. With each passing wave, their confidence grew until the two joined Tera where the water was deep. They let the waves roll over them, soaking them and pushing them back to shore. Every time they were pushed back, they trudged even deeper, fighting the ocean's push and pull. At one point, Drathanar lost his footing just as a wave hit him, causing him to tumble over himself, his limbs sprawling as the wave swept him all the way to shore. Aniria let out a burst of laughter but just as quickly stifled it with her hands. Even so, a smile bled from behind her attempted cover.

It was a sight Salevari hadn't expected but was glad to see. Though she hadn't known the young viatari until after tragedy had struck her, she had heard often from the likes of Victria and Thuradin how she had been the definition of optimism and joy. The loss of her brother and fiancé during the siege of Aleganthia had dramatically changed her into a somber, vengeful shadow of herself. That shadow was all the Chancellor had ever known. Until now.

Having suffered tremendous loss herself, Salevari knew it wasn't always time that allowed for wounds to heal, but rather a specific catalyst; an event, a distraction, something or someone new to fill the hole of what had been. Watching Drathanar lift himself back to his feet, spitting out a mouthful of salty water as he waved at Aniria and waded back to her, her lips curved by their own accord. Oh yes, there was a catalyst here, she thought. And she was only too happy to encourage her ever faithful, dependable general to be that catalyst.

She glanced over to her left, where Zael sat, looking bored. He too had served her well during a time of great need. Yet, for him, it seemed duty was the only thing on his mind.

"You can go into the sea too if you wish," she offered. "We are safe here for now, and it looks like fun."

Zael shook his head. "I have no time for games."

Salevari thought they had nothing but time right now but decided not to mention that fact; instead choosing to watch a small cast of hermit crabs trying to scuttle through the foaming surf. They never made it far. Individually, they were too weak to counter the push of the waves, even when those waves were right on the cusp of being pulled back from whence they came. She didn't know how these creatures normally behaved, but she couldn't help but think that if they banded together, they might be able to counter the feeble strength of a dying wave just enough to enter the oceanic realm. Then, the world would be before them.

With a sniff, she turned her gaze. If a creature as simple as a hermit crab couldn't think to band together in the face of overwhelming odds, what chance did they have of convincing the humans to do the same?

Finally, after some time, Drathanar, Aniria, and Tera returned to shore. They collapsed onto the sandy beach and let the sun dry their soaked bodies. As they recovered, Simon, who had gone off to scout ahead, returned and sat next to Salevari.

"I believe I know the best way for us to approach Halding Port, but we're going to need a few things."

"What's your plan?"

"I know little of the ways of coastal humans, and I suspect they know just as little about us plainsmen. We can use that to our advantage. We have nothing similar when it comes to an elite class like the one Tera mentioned for Halding Port, but we do have chiefs, and we can use the title of chief to present ourselves as nobility from the northern towns. I believe that could pique the interest of the elite in Halding Port and may allow us easier access to their Grand Admiral."

Salevari nodded. "I assume you'll present yourself as chief then, since you were one in the past. What about the rest of us?"

Simon glanced at her with a knowing smile. "You'll be a chief's wife, of course."

"My, Simon," Salevari took on a mockingly bashful air. "Is that your idea of a proposal?"

"Please," the human chief scoffed. "No need to flatter yourself. It's only a practical solution. Being a chief's wife will have perks you may need to lead us in this mission. As my wife, you will have as much access and weight in your words and desires as I would. Otherwise, you might be ignored simply for being a woman."

"Humans," Salevari shook her head, lifting her eyes to the heavens. "So silly the way they think of the other sex."

"Be that as it may, that's how we are."

"Then, what about the others?"

"Aniria has a pretty face—"

"You *are* a judge."

"Quit interrupting," Simon frowned. "Think tactically. That's all this is."

The viatari sighed but nodded. Simon was right, and clearly not in the mood for her light-hearted teasing.

"With Aniria's looks, we can pass her off as either our daughter or as another noblewoman. Drathanar and Zael can be our bodyguards and Tera will be a lady-in-waiting for Aniria."

"Why not have Drathanar act as Aniria's husband or something similar? With such a pretty face, Aniria is sure to attract some elite bachelors."

A smug grin lined Simon's face. "Exactly. A man who feels the need to prove himself is a braggart with a loose tongue. She will be able to siphon information with ease if we need her to."

After giving it a moment's thought, Salevari found that she liked the plan. It was practical and seemed to have a solid chance of success. As long as the viatari could pull off being human. That was her one worry. Aniria might do well enough, having been raised in Aleganthia. The viatari of that city often donned their human illusions when traveling through the plains. They were accustomed to this sort of playacting. Dalyrans, living in isolation within their canyon-city, had no need to pretend to be human. They didn't practice with their human disguises, nor did they know how humans really acted among themselves. Simon seemed to read her thoughts.

"Do not worry, dear wife," he said sarcastically, though he

gripped her shoulder in a reassuring manner. "I will teach you what to do, how to do it, and everything else you need to know. We'll make a human out of you yet."

Laughing, she accepted his confidence as her own. "It's a good plan. But you said we needed some things to pull it off?"

Tera, having dried off, meandered over and joined the conversation. Salevari welcomed her. This was a topic with which she valued the wanderer's added input. Besides, involving her in these plans would be a good distraction, one that could help shake off the sullen air that seemed to linger around her with every step she took these days.

"Well, we can't present ourselves as nobles with you and the others dressed in your viatari armor. We need to make you proper outfits—dresses—ones that a noblewoman from the north would wear."

"But what *would* they wear? You said yourself there are no nobility among your people."

"True, but I have an idea of what someone in that position might wear, if someone like that were to exist. They won't know the difference. You and Aniria will only have to *look* the part. I need supplies to make the dresses, however. And time. And we need horses. Nobles don't walk when they travel."

"What you're saying is we can't just continue on our way to Halding Port like we have been. We need to make our preparations somewhere else?" Salevari asked with a frown. "That would delay us for days, if not weeks."

"Not if we got the supplies from somewhere where we could *also* focus on our task," Tera suggested, her eyes lighting up. "Like Donsea."

Salevari looked at her. Tera had a knowing smile on her face that said plainly that she was suggesting the only correct option. And she knew it.

"Donsea won't care that you're viatari," Tera continued. "So we don't have to worry about appearing human with them. We don't have to pretend to be nobles from the north either. While Simon and I make ourselves busy gathering the supplies we need and making the dresses you need, you can speak with the leadership there and earn their favor for our cause. It'll be like a test run for the real challenge anyway. The people of Donsea don't harbor the same resentment for the vashi that Halding Port does. They'll have horses to sell as well."

Simon and Salevari shared a look.

"She has a point," he finally shrugged. "It's our best option."

Salevari spent a moment longer staring out into the ocean as she let her thoughts settle. The sun was already drifting toward the horizon. No matter what they chose, they wouldn't reach either town before nightfall. She wanted to go to Halding Port straight away. It was their main target, the one ally that would surely help them the most. But she could think of no counterarguments to Tera's proposal. She was right. Donsea would give them the time and foundation they needed to approach Halding Port properly, giving them every chance for success. And they *needed* to succeed. Besides, she shrugged to herself, perhaps Donsea had more to offer than a fleet of fishermen. There was only one way to find out.

"Very well," she finally conceded. "We make for Donsea."

Tera grinned widely and Simon clapped his hands. Both humans lifted themselves onto their feet.

"No time to waste, then." Tera said, a familiar confidence creeping back into her voice. "Without horses, it will take us a few days to make it to town, so we better get moving."

Salevari agreed. Once everyone had shaken off any clinging sand, they turned back the way they had come and followed their own tracks westward. The ocean roared encouragement with every step they took.

CHAPTER EIGHT

It took several days for them to reach Donsea. At night, the viatari ventured out into the grassy swamplands to the north to find something to feed on. During the day, if they were lucky, they could catch some fish or small sharks that wandered too close to shore. But this proved insufficient for keeping them from tapping into the small bags of live critters they carried with them in order to stave off hunger. The humans had an easier time, capable of carrying more dried meats and bread than the viatari could live animals.

Water was also difficult to come by. Salevari thought it ironic that they were forced to ration their supply in order to have enough for their journey when there was a giant, endless pool of the stuff right next to them. Of course, it was undrinkable.

Still, they trudged on under the beating sun. They took breaks to rest occasionally, but otherwise never stopped. Even at night. By the end of their journey, their feet were sore. Their supplies were low. They were exhausted. In that moment, Salevari would have liked nothing more than to collapse onto a bed—even the floor would suffice—where she could escape into a dreamless void for an unspecified amount of time.

Seeing the small port town from a distance had filled them with a final spurt of energy. Donsea was exactly as Serania had described it. A simple palisade surrounded the town, offering protection. As they approached the gates, however, Salevari didn't see many guards stationed around it. Those that were there waved them through without so much as a glance. She thought this was rather lazy and spoke volumes about the laxness of security here.

She still had difficulty understanding what kind of place Donsea could be if it wasn't just a simple fishing village. Tera seemed to believe that they had something to offer. Salevari would wait to pass final judgment, but right now she couldn't see it.

This was a clean town, that much was certain. The gravel pathways were flanked by tall palm trees that offered a fair amount of shade to those who meandered under them. And meandered was the word to use, Salevari thought. The few people they did pass walked slowly, as if without purpose. Often she and the others would have to navigate around the town's denizens as they continued down their straight path deeper into Donsea.

Past the palm trees were rows upon rows of neatly built wooden houses, each lined with a porch. People sat in rocking chairs, watching them pass by, pipes hanging loosely from their lips or in their hands, smoke drifting aimlessly.

Though Tera had told the viatari they didn't need to, they had assumed their human forms, and Salevari was glad to have done so. Eyes were everywhere. She felt that everyone was watching them. Prejudice against her kind might not exist here like it had with the people of the plains, but she knew humans hated things that were different from them. Until she personally gauged how things were here, she didn't want to take the risk.

Her appearance wasn't too different from her regular look. Rather than the natural silver hair every viatari was born with, Salevari always opted to maintain her hair in its illusionary black. She thought it matched well with her vivid red eyes, at times making her seem even more intimidating. Now, however, her eyes were a deep shade of blue. Her fangs had softened into the flat teeth humans had. Glancing over her shoulder, she studied her fellow viatari and barely recognized them.

Aniria's hair had turned blonde, melding well with her green eyes. Her face was also spattered with freckles, a feature rarely seen on the viatari. Drathanar, who Salevari had only occasionally seen in his human form, had taken on an auburn hue for his wild mane. His eyes were a deep shade of brown. Zael, like Aniria, now sported blond hair, but his eyes were gray, his expression as stern as ever.

They took a few turns along the gravel path as time went on, passing through a central plaza where the town's inhabitants seemed to all converge. Markets were set up along the edges of the buildings, selling a variety of items from food to handmade jewelry made of seashells, to clothing. There was a fountain in the center that spewed water high, spraying those who sat around it with its cool touch. They didn't spend much time there, though. Soon they were once more making their way through a labyrinth of palm trees and wooden houses.

"Where are we going?" Salevari finally asked. She was eager to reach their destination, if only so she could take some weight off her feet.

"A friend's house," Tera answered. "I'm sure you've heard

of him from your daughter."

She had. They were to meet the man called Thomas, then. Salevari had to admit, she was curious about this human. Serania had mentioned his eccentric nature, and how perceptive he was. If half of what she had heard was true, there would be no deceiving him. He would know they were viatari the moment he set eyes on them. As she understood it, though, that didn't matter.

They soon came upon the so-called house that he lived in. It was as much a precarious dwelling as Serania had described. The uneven three-storied building was made of a mixture of brick and uncut stone, glued together with thick layers of mortar. Rotting planks of wood filled in the gaps where brick and stone were missing. The roof was mostly wooden with a few random patches of thatch. Two tin chimneys jutted out from there, thin trails of smoke rising into the sky. It was a mess. Salevari had no idea how this house could remain standing, much less how somebody could live in it.

"Come," Tera beckoned for everyone to follow. "Looks like Thomas is in. We'll have him put us up while we're here. I'm sure he'll be more than happy to help once he hears the reason for our presence."

"You expect me to confide in him our task?" Salevari asked with some bewilderment.

"If you want his help, I do," Tera replied curtly. "Don't worry. Thomas is a friend. Anything we tell him will not be shared in some gossip mill without our permission."

Tera approached the front door, rapped sharply three times, then barged in without waiting for a response.

"Come on out, then, you sack of mussels," she shouted, striding deeper into the house. "You have guests!"

A dark-skinned man with thick, disheveled hair and wild

eyes came stomping down the stairs as Simon, Salevari, and the rest of the viatari stood awkwardly just outside of the door's threshold. Salevari noticed that the descriptions given to her of this man were far from lacking. As he spun around to regard the strangers outside his home, her eyes roved over the barrage of white ink tattoos covering his body. She even recognized the few fish tattoos Victria had mentioned which swam around his right bicep with each movement he made.

Thomas smiled, revealing several rotting teeth and gaps where others had once existed. His gaze seemed to linger on Salevari, almost like he recognized her.

"Ya be waitin' fa an invitation?" He asked, turning to follow Tera. "Ya be waitin' a long time."

He disappeared around the corner, going into the same room as Tera. Laughter came from within as the two friends greeted each other. Salevari shared a glance with her companions, shrugged, then stepped inside.

"I not be expectin' to see ya so soon," Thomas said amusedly as she rounded the corner into a dining room with a single, long wooden table and several high back chairs surrounding it. "Last time it took ya years to come an' see ya old friend."

"Last time I was busy wandering the whole world," Tera replied with a light-hearted shrug. "I'm a little less busy this time around."

"Hah! I can't imagine life with da viatari bein' anyting but busy."

"Yes, well, it certainly has kept me grounded if nothing else. Though, with recent events, . . ." her voice trailed off. A dull fog shrouded her eyes. She brought her arms across her chest and shook her head, her easy-going smile returning, though it didn't stretch as far. "Speaking of the viatari, allow me to introduce you to your guests."

Tera motioned for her companions to join her, pointing out each one as she spoke. "They've come to The Southern Isles with an important task. The two ladies are Salevari and Aniria and the two standing over there trying to look intimidating by the doorway are Drathanar and Zael. Simon is a human, in case you weren't sure."

Thomas guffawed. "A plainsman. Nah every day I meet one of ya, mon."

Simon frowned as he regarded their host and asked, "How is it you know that I come from the plains?"

The fisherman scoffed and took a seat at the table, beckoning for the others to do the same. "Easy. Ya ain't got da smell of da sea on ya."

As Tera left for the kitchen to make salted tea for everyone—a refreshment, it was insisted, that would give them back all the energy they had spent during their journey—Thomas took his time studying each individual at his table. His brown eyes, bordered by white ink, were piercing. Salevari felt like he could see through her. A light chill settled over the nape of her neck. Simon wasn't enduring the silence too well, either.

"We're wasting time here," he finally said, rising from his seat suddenly even as Tera returned with a tray full of small clay cups. "We can stay at any basic tavern in town and accomplish our task. We need not waste time with this fisherman who would rather be floating on a plank in the sea."

Thomas closed his eyes and clicked his tongue. "Ya paint a pretty picture, mon, perhaps ya should paint it fa yaself. Ya plainsmen be so tightly wound, so busy, like da ropes holdin' da boats in place at da docks. Too much pressah and ya snap. Relax, mon, and share wit me what be worryin' ya so."

While the two men argued, Tera finished passing out the

strange beverage. Salevari sniffed hers and winced. The tea was named appropriately. She just hoped there was something else mixed in that would keep it from tasting like the ocean. As the hot liquid touched her tongue, a faint sourness mixed with salty overtones overwhelmed her tastebuds, creating a refreshing combination. Before she knew it, she had downed the whole drink, wishing she had more. She had to admit, Thomas was right. She felt energized, like she could make the journey between Donsea and Halding Port in a single night. With a new resolve, she decided she needed to take charge of the argument happening beside her.

"Simon, that's enough," she said in a voice that brooked no argument. The human chief frowned and focused on his drink. A slow grin crept across Thomas' face like frost as he turned his attention to the Dalyran Chancellor.

"To business, den. What brings ya to me 'umble abode, viatari?"

"We've come to recruit the coastal humans to our war effort. . . ." She explained the events that led up to their arrival. She spoke of the coming darinsha invasion. She explained their inability to send reinforcement to the vashi directly and how a plan had been hatched to recruit the coastal humans to be those reinforcements instead. She even shared some details of their plan for Halding Port, explaining how they would have to spend some time here in Donsea preparing for that grand prize. Thomas listened attentively. Salevari didn't think he blinked even once as she went on about their task and their desired outcome.

By the end of her explanation, she was exhausted again, her mouth dry. She looked down and saw that her cup had been refilled. With a grateful nod to Tera, she sipped the rejuvenating drink as Thomas absorbed all the information she had thrown at him.

The fisherman thought with his eyes closed. Even without his piercing gaze, the stylish white tattoos marking his face made it look like he was still watching them. Finally, eyes still closed, he let out a long, low whistle.

"It be a hefty ordah ya be puttin' in, viatari."

Salevari hadn't been sure what sort of response to expect, but it wasn't this. She raised an eyebrow. "In what way?"

"I'm sure ya know da history between da humans of da coast and da vashi," Thomas' eyes opened slowly as he spoke. "While Donsea don' harbor hatred 'gainst da vashi da same way as Halding Port, dere still be some feelings dere. Not fa me—" he put his hands to his chest, cracking a smile. "I be makin' me own deals wit da vashi. Dey be alright wit me and I be alright wit dem. Dat's why dey let me fish in deir waters. But I be da exception."

"Let's say we could get over this hatred between vashi and humans," Salevari suggested. "I would think a common threat would be enough to persuade a rational mind. Would Donsea be able to offer anything to assist the vashi if the enemy were to attack tomorrow?"

It was a veiled question. One meant to see if Donsea really had anything of value for their war effort while remaining innocuous. It was not as inconspicuous as Salevari might have hoped, however. Tera shot her a warning look. Thomas' eyes narrowed, though his grin remained fixed on his face, taking on the appearance of a shark.

"Ya tink we be a simple town of fishahmen and not'in else."

Salevari shrugged unapologetically. "I can only go off of what I've observed so far. I've seen no fleet, no military, and lax guards at your gates. Tera says I shouldn't underestimate you; but so far, I fail to see why."

Tera groaned, lifting her eyes to the ceiling, but Thomas reached out and patted her hand consolingly. When he spoke again, he spoke slowly, as if chewing on every word before it left his lips.

"Dere be other ways of fightin' on da seas dan wit big fancy ships," he said. "Perhaps ya should listen to ya friend here. No point in havin' a guide if all ya do be castin' her aside."

Their eyes met. Salevari felt an urge to look away but fought it. Though there was a vestige of remorse for asking the question the way she had, she wouldn't be cowed into offering some sort of apology. Finally, after several minutes, Thomas slapped the table and cackled.

"Besides, I ain't be da one to offer Donsea's services. Ya need to speak to da Boss if ya wanna win us ovah."

Salevari blinked. In an instant, the tension that had built up in the crowded room evaporated as if it had never been there to begin with.

"Who is the 'Boss'?" she asked. "How difficult would it be to get an audience with him?"

Thomas scratched at the fuzzy tuft of hair on his chin as he considered how to answer, "It be pretty easy. Da boss, Hadreen, he be called, don' do anyting all day. He be lazier dan me, as da plainsman here might say. I can speak wit him tonight and get ya before him." The shark-like grin reappeared. "But ya best be prepared when ya go to treat wit him. He be a laidback kinda guy, like me, but he be vicious when pushed. Dat's how he came to be da Boss, after all."

Thomas collected the empty clay cups and brought them back to the kitchen. When he returned, it was with a platter stacked high with live, flopping fish. In his other hand he balanced two smaller plates crowded with fried fish fillets, some cooked shrimp and a thick slice of bread. He handed these to Simon and Tera after setting the larger platter in the middle of the table.

"Apologies, plainsman. Dat fish be from yestahday's dinnah an' cold, but it still be good. Tera can vouch fa me on dat. As fa da viatari, I know how ya like to eat."

Grudgingly, Simon nodded his thanks and dug in. Salevari reached for a fish, ignoring its gulping gasps for breath, and bit into it, consuming the life-energies within. A trickle of warmth spread through her body and her strength returned. The fish withered in her hands, deflating like it had been dried. She tossed its remains back onto the platter and reached for another, her companions doing the same. As energy coursed through her limbs once again, curiosity drew her attention back to the subject at hand.

"What can you tell me about Hadreen?" Salevari asked, baring her fangs toward another hapless fish.

"To undahstand Hadreen is to undahstand da history of Donsea," Thomas leaned back in his chair, putting his fingers together. A distant gaze entered his eyes as if his mind was no longer in the present but dwelled on old memories. "Donsea wasn't always dis perfect clean town. It used to be a slum, full of da worst kinds of people. Crime be rampant. Murdah on ev'ry block. Ya had to be hard to get by here. We had our leadahs, but dey was weak or corrupt or both."

His eyes softened for a moment. "Den came Hadreen wit his crew of outlaws—fa dat's what dey were. Dey be a gang. Dey happened upon Donsea and were all but ready to pillage dis place. Da leadahs came out to meet wit him and offered someting fa Hadreen to leave dem be. To dis day, I don' know what deir offer be. But it clearly wasn't enough fa Hadreen.

"Hadreen sensed deir weakness, must 'ave realized he

could 'ave more dan just da loot a raid could provide. He could take an entire town and live off its wealth as its leadah. So dat's what he did. He killed da old leadahs where dey stood and took his place at da helm. Ovah time, he purged da city of all criminal activity dat wasn't endorsed by his own syndicate. He became da master of Donsea, da big Boss, and no one dared challenge him. He improved our lives, tore down da slums and turned dem into propah livin' places. He had his crew plant trees, make da place pretty, ya get da picture."

Thomas waved a hand as if the details were becoming a nuisance.

"Point is, since dat day, no one be challengin' his rule because dey know if dey cross Hadreen, it be *deir* heads put on spikes at da gates fa all to see. Or it be dey who be tied up wit chains and tossed from da docks to feed da sharks. Ya either work wit da Boss on his terms, or ya die."

Salevari tossed back the last of the withered fish. Thomas painted a vivid picture of a hard ruler, perhaps even a ruthless one, yet he also claimed that Hadreen maintained the same relaxed temperament that he himself had. She wondered how much of the eccentric fisherman's word she could take on face value and how much she would have to discover on her own. One thing was certain, though. When the time came to meet with this Hadreen, she would have to tread carefully.

With his story told, Thomas rose from his chair and clapped his hands. "I speak wit him tonight fa ya. I let ya know when he say he wanna meet. In da meantime, ya welcome to stay in me home. Explore da town. Take out a boat an' fish. I'm sure Tera already told ya, but I'll say it again. Ya are welcome to roam about town in ya viatari forms. Ya ain't da first we seen here, and dere be no bad blood wit ya people."

"Thank you for your hospitality," Salevari inclined her head.

"We will stay in our human forms, though. We'll need to be able to maintain them the entire time we're in Halding Port. Might as well get used to it. Aniria, Zael," the two viatari stood, waiting for her command. "Go walk around town. I want to hear more about what Donsea is like from your own perspectives. See what kind of feel you get from this place."

The two nodded and took their leave.

"I'll go out as well," Simon said, slowly lifting himself from his seat. "There are several materials I need to purchase to create the style of clothing you'll be wearing in Halding Port, and it'll take several days to shape them and fit them to your size. We also need to buy horses." He glanced at Tera. "I'd appreciate if you came along to help me haggle with this town's merchants. Even with all the dwarven gold at our disposal, I want to be sure we get a fair price. I don't like the idea of being taken advantage of just because I smell like the plains."

Tera agreed and stood to leave with him.

"Take Drathanar with you." Salevari called out before they could leave.

Simon glanced back with a raised eyebrow.

"For your protection," she reassured him. "Donsea may be safe from its own people, but we don't know if there are any forces from The Turned One at play here and I cannot afford to lose either of you."

Simon thought for a moment, then finally nodded. Drathanar joined them without a word and the three left the house. Now Salevari sat at the table alone with Thomas standing over it, an amused look on his face. Salevari tried to think of a way to excuse herself. She had nothing more to say to the fisherman, but she also had nothing to do, having delegated all the tasks she could think of to her companions. She sat there, silently, meeting the penetrating gaze of the peculiar human before her with her own

Luckily, the awkward moment was broken by Thomas as he proclaimed, "I be headin' out as well."

He ambled slowly for the door leading to the central hallway but stopped right at the threshold. He looked back at the Chancellor with something akin to nostalgia. "I must say, it be a pleasah speakin' wit ya. I know now where ya daughtah be getting' her good looks."

With that, he left the room. Salevari wasn't quite sure what to make of that comment. Was it a compliment? A veiled threat? But as she thought more about it, she relaxed. She shook her head and even let out a soft chuckle as she realized her daughter had had to deal with this man. This same insane man. Through Thomas, a new and unique connection between them had unwittingly formed. When next they met, perhaps they would even understand each other a little more.

She sighed wistfully, finally lifting herself from the table. She decided she would join Aniria and Zael. There was nothing else for her to do besides wait alone and impatient in this strange house, which she did not want.

As she left the building and ventured out into the sun, thoughts of her daughter persisted. She hoped Serania was doing well, that Felix wasn't giving her too much trouble. She knew her daughter's capabilities and had every confidence in them. Still, her task was substantial and so important. And there were so many unknown factors. There always were. She longed for the day where thoughts of her daughter weren't always tainted with worry. The day they would be able to relax under the sun in a peaceful world.

Until then, she thought, resolve returning to her step along with a renewed sense of focus, there was work to be done.

CHAPTER NINE

The better part of a week passed before Thomas brought them the news they wanted to hear.

It had been a busy and productive time for them. On the first day, Simon had ravaged the town, buying up vast quantities of silks, bolts of linen and wool, as well as a variety of needles and spools of thread. Tera had purchased six horses and rented out a stable to house them before joining Simon in his mad quest to create a line of high-class dresses as quickly as possible.

Many sleepless nights were then spent with Simon bent over these materials with a needle and thread, connecting different fabrics together after shaping them as his vision saw fit. Tera would then take the completed pieces and carefully add intricate designs, her fingers moving diligently back and forth wherever Simon directed. By week's end, they had five elegant dresses ready for Salevari and Aniria to try on.

Salevari stood on a stool with Aniria next to her. Both viatari stared at their reflections in a wide full-length mirror Thomas had hanging up against the wall of the second floor of his house. Both wore the same uncomfortable expression. Simon and Tera were crouched down, inspecting the fitting, remeasuring lengths, adjusting the hem of each dress.

The dresses themselves were light and soft. That much Salevari could appreciate, since the climate in this coastal region had proven to be relentlessly hot and humid. She was used to the aridity of the desert. Still, despite their comfort, she struggled to adjust to the sense of restraint the attire imposed. She tried swinging her arms back and forth, but her sleeves clung tightly. The mobility she needed just wasn't there. That would be a problem if it came time to defend herself. She mentioned this to Simon with a disapproving frown.

Simon finished inserting a series of pins along a folded section of the hem and shrugged, "You're not supposed to fight in these. You're supposed to be the wife of a chief. A noblewoman, some might say. You must be the picture of grace and elegance. Even we in the plains have our manners."

"Well, what am I supposed to do if we run into our enemies? Charm them with my grace and elegance?"

Aniria snickered.

"As I am to play your husband, I would defend your honor and protect you with my life," Simon replied, a note of humor in his voice. "But that is why we also have Zael and Drathanar in our party. Their job will be to keep you and Aniria from harm."

"Besides, as Simon's wife, you will not have the freedom to explore the city in search of The Turned One's agents yourself," Tera added. "You'll need to remember your role when we enter Halding Port. You must delegate the more labor-intensive tasks to us. Your sole priority will be the Grand Admiral, trying to gauge his wants and needs. Aniria will have the same focus, except with the other elites."

"I hope the elites of Halding Port enjoy dour women then," Aniria sneered, regarding the layers of cloth that now wrapped around her body with venomous eyes. "I don't intend on putting on a show as a silly, cheery flirt."

Tera raised an eyebrow. "They might prefer that, actually. They'd see it as a challenge. You might hear lines like, 'oh, how you remind me of the seas.'"

A chuckle came from Simon. "If I didn't know any better I would say you're speaking from experience."

A sly grin flashed onto Tera's face as she took a moment to dramatically flip her curly blonde hair back. "What can I say? I seem to be blessed with genes of beauty that rich old sailors look for."

They all shared a laugh. Salevari's smile quickly faded though as she once again caught her own reflection. In such alien attire, she hardly recognized herself. While she wouldn't go so far as to say she *felt* beautiful, there was certainly an attractiveness to her now that the dress emphasized, which her regular armor could not. She couldn't put her finger on it. Perhaps it was the dress itself that magnified her own beauty with its own. Simon had done a wonderful job in making his vision a reality, after all.

"You are quite the seamster," she noted. "While I am not used to clothes like these, even I can appreciate the skill and effort it has taken to create it. I'm surprised such a talent has come from you, Simon."

There was no response from the human for a time. He focused on his work with a grimace. Finally, with a guarded tone, he said, "I learned how to do this from my wife. Yes, before you ask, I was married once. She's gone now."

Salevari opened her mouth to offer her condolences, but Simon raised a hand quickly and vigorously shook his head.

"It happened a long time ago. There's a reason I don't talk about it. I don't need or want your sympathies."

She shut her mouth but still regarded her companion with some sympathy. She knew what it was to lose part of one's soul and heart, for that was the only way she could describe the utter pain she felt when she lost her own husband. Even now, more than one thousand years later, an aching hole still dwelt in her heart when she thought of him.

"Anyway," Simon continued. "Making clothes like this was a pastime we often partook in. We would compete to see who could be more creative with their final product. Then, we would give the dresses away to the young maidens of the town whose needs were greater than ours." He stopped his work, his eyes unseeing as he briefly lost himself to memory. A quick shake of the head brought him back. "I'm only glad I seem to have retained the skill, despite my lack of practice over the years."

There was a moment of silence where Simon and Tera simply worked diligently on their tasks while the viatari stood there awkwardly, staring at themselves in the mirror. After a few minutes of this, Aniria turned to Simon with a gentle smile. "They really are well made. I'm grateful for your work."

Simon grunted and continued with his deft movements.

They spent the next few hours trying on the remaining dresses. With conversation limited and nothing else going on, Salevari had nothing to do but continue reflecting as she stared into the mirror. Her thoughts remained on the idea of beauty.

There was a time, long ago, where she had made efforts to appear beautiful. Times where she had sought out someone to recognize her beauty. It was how she had finally found her husband. Or, rather, how he had found her. She sighed wistfully, remembering the life they'd spent together. They had created a beautiful daughter who, to this day, worked hard for the betterment of the world. She knew, if he were still alive, Serania's father would be just as proud of her as she was.

But that was the past.

Now, she didn't care for beauty, only for what was practical. Her husband was long dead. And with him the part of her that concerned itself with such trivial things.

Finally, Simon declared they were done. The humans helped the viatari take off their dresses, giving them privacy to get back into whatever outfits they had been wearing before. Salevari let out a sigh of relief as she donned a loose white shirt and tight black trousers, a common style of dress in Donsea. She could tell Aniria felt the same.

Once dressed, she made her way to the living room and began putting on pieces of her armor, just to feel its protective hold around her body.

That's when Thomas barged in.

He strode into the living room with a large, toothy grin. His chest was bare today and his linen trousers were torn and muddy around the ankles.

"Good news," he said proudly as Aniria, Simon, and Tera joined them in the living room. "I done got ya a meetin' time wit da Boss. He be seein' ya tonight. All of ya."

With that said, he glanced around confused. "Where be da other two?"

"They went out to town again," Salevari answered, tightening the straps of her greaves. "Exploring the docks, I believe."

"Ah," Thomas' smile broadened as if this made all the sense in the world. "Lots to see dere. I can spend me whole day dere."

"I will share the news with them when they return. So,

tonight?"

Thomas' expression remained blissful. His eyes locked with hers. There was a gleam in them, as if he was excited for what was to come.

"I hope ya be ready."

The Chancellor nodded. She may not know much about beauty anymore or the strange customs and mannerisms of human high society, but she knew how to speak to people in charge. She knew how to negotiate, how to get what she wanted. This environment was where she thrived. She was eager to return to it.

When the sun set, Thomas led them through Donsea's well-lit pathways. The town was eerily quiet and empty. Salevari doubted everyone could already be indoors and in bed. Surely, there was some form of night life in this fishing town.

They were led to the central plaza, where they had gone through on their first day to reach Thomas' house. Salevari hadn't noticed it the first time, likely because there'd been a plethora of new sights, sounds, and smells assaulting her senses at the time, but on the far side of the plaza was the town hall, a towering wooden structure.

It stood at least two stories taller than any other building. Its roof rose high in a long curving slope, hanging well past the entrance and coming to a point at the end. If Salevari didn't know any better, she would have thought the roof was just the hull of a large ship flipped upside down. Windows along the building glowed with light and a soft buzz of conversation came from inside as the doors swung open. Inside, the space was filled with the folk of Donsea.

"Is this not going to be just a meeting between us and Hadreen?" Salevari asked.

Thomas shook his head. "Nah mon. Much of da town wanna hear what ya got to say. Dey'll all be dere."

Great, Salevari thought, so she would have an audience. She shook her head, trying to focus. It didn't matter how many spectators there were, in the end. The only one inside who mattered was Hadreen. She would ignore the others.

"Remembah," Thomas said in a low voice as they approached the entrance. "Be mindful of how ya approach any subject wit Hadreen. He can appreciate a little fire, but it needs be done wit respect."

Salevari nodded. She had spent their time here imagining countless scenarios for these negotiations, countless talking points that Hadreen might make that she would have to answer when it came to why Donsea should fight. Despite her preparations, though, she expected to be thrown off guard. That seemed to be something that just came with this town. The key would be to keep her wits about her when it happened, controlling any exterior signs of doubt. They needed Donsea, but Donsea didn't know how badly they were needed. She planned on using that.

They entered the town hall. The place was flooded with torches and braziers all along the walls so that the entire space was well-lit. The first thing Salevari noticed was that everything in here was wooden. Polished floors gleamed under the light of the flames. Several carved sea creatures either stood on pedestals or hung from the walls. They varied from diff-erent types of fish to sharks to octopuses to crabs. They were skillfully carved, with intricate detail put into each one, and painted so that they stood out from the dull brown walls they hung upon. Along with the carvings were several works of art. These weren't typical paintings like Salevari was used to seeing, however. They were an assortment of nets, seashells, and sand, strategically placed and assembled to form an abstract theme. They were primitive, but impressive. Looking up, she saw that the ceiling rose high and appeared hollowed out. Thick crossbeams lined the length of it, making her suspicion of the roof really being the flipped over hull of a ship all the more credible.

The townsfolk stood along the walls or up on the second floor where a balcony lined the edge for them to lean against. All eyes were on the newcomers. No one spoke.

Ahead, near the end of the spacious hall, situated on an elevated platform, was a large, plump, pale-green couch covered with a myriad of pillows and cushions. Laying on his side, propped up by an elbow, watching them approach, was Hadreen.

Despite his unassuming posture, Salevari could tell he was a large man. Muscles rippled under his dark skin, exposed for everyone to see as all he wore was a thin leather vest, which he left open along with the same type of torn trousers that Thomas liked to wear. His thick hair was pulled back into a series of tight braids that ran down his head, touching his shoulders. Each braid was decorated with a pattern of sea-shells and crab claws.

To his side knelt a servant holding a substantial platter stacked high with an assortment of food. Hadreen reached for a morsel as he continued to stare. Slowly, he plucked a shrimp from the stack and dropped it into his mouth—head, shell, and all—maintaining eye contact the entire time.

Thomas motioned for the viatari to stop. They stood where they were, the two parties studying each other. Silence reigned for several minutes, save for the sound of crunching shellfish, until finally, the Boss of Donsea spoke, his voice smooth and silky.

"Me friend Thomas say ya been askin' to see me. Now, here ya are. Tell me, viatari, what brings ya here?"

The viatari glanced at each other and nodded. Together, they shimmered and allowed their human illusions to fade away. Their silver hair returned—though, Salevari kept hers black—along with piercing red eyes. A ripple of soft murmurs broke out among the townsfolk.

Hadreen chuckled as he reached for a mussel this time, slathering it with a pungent red sauce before slurping it down. He smacked his lips appreciatively.

"We've come to Donsea to ask for an alliance," Salevari started. She spent some time explaining the threat they all faced from the darinsha as well as who the darinsha had aligned themselves with. Though it might have been considered an incredible story by those who'd done nothing but keep to themselves all these years, she spent every effort to portray, in detail, the type of beings The Turned One and the Creature were. If anything, this was a vital part of the negotiation. If the people of Donsea didn't believe in the reality of the threat the corrupted acolytes posed, there would be no reason for them to join the fight. The force in her voice wavered as she looked around the room. Smug grins lined the crowd. They had already heard this news.

"Spare us da details," Hadreen groaned. "Wanderers come here all da time. We 'ear 'nough of da world's troubles. We already know of dese acolyte tings and what dey been doin'"

"Then you know the grave threat they pose to us all," Salevari said. "If they have their way, they will take the Southern Seas. That is what they intend by having the darinsha invade vashi waters."

Hadreen sighed, rubbing his eyes and yawning theatrically. Finally, he waved away his servant, and the platter of food was taken out of sight.

"So?"

Salevari had to take a breath. Her immediate response would have been to scream out "What do you mean 'so'?" but she had a feeling that wouldn't have been the wisest reaction. Instead, she tried once more appealing to reason.

"Like I said, they intend to take *all* of the coast. That includes Donsea and Halding–"

Hadreen held up a hand and Salevari fell silent, though she pursed her lips, her hands gravitating to her hips.

"We done already 'eard dat," the Boss said. "What I wanna know now is why we should care. What be in it fah us?"

Salevari scoffed and crossed her arms. "I would think the safety of Donsea would be enough reward. I would think not seeing this place go up in flames would be the end you strive for every day."

A smile crept over Hadreen's face, but there was no mirth in it. A dangerous glint entered his eyes. "Donsea can take care of itself. If dese darinsha be as real as ya say, we can take dem out like all da enemies I taken out before."

"The darinsha will not come to you with a few criminals," Salevari countered. "They'll come with an army. And if no one moves to aid the vashi when they need it, there will be no one to aid you when it's your turn."

Hadreen waved dismissively, his face scrunching up as if he smelled something repugnant. "Da vashi be a powerful people. I'm sure dey can take care of demselves, just like us."

Salevari doubted this. Donsea still appeared ill-prepared to handle so much as a raiding party with the type of defenses she'd observed. Not even Zael and Drathanar's excursions into town had revealed much in the way of hidden defenses. She still didn't believe this town of fishermen had much to offer the vashi anyway and suddenly felt silly that she was trying so hard to get their help. Perhaps it would be best if she just walked away. And then she smiled. Perhaps that was all she needed to do to get what she wanted. These people were like children, as far as she was concerned. Maybe she needed to treat them as such.

She shrugged. "If you say so. I guess I'll never find out. Regardless, I can see I'm wasting my time here. Even if you *were* willing to help, I don't see what Donsea can offer the vashi anyway."

Her words had their desired effect. Thomas and Tera shot a warning glance her way, but she ignored them. The crowd grew restless, murmuring with some dark undertones now. Hadreen's eyes narrowed. His lips curled into a snarl.

"Ya be undahestimatin' us," he growled. "We 'ave much to offah da world. We be some of da best sailors 'round. We 'ave trackers who can tail a fish fah miles in da ocean. I'd like to see ya find someone like dat in fancy Halding Port."

Again, Salevari shrugged and turned as if to walk away. "Trackers and sailors," she called back. "Sorry to tell you this, but I don't find that too impressive. Now, out of respect for your time and mine, I think we'll just move on to Halding Port where we should have gone to begin with. At least they have a fleet of warships to offer."

She could only take a few steps before Hadreen rushed forward, grabbed her shoulder, and spun her back around to face him. His face was livid, but she could tell through the look in his bloodshot eyes that he was calm in mind, still calculating his options.

Normally, she would have balked at anyone trying to make such a move on her. She had to fight her natural instincts to grab Hadreen's hand and rip it out. She wasn't the only one.

Zael and Drathanar's hands hovered over their weapons, ready to draw them if the situation escalated.

Finally, Hadreen's easy grin returned. A flicker of recognition entered his eyes as he saw through Salevari's ruse. The scent of oily shrimp was heavy on his breath as he spoke. "Ya make a hard bargain, viatari. Donsea will aid da vashi with whatever dey need in deir comin' war. Let it not be said dat when da world came togethah, we only kept to our fishin' lines. But dere be one condition."

"And what might that be?"

"Ya see," Hadreen circled her now, sizing her up. "We rarely seen da viatari, bein' as far south as we be, much less tested dem. We don' know much about ya people. If I'm gonna be riskin' Donsea in dis war, I wanna make sure da people I be riskin' it fah be worthy."

"What are you proposing?"

"If ya want Donsea as an ally, ya must have ya mettle tested. We be havin' a sailin' race."

Now it was Salevari's turn to think. She knew nothing of the ocean, nothing of sailing. Surely Hadreen knew that. "My people are not a seafaring one. It seems hardly fair to challenge us in something you will clearly win at."

The Boss nodded solemnly. "It be true. Ya stand no chance 'gainst even da greenest of sailors. I don' expect ya to win. I just wanna see ya at da sails, see how well ya can adapt from da forests to da seas. Ya don' 'ave to beat us. Ya just 'ave to finish. I wanna see how much fight be in ya."

If they didn't have to win the race, Salevari thought this proposal posed little risk. After all, how hard could sailing be? She had observed the ships at the docks going about their daily routines for the past few days. She had watched fishermen set out every night and come back in the morning, their boats laden with the catch of the day. If she didn't have to be a master at it, perhaps she could learn quickly enough to be adequate.

"I accept your challenge," she said with a confident air. "When do we race?"

Hadreen's smile extended, his teeth gleaming in the fire-light like pearls. "Why wait? We race right now. Tonight."

CHAPTER TEN

The townsfolk surged together towards the docks. Hadreen marched confidently in the front. Salevari wished she could feel the same, but the more she thought about what she had just agreed to, the less confident she felt.

She knew nothing of sailing, nothing of boats. She'd never even seen the ocean until a week ago, much less been in it. The closest experience she'd had to what she was about to do was drifting down the Granian River with Serania in her canoe. That had been a long time ago, and she hadn't even really participated. Serania had done all the work.

Without realizing it, she lagged behind as Hadreen marched on until she was walking beside Thomas. The man might be crazy, she thought, but he would know more about the sea and sailing than she ever could. If ever there was a time to seek his advice, it was now.

"Thomas, what have I gotten myself into here?"

The fisherman whistled a single, long note. "Dat be da question, viatari. Ya evah been on a boat before?"

She shook her head.

"Well, it be pretty simple. Likely, ya be racin' wit our sloop hybrids. Dey be sailin' ships but also have two sets of oars fah when da wind die down. It takes four to sail her but runs bettah wit eight."

"I don't have eight companions to sail with."

"Remembah, da Boss ain't expectin' ya to win. Only to finish. So long as ya have three other viatari to sail wit, which ya do, ya'll be fine."

Salevari nodded. The odds were stacked against her, but that was a given. Thomas was right. As long as they could just finish the race, they would be fine. "What else can you tell me about how to sail this ship?"

Thomas' eyes flashed excitedly as he spoke, "It be simple. One of da crew needs to always be on da ruddah to steer da ship. Two more to man da oars when dey be needed. One person to man da sail when da wind be blowin'. If da wind be behind ya, sailin' be pretty straightforward–ya just pull on da sail to catch it. If da wind be blowin' toward ya, ya gotta go against it at an angle to let ya sail do its job. Zigzag back and forth. We call dat tacking."

"How do I control the sail?" Salevari asked.

"Dere be winches on da boat's railin'–little knobs–ya know it when ya see dem. Ya run da rope from da corner of da sail through da winch. Tie it 'round a couple times, den use da levah to pull or push da sail away from ya. Dere be a winch on both sides of da ship, dependin' on which way ya need to turn."

Thomas went on to describe all the parts of the ship, from the keel to the boom to the different ropes, called halyards, attached to the mast. He explained how to furl and unfurl the sail, how to tell where the wind was blowing, and what it looked like when the sail caught the wind.

By the end of his explanation, Salevari's head was swimming with information. She felt more confused than before, but she hoped once she saw what she was working with that some of the things he had said would click in her head.

There was a wave of excitement as the crowd reached the docks. Bets began to be placed. Hadreen would be the winner, that much was certain, so the focus of the bets turned to whether or not the viatari could actually finish the race.

Two medium-sized ships were boarded by some of the townsfolk, who began to inspect its different parts, making sure everything was in order. They were unlike anything Salevari had ever seen. The body of the vessel was long and wide enough to fit three. The bow and stern both curved upward and inward, like wooden waves threatening to wash onto the deck. Two holes were on the side well above the waterline with the oars' blades sticking out. A single mast rose high from the ship's center, its canvas sail folded and securely fastened.

As the townsfolk went about their work readying the vessels, Hadreen turned to Salevari, his demeanor completely different from how he had been in the town hall. Excitement oozed from his veins like sweat. Meanwhile, her stomach was in knots as she continued to stare at the two vessels bobbing in the water.

"I done have me crew picked. Have ya decided who be sailin' wit ya?"

Salevari shrugged. "I suppose if this is a test of the viatari, only my viatari companions should assist me."

Hadreen nodded approvingly, "Wise choice. My men be makin' sure everyting onboard be in ordah. Once dey finish, we hop aboard ourselves and start da race."

Donsea's Boss grinned smugly, turned, and walked away. Salevari glanced at her companions. They looked back at her steadily, but she could sense their dread with every shallow breath they took.

"We will all be novices in this task," she said, trying to keep her voice steady. "I expect nothing more from you but to do what I ask when I ask. With any luck, we'll come back to shore in one piece."

They all nodded.

"I will control the sails. Aniria, you steer. Zael and Drathanar, you'll man the oars."

Again, they nodded. Then, they waited, each dwelling in their own thoughts as they imagined everything that could go wrong with this alien task ahead of them.

After a few minutes, the inspectors were satisfied with the status of each sloop and disembarked, letting Hadreen, Salevari, and their crews take their place. As the viatari settled into their assigned positions, the townsfolk stepped up and unfastened the ropes from the mooring, letting each sloop float freely. They then took long, thick poles and pushed both ships out of their slips into open water.

"Good luck!" Salevari heard Tera call out from the docks as they continued drifting into the waves.

Immediately, her stomach lurched as the ocean rocked their ship. The waves were small and gentle, but the movement was amplified. She took a few deep breaths, forcing down the sick feeling and looked ahead. Before them were two small dinghies floating in place about fifty feet apart.

"Dose ships be da startin' line and da finishin' line," Hadreen called out from the helm of his own vessel. "Once we cross ovah, da race be on. Just beyond da horizon be a small island. One of me men has gone ahead to light da bonfires so we can see it in da dark. We circle da isle and come back here. Whoevah crosses da line first be da winnah. Do ya understand?"

"Yes," Salevari called out. "Though, who crosses this line first is not my priority right now."

Hadreen laughed. "I done 'eard a lot about da viatari from others. Ya may yet make dis race interestin'." His smile faded. "Out of fairness and because I don' want ya runnin' me ship aground, I be warnin' ya. Da waters be shallow 'round da isle. If ya get too close, ya run da risk of ya hull smashin' into da sandbanks. Ya need to keep ya distance from it when ya make ya circle."

Salevari nodded. "I'll keep that in mind."

"Den, prepare, viatari. Soon, we begin!"

Slowly, the two sloops drifted closer to the starting line. There was no wind, Salevari noticed, which meant this race would begin with the oars. She took note of everything on the ship while she still could, finding the winches Thomas had described as well as the rope she would need to keep hold of to control the sail. She looked one last time at her companions and they all nodded to each other. They were determined and ready.

They reached the starting line. The fishermen on each dinghy cheered loudly, waving their arms back and forth.

"Oars!" Hadreen called out.

"Oars!" Salevari mimicked.

Hadreen's crew of eight worked like a well-oiled machine. Together, they slid their oars out from the deck, putting the blade of each one into the water at the same time. With a steady, cadenced grunt, they began to row and pull forward through the waves.

Zael and Drathanar might have been a few men down, but they didn't let that slow them. They sat on their own benches, manning an oar with each hand. Together, they pushed out the shafts until the blades were in the water. Without speaking, they pulled back, lifted the blades, pushed them forward, dipped them back into the water, and pulled again. Salevari felt their vessel surge forward.

A confident smile stretched her lips. With one stroke, Zael and Drathanar had covered the distance Hadreen's men had done in three. Within a few minutes, the viatari were well ahead, Zael and Drathanar working steadily, using their viatari strength to propel themselves forward at an impressive pace. Salevari took great satisfaction in seeing Hadreen's wide-eyed look of disbelief as he could do nothing but watch the gap between them grow. He yelled at his crew to increase their own pace, but it wasn't enough.

Soon Salevari couldn't hear his yelling, only the crashing of waves against their hull as they continued to power forward. Sea spray splashed on deck, soaking them. The water was freezing, but invigorating. It kept them focused on their task, providing a bulwark against fatigue.

Salevari glanced behind her and saw that Hadreen's ship was now just a dull, white speck in the distance. Were it not for the brightness of the full moon and the countless stars in the sky, she wouldn't have been able to see it at all. As far as she was concerned, they were now alone in this vast ocean. It was a strange, ominous feeling as she looked out and saw nothing but darkness.

As time passed, she began to search for a silhouette of the island they needed to circle but couldn't make anything out. She heard some splashes in the distance but no sign of what might have caused them. It could be something as innocent as a few fish or something deadlier prowling around them, following them, waiting for a chance to strike. Salevari felt a primal fear work its way through her that she had to force down. There was a deadliness to this place that she never would have understood until now. She hoped this was just her own mind playing tricks on her, that this sense of danger and fear was imagined. But the feeling remained. Worse was the helplessness that accompanied it.

"Light in the distance!" Aniria called out, spitting out a mouthful of seawater as another wave sprayed them with its contents.

Salevari broke out of her trance with a gasp and turned to see it too. Faintly, far to their left was a flickering light that could only be the bonfires Hadreen had mentioned would mark the isle's location.

"We'll keep a wide berth around it," she called back. "Keep your eye on it, Aniria, I don't want to accidentally get stuck out here."

Aniria nodded and they continued on, Zael and Drathanar refusing to show any sign that they were growing tired.

We can win this, Salevari thought. The wind remained still. If she didn't have to worry about working the sail—something she was dreading the more she eyed the contraption—they could rely on brute strength to bring them to the end. The viatari would not only finish the race but win it by a large margin. Even the best sailors couldn't match up with the strength of the viatari. If that didn't prove their mettle to the Boss of Donsea, she didn't think much else would.

They kept the light aligned to their left, taking their time circling it. After several minutes, they completed their orbit and now rowed for the distant shore. Back towards Donsea. The race was theirs.

Then Salevari felt a strong gust hit her face, blowing her hair back forcefully.

She blinked hard as the gust proved not to be a lone punch

from the sky, but a continuous tumult that made the waves rise higher and push more violently against them. She struggled to maintain her footing as the deck rose and dipped violently beneath her.

"Chancellor, the oars are useless," Drathanar called out through gritted teeth. "I can't get a steady pull on the water with this wild movement!"

"Nor can I," Zael grunted.

"Oars in," Salevari ordered. With a series of clatters, the two viatari pulled their tools in until only the blades stuck out from the side of the ship. She sighed. Zael and Drathanar had done brilliantly. Now it was her turn to contribute.

She moved for the mast, stumbling back and forth as the ship continued to rock, and numbly untied the ropes fastening the sail to it. She kept her grip tight as she spread the sail along the length of the boom. Securing the foot of the canvas to the boom with the same rope that had secured it to the mast, she took the corner line Thomas had told her she would need and made her way to the portside winch. She remembered the fisherman's advice as she struggled to tie the rope around the metal knob.

"Ya wanna make sure ya don' lose dat line. Ya lose da rope to da wind, ya ain't evah gettin' it back. Da wind will keep it flappin' in da air out of ya reach and ya'll be dead in da water."

Salevari tightened her grip. She would hold onto this rope no matter what, though it was certainly a difficult task when her hands and the cord alike were cold and wet. Once she managed to wrap it around the winch a few times, she found the lever. She cranked it with one hand, keeping hold of the rope with the other. Slowly, the boom turned port-side, the tall, triangular sail curving along with it. She felt a rough tug on their ship as the wind caught their sail enough to get them moving.

"Aniria," she shouted through the howl of the wind. "Swing us to the left until I say!"

Their vessel moved forward slowly, then began to drift in the proper direction. As the angle of the sail grew steeper against the wind, they gained more speed. It was just as Thomas had described. Salevari didn't understand how it was possible. By her thinking, if the wind went against the sail, it should be impossible to use it, or it would at least push them in the opposite direction, but she was no sailor. If Thomas said she had to zigzag through the wind to maintain their speed, she would zigzag as best she could.

"Straight ahead!" she ordered.

Aniria pushed against the tiller until it was in a straight position. Zael and Drathanar watched in wonder as Salevari fought the wind and the ocean at the same time, working with a single cord of rope and moving between winches portside to starboard then back again, ducking beneath the swinging boom as she did so, all while maintaining her footing on the slippery, swinging deck.

But as efficiently as they all thought they were working, it wasn't enough. Zael kept a lookout behind them and soon saw a white speck emerge in the distance.

"They're gaining on us!"

While the oars gave the viatari an advantage because of their strength, the wind proved to be the boon Hadreen and his crew needed to even the odds. They had covered the remaining distance to the island quickly by using their sail to its full effect while the tempest blew in their direction. Now that they were going against it, they too were tacking, swerving left to right and back at an impressive rate.

Far ahead, Salevari could see Donsea's lights dotting the

shore. In the surrounding darkness, it was like a blinding beacon. She renewed her efforts, doing her best to continue their tacking movements, but Hadreen's crew was better.

She estimated they were about halfway between the isle they had rounded and the finish line. At this rate, Hadreen would overtake them and win the race handily. She bared her fangs and grunted with renewed effort as the boom swung around once more to the starboard side. She cranked the winch lever furiously, wishing the sail would just catch the wind properly.

Hadreen had said all they had to do was finish the race. That would be enough to earn his respect, something she realized she wanted. He had irked her with his aloof attitude initially when she had warned him about the grave threat they faced, but she still wanted his respect. There was something about this Boss of Donsea that resonated with her, made his opinion valuable.

She didn't want to just finish this race. She wanted to win.

"Ahoy!" Hadreen's voice reached them faintly from behind. "Ya had me worried dere da way ya took off like dat. But it seems even da mighty viatari can't push deir way through da might of da sea."

At this rate, he would pass them in minutes. Salevari couldn't let that happen.

"Oars!"

Zael and Drathanar shot her a look.

"We can't row in these conditions," Zael shouted over the wind.

Drathanar added, "Besides, the oars will drag along the water and slow us down."

"I can't keep us ahead with this blasted thing," Salevari admitted. "It's beyond me. The best thing we can do is try to use the oars and our strength to maintain our distance from the humans. If we can get just a few good strokes, it might make the difference."

With a nod of understanding, the two viatari took their places. They deftly pushed out the oars and began rowing. Salevari continued her attempts to catch the wind with the sail. She felt their vessel surge forward, then briefly slow down, only to speed along the waves again. This inconsistent momentum continued and seemed to be enough to slow Hadreen's gains. But only for a time.

The Donsea Boss quickly noticed what they were doing. Salevari could hear his laughter in the wind. "A bold strategy, viatari. But not enough, I tink!"

In the distance, the two dinghies marking the finish line came into view. They were close. She glanced behind her and saw Hadreen pulling up just off their stern.

Within that brief moment of distraction, she felt the rope slip out of her hand.

Immediately she lunged for it, but the wind already had its prize and refused to give it back. Just as Thomas said it wouldn't. All she could do now was watch it flail high in the air where it would remain so long as there was wind to keep it there. The sail fluttered uselessly.

"I've lost the sail," she yelled out. "Double your efforts on the oars!"

Zael and Drathanar grunted as they tried to find some grip with their strokes, but they remained inconsistent. The waves were too choppy. They could still move, but not nearly at the speed that they had started out with.

The bow of Hadreen's ship became visible on their starboard side, creeping up closer with each passing second. Salevari could see the Donsea Boss manning the sail with his men, grinning broadly at her. He saluted smartly and turned back to his work.

"Aniria," Salevari growled.

"Yes?"

"Turn into them."

"What?"

"Ram them!"

Aniria glanced between the two vessels. She looked like she wanted to voice her thoughts about the order, but with an uncaring shrug, pushed the tiller as far as it would go, bringing their ship into a collision course with the humans.

Hadreen saw it coming.

"Nice try!" He gave a series of quick orders using sailor terms that Salevari couldn't follow. Instantly, his vessel slowed down, retreating behind Salevari's, allowing her to pass across its bow safely. After another series of orders, it veered left and surged through the waves, passing the viatari with ease. Salevari stared, bewildered, as he waved happily and con-tinued his way to the finish line.

"Turn back!" Salevari demanded "Turn back toward the finish line. Zael, Drathanar, with as much strength as you can, push us through these waters and across that line."

The three viatari worked hard to carry out her orders but they had lost a lot of speed with their aggressive maneuver. With Hadreen now in front, there was no hope for them to win the race. But that wouldn't stop them from trying.

Straining against the raw power of the sea, Zael and Drathanar pulled on their oars, doing what they could to send their ship forward. Within minutes, they were crossing the finish line marked by the dinghies. But Hadreen had already crossed well before.

The race was over.

They had lost, and Salevari couldn't help but feel disappointed. However, this was the expected result. In fact, the viatari had done better than anyone could have imagined. But that wasn't enough to console the Dalyran Chancellor. She was silent and brooding as men from Donsea set out and boarded her vessel to help bring her back to port.

Once the sloop was moored, the viatari disembarked. Immediately, Salevari's legs began to tremble beneath her. The ground seemed to sway up and down, despite her knowing that was impossible. She fought the urge to fall to her knees, if anything to conserve what little pride she had left. Her companions were not of the same mind, and each fell onto their backs, breathing hard, dizzy and wet from sweat and ocean spray as they recovered from the aftermath of the strenuous effort they had given.

"I must admit, viatari, I be impressed." Hadreen walked over from his end of the dock and embraced the Chancellor, shocking her out of her stupor.

"I lost." She said numbly.

"Ya mon, I told ya ya would. Did ya really expect to beat us when we been doin' dis our whole lives?"

Salevari shrugged.

Hadreen chuckled and clapped her shoulder. "Ya completed da race like I wanted. Not just that, but ya gave me a run fah me money. I be a man of me word. Da people of Donsea would be honored to ally wit ya and all dose involved in da struggle fah our world."

Salevari took a moment to gather her thoughts. Hadreen was right, she knew. There was no chance in defeating these sailors at their own game. She had fooled herself into thinking there was and that was on her. But if there was anything to take away from this race it was a new appreciation for what the people of Donsea were capable of.

"I have a new respect for the sea and what your people can do," she admitted. "I am happy to have Donsea with us. And I'm sure the vashi will appreciate the support."

Hadreen laughed without restraint. "Ah, the vashi. It'll be interestin' to work wit dose fish-men. I be sendin' Thomas to begin talks wit dem soon. But fah now, we must celebrate dis new friendship."

He turned to the townsfolk who had crowded the docks as both ships arrived.

"Drinks on da house tonight! Kitchens, fire up! We eatin' good 'til da mornin'."

Everyone roared their approval.

Salevari relaxed. The disappointment she'd felt earlier faded away, a forgotten memory. Now all she could think about was the euphoria stirring inside her as she considered what she'd just done. Sailing had been an exhilarating experience and a challenge. Now that the stress was gone, she couldn't help but feel an urge to try her hand at it again.

A wave of exhaustion quickly changed her mind. Shaking her head, she felt wet, sticky hair slap her face. Hadreen may have wanted to celebrate their new friendship, but all she could think about was how much she wanted to collapse onto a bed.

After that. . . .

Well, she thought with a tired smile as she helped her companions back to their feet. *No harm in enjoying the night a little.*

CHAPTER ELEVEN

A week had passed since Thuradin's altercation with Hork. Since that day, Lyrie had made every conscious effort to keep their paths from crossing again and Thuradin had done the same. The dwarven grid was awash with rumors of what had occurred. Only a few had actually seen the event play out from the beginning, but that didn't stop their stories from evolving into something far from the truth.

Thuradin was making his way back to his tent from the camp's perimeter when he heard one such rumor being shared between a pair of dwarves and their human counterparts. He had been out all night on sentry duty and was already ill-tempered from exhaustion. Hearing them speak his name and slander it was simply too much. He stopped in his tracks, debating whether he should confront them.

"I hear he wanted ta duel Hork for the right ta his wife," one of the dwarves said in a low voice that nonetheless reached Thuradin's ears. "When Hork refused, the old commander blew a fuse and tried ta fight him anyway. Lyrie had ta pry him off. Hork didn't throw a single punch."

The humans whistled and shook their heads. Thuradin grumbled and marched away quickly before they noticed his presence.

He was angry more at himself for having lost his temper than at them for gossiping. It was what dwarves did, after all. They were notoriously poor at keeping secrets unless those secrets involved mining node locations or brewing recipes. Spreading rumors for them was a way of passing time. And his story wasn't the only one being passed around.

Not much had changed within the camp since the day they had set out to rescue Veliris. As time passed, people settled back into a mundane routine. There were no signs that another battle would take place any time soon and the siege's progress appeared to have stalled. Everyone noticed it. Then, rumors began to circulate concerning the camp's leadership.

Whispers spread like a plague, some from the humans and burrowers but mostly from the dwarves, that Felix had lost his nerve. They didn't know why or understand it. Felix had always led his people well as far as anyone remembered. But something had happened, they knew. Something that had provoked a change. Questions were also beginning to pop up concerning the whereabouts of certain well-known viatari. It was only a matter of time before a connection was made.

The thing was, Thuradin thought, those whispers weren't so much rumor as they were truthful observation that any common warrior could make. He couldn't fault them for this. But he could keep them in line. He made a point of doing just that as he heard one of these whispers from a small group of dwarves sitting huddled outside their tents.

"That's enough out of ye lot," he said gruffly.

He may not be commander of the royal guard anymore, but his legacy still commanded respect—especially now that he was no longer considered an exile. The dwarves looked up at him, embarrassed. No doubt, they had been busy sharing whispers about him as well and hoped he hadn't heard.

"Have ye heard from Felix, commander?" One of them asked.

"Ye need nae call me 'commander' lad," Thuradin said. "Just 'Thuradin' is fine. As for Felix, I saw him a few days ago. As ye should know, his job isn't an easy one. It takes much time and planning ta envision how we can take those peaks from the enemy."

He emphasized his point by lifting his finger and directing it straight at the looming peaks in question. The group of dwarves nodded somberly.

"In the meantime," he continued. "I'll nae risk having morale damaged because ye find yerselves with nothing ta do but whisper inta each other's ears like a couple of old she-rams. Keep ta yer tasks and the day for action will come."

Again, the dwarves nodded, this time sufficiently cowed. Thuradin grunted, then turned and continued on his way. It was a little lie he had told, but necessary. He *had* seen Felix the other day. But the elder viatari had been in the same stupor as the day when the devastating news of Victria's capture had been brought to him. Though he had confidence in Felix's levelheadedness to win through in the end, there was a part of him that wondered if he, one of the original viatari, was finally breaking.

After a few more minutes navigating his way through the sprawling pathways of the dwarven grid, Thuradin found himself back in his own tent. He took off the heavier pieces of his armor—his chestplate and spaulders—then swung himself onto his cot and let out a contented sigh. Now it was time for sleep. His head was heavy, his eyes heavier. He could feel his thoughts drifting almost out of reach when he noticed a shadow smiling at him from the corner of his tent. He bolted up into a sitting position, instantly alert and awake.

Morteth's body was wrapped in a light cloak that matched the tent's canvas. "Well, commander, it's nice ta see ye take some weight off yer shoulders."

Thuradin groaned and fell back onto his cot. He brought his arm over his eyes so he didn't have to see anything and asked, "What is it, Morteth? Can it nae wait?"

The assassin stepped out from his corner, letting his cloak fall from his body and pulled a chair over to sit down. Thuradin was surprised he hadn't noticed him upon entering. He was notorious in the Dwarven Kingdom for his ability to blend in with his surroundings and Thuradin had been tired from a night of sentry duty, but still. If Morteth had been paid by anyone to end his life, he would have entered his tent to close his eyes for the last time, he was sure of that. Perhaps he had become a bit too lax in his old age.

"I 'eard about yer li'l spat with our dear friend Hork."

Thuradin groaned again. "The rumors have gone far beyond what actually happened."

Morteth laughed and nodded knowingly. "Aye, they always do. But I'm confident in me own mem'ry of the event, seein' as I saw it 'appen before me eyes."

"Consider me shocked."

"Anyway, after tha' I figured I'd give ye some time ta let yer thoughts an' emotions settle before I asked."

"Asked what?"

"Why, asked if ye've reconsidered the generous offer I made ye all those months ago, of course!"

"Ye think—"

"Now, commander," Morteth interrupted, holding up a

finger. "Before ye give me yer answer, know that this is the final time I'll ask. If ye 'old off from givin' me an answer in any way, I'll consider it a rejection and ye'll never 'ear this subject leave me lips again. Even if ye change yer mind later and come a-callin'."

Thuradin grit his teeth. Of course he would reject this offer. He had every time in the past as well. What in Azar made Morteth think he would ever stoop so low as to agree to putting a target on Hork's back? He was about to tell the assassin off in the clearest and vilest terms he could think of when he stopped himself.

He thought back to his encounter with Hork. He remembered the look on Lyrie's face, not just then but every single time he had seen her in his company. Her downcast, terrified eyes. And she *was* terrified, that much was certain, though she refused to admit it. He wondered how many more centuries she would have to live like that.

In his mind, he saw Hork raise his hand against her, saw her flinch. Feelings he couldn't recognize bubbled up in his gut, making him feel like he'd eaten something that hadn't cooked all the way through. Nausea made his head swim, even as he continued to lie on his cot. But in his mind he felt clarity like he had never felt before.

"Perhaps. . ." he heard himself say, but his voice sounded muffled, as if someone were trying to block his ears. "Ta free her from this captivity . . . action must be taken."

The smile on Morteth's face widened and he nodded slowly, his eyes gleaming.

"Aye, 'tis a noble act ta grant a friend their freedom. I'll draw up some plans and methods for me approach on the target and then share 'em with ye at a later time so ye can choose which one ye like best."

Thuradin shot him a confused look, his head still spinning. "Why do I need ta know what yer plans are?"

"Oh, believe me," the assassin answered, wrapping his cloak around his body once more. "I could stroll over an' take out the target right now if ye wanted. I imagine, however, that it'd be too much for yer lassie ta witness me work. She might end up traumatized for life. Believe it or nae, I can be pretty brutal with how I go' 'bout it. Certainly too brutal for ye. So, I'll think of some tamer ways ta . . . liberate yer lass. All ye have ta do is approve them. Until then—" Morteth ducked out of the tent and was gone.

Thuradin closed his eyes. He was exhausted and wanted nothing more than to sleep, but there was no way sleep would come now. Had he done the right thing? He wasn't sure. Something in him certainly made him feel like this was the right path forward. There had been that moment of clarity. He no longer had it, but he held on to the memory of it. Had it not been a sign. . . ?

He felt himself dozing once more when a loud, piercing horn broke through his subconscious and jarred him back awake. He bolted upright and listened. The horn sounded again. Three blows of the same high note. All hints of exhaustion evaporated as Thuradin jumped out of his cot and quickly strapped his chestpiece and spaulders back on.

The camp was under attack.

He burst out of his tent, still fiddling with a few straps as he ran for the camp's perimeter where the horn had sounded. Around him, other dwarves poured out, the same eager look on their faces. He was sure other parts of camp were mobilizing just the same.

"Why, hello there father!"

Thuradin kept running but glanced over his shoulder to

see his daughter, Myrna, catching up to him on his left. Her thick, black hair tied up in its usual tight bun bounced with each step she took. Her fierce green eyes were steady and eager, not an ounce of fear or panic in them. She was ready for battle, her sword and iron buckler already in hand.

"Myrna, lassie, funny meeting ye here."

A brief chuckle passed between them as they ran together. "Aye, if only we could meet someplace other than the field of battle or during sentry duty, we might be able ta actually spend some quality time together."

Thuradin shot her a look of surprise. Sometimes it shocked him how much closer the two of them had gotten after spending so many decades estranged. They still weren't as close as he would have liked, her formality when she called out to him was proof of that, but the fact she called him anything at all was a step in the right direction. "I'd like that. Got anything in mind?"

"The humans tell me fishing is a rather calming recreation." The mirth left her voice. "Do ye think The Turned One has sent her full force against us?"

Thuradin shook his head as they rounded one of the last corners of camp and began crossing an open field. Ahead of them lay a cluster of trees. Just past this thinly packed copse would be the sentry line that had made the call for aid. Whatever had prompted it, they would find out soon.

"It's just a raid," Thuradin guessed. "If that blasted acolyte wanted a fight, she would have given us one months ago."

As it turned out, he was correct. The two dwarves emerged from the other side of the tree line and took in their surroundings.

Only a short distance away, a small band of dwarves and humans had pulled together, forming ranks, as a pack of corrupted burrowers and humans smashed into them. The enemy was much larger than their uncorrupted brethren, and much stronger. The weight of their charge alone was enough to break through the thin line of defenders, scattering them. The skirmish quickly fell into disarray as every dwarf and man fought for himself.

More sentries poured in from the camp's perimeter to join the fight, but at this rate some would join too late. Thuradin and Myrna rushed in to help however they could. Thuradin pulled out his twin-axes and let loose a war cry as he rammed into the nearest opponent he could find. He sent the corrupted human flying, immediately turning to block an incoming attack from another. He looked into the black eyes of the human foe and grunted with effort as he pushed the blade away. The human pulled back to swing his sword again but found himself face first in the dirt as Myrna bashed him from behind, knocking him down with her iron buckler. Thuradin moved in quickly and finished him off before he could recover.

Together, they rallied the remaining sentries into a defensive line that curved away from the camp. If they continued fighting as they were, there was no telling how this battle might end. Their best chance at repelling the invaders was to maintain their lines and their discipline. After a few more minutes of chaotic fighting, they managed to pull in a few more dwarves and locked shields with them, forming a strong foundation that others could build off.

The enemy was strong, especially empowered by The Turned One's essence as they were, but Thuradin was confident they could be easily turned back. They simply didn't have the strength to break through the camp's perimeter with their meager numbers.

Then the darimun came.

Thuradin saw them crest the hills to their right, charging down in a mad craze. Their large bestial bodies, corrupted by the Creature oozed a purple essence like a haze. Their yellow eyes were on fire with bloodlust as they bared their fangs, ready for the kill. He felt a jolt of worry. The darimun were charging for their flank. There were only five of them, but that was enough to devastate the defensive line they had only just set up.

Realizing there was no way to counter this charge, Thuradin braced himself, making sure he stood between the incoming attack and Myrna. The darimun crashed into the sentries like a rockslide, sending many flying into the air. A few dwarves met their end between the jaws of these corrupted beasts. A few others tried to group up to fight one of the darim together but were quickly scattered as another jumped into the fray.

Thuradin leaped out of the way just as the darimun charged in, grabbing Myrna and pulling her with him. They avoided the brunt of the attack but now they were alone again, facing off against several dozen corrupted humans and burrowers who still surrounded them. Both sides held their ground, waiting for the other to make the first move.

Luckily, no move had to be made. The darimun were wreaking havoc among the defenders, but within minutes one of them fell with a pained howl, never to rise again. Thuradin glanced around and quickly spotted the reason. Ten viatari had emerged from the nearby woods and fell upon the enemy.

They swarmed the darimun, dodging their powerful attacks with ease. The Creature's minions were a force of brute strength to be reckoned with, but even they were no match for the viatari's supernatural strength and agility without having numbers on their side. Within minutes, all five of them were killed, the viatari having managed to mount them and crack their necks.

Seeing this, the remainder of the raiding party shrank back with uncertainty. Recognizing the opportunity, Thuradin let loose another war cry and charged at the nearest foe, digging his axes deep into a burrower's belly. The burrower grunted painfully and fell. The others turned and ran.

The sentries moved to pursue them, but Thuradin held up a hand.

"Hold!" he ordered. "Let them go. We'll nae give them the satisfaction of leading us inta an ambush."

The remaining defenders nodded, breathing hard, and let their shoulders droop as they began to feel the weight of their armor and weapons. Several humans collapsed to their knees, their hands trembling as adrenaline wore off.

Thuradin surveyed the scene before him. About a dozen of The Turned One's warriors lay dead, plus the darimun. He counted ten of their own had fallen. He grimaced. For a raid, it had been an effective effort. If not for the viatari arriving when they did, the camp's perimeter might have been broken. Who knows what might have happened then?

Myrna approached him, panting and bloody from the enemies she had slain, but otherwise unharmed. Thuradin clapped her on the shoulder.

"Ye fought well."

She shrugged off the compliment, her mind already focused on the future. "Sentry duty has been a dull affair up ta now. Do ye think we should be expecting more of this?"

That was a question that also bothered Thuradin. In all the time their forces had been camped in these foothills, The Turned One had never sent any sizeable raid to harass them. Why had she started now?

"Search the bodies," he ordered to anyone still within earshot. "I want ta know if any of them was carrying anything of interest."

The closest sentries nodded and carried out the order, digging through pockets, feeling every part of the stiffening bodies for anything out of the ordinary. Thuradin joined them. It was gruesome work. Despite them being enemies, there was still some faint feeling in the back of everyone's mind telling them they should show respect for the dead. But duty came first.

It didn't take long for Thuradin to find what he was looking for. There had been a reason behind the raid after all. It had acted as a delivery service. He knelt next to the last burrower he had slain and retrieved a tuft of silver hair tied around his bony wrist. The dwarf inspected it grimly, already sure of what it was. There was nothing else it could be.

These strands of silver came from the head of a viatari.

He turned to Myrna, who had seen what he'd retrieved and now stood where she was, a grave look on her face.

"I think we'll have ta put our fishing trip on hold for a little bit, lassie."

Felix was beyond frustrated.

He had spent days doing nothing but thinking and planning and analyzing the wretched mountains they had to take. He had developed several ideas on how to approach the task, envisioning several scenarios of what a battle might look like within its tunnel systems. Despite this effort, Serania had rejected every single one of them.

Out of respect for his sister, Felix had decided to share his plans with Serania since she was now his second-in-command. He was beginning to regret that decision.

Now, the two viatari hunched over the table in the central command tent, poring over maps and stacks of reports listing their numbers and the whereabouts of their forces. They continued throwing ideas at each other but made no real progress. Felix couldn't help but think that every day wasted like this was another Victria had to endure pain and torment. He couldn't dwell on it for long though, else he'd fall into despair, and then he'd really be useless. But the dreadful thought and feeling remained in the back of his mind.

They were so focused on their work they hardly registered the horn calling for aid from the camp's perimeter when it sounded.

Serania looked up with sudden alarm. "We're under attack."

"So it would seem," Felix waved his hand dismissively.

"This is the first time she's attacked us. Don't you think we should see what's going on?"

"There are more important matters we must attend to," he glanced up sharply. "I trust the sentries to do their job. Now—"

He pulled a map that showed a layout of the mountain path leading into the Three Spires. "What if we send our entire force of burrowers to climb the smaller mountains surrounding the Three Spires and have them dig out a tunnel that burrows directly into their already-existing tunnel system? While they do this, I can take the remainder of our forces and charge up the main path. We would take the brunt of the fighting for a while, but once the burrowers finish their tunnel, they can come in from behind and surround the enemy. Then it is just a matter of slaying them all."

Serania shook her head. "There would be no way to coordinate such an attack. We have no clue where the Spires' inner tunnel system is from the outside, so the burrowers would be digging blindly. We don't know how long it would take for them to carve out such a tunnel either. What if it takes days? Weeks? Can you fight The Turned One's forces for that long? It's just not feasible."

Felix frowned. He was definitely losing his patience, but he also couldn't argue with what had been said. Serania was correct in her criticisms, much as he loathed to admit it. He shook his head. These mountains were proving difficult to figure out. And if he couldn't think of a way to take them . . . he didn't want to finish the thought.

"Could we not send a small, elite force to infiltrate the mountains with the sole intention of rescuing Victria and the others like we did for Veliris?" Serania asked.

Now it was Felix's turn to shake his head. "I have already sent scouts up to the hot springs. That area is now being guarded by a sizeable force, according to them. Our previous raid seems to have revealed to our enemy one of the few backdoors she unwittingly left open for us to take advantage of. She will not let us infiltrate her domain so easily again."

As he finished saying this the tent flaps flew open and Thuradin and Myrna stepped through, an urgency in their step. Thuradin spotted Felix and marched up to him. The dwarf saluted, then hesitated as if to gather some courage. As if he wasn't sure he wanted to share what he had to say.

"We were raided by the enemy. We took some losses but pushed them back in the end. I had our remaining sentries search the bodies ta see if they could find anything important that would give us a hint at the reason behind this raid and we found this." Taking a breath, the dwarf held out his hand.

A tuft of silver hair sat limply in Thuradin's palm. Felix's mind went blank, like it had been numbed. He reached out for the strands and took them, rubbing them absently between his fingers.

It was Victria's. He was certain of it.

His knees felt weak, but he managed to keep his footing. Anger surged through him. His imagination went wild as he thought of what the enemy could be doing to her. They took this hair from her. They wanted him to know.

"It is no longer up for debate, Serania," he said resolutely, looking up with cold determination. "I am no longer asking your opinion, I am telling you what we will do. We are going to assault the Three Spires. That assault will not end until Victria is back with us. We attack tomorrow."

"And here I thought our goal was to stop the corrupted acolytes," Serania muttered.

Ignoring the quip, Felix turned to Thuradin, who stood at attention. "Thuradin, I want you to gather the heads of every faction in this camp. We must discuss strategy and I want each of them here so we are all on the same page."

The dwarf nodded, saluted, then left the tent, his daughter following close behind. Felix moved to leave as well.

"And where do you think you're going"? Serania asked.

Felix answered without breaking stride. "I leave to speak with the acolytes. I will need their help with tomorrow's battle."

He pushed through the canvas flaps and walked the short distance to the acolytes' tent. Thuradin's report had been troubling, but it also made one thing clear in his mind.

They could no longer afford to wait.

Action had to be taken. Felix wasn't sure a frontal assault would yield favorable results. He might lose the whole of his army. Or he might not. Perhaps he was overestimating the enemy's strength. Regardless, so long as he achieved his aim, he was ready to accept whatever cost that might take. No price could be too high.

He scowled. No, there was at least one cost that was too high. He couldn't shake the feeling that the path he was taking wasn't the right one. But it was the only one he could see. With any situation there were always multiple paths one could take to reach an end result. In this case, every other path ended with him losing Victria, and that was something he wasn't willing to do.

CHAPTER TWELVE

The acolytes' tent was no different from the last time Felix had visited, though a different set of guards saluted him as he entered. Ethereal tendrils still mixed together like they had never stopped, creating the same vivid colors. Had he not known any better, the elder viatari might have thought time had stood still within these canvas walls.

As quickly as the thought came, it was gone. Felix's mind was roiling in turmoil. Serania, who had followed him from the command tent, looked around in awe. She studied the bright, energized tendrils interacting with each other, her eye following even their smallest movements.

"Ah, Felix," The First One said serenely. "We have been expecting you. There is much to discuss; however, I sense you have an urgent matter in your heart that you wish to bring up first."

The elder viatari nodded, his lips a thin. He held out his hand, strands of silver still sitting in his palm. "What do you make of this?"

The four acolytes reached out, enveloping the viatari's hand with their light.

"These strands appear to have belonged to Victria," The First One said softly, withdrawing his tendrils. The others murmured their agreement. Felix fought back the urge to scream as his fear proved correct.

Faenerus asked, "You intend to move forward with your assault on the Three Spires, then?"

Closing his fingers around the silver strands and gripping them tightly, Felix nodded. "We can no longer afford to wait. If they can get close enough—have enough control over her—that they can take what they want like this, I dare not imagine what else they can do. We attack tomorrow at dawn."

The acolytes were silent for a moment, their tendrils flowing in a rhythmic dance. They almost seemed to be hesitating.

"We must confer on this matter," The First One finally said. Silence filled the tent once more as each acolyte's tendrils mixed together aggressively, creating a connected ball of pure light.

Felix frowned, staring into the light despite the fact that it hurt his eyes. He didn't understand what there was to discuss. The First One had said he and his siblings would give their aid once he came up with a plan of attack to rescue Victria. They had given him their word. Heat rose to his face at the prospect that they might turn back on it. Serania gripped his arm comfortingly, bringing him back from darkening thoughts.

"We will aid you in this battle, as promised," The First One spoke, his voice booming with authority, filling the spacious tent. "But there is information we must share with you before that decision can be final. Something we have only just learned."

Felix raised an eyebrow but kept his mouth shut. He couldn't begin to guess what more could be said. Still, he kept his impatience in check. He would hear them out.

"We have broken through our sister's wards," it was Scorpus

who spoke, his voice a cascading wave. "We have learned her plan in detail."

The atmosphere grew heavy with tension as the two viatari leaned in to hear the result of months of effort and patience.

Deep tones from Faenerus burst forth, "Our sister, devious in her planning, intends to awaken the First Gods."

The viatari shared a confused glance.

"Is that not a good thing?" Serania asked. "If the First Gods created all of Azar, including us, would they not help us and defend their creations?"

A trembling answer from Veliris, "No."

"Our sister was not idle during her slumber, as I originally thought," The First One explained, his words bitter as they floated out from his artifact. "She spent those many centuries digging into our world, like the roots of a weed, spreading her corruption into Azar itself. Her influence now runs deep, touches everything that exists."

"I must admit my confusion," Felix interrupted. "I was under the impression that the First Gods had left Azar; vanished without a trace."

"That is also what we believed," The First One's tendrils shook somberly. "Another inaccurate assumption, unfortunately. I cannot say how our sister has discovered their existence, as I cannot feel their presence myself, but the First Gods never left Azar. They remain here, buried deep beneath the world, asleep for countless millennia."

"And The Turned One is able to reach them through the roots she has grown." Serania stated flatly.

"Ah, you see the problem," Scorpus mused. "We cannot be sure for how long, but it is likely she has been feeding them her corrupted essence since the end of our last war with her."

Bewildered, Felix shook his head, the beginnings of a headache taking shape behind his eyes. He pinched the bridge of his nose. This was a lot to take in, but he failed to see how it related to his plans for assaulting the Three Spires.

"Surely, the First Gods cannot be corrupted," he ventured.

White tendrils quivered in disagreement. "Any-thing can be corrupted, given time. If my sister's plan sees fruition, the First Gods will rise again to roam Azar. But it will not be a happy reunion. They will be corrupted shadows of their former selves. Empty husks. They will embody hatred, violence, destruction, chaos; the complete opposite of their true natures. For all intents and purposes, the First Gods will be dead—are already dead. If they awaken to do our sister's bidding, they will be nearly unstoppable. They will bring this world into an unprecedented era of chaos and destruction that we cannot fathom."

"So that is the endgame," Serania let out a heavy breath. "Then we must stop her before she can carry out this plan. How does she intend to do it?"

"With the Purity Scepter," The First One planted a tendril on the viatari's forehead. They felt his presence force its way into their minds. It wasn't an un-pleasant feeling. An aura of peace and calm pulsed through their consciousness like a warm flame. They heard the acolyte's voice speaking in their head as an image formed within their mind's eye.

This is the Purity Scepter, he explained. In his thoughts, Felix saw an image of a dull-gray metal rod that narrowed into a sharp curve on one end, like a hook. On the other the rod flared out, shaping into several curves, like an eagle's claw. Within that claw sat a faintly glowing red orb.

Veliris' sky-blue tendrils hovered close to Felix's head, as if it could see what he was seeing just by proximity. "With this item, our sister would be able to rouse our creators from their sleep. There is a process to undergo. She must first find the Scepter and take it to the Temple in the Eastern Wald. Then, she must pass the test of the Guardians, those who protect that sacred edifice. That would be no easy task for her, as the Guardians look for purity of heart in those they test before allowing them into the Temple. After that, there is an ancient incantation that must be spoken at the Mountain of Beginnings. The point is, however, that we must keep her from obtaining this Scepter in the first place."

"Why have we not heard of this before?" Felix demanded.

The existence of this tool has only ever been rumor, The First One responded. *Our sister seems to believe that it truly exists. That is enough to make me believe in its existence as well.*

"Are we sure that she does not already have it?"

If she does, there is no reason for her to dwell within the mountains.

The First One withdrew his tendrils from the viatari, a faint ghost of his presence lingering with them like a dream soon to be forgotten. His voice once more filled the tent for all to hear.

"So, we must keep her from obtaining the Scepter by keeping her contained within the Three Spires." Felix began to pace. What had been shared here was extremely important. Any other time, he would've given it his full attention. As it was, only one thing bothered him about this recent revelation. "My next question, then, is how does this conflict with my plan to assault The Turned One's base of operations tomorrow?"

"It is exactly because of this shortsightedness that we share this information," Scorpus mused.

The First One's tendrils snapped like a whip, admonishing

his brother. "You must understand, Felix, that while containing our sister within her stronghold is not the optimal long-term solution, it is the best option currently. The only other one is to conquer the Three Spires flat-out in a decisive victory, thus defeating The Turned One *and* the Creature for good."

"Then, we are in agreement."

"We are not, young viatari," Faenerus' voice barked. "If you make this assault but cannot win the battle, what then? What happens if your losses are too great from this venture that we can no longer maintain a siege?"

Frowning, Felix shook his head dismissively. "It will not matter what our losses are if we win, which I intend to do." Serania shot him a disapproving look but said nothing.

The acolytes seemed to collectively sigh, the atmosphere in the tent vibrating with their power.

"So be it, Felix," The First One said, slightly dejected. "We will join you in this battle in the hopes of a complete victory; but remember what I warned you before," his presence seemed to grow, a stern edge entering his voice. "We cannot risk capture by the enemy under any circumstances. If there is any determination by us that victory has slipped through your grasp, we will not hesitate to withdraw from the field with or without your approval. Do we make ourselves clear?"

Felix frowned. He had agreed to these terms before, and he would agree to them now, not that he truly had a choice. In the end, it would not come to that. He would make sure of it. He nodded.

"Then we hope for your success tomorrow, and we will endeavor to help create such a result."

The two viatari bowed respectfully, then turned to leave. Before Felix could exit, however, The First One called out to him privately in his mind.

You take great risk with this action, Felix. If we fail here, and my sister is given free rein to carry out her plot, our war is all but over.

The elder viatari hesitated. The acolyte's words weighed on his mind for a second, but only a second, before he pushed his way out of the tent and made his way back to his own.

He did not look back.

A ring of figures surrounded the long wooden table within the command tent. Their somber faces were lit by the gently swinging braziers hanging overhead. Each one had the same uneasy expression. They all knew the reason for their presence: to plan for the next battle. They also knew, based on their last assault on those cursed mountains, that this next attempt would be nothing short of a grisly affair. Their only hope was that their viatari ally, the one who had summoned them, who led them, had devised some clever scheme that could bring victory.

Felix entered the tent, Serania following in his wake. Shadows hung under his red eyes, but a determined fire still fueled him, staving off fatigue. He made his way to the head of the table and regarded each leader present.

There stood before him six different heads and their retinues. Across from him proudly stood Garadin Stoutshield, Thuradin's cousin, once more in the service of King Dunkell. Felix was glad to see him. Garadin had proven himself a friend of the viatari more than once, helping them defend their city of Aleganthia from The Turned One's forces in the past. Even when he had been on the Council, an anti-monarchist faction within the Dwarven Kingdom that had nearly led the dwarven clans into civil war, he had been open to the viatari's desire to speak of peace. Now he stood, with

Thuradin and a small band of dwarven guards behind him, a somber but confident expression on his face as he swept his shoulder-length black hair out of the way.

To Garadin's right stood Brap, son of the burrower High Chieftain, Gruk-Gruk. He stood in the place of his father while the High Chieftain oversaw the reconstruction of the dwarven capital and farming communities alongside King Dunkell. Felix hadn't spent much time interacting with the burrowers so far, but they had certainly proven themselves useful to the war effort. He was glad to see them represented at the table.

To the left of the dwarves stood Kent, leader of the humans. He and Simon had been instrumental in bringing their people together with the viatari, bridging the gap that centuries of hatred and violence had created. Now, virtually all of the human towns of the plains had joined the fight against The Turned One. While Kent led them all as their head chief, each town and region had its own representative who stood with him now at the table. A few glanced Felix's way, still unsure how to feel about being so close to a viatari without having to fight for their life. Not all of them were like this though, as some of the chiefs watched the elder viatari with a degree of admiration.

Next to the humans were the vashi. Since Cotovas, who had been leading them before, was now dead, Avmoshir had appointed Esseld, commander of his border forces, to represent his people present in the siege. The vashi were a strange looking people in Felix's eyes, and he was sure they thought the same of him. Each one wore their thick locks of hair in bulging braids, some decorated with seashells or tied with lengths of seaweed. Their bodies, rippling with muscle, were surrounded by a thin layer of a mucus-like substance that kept them hydrated while they were out of the water. Their lower bodies were multi-colored and scaled, each one differing from the others. Despite their odd appearance, Felix was glad to have their skills. Their waterseers had especially proven useful as healers alongside the dwarven Enurg'en.

Finally, he looked to his right where Drathanar and Salevari normally would have stood to represent the viatari of Dalyr. In their place stood Serania, still glowering at him with severe disapproval. She kept her mouth shut, however, waiting for him to at least lay out his grand strategy before she attempted to shut it down.

"I would like to thank each of you for coming here in such short notice," Felix began. "As you may have surmised, we are here to discuss our next assault on the Three Spires. Our objective here is simple. We will march into those mountains and utterly defeat the enemy, ending this war with one swift strike."

He walked over to a shelf holding a variety of scrolls and pulled one out. Unfurling it, he laid it out on the table for all to see, putting weights on each corner. The scroll depicted a closer look at the Three Spires and the nearby foothills, detailing the path leading into the depths of those peaks. The map had several ink scratches along the path, marking fortifications the enemy had placed as well as fresh scribbles which pointed out various traps they had encountered during their last assault. This was a map they were all familiar with. They had spent hours studying it already.

"If I may, Felix," Garadin spoke up, stroking his trimmed beard. "We all know what happened the last time we tried this sort of thing. Why would we try another direct assault when the last one was a disaster?"

"Our last assault was no disaster," Felix countered. "Our attack served its purpose. We attacked to provide a distraction, not to take the mountains."

"We lost a lot of good warriors in that distraction."

"Yes, and many of those deaths exposed the locations of enemy traps. Even if they are rearmed, we will be able to approach more cautiously this time. That should mitigate our losses."

"And if the enemy has set new traps? They've certainly had the time ta do so."

"The mountain pass does not provide much space for such a move," Felix said, his eyes staring hungrily at the parchment before him. "I do not believe they will have the capabilities to randomize trap locations as you suggest. No, at best, we will have to deal with the ones we suffered through last time. This time, however, we will have a team dedicated to disarming each trap as we approach. That is something I think you dwarves will have some expertise in."

Garadin grunted. "I can find the right engineers for the job."

"Excellent," Felix moved on. Now was the time to lay out his strategy. He hoped everyone would accept it without question. There was no time for debate as far as he was concerned.

"As I said before, last time we assaulted the Three Spires we went in as a distraction. We always knew that we would not reach the Spires' entrance, that we would pull back at some point. That will not be the case this time. With everyone knowing the stakes that this could be the final battle, I believe we all will fight harder and smarter. We will be fighting to win. This mindset will help us push farther than we would have before."

Every pair of eyes was on him. He could feel them. But he didn't stop, didn't let their visible doubts give him pause. He kept his own gaze glued to the map, imagining the battle in his head even as he described it.

"We will assemble in the valley. The enemy will see our approach and be ready for it. I will not deceive you by saying this battle will be easy—it will not be. This will likely be a long, difficult affair that requires all of our combined efforts to take each switchback. The bulk of our forces will make their way up the path as before. I expect stiff resistance, especially in the first few hours of the fight."

"We cannot fight all day," Kent interrupted. "While you may have a limitless amount of strength and stamina, and the dwarves perhaps more than us, our forces will be spent before we reach halfway up the mountain if we're fighting in bottlenecks the whole time."

"That is where the burrowers come in." Brap stood a little straighter as Felix mentioned his people. "The burrowers will take the majority of their warriors and scale the mountain's face. As our forces draw attention to themselves on the main path, they will fall upon the enemy's flanks while we move up the switchbacks. The enemy will have no counter against them and will be forced to fall back. This will allow our progress to go much faster than last time. We continue this method of attack all the way up until we reach the Spires' entrance."

"And what of my people?" Esseld asked, his words heavy and accented. "We cannot fight ssso fiercely out of the water. I fear we will be of little ussse on thossse mountainsss."

"Which is why you will be the reserve," Felix pointed out the foothills. "The acolytes have pledged their strength in tomorrow's assault. They will use their powers to strengthen us or attack the enemy directly at their discretion. As they already warned me, they cannot risk capture. Your people will help ensure their safety. If the enemy has any reserve forces of their own waiting to ambush us from behind, it will be your job to defend the acolytes as well as the rear of our forces."

"And what happens when we enter the mountains?" Garadin

asked. "We have no maps of the interior, no knowledge of their tunnel system. There could be more traps within that we know nothing of. They may even induce a cave-in just ta keep us out. We won't even have support in the air at that point with yer people's Lyruun riders."

Felix nodded, "It is true we will be more or less blind when we enter those tunnels. That is something that cannot be helped. My hope is that the enemy will be so spent trying to keep us out that there will be little resistance once we've actually entered the mountains. Either way, at that point we will have to play it by ear and use caution. Once we are in, our goal must be to find the location of The Turned One and the Creature. If we can drag them out of their caverns or perhaps bring our own acolytes to them, they can do what must be done to put an end to our enemy for good."

The elder viatari finally took a breath as he continued to peruse the map. Had he forgotten anything? As he described his strategy out loud, it had sounded more promising. Could this be the way, the true way, to end this conflict?

Arms crossed, Serania cleared her throat. "You better tell them the real objective of this assault or I will. They deserve to know."

All eyes fell on Felix once again, suspicion in them. He regarded them cooly, unwavering. "With this assault there is also the chance to rescue several of our own who were captured by the enemy during our raid to save Veliris. I do not deny that it is my desire to get them back. Even if all we get back are their—corpses." He choked on the last word but played it off as a sudden cough. He took a swig of water for good measure.

"Are there any questions or objections to this plan of attack?"

There was a moment of silence. Everyone looked around the tent as if to gauge what the others were thinking. One by one, they nodded.

"It is settled, then." Felix almost let out a sigh of relief but kept control of himself. This was not the time to show how desperate he had been for their approval, how anxious he really was for this coming battle. It would have been seen as a sign of his uncertainty, of his recklessness. Which he was not. Everything in his mind was telling him this strategy was sound. Barring any surprises thrown their way, tomorrow would be the end of this terrible war. Even now, he was racking his brain for what surprises *could* come their way so that he might be able to counter them.

One by one, each faction left the tent to go spread the news among their respective warriors. After a while, only Serania and Felix remained. Her accusing gaze never wavered.

"I hope you know what you're doing, Felix," she said softly. "You're risking a lot here."

The elder viatari nodded. He knew the risks. They were worth it to him.

"Are you sure this is the path you want to take?"

An image of Victria, withered away and chained to a stone wall entered forcefully into his mind. She was hardly breathing. Her normally vibrant silver hair was dull and matted. Her eyelids fluttered and he saw her lips move. A single name escaped them. His. A mixture of pain and resolve pierced his heart as lethally as an arrowhead.

He glanced at Serania, doing his best to exude confidence as he grinned, but the pain inside was too much to hide as he croaked, "This is the only path there is."

CHAPTER THIRTEEN

The sky was still dark when the camp began to stir. Dwarves, humans, vashi, viatari, and burrowers alike woke in silence, milling about their individual camps, putting on their armor, their eyes bleary from a troubled sleep—the small amount they'd been able to grasp, anyway. Each individual knew what was to come today, knew what was being asked of them. The only thing they didn't know was whether they would return by the end of it.

Thuradin groaned as he finished tightening the straps of his greaves and splashed his face with a cold handful of water to chase away the remnants of sleep. Borim did the same next to him. With a knowing look from having shared many a battle together, the two dwarves grabbed their weapons and together made their way through the neat rows of tents to the kitchens. Other dwarves trickled in from their shelters, stumbling along in the same direction. Thuradin was sure the scene was similar all throughout camp.

There would be one final meal they all shared before they

were organized and sent out to battle. Long lines snaked from the kitchens as warriors of all races waited their turn, bowls in hand, to receive what for many would likely be their last meal. As their bowls were filled with a steaming pool of rice porridge topped with slices of pork, ram meat, egg, and a mixture of pickled vegetables, they made their way to one of the numerous wooden tables to eat. There was silence in the air, save for the clattering of wooden spoons against bowls and the occasional slurp. Some looked nervous, others grunted appreciatively, eagerness in their eyes as they spooned the hearty breakfast into their mouths.

Thuradin and Borim sat across from each other. They were soon joined by Myrna. She and Thuradin caught each other's eye. For a moment, it was just the two of them. Each one recognized the potential fate the other could face this day. For Thuradin, he saw his daughter as he remembered her, a child looking up at him with an eager grin, reaching her arms out for him to pick her up, the armor she was wearing far too heavy for her small shoulders. Myrna looked lost in thought as well as she stared deep into him, working her jaw as if chewing on the sentiments she wanted to let loose. He gripped her shoulder firmly, squeezing, hoping his pride, worry, and love could be felt by her even with this simple gesture. They turned their attention back to their food and ate. The porridge was hot and creamy and was complimented nicely by the salted meats, but to Thuradin it was as dry as dust.

This shared meal continued for another two hours. By the time the first rays of light colored the sky a dull pink, most of the camp had finished eating and were making their way for the clearing just outside of camp to form up with their respective companies and troops. Banners fluttered in the wind, each with its own insignia. The sound of thousands of armored boots treading on grass filled the air. Horses nickered and rams bleated softly to each other as they carried their riders slowly forward. The first few crows, spotting the forces gathering below them, began to circle eagerly, though they were quickly chased away by Lyruun riders.

A massive stone sat in Thuradin's stomach as he followed everyone out. It was a familiar weight that always came before battle. How many times had he carried it with him? He brought his fist to his palm, punching it several times, and let out an exhilarated breath. Fire flowed through his veins. His muscles tremored in anticipation of what they would have to do. He was ready.

Horns sounded a low deep tone. Their call filtered through the air, carried to everyone's ears by the wind. As one, the combined forces of Azar marched against the Three Spires.

Felix sat on his horse on the crest of a line of hills overlooking the valley where his army had gathered. From here he could see everything; the full size of his forces; each individual banner they flew, all different colors and styles; the mountain path they would have to climb; everything. He saw some movement ahead of his warriors as The Turned One's forces made their own preparations, aware that battle was once more upon them, but they made no move to sally forth from the mountains. This would make their own advance much easier, Felix thought. The battle would be met on the switchbacks themselves rather than the valley first as it had last time.

Next to him sat Serania as well as several viatari, dwarven, and human riders who would act as messengers for whenever Felix needed their services.

The sun was now fully in the sky, rising steadily, spreading its glow and warmth to all below. Horns blew, their calls faint to Felix's ears. Two separate regiments of warriors began a steady march forward, mostly consisting of dwarves and humans, with viatari archers interspersed among them. Their armor glinted in the sunlight, even as clouds of dust rose up around them.

Another horn.

A third section of the army, this one made up entirely of burrowers, spread out in a long line and trudged their way straight toward the mountain face. They began to climb the steep incline just as the dwarves and humans reached the mouth of the first switchback. The enemy remained clustered in a defensive position near the top of this section of the pass, waiting for them.

Back in the valley, the vashi forces separated into four different troops and stood at the ready in half-mile intervals. Behind each troop sat an acolyte, stationed on the grassy field. A smattering of viatari Lyruun riders stood guard behind each one, ready to airlift them back to camp if they were ordered to do so.

Felix was curious to see how the acolytes would influence the battle. He didn't have a good understanding of each one's power yet, save The First One's, which he had seen first-hand in Aleganthia. The First One's powerful aura would be a boon to his forces climbing the mountain and negate the effects The Turned One's corrupting aura would normally have on her own. While such a blessing was nice to have in this particular battle, it wouldn't have a direct impact on the enemy's forces or their numbers. He hoped the other acolytes were bestowed with more practical abilities.

Looking back at the column of dwarves, he saw that they were approaching cautiously, their eyes on the enemy ahead. The first rank held their shields out and locked together.

They took deliberate steps forward, the right flank curving inward to avoid a certain section of the path that had been marked as a trap on Felix's map. Once they had passed the spot, the line refilled the width of the trail and continued forward.

Felix's stomach twisted with every step they took, anticipating the moment the two lines would meet and the bloodshed begin. He wished he could be down there right now, leading them personally. However, he was needed here to direct things; especially if something–

A flash of light. Then more. Followed by plumes of smoke. Seconds later, faint booms reached his ears. Serania gasped. Felix's mouth fell open as a gust of wind mercifully pushed the smoke away, erasing it from existence. A bloody picture unfolded.

One moment, the dwarven and human columns had been advancing up the mountain path, about to reach the enemy waiting for them at the top of the switchback. The next second, the first few lines of dwarves had been obliterated in a series of explosions. Enemies had come out all along the mountain trail seemingly out of nowhere and surrounded those who remained. Those waiting atop the switchback charged down, forcing the dwarves to fight on three sides.

Thankfully, by this point, the burrowers climbing the mountain face had reached the lip of rock leading onto the pass as well. They jumped into the fray, freeing the dwarves' right flank and putting pressure on the enemy's. Just as Felix had wanted.

The enemy's attack had been brutal. Sudden. But the dwarves soon freed both flanks from the initial pressure and turned their attention on the foes directly ahead. Slowly, they pushed the enemy back and within minutes took the first switchback. The Turned One's forces broke contact and retreated up the next one. Dwarves and humans followed, with the burrowers beginning the next leg of their climb. A trail of dead were left in their wake.

"Those explosions were not marked on the map." Serania stated flatly.

Felix nodded, his lips twisting into a snarl. Explosives going off where they had could only mean one thing. The Turned One's forces had made the time to lay out new traps, despite the limited space the mountain passes provided. There could be more uncharted traps that his army would walk blindly into. The losses from them could be catastrophic, or they would bleed him slowly over time.

Either way, a part of his subconscious tugged for his attention, as if suggesting that he should pull away from this battle. They weren't prepared to deal with this kind of surprise. If they repeated their mistakes from the last battle, there would be no army left by the end of the day.

To continue onward was suicide.

Yet, another part urged for him to push forward. Determination would win the day. He had known there would be losses. Heavy losses. He had underplayed this fact during the war meeting but deep down he had known this is how it would be. The acolytes had known it too, seeing into his mind and heart as they had, and they hadn't stopped him. This was a gamble, but it was one that was still worthwhile.

They would continue on. In the end, they would take the Three Spires. Felix nodded again, now to himself. Even if it led to the utter annihilation of his army, so long as his goals were met, he would let this battle play out to the bitter end.

The first switchback was taken.

Thuradin took a moment to lean on his knees and catch his breath as a vanguard was formed to continue up the path ahead of the main force. They had been caught off-guard by the sudden explosions. They wouldn't let the bulk of their forces walk into a trap like that again. The vanguard marched bravely forward, chanting a war cry. Ahead of them, a few lightly armored dwarves scurried forward with small pickaxes and wooden mallets, inspecting the path ahead. The dwarven engineers, despite having missed the first trap would be instrumental in discovering other hidden ones—at least, that was the belief. They tapped lightly on the surrounding rock with their tools, listening hard for some telltale sign that danger awaited the main host. It was slow progress.

Lifting himself back up, Thuradin went on with the main force, his ears still ringing. He tried to think back on what had just happened, but it had all been so confusing.

The dwarven column had walked into a trap, that much was obvious. But it wasn't one that should have existed. It was almost a certainty now that there would be more uncharted traps ahead. They had to be more cautious with their approach if they wanted to minimize losses. That one series of explosions alone had vaporized the first four ranks of dwarves and threw half of the following two ranks off the mountain. They couldn't afford to take hits like that all day.

Then the enemy had attacked. There were tunnels built into and hidden along the mountain face. It was how the enemy had so quickly and easily surrounded them on such a narrow pass. This pincer attack had led to more dwarven losses as confusion reigned throughout the column.

Thankfully, Felix's plan to have the burrowers climb the mountain face to flank the enemy proved enough to relieve the pressure almost immediately and the dwarves wasted no time with pushing the enemy back.

It was a devious ambush. And Thuradin was sure they could expect attacks like this for the rest of the day.

Sure enough, just as they reached the center of the second switchback, a segment of mountain the vanguard stood on crumbled beneath their feet. The dwarves yelped but could do nothing as gravity began to pull them to their deaths.

As suddenly as the ground had begun to crumble, however, it reformed and solidified. The vanguard stood where they were, still as statues, unsure of what had just happened and what they should do next.

"Forward, lads!" A dwarven officer called out. The vanguard regained their composure, reformed their lines, and continued marching up the mountain.

But only for a short time.

Just as Thuradin had suspected, there were several more new traps ahead. Holes appeared all along the mountain face to their right as if curtains were being swept aside. Corrupted burrowers, their bodies enlarged and powerful and covered in scale armor, their eyes black, rushed out with a gurgling war cry. Humans followed silently, their own eyes the same corrupted black and their movements swifter than normal.

Metal clashed against metal and an incessant din of yelling took hold. Thuradin felt a war cry rush from his own throat as he deflected an oncoming sword, bringing an axe around and lodging it into the offending human's spine. His opponent's back arched, a silent scream on his face as he crumpled to the ground, unmoving.

Thuradin ripped his axe out and looked for his next kill. He fought in formation with his fellow dwarves, their shields keeping the enemy from smashing through while he lashed out with his axes, looking for the smallest of openings to do the greatest damage.

He had only just raked his serrated blades against the neck of a burrower when he felt the air whistle around him. Several dwarves next to him grunted in pain. Some fell to the floor, wrestling with long, protruding shafts, goose feathers at the end. Others lay eerily still. Looking up, Thuradin saw a line of black-eyed humans staring down at them from the mountain pass above. They pulled back on their bowstrings, arrowheads gleaming in the sunlight.

"Shields up!" he cried out.

Immediately, the dwarves around him obeyed. While the front lines continued to maintain their shield wall against the immediate enemy, all while pushing back on them, the inner ranks lifted their iron slabs high overhead, interlocking them to form a single large shell.

Not a moment too soon, Thuradin ducked beneath the formation. A series of thunks sounded overhead. Then another. The dwarves kept their shields up despite the fighting raging around them, their arms steady and faces defiant, as if they dared the arrows to punch through.

Crouched, Thuradin pushed his way around the many bodies holding back the onslaught of deadly missiles. Sweat and blood filled his nostrils. Occasionally, his foot slipped as he accidentally stepped on someone's stiff body. He tried not to think about those times.

Finally, he reached the rear of the dwarven column, but he need not have wasted his time or energy. The humans he had meant to order into firing their own arrows at the mountain pass above were already doing so, as were the viatari. Unfortunately, their shots fell short or bounced off the rock wall above them, the enemy being just out of range.

The human column itself was in some trouble. They didn't

have the benefit of a protective formation like the dwarves. Those who had shields raised them, trying to protect their fellows, but the thin wall they created had far too many gaps in between. Arrows slithered their way through, often finding their mark. On top of this, the humans were also being flanked by the enemy and struggled to maintain their lines. Kent stormed between his men with a mad gleam in his eyes, shouting orders with gusto and doing what he could to keep his warriors from running. But there was only so much he could do. Corrupted burrowers were much larger than humans and proved to be much stronger. They wreaked havoc within the lines before being felled themselves.

As before, their own burrowers came to the rescue just in time, having made the climb to the next switchback. They rushed in, alleviating much of the pressure that had been put on the flanks, hacking and slashing into their corrupted cousins with a mad glee. They ran into battle only lightly protected with armor, however, and no shields to speak of. Arrows found easy marks among them and several fell with each volley sent their way. Some burrowers danced along the path, swinging their cudgels and daggers haphazardly, making themselves as elusive a target as they could, but they couldn't evade the missiles forever.

A screech from above.

Thuradin glanced up again and felt his heart beat with a fierce satisfaction. Lyruun riders dove upon the entrenched archers, their long wings opening up and catching the wind just in time for them to glide along the enemy's lines. From their serpentine maws burst forth clouds of green mist that melted the skin of those it touched. The corrupted archers only had time for one horrific howl of pain before their lives were snuffed out.

Seeing the threat from above eradicated, the dwarves broke their defensive position and pushed hard against the remaining enemies before them. The Turned One's servants fell by the dozen as dwarven swords, axes, and hammers found their mark. Roaring with one voice, they steadily made their way to the next switchback.

A few surviving enemy archers tried to fire at the Lyruun riders, but the flying serpents were too fast, and their missiles sailed harmlessly through the open air. Thuradin thrust his axes up and laughed madly. So long as they maintained their superiority in the air, the enemy wouldn't be able to do anything but fall back.

Felix adjusted himself in his saddle. He licked his lips eagerly. His eyes devoured the battle with a studious nature as it unfolded. With the Lyruun riders causing so much damage against the enemy, ending the war with this one desperate battle seemed to have become a real possibility.

His intuition so far had been correct. His plan to have the burrowers carry out continuous flanking attacks against the enemy by climbing the mountain face directly was yielding results. The dwarves and humans were taking losses, but they were fighting with an impressive display of bravery and resilience.

And now the acolytes had joined the fight in earnest.

After the initial explosions, Felix had called for a messenger and sent them with orders for the acolytes to join the fight as they saw fit—to use their powers at will. And not a moment too soon. One of the traps the dwarves had triggered would have caused an entire section of the mountain pass to crumble away, taking the dwarves who had triggered it as well as a large part of the army still making their way up the pass below in a bloody rockslide if Faenerus hadn't intervened.

Felix didn't understand how it worked, but he saw the pass crumble, saw the dwarves begin to fall, then saw Faenerus' artifact flash a brilliant red. The next moment, the collapsing rock had resolidified, and the dwarves continued their push forward.

It appeared he was the only one pleased. Looking to his right, he saw Serania's grim face and raised an eyebrow. She shook her head.

"We may be making progress, but the enemy can keep up this resistance along the whole mountain. Even with the acolytes' help, we will suffer far too many losses for us to maintain any sort of siege afterwards."

"That is only if we are forced to retreat," Felix countered, bringing his eyes back to the battle. "We will not need a siege if we win the day."

There was a flash of green from Scorpus' position. Thin layers of low-hanging dark clouds sailed across the valley and hovered over the mountains, almost hugging the passes. A misty rain followed. Even as the rear-guard, consisting mostly of dwarven Enurg'en and vashi waterseers, moved into position to heal any wounded left behind by the main force, the wounded lifted themselves up. There was some confusion as everyone wondered how such a miracle could be possible. Then, remembering their situation, the healed warriors gathered together and marched off to rejoin the main host. The Enurg'en and waterseers stayed back for a little longer just to see if there were any others who could benefit from their healing powers before deciding there was nothing left to do and moved on.

Just as quickly as the rejuvenating shower came, it stopped, and the clouds dissipated.

Once more Felix looked at Serania. "It seems we won't have as many losses as you think if we can have our wounded healed at such an impressive rate."

"I don't think that rain raised our dead, Felix."

Two more flashes, one from Veliris and another from Faenerus shot out into the sky as the battle progressed. Tree roots crawled at a swift pace from the nearby woods toward the Three Spires, rippling up the mountain pass. When they reached the battle, they erupted from the earth but only where the enemy stood. Thick roots wrapped themselves around dozens of The Turned One's servants and dragged them down into the mountain itself. They became one with the stubborn stone.

At the same time, another blanket of clouds formed along the Three Spires, though this one was much higher. Lightning flashed and balls of fire fell from the sky, crashing directly where the enemy's forces were at their thickest. Many burrowers and humans were thrown from the mountain or crushed by the falling missiles. Many were set aflame and died writhing.

It was an awesome display of power, but Felix couldn't help feeling a slight sense of unease. Before now he had never truly known the extent of the acolytes' powers. Now, he was just glad they were on the same side.

The sun hovered at its zenith, beating down on the two armies below, marking noon. They had been fighting since the morning, and it was beginning to show. Attacks came slower. Defenses were harder to maintain. Many died from simply being too tired to fight. But the battle had continued to progress even as the combined forces of Azar found themselves fighting along the midsection of the Three Spires.

Thuradin gasped for breath, his lungs burning with effort.

His arms were heavy, defiant every time he wanted to raise them, whether it was to defend himself or strike at an opponent. His mind was dense with fog and numb from the constant fighting. He wasn't sure how many switchbacks they had taken, how many miles they had hiked and fought uphill, how many losses they had suffered. What he had seen from this battle, however, had been enough to fill him with a dread he had never experienced before.

Fire from the sky. Sudden explosions that left one dead before they knew it. Gnarled roots coming up from the earth and devouring those they grabbed onto.

He had fought in many battles throughout his long life. Too many to count. He knew how terrible war was. Once a battle was over and the adrenaline rush was spent, all one could do was remember the faces of the slain. The heavy scent of blood would register and never seemed to leave. The realization of the kind of affair he had just undergone always settled in like a nauseating sickness upon his mind.

War was ugly. War was brutal. But what he was seeing here was neither. This was hellish.

Where often one's fate was decided in battle by a combination of strength of arms, fighting skill, bravery and, most importantly, luck, there was none of that here. This was chaos. There was no order to this fighting, no control. One could fell more enemies than they could count and be vaporized by fire the next second by no fault of their own. One could yet have seen the enemy and find themselves the unfortunate recipient of a cluster of falling rocks from the battles above. There was no control.

Thuradin didn't like it. In fact, he *hated* it. This was no fight he ever wanted to relive. This was an ordeal he wanted to survive and immediately put behind him.

Still, they were making progress. Their purpose here was not yet done. They would continue fighting until the enemy was destroyed or they were. Thuradin brought to his mind a terrible image of what he imagined Victria's situation to be. He thought of her in pain, bonded, yet holding out hope. It fueled his tired limbs. He was fighting for her, just as she had fought for him so many times before. If this hell was what he had to endure to save a friend, he would endure it.

Another large explosion ahead. Thuradin braced himself and managed to keep his footing, though others weren't so lucky. Looking ahead, he saw a large horde of The Turned One's forces waiting for them to approach. This time, however, darimun were interspersed among them.

They had fought countless burrowers and humans and even the dwarf-sized crab-like creatures Thuradin had seen following the darinsha leader like a pet. These last had proven to be formidable, their armor hard, their claws deadly. They could crush through a dwarf's thick plate armor in seconds, cleaving their bodies in two. But they hadn't run into any darimun until now.

These servants of the Creature, once regular beasts of the wild, were corrupted and perverted versions of their previous selves, marked by yellow eyes, grotesque and enlarged features, and an ever-present aura of purple mist that seemed to emanate from their own bodies. Thuradin was thankful a vast majority of them had been slaughtered during a pitched battle Salevari had won against them a year ago, ending their rampage of the plains south of Aleganthia. If she hadn't won that fight, they might have been facing more throughout the duration of their siege. There wasn't enough wildlife within The Three Spires, it seemed, for the Creature to replenish his forces as quickly as he might have liked.

As it was, even with their small numbers, this would still be a problem. The darimun could rush through their lines with ease. Many would fall to their deaths over the side simply by the beasts running down the pass. Even the viatari they had mixed in with their dwarven and human columns wouldn't be as effective a counter against the darimun with such limited space available.

A large shadow passed overhead followed by a strong gust of wind. Then a chorus of pained screeches.

Thuradin looked up and dove out of the way.

A Lyruun crashed where he had just been standing, its fanged maw hanging open, its reptilian eyes bloody and unmoving. Its wings were shorn and bloody gashes covered the length of its scaled body. The Lyruun's rider was no worse for wear, her body a broken mess of bones. She lay next to her mount, unmoving, red eyes glazed over with a look of shock.

Looking up, he was met with a horrific sight. More Lyruun fell from the sky. Several crashed into the dwarven and human columns, crushing many and sending up large plumes of dust. One exploded on impact, sending green mist gushing forth from the impact zone. Many of their own forces were caught up in it, including Kent. Howls filled the air. A mad dash ensued to escape the area, but it was too late for too many. They clawed at their bodies even as the mist ate it away. Kent managed to find enough strength to crawl a few feet as flesh fell from his bones before he finally collapsed, never to move again.

Thuradin didn't have time to lament the loss of the human chief, nor to dwell on how bravely he had fought and how terribly he had died. There were more pressing matters, such as the cause for all this mayhem.

Above them soared a large shadow shaped like a giant bat with dull red eyes. Thuradin had seen it before. His veins ran cold. This same shadow bat had rescued The Turned One just before Felix had been able to capture her after they had successfully taken the city of Garon.

Now it had returned to decimate the Lyruun riders. The viatari mounts were tiny things compared to this giant shadow. Its wings caused gust storms below, blowing several people off the mountain altogether. It snapped at the fluttering Lyruun with its large vampiric maw and gouged into their bodies with talons of shadow, sending several flying serpents spiraling to the ground at once.

The Lyruun riders tried their best to rally against this new foe, but their green and blue mists proved ineffective. With nothing else to do and seeing too many of their fellows fall to their deaths, the remaining riders turned and fled.

And with that, Thuradin knew the battle was lost. The realization rushed through the whole of the army like a plague. Without waiting for orders of any kind from their officers, horns sounding for a retreat pierced the air.

The vanguard quickly turned into a rearguard, ensuring the main host could make their escape back down the mountain without the enemy running them down from behind. The Turned One's forces smashed into them and, despite the destructive force the darimun provided, the vanguard's line managed to hold. But they would not survive long.

With one last look up the mountain pass, Thuradin turned and ran for his life.

Felix couldn't believe what he had just witnessed.

He had been confident, jubilant even. The battle had progressed all the way up to the midsection of the Three Spires, only a few switchbacks away from where the entrance was supposed to be. With one or two more hours of hard fighting, they would be through and then they could scour the tunnels within to search for Victria. He had been all but ready to urge his mount forward so that he could lead that search.

Then the shadow had come.

The bat-like creature had peeled itself away from the face of the leftmost peak of the Three Spires. Felix hadn't even been aware of it until it began to move.

With a few flaps of its powerful wings, it had reached the battle raging on the central peak and devastated the Lyruun riders who had been controlling the sky until then. The viatari had tried fighting back but to no avail and were soon soundly defeated, fleeing with what forces remained.

Soon after, horns sounded from the main host as the giant shadow continued to hover above them. Felix's army retreated.

Each section of that mountain pass and its switchbacks had been fought for and won with blood, and within a few minutes that blood proved to have been spilled in vain. And Felix was the one who had ordered for it to be spilled, knew it would be spilled, allowed for it to be spilled so he could have his chance to rescue someone dear to his heart.

He hung his head, now in a sudden fit of pain. He clenched his eyes shut but then forced them open, unwilling to look away from what he had done. His hands filled his vision. Blood covered them. Rivulets of crimson ran down the lines of his palms, spreading to his wrists where they then dripped onto his horse.

His thoughts turned to Victria. She would remain trapped now, imprisoned. Tortured, most likely. She had put her hopes and trust in him. Thought that he would find a way to free her. And he had failed.

How could this have happened?

Drawing his attention back to the battle, he saw that his remaining forces were making their way down the last of the mountain passes and were spilling into the valley, running as fast as they could back to camp.

Out of his peripherals, he saw movement. The Lyruun riders assigned to each acolyte had finished securing their assigned artifacts to their mounts and were now lifting them into the air. The vashi positioned to guard them retreated. The acolytes swung ominously from thick ropes, tendrils nowhere to be seen as they withdrew from the field.

CHAPTER FOURTEEN

Victria awoke with a start. Her head throbbed. She tried to bring her fingers to the point of pain but found she couldn't move. Her wrists were shackled, connected to a thick iron chain that was staked into the cavern wall, keeping her arms suspended above her. Her legs were folded under her uncomfortably and overlapped with more iron chains, their anchors digging deep into the stone floor. Her breaths came in rapid gasps as she tried to remember what had happened.

They'd been captured, that much she knew. Drake had ordered for them to be taken deeper into the mountains and their guards had obliged, shoving them all the way up the jagged stone steps leading back into the Three Spires. They had followed the tunnels for a time, then . . . nothing. Victria suspected the guards had struck them from behind, rendering them unconscious so they couldn't observe the path they had taken to get here.

And where were they, exactly?

There wasn't much to look at. The cavern they were being held in was dimly lit with a series of braziers suspended by thin chains lodged into the ceiling and a line of torches interspersed along the wall. They all flickered with the same purplish flame.

The cavern was unnatural. The floor and ceiling were too smooth, forming a perfect oval. It was as if the stalagmites and stalactites that normally decorated the innards of a mountain had been shaved off completely. Or they were never there to begin with.

Looking to her right, she saw her friends chained to the wall in the same way she was, evenly spaced so no one could touch anyone else. They were still unconscious, their heads hanging limply forward or to the side.

Victria continued taking in her surroundings. Her observations would be vital if she was going to come up with a means for escape. Before them lay a single metal table that shone ominously under the dim, flickering light. It hung suspended by the same type of chains that held up the braziers. The table swung back and forth gently as if someone had only recently been sitting on it.

On the other side of the cavern were a series of shelves carved directly into the stone wall. They were laden with numerous glass vials and jars, all of varying sizes, as well as several worn iron pots and pans. Their contents were too far away for her to discern, but many gave off a sickly, pale glow that discouraged her curiosity.

There was only one exit as far as she could tell. A simple wooden door stood obstinately to the side of the shelves and partially in the shadows. That would be how they got out. But there were obviously too many unknowns to simply break their chains and burst through the door.

How many guards were outside? What *type* of guards were there? And if they made it into the tunnels, which way would they go? They could end up going deeper into the mountains, easy enough for The Turned One and her subjects to recapture. And if there was one thing Victria was certain of, there would be no do-overs. If they failed to escape, they were stuck here.

But first, if she was going to try anything, she had to break out of these chains. She took a breath, calming herself, and focused on the iron bonds keeping her immobilized. She summoned the strength within her and pulled her arm down with a quick jerk, expecting the iron links to snap and grant her immediate relief.

The iron held.

She tried again with more effort. She snarled, groaning as the iron dug into her wrists. Sweat beaded her forehead and the small of her back from her efforts, despite the cooler temperatures within the cavern. She tried her other arm but found those chains to be just as stubborn. She tried moving her legs, but discovered the bonds were wrapped so tightly around her folded limbs she couldn't move them at all.

Her breathing came out in panicked shudders now.

How could she not break these simple chains? Had they been reinforced somehow? Even dwarven craftsmanship was no match for a viatari's strength. No, it wasn't the iron. The iron was normal. It was her.

Closing her eyes, she reached inside and tried to summon her strength once more. This time, she noticed something odd. It was as if a nail had been driven deep into her mental state, blocking her from harnessing her natural abilities. Every time she would feel a surge of power almost flow into her limbs, the nail would catch her attention, distract her, and the power would fade.

Someone had done something to her, and she didn't know

what, but it had taken away her strength. She was trapped here. Truly trapped. And she was sure whoever had done this had done the same to her companions as well.

She looked their way, unable to hide the horror in her eyes as she noticed a thick, solitary worm-like creature attached to each one's forehead. It pulsed, twitching as the viatari came to. A thick pool of mucus the parasite had created around its mouth kept it stuck to the one spot.

Now that she had noticed them, Victria thought she could feel a worm pulsing on her own forehead. Her skin prickled. A shiver shook her to her core. This thing had to be what was blocking her from summoning her strength. How was she supposed to remove it?

Natiari and Tessa groaned as they woke up. Madira yawned. They blinked blearily, then seemed to remember their situation. Tessa pulled on her chains, yielding the same non-result. The three viatari struggled for a few more minutes before finally realizing it was useless. They looked at Victria, their fear and uncertainty plain.

"Where are we?" Natiari whispered.

"I don't know," Victria answered truthfully.

"Why can't we break from these damned—" Tessa grunted as she tried to free herself again, "—chains? I feel like I have no strength."

"Look at my forehead," Victria said, her voice pitched just a bit too high for her own liking. She chided herself silently. She had to be strong, even if she didn't feel like it, for her friends. She had gotten them into this mess. Now she had to get them out. In the meantime, it helped no one to put her feeling of helplessness on her sleeve for all to see. "We all have one. It seems to be blocking us, subduing us somehow."

A look of revulsion took hold of each viatari's face as they noticed the parasite.

Trying to shake it off but having no luck, Natiari asked, "Madira, have you ever seen something like this in your gardens?"

Looking sick, the Dalyran shook her head. "No, this thing is unnatural. Look at how it pulses with our movements. It's like it's feeding on us in some way."

"Whatever it does," Victria said. "It's keeping us from breaking our bonds and escaping. We can do nothing so long as they're attached."

"So, what do we do?" Tessa asked timidly. Her eyes began to water, but perhaps that was a trick of the purple flames flickering beside her

"They can't keep us subdued like this forever. There must be a reason we're here. For now, we just have to wait for an opportunity where we can make a move."

Natiari scoffed. "Well, then, to pass the time maybe we can speculate why they took us prisoner in the first place. That should be fun."

"That human, Drake," Madira said softly. "He said The Turned One doesn't normally take prisoners."

"So we're special," Natiari drawled. "Wonderful."

"I don't think The Turned One is accustomed to dealing with our kind. We've surprised her with our resilience." Victria thought hard, ignoring Natiari's quips. If it helped her accept their current situation, she wouldn't stop her. "Perhaps she intends to learn more about us."

"Why would she care about us?" Madira asked.

"Not *us* specifically, but *us*, as in, the viatari."

Tessa sniffed. "What if she means to corrupt us like she did the humans and burrowers?"

"She can't," Victria said confidently. "It might be a weakness of ours, but remember how her essence nearly killed Felix? Our bodies can't harbor her corruption like the humans and burrowers can. Something about our biology makes us want to die rather than serve as some mindless slave."

"Maybe that's what she wants to learn about, then," Madira guessed.

"Bravo."

A slow, methodic clap came from the cavern entrance. Limping slowly out of the shadows, hunched, emerged a burrower, but it was one unlike any Victria had ever seen.

Intelligence gleamed in his single eye, his other nothing but a gaping hole. A crooked grin lined his face, revealing several missing teeth and others that were rotten. The remainder of his face was disheveled. Uneven facial hair grew in random patches along his sallow cheeks. His oval shaped head was home to only a few scraggly threads.

Burrowers were known for only dressing as their needs dictated. They wore loincloths most of the time and armor only where it was most needed. This burrower, however, wore a long, white robe that dragged on the floor behind him. Cords of multi-colored thread wove together in strange patterns all throughout.

He inspected each of the viatari with his single eye, chuckling and clapping gleefully as he did so.

"My, you all look like such *fine* specimens." He bowed with surprising grace. "Allow me to introduce myself. I am Gar'Gir, and I shall be your host."

The viatari couldn't hide their shock.

"Yes, yes," Gar'Gir waved his hands absently as he paced before them. "I know how shocking it must be to meet a burrower who can not only speak but speak well. One who can think properly. My own kind would be just as appalled, though their ignorance is no fault of their own. It's in their blood. Perhaps that is why they exiled me."

"Then how–?"

Gar'Gir stuck his face inches away from Madira who had been about to ask the question. A terrifying snarl now dominated his features along with a series of deep wrinkles carved into his forehead. His movement had been quick. Too quick for someone who appeared crippled. It was clear there was more to this burrower than what his appearance would have them believe.

He spoke slowly, trying to suppress some inner rage, "You will speak only when I allow you to. Do not interrupt."

Madira nodded, choking back a sob, her eyes wide and terrified. She looked away as he breathed onto her, her body shuddering involuntarily.

"As I was saying," Gar'Gir stood up and resumed his pacing, maintaining eye contact with each viatari as he passed. "My own kind wouldn't recognize genius if I spat it into their faces. That made it easy when I turned them all over to my master for her to corrupt as she willed. Hence, why I am here today, serving her great vision, for she recognizes talent when she sees it. And now she has given me the great honor of learning all that I can from you four special viatari."

The burrower's tone was light, his face once more paternal. He spoke as if he were giving them the best news imaginable, but his words did nothing except fill Victria with dread. It was the fact that he was being so forthright with this information, like he had nothing to hide, like no one would ever know the events that transpired within this cavern that unnerved her.

As Gar'Gir continued spouting about how educational this journey would be for them all, Victria's mind wandered. She thought of Felix, regret welling up inside her heart like a bleeding wound. She thought of all the times she could have shared her feelings with him. She imagined his face; his handsome, stoic features. She still believed he would be able to rescue them. She knew he would at least try. But if he should fail. . . .

Gar'Gir's visage filled her vision as he brought his shriveled face close. The fear Felix wouldn't arrive in time became tangible. Her tongue sat dry and heavy in her mouth as she gazed into the burrower's single orb. It was clear she and her companions would be forced to undergo horrors that were, as of yet, unimaginable. How long could they survive this place? The viatari body was strong. It took a lot to kill any one of them. But a physically strong body wasn't all there was to their resilience. If their will was broken. . . .

"I see some shred of hope in your eyes still," Gar'Gir's terrible voice reached deep into Victria's mind, his breath rotten and hovering around her nose like a dense fog. Her eyes narrowed, a wall of defiance overshadowing the pool of self-pity she had been wallowing in. Something in the way he had said this had sparked a desire to fight. She *would* fight, she decided. She wouldn't let this single mad burrower extinguish the fire she felt burning inside her. In the end, he would be the one who broke. And she would be the one to ensure that.

Gar'Gir laughed, a grotesque sound that echoed in the darkness around them. "Oh, I will enjoy breaking you, viatari. In fact—" he moved for her chains.

Yes, Victria thought. This would be their moment. While she wasn't strong enough to break the chains herself, she was still strong enough to throttle this single burrower. To choke the life out of him. Once he unbound her, that's exactly what she would do.

But just as he was bringing a key to the shackles binding her wrist, he stopped.

"Oh my," he slapped his forehead, a grin playing on his lips. "How silly of me, I almost forgot! What a mistake. I will have to be more careful with how I proceed."

The burrower turned away and limped toward the shelves on the opposite end of the cavern. He inspected several jars, looking for the right one.

"Aha!"

He grabbed one of the larger ones, full of a thick substance. With long, gnarled fingers, he reached into it and plucked out a slender, wriggling worm. Then, he replaced the jar and returned before Victria, holding the creature up for her to see.

"Drainwyrms," he said. "Very useful for my studies. You already have one on you, in case you haven't noticed already. One was enough to sap your strength, allowing for these simple iron chains to restrain you. Just as I predicted. Now, if we put two—"

Victria wanted to scream as Gar'Gir placed the slimy wyrm on her forehead. She felt a slight prick. A trickle of mucus slid down her forehead onto her nose. Then, her energy drained from her completely. Her head lolled to the side. She could do nothing but shift her eyes toward her tormentor, watching Gar'Gir as he undid her bonds.

"With two," the burrower continued. "You become as helpless as a newborn. Very useful for when I have to move you. As I'm sure you know, I would be no match for you in a fight." He looked pointedly at her before moving to free her legs. "I'm sure you were just itching to pounce on me as soon as I inserted that key, weren't you?"

Chuckling, Gar'Gir then hoisted Victria's limp body over

his shoulder, carrying her to the metal table hanging in the cavern's center.

Victria couldn't fight it. Couldn't speak. She heard her friends yelling abuses at Gar'Gir but he ignored them and instead whistled a happy tune as he lay her down on the cold metal. She felt leather cords wrap tightly around her wrists and ankles. A drainwyrm was plucked from her head and she felt some energy come back. She shuddered and gasped as a feeling of helplessness overwhelmed her.

Blood flowed back into her lower legs, but the prickling pain from that was quickly forgotten when she saw Gar'Gir move back toward the shelves and grab a different jar. He placed it on the metal table right next to her head, then stood there for some time, relishing in what he was about to do.

"Whatever–you're doing–don't," Victria sputtered. Her body trembled and she couldn't stop it. Couldn't control it. She hated this feeling. But the unknown of what was about to happen was proving too much. Fear clawed at her like a beast.

Gar'Gir brought his gaze down to her and smiled reassuringly. "Oh, viatari, why do you tremble? I am not some savage barbarian like others of my kind. I would not dare lower myself or you to their levels by carving into you like some piece of meat. I told you, we are here for an educational experience. We will both learn *so* much. But you can't learn much if you're too busy screaming because your toes are being cut off, now can you?"

Victria didn't respond. It was all she could do to keep herself from crying out. Her eyes followed his gnarled fingers as he undid the lid.

"Still," Gar'Gir continued as he looked inside the jar and marveled at its contents. He pulled out a small, white, wrinkled worm. Its head was pink, with small but vicious fangs protruding out of it. "I cannot deny that some of our experiments will bring about a great deal of pain. We already know your kind can take a lot of physical damage without suffering death. But there are degrees to pain." A faraway look entered the burrower's eye as he continued talking. "Pain is such a beautiful thing. I want to know everything about it. And you," his eye refocused as he hungrily slid them along the length of Victria's body. She shuddered, glad that she and her companions had at least been left with enough clothing to maintain some sense of dignity, though much of her body remained exposed. "Why, you provide the perfect canvas. Now, let us begin."

Gently, he lowered the writhing wyrm until it touched Victria's arm. She tried to shake it off, but too late. The wyrm bit into her flesh and continued biting, digging in deeper until it was under her skin. It continued gnawing, moving up her arm.

The pain was sharp, irritating, but small. It was no sword thrust into her midsection, but it was persistent, and worse was the knowledge that something was digging its way freely inside her.

Victria clenched her jaw, keeping her mouth shut. She would not cry out. She would not give this sadist the satisfaction. She lay there, shaking, her fists clenched, nails digging into her palms and producing blood as the wyrm continued tunneling its way through her flesh.

Gar'Gir placed down another one, this time on her stomach. Victria couldn't help but gasp as it dug into her and the burrower smiled.

"Skinwyrms," he said, putting down his jar and taking out a worn journal along with a well of ink and a raggedy quill. He opened it up to an empty page and wet the tip of his quill before looking back at Victria. "One is usually enough to have a man screaming. Even burrowers cannot withstand them for long. You, however, took two before making any sort of sound. Impressive, but not entirely unexpected for such a strong specimen. Now, tell me," he leaned forward, watching the skinwyrms' progress. "How would you describe the pain? What can you compare it to? Can you feel their little bodies and their every movement or just the tear of their mandibles scraping against your flesh. . . ?"

There were more questions Gar'Gir asked, but Victria couldn't hear them. She couldn't hear her friends anymore either, though she suspected they had quieted down in horror as they witnessed what she was going through. No doubt, they realized they were in for the same treatment. Fear would settle in. Perhaps they were already trembling as she had—still was.

The pain from the skinwyrms grew exponentially as Gar'Gir continued placing more of the things onto her body, but soon even that disappeared as her mind focused on two thoughts.

Regret returned, but now it was more focused on the fact that she had brought this fate upon her friends. They had wanted to fight. They would have all died, but that would have been their choice. Now, everything that happened to them was beyond their ability to choose. None of them had control, and that was her fault. And in the end, they would die anyway.

By surrendering, Victria had bought them all time to suffer.

Felix will save us.

The thought repeated itself in her mind. She wanted to believe it, willed herself to be defined by it.

As long as Felix saves us, whatever happens here will just be nothing more than a nightmare, something for us to forget in the future. We just have to survive.

She was so adamant about this thought that she convinced herself to believe it. She held onto it, like a piece of driftwood barely keeping her afloat in a thrashing river of pain sweeping her ever closer to the edge of a cliff.

CHAPTER FIFTEEN

Five figures rode steadily down a long winding road. They drew the eyes of all they passed, be they merchants, patrolling guards, or simple folk living on the highway to Halding Port. Salevari fixed her hair, which a gust of wind had misplaced, doing her best to keep her eyes forward, doing her best to look . . . regal, whatever that meant. Passersby murmured to each other as their horses clopped along, especially the merchants.

"Fine silk, that is."

"Aye, a pretty penny tha' would cost. And tha's *before* it be shaped into a dress. Can't imagine the cost now."

Salevari didn't have much to compare her current attire to, what with everyone in Donsea wearing loose-fitting shirts and trousers or the bare minimum of loincloths for much of the day, but now that she was seeing more of the countryside, and what others wore on a regular basis, she had a better understanding of just how much Simon had endeavored to make her and Aniria stand out.

Their dresses carried a brilliant sheen under the bright sun.

White, yellow, and bright blue threads, which formed patterns along their sleeves and midsection glimmered as if they were made of gems. Salevari couldn't help but feel a trickle of pity for the humans they passed. Their own garments were dirty, simple, made of a lightweight linen. Some of the merchants carried themselves with slightly better and more fashionable attire, but even they stood in awe.

They were royalty, as far as anyone could tell. Just as Simon had intended.

It had taken them two more weeks in Donsea after their sailing race before they finally set out for Halding Port. Though Simon and Tera had finished Aniria and Salevari's wardrobe much earlier than that, time had to be taken for the viatari to learn the proper etiquette, mannerisms, and cultural queues of upper-class society.

Simon was mostly responsible for this. He taught them how to eat properly; which utensils to use and when; how to curtsey, how to speak, and most importantly how to politely reject someone's advances—a skill he suspected they would need against Halding Port's elites. They even had extensive lessons on human history in the plains, how certain customs and festivals originated, and the common values that glued each town together.

It was extensive work, and Salevari and Aniria hadn't been the best of students, too willing to show their superiority as viatari to partake in the need for this subterfuge. Eventually, Simon and Tera won out. There would be a time to show the people of Halding Port who they really were, but if they didn't earn their trust beforehand, there would be no opportunity to do so without risking a prejudiced reaction from the beginning. After that, the viatari fell in line until they finally had their crash course in humanity engrained into them.

Now they were only hours from Halding Port. They had been riding for days, forced to travel northward first before rounding about and finding the road that led from the plains to the city. From there, they made their way at a leisurely pace. The viatari took on their human forms, careful to maintain them even when they ate and slept.

Word quickly spread of the nobles from the plains traveling south on the main road. Attracting attention wherever they went, whispers of their presence started spreading and traveling faster than they did. This was also what Simon had wanted. The people would see them, make glowing assumptions about them, then spread the word. In this way, they would gain a sense of prestige that didn't really exist long before they ever set foot in Halding Port.

As the formidable walls and spiraling towers of the sprawling city came into view, Salevari spotted a lone rider in the distance. Their sixth member, Zael, whom they had sent ahead to announce their arrival was trotting back to them.

They waited for him. Upon reaching them, he patted his horse's neck, looking pleased. "They know we're coming. I suspect we may have some sort of escort when we enter the city. I've been assured the Grand Admiral is eager to meet us."

They all shared a pleased grin. Simon's plan was going exactly as he predicted. But as their faces relaxed and they continued making their way toward the bustling harbor, Salevari felt a slight flutter in her chest. Simon's plan was working so far, but the next step in it would depend solely on her and Aniria's performance. Her knuckles whitened as she gripped the reins tightly. Her mount bucked its head in protest with an annoyed nicker.

Salevari was confident she could make the people of

Halding Port hear her request. She was confident she could convince them that it was in their best interest to help the vashi and let bygones be bygones. The one thing she wasn't confident about, however, was her ability to act human.

She knew their history now, knew their culture, their customs and mannerisms, but it didn't come naturally to her. It felt wrong and unnatural pretending to be something she was not. Sometimes, watching Aniria go about in her human guise, she marveled at how easy the Aleganthian made it look. Still, despite this self-doubt, she knew she had to swallow her pride and this desire to reveal her true self. The time for that would come eventually, as she was constantly being reminded by the human chief riding next to her, but she would have to practice patience until then.

Her thoughts turned to Simon, who caught her eye as they continued on down the road. She was to play his wife. Devoted. Submissive, even. She felt her lips twist at the thought, as if an offensive odor had passed under her nose. She got along fine with the former chief these days, but she still detested this part of his plan, especially when she had the fleeting thought of what her true husband would have said. Even if it was a ruse. Still, she knew her duty. If he had any ideas about putting his hands on her in any way that she didn't immediately approve of, however, she would be quick to remind him who held the real power in this "marriage."

As they approached the city, the number of gawking passersby grew. By the time they were outside Halding Port's gates, being ushered through by a cohort of guards, there was a throng of people both inside and outside the city. They crowded around the small party of strangers, everyone trying to lay their own eyes on the rumored nobles from the northern plains who had traveled all the way to their coastal city for . . . who knew what? That was the mystery, as far as the people of Halding Port were concerned. The crowd buzzed with excitement.

Salevari somewhat understood the feeling in the air, but something felt off. They were new here, foreign. Some curiosity was to be expected. But the city looked positively ready to explode. Guards wearing chainmail and carrying large kite shields formed lines on either side of the newcomers. They locked shields and stood firm as the crowd began to push against them. A few guards pulled out wooden rods from their belts and started swinging at anyone who got too close or too rowdy.

"Simon, is this normal?" Salevari asked. She leaned in close to speak into his ear, the crowd around them making the air churn with noise.

Simon shook his head. "This is beyond what I expected. Something seems amiss here. They're not protesting our arrival, but they're also far too excited for it. It's almost as if . . . they've been expecting us."

"Wasn't that the point of us making a grand show of our traveling from the north?"

"No, not like that. I can't explain it, but our presence here seems to have brought some strange new hope into these people. Now the question is, what is that hope, and why are they so desperately clutching onto it right now?"

Salevari allowed a guard to approach her mount and grab the reins, leading her deeper into the city. The same was done for her companions. As they were led through, more people came out and lined the streets, cheering them on while jeering at the guards. It was entirely bizarre. Salevari had the feeling that Simon was right in his initial observation. Their arrival may have been the cause of this, but something else must have happened here beforehand to make it carry such importance to begin with.

She leaned in close to Tera and shouted over the noise, "I thought you said these were an orderly people."

The human wanderer shook her head, just as bewildered as she was. "They weren't like this last time I was here. Something's changed."

Before Salevari could think too much on it, the city guards stopped them just outside of a tall iron-wrought gate. A thick wall stretched out on each side down the entire block they were on and disappeared around the corner. Before them stood a short, bald man whose eyes closed when he smiled, as he was doing now.

"My lords and ladies," he said, bowing deeply and with much flourish. "On behalf of our Grand Admiral, I welcome you to Halding Port. Please, if you would follow me inside past these gates, we can make our introductions away from this noise."

The crowds booed at the bald man, but he paid them no mind, keeping a smile plastered on his face as he turned and waved his hand forward. The guards swung the gate open, allowing Salevari to urge her mount through.

She gasped.

In front of her was the grandest building she had ever seen. It was a three-story palace that stretched out as wide as the walls went. Countless arching windows pocketed each floor, lined with gold. The roof slanted upward then leveled out, its red tiles layering on top of each other like scales. Sitting on the roof's edge was a line of statues. Many were of men: bulky, strong, fearsome looking; but some depicted creatures of the sea and other unfamiliar monsters.

The palace was not the only thing to marvel at. The path

before them was neatly laid with gravel. It looked like it had been smoothed to perfection. The grass around them, too, was cut short and glowed under the sun, the vibrant green color almost too bright for their eyes. More statues lined the path. Some depicted humans in varying poses, some beasts, but many more were of ships.

These ships were unlike any Salevari had seen in Donsea. They were behemoths. Tall masts soared from long decks. Hulls dug deep into waves molded from stone. Ballistae were lined along the sides, ready to fire. If the statues were this impressive, Salevari was all the more excited to see the real thing.

Servants ran around constantly, carrying out their work. Some trimmed the lawn, kneeling and bearing their faces just over the ground to ensure each blade of grass was the same height. Others trimmed bushes, establishing uniformity. Still others held strange raking tools and rushed past the viatari as they cantered toward the center of the courtyard. They then busied themselves with brushing their rakes across the gravel path, erasing any evidence that it had been disturbed by horse hooves.

A handful of young boys rushed out of a large wooden stable built away from the palace, along the wall where two sections met in a corner. They approached Simon, Tera, and the viatari, grabbing the reins from them.

Another servant stood by Salevari's horse, waiting to take her hand. She hesitated for a moment, unsure of what she should do. While the dress she wore was not as flexible as she was used to, she was still able to mount and dismount on her own. Still, she was supposed to be a noble woman. And noble women didn't do anything for themselves if they could help it—as Simon had drilled into her brain. She despised the idea of how helpless this made her appear but pushed back against her natural instinct to prove herself.

She took the boy's hand, felt him steady her as she swung her leg out over her saddle and down to the ground. He held on until her other foot was also freed from the stirrup. Bowing, he turned and followed the other boys back to the stable, horses in tow.

"Now," the bald man's smile had faded enough for his eyes to open, though its shadow remained. "If I may, my lord."

Simon motioned for the man to continue.

"I am Aethel, usher to the Grand Admiral. I ensure this palace runs in an orderly fashion and that all of the needs of our lords and ladies are met."

Simon held his head high, a haughty expression on his face as if he was used to always getting what he wanted as he proclaimed, "I am Simon, chief of Halshire. Behind me is my wife, Salevari, and our daughter, Aniria." Both viatari offered their hand as Simon had taught them. Aethel took them one at a time and placed his lips just past the knuckle of their middle finger. Shivers ran up Salevari's arm at the feel of his lips.

Simon continued, "The two others are our protectors, and the woman is our daughter's lady-in-waiting."

Aethel raised an eyebrow. "Only two guards to protect you during your travels? It must be an easy road from the plains to our humble city."

"It is a long one fraught with danger," Simon sniffed, looking down his nose at the usher. "But our guards are extremely capable warriors."

"I see," the smile Aethel initially had outside the palace gates crept back in, forcing his eyes shut. "You must be exhaust-ted after such a long journey. Come. Let me show you to your quarters."

They entered the palace, and again Salevari felt a gasp escape her lips. As magnificent as the outside of the building was with its perfectly cut stone, series of columns built into the walls between windows, and lack of vines or other touches of nature trying to creep its way back into control, the interior was stunning.

A grand staircase, steps partially covered by a red rug, met them in the middle of a vaulted hallway. The marble steps led them up to the second and third floors where smaller hallways branched out toward the palace wings, crossing and intersecting with other parts of the building. Enormous portraits hung on the walls depicting stoic-faced men in finery or military uniform. The colors were vivid, and the men looked realistic. Salevari thought they might actually be staring at her as she passed under their gaze.

Regrettably, she couldn't take in much more than that, as Aethel wasted no time in leading them through the twisting labyrinth of halls.

After a while, Salevari had to ask, "Such a grand building. Is this all for the Grand Admiral?"

The usher laughed. "By the waves, no. While the Grand Admiral has the largest quarters we have to offer, we house all of our nobility here, most of the fleet's admirals, some captains, and guests and dignitaries when we receive them—such as yourselves."

"So none of your nobility live in the city among the people?" Simon asked.

"That is correct!" Aethel chirped. "Now, here is where you will be staying. I do hope it is sufficiently comfortable. I'm afraid we are unversed in what the nobility of the plains might be accustomed to."

Aethel swung open a set of hand-carved double doors and stepped aside.

For the third time that day, Salevari was unable to control her reaction, a hand flying up to cover her open mouth, as she beheld the rooms they would stay in.

The main hallway led into a large living space, filled with chairs and couches all adorned with plump cushions and pillows. A small fountain bubbled cheerfully in the room's center. Moving to the windows, Salevari could see the beach clearly for miles. The ocean spread out before her, uneven white lines marking waves.

There were several doors throughout the suite, each promising a room of exquisite comfort. Large beds with mattresses and pillows stuffed with, according to Aethel, the softest of goose feathers lay in wait for their use. The closets connected to these rooms were large enough to be considered a room themselves. Yet the most surprising part was what Aethel called "indoor plumbing."

He gave them a demonstration.

Salevari couldn't help but stare in wonder as he turned a silver knob and water poured out of a faucet into a basin where it was then drained and sent off elsewhere.

"I'm not surprised you are so shocked by this," Aethel shrugged. "Even we have only recently developed the technology necessary to do this. Such a concept must be alien in the plains."

"Indeed, it is," Simon groused. Whatever resentment he had in his voice, Aethel chose not to notice as he hummed a cheery toon and continued with his tour of their quarters.

"I'm sure you'll enjoy the warm comfort of your baths, then!" He called out, leading them to another double door.

He swung it open and steam poured out. Upon entering, Salevari nearly fell to her knees but finally managed to control herself. Inside was a large pool built into the floor. Hot water endlessly poured from a series of pipes on the other side. She was amazed. The water was hotter than she thought possible, having only bathed in cold rivers. There was enough space within the pool that their entire party could bathe here and leave enough room for each one of them to have some privacy.

Once he had finished with their tour, Aethel stood just outside of the doorway leading into their quarters. The same fixed smile hadn't left his face once. "If there are no questions, I will leave you for a time so that you may rest, relax, bathe, do what you will. I'll make sure some food is brought up, as well. Unfortunately, I believe the Grand Admiral is too busy this evening to dine with you, but I shall go now to see if he can at least meet with you briefly before the day is done."

Without waiting for an answer, Aethel bowed, turned, and disappeared down the winding halls.

Simon closed the door and stepped away, walking as if in a trance toward the living room where he collapsed onto one of the several couches available. They all hovered where they were, stunned at the grandeur they had been given with such nonchalance.

Finally, the human chief shook his head and spat in disgust. "To think, the people here live like this and it's normal, while mine have to dig in the dirt—when we're not fighting for the survival of our world, that is."

"Now, now," Tera patted his shoulder consolingly as she moved to claim one of the adjacent rooms. "The *elites* live like this. I've been through this city enough times to tell you that what we've been given is not the norm. I'm sure if the people knew about this extravagance, they would riot."

Simon grumbled, "Still, it feels wrong to enjoy these luxuries when I've done nothing to earn them."

"You're a chief," Tera called back from within her freshly claimed room. "You're a lord, as far as they're concerned. You'll be given what they decide you'll be given. No sense fighting it."

They spent the rest of the day refreshing their memories about the stories they would tell if anyone were to ask them for personal details. Salevari, Simon, and Aniria in particular worked hard to make sure theirs were aligned.

At one point, Drathanar poked his head into the room where they were rehearsing their answers.

"We might have a problem," he said uncertainly. "There's only five rooms but six of us. There aren't enough beds for each of us to have one."

"Well, one of us will just have to share with someone else," Simon shrugged.

Drathanar and Aniria's eyes locked, a look passed between them, a shared thought. Then Aniria looked away, her face reddening. Salevari grinned but said nothing. Instead she brought all the attention back to Simon.

"I hope you're not suggesting we sleep in the same bed just because we're acting as husband and wife."

Simon's eyes widened as he sputtered a response, "I—I would never dream of it!"

They all laughed and Drathanar took the chance to slip away unnoticed before anyone could see how red his own face was.

As evening fell to dusk, Aethel returned.

"I hope you've had a moment to rest and relax," he said, bowing. "It seems the Grand Admiral is quite the busy man today; however, he has found an adequate window where he can meet with you briefly. He's eager to greet and learn about our visitors from the plains."

They followed the usher once more through a series of twisting turns within the palace. Salevari was glad they had a guide. If she had to try to navigate her way through here alone, she was sure she'd have been lost within minutes.

Soon they found themselves on the top floor, near the center of the palace. Aethel knocked on a pair of wide, oaken doors before them. A booming voice called them in.

The doors were swept open and the first thing Salevari noticed when she stepped through were the shelves upon shelves of leatherbound tomes and piles of scrolls carefully tucked away, as well as a series of ship schematics, maps, and stacks of paper cluttering a large, wooden desk sitting in the middle of the room. Behind it sat a man with a thick, bristling mustache. Some gray hairs made their presence known within the thick wall of whiskers, but the majority remained a soft brown.

The man looked up from whatever he was working on, a letter, thought Salevari, and laid eyes on them. An eager grin broke out on his weathered face. He lifted himself up and walked over, laughing with every step he took.

He was a tall man, towering over them all. His bulking muscles made him twice as wide as a normal person and his rough hands told Salevari that he was accustomed to hard work, despite the multiple golden bands adorning his fingers. No doubt, he had been a sailor at some point. His storm-gray eyes roved over each of their faces, finally landing on Salevari's where they lingered. She raised an eyebrow.

"I must say in all the years of me life, I don't think I've seen me a vessel as beautiful as the sea 'til now." He took her hand, bent down and kissed it, the bristles of his mustache tickling her knuckles. Salevari fought back the urge to jerk her hand away.

Simon cleared his throat. "That would be my wife, Salevari, Grand Admiral. I am Simon, chief of Halshire."

"Hm?" the Grand Admiral straightened back up, his eyes meeting Simon's. Something seemed to click. "Right you are, and quite a prize you've got there." He extended his hand, which Simon took. "No offense intended, chief. Me name's Fradrick. As you know, I am the Grand Admiral of this here city."

Once introductions were complete, Fradrick smiled broadly, clapping his hands.

"Lords and ladies of the plains," he shouted, hands raised to the sky dramatically. "Not often do we get any sort of plainsman to visit us, but nobles? I must admit I was intrigued when I heard rumors of your presence approaching our coast. That's why I'm so excited to meet you. There's a lot we can learn from our brothers up north."

"The feeling is mutual," Simon said. "That's why we set out from Halshire to begin with, to learn more about our southern . . . cousins."

Fradrick's jovial smile reached his ears. "Ah, only a shame we can't speak more now. I'm still up to me ears in paperwork—the curse of running a city—otherwise I'd have dinner with you all and barrage you with a volley of questions."

The Grand Admiral threw his head back and laughed loudly. "That said, to commemorate your arrival here I plan to throw a feast. It comes with perfect timing as our yearly Admiral's Ball quickly approaches as well. I don't know yet how long you intend to stay, but you would do me a great honor if you and your family were to attend."

Simon inclined his head. "Thank you, Grand Admiral—"

"Please, call me Fradrick."

"—Fradrick, then. We would be honored to attend. A ball in a grand palace such as this would be a special memory for us to always cherish."

Fradrick clapped Simon's shoulder happily and let loose another burst of laughter. "Excellent! Well, I'll not keep you. I'm sure you're still tired from your journey. Aethel will show you the way back."

The usher bowed. "If you would follow me, please."

"Before we go," Salevari said pointedly, "I'd like to know how we might go about leaving the palace to explore the city. I do not wish to be kept indoors for the length of our stay—no matter how grand it is."

The Grand Admiral's spirited face turned back to her. His eyes relishing the opportunity to absorb her beauty once more.

"But of course! I'll personally give you a tour meself. But tomorrow, if that will please your ladyship."

Salevari flashed a brief smile, if only to throw Fradrick a bone, and curtsied before turning and following the others out of his office.

They followed Aethel back to their suite with not a word said between them. When they returned, the usher lingered for a moment just inside the threshold, his wide grin an ever-present feature.

"Is there anything else I can get for my lords or ladies before you retire for the night?"

"That will be all, Aethel, thank you." Simon said with some curtness.

Aethel bowed, reaching for the doors and closing them as he backed out of the room.

"My lord."

* * *

Aethel shut the doors with finesse, barely making a sound.

Quickly turning, he made his way through the palace without a second thought, turning left and right down hallways he had passed through since childhood. He soon found himself near the palace doors leading out into the courtyard. There, an older man with a tired look stood at attention, a sense of poise and posture about him despite his exhaustion.

"Retiring for the night, sir?"

"Yes," Aethel yawned. "Will you oversee the final walk-through for the staff?"

The man bowed. "It will be my pleasure. Good night, sir."

Aethel bid the man goodnight and pushed his way outside. He made a beeline for the gates leading into the city proper and soon found himself walking down cobblestone streets filled with drunkards already asleep leaning back against whatever wall they could find. Workmen passed him, tired from the day and heading home themselves. Ladies of the night fished for their next customer with the soft brush of their fingertips.

He ignored them all, keeping his eyes passively forward. He walked with purpose, like he had somewhere to be.

After traversing several busy plazas alive with a nightlife of hot stall foods and music and dancing, he ducked into a dark alley and found himself going down a poorly kept stone pathway. Few ever traveled this way, he knew.

Within minutes, he had entered a graveyard, one of Halding Port's oldest. The gravestones here were weathered, many listing to the side, most of them marking the final resting place of hundreds who had died during the humans' war with the vashi. By now, many of their names and the year they had died were barely legible on the stone.

It was dark. The moon rose like a watchful eye as Aethel

inspected one grave after another. This was the hardest part. He always forgot which series of graves marked the line he needed to follow.

Finally, with a grunt of success, he found the ones he needed and made his way down the row until he found what to any average observer looked like a freshly dug grave. The soil was loose, a stark contrast to the patches of grass that grew on its neighbors.

With confidence, the usher leaned against the gravestone, pushing it to the side. The stone gave way, bringing with it a large square of dirt and revealing a hole with steps leading down into the earth. Not wasting a moment, he descended into the darkness, making sure the gravestone swung back into place so that the entrance was once more hidden. It was pitch-black now, but all Aethel had to do was follow the steps down and he would find himself before a simple wooden door, which he eventually bumped into as he stumbled off the last step.

He fumbled for the handle. Upon finding it he twisted it down and pushed the door open, light flooding his eyes. Squinting as he walked into a new set of tunnels lit by torches, he found himself in a large circular stone room with several hallways built along its perimeter leading to other tunnels which connected a vast network of storage rooms.

As he walked across to the other side of the circle, he passed several men going about their labor in silence. Some hefted wooden crates from one side to another, stacking them together. The crates were marked with the symbol for grain but otherwise were nondescript. Others worked directly with exposed piles of the foodstuffs. The nearby torches gave the granules a discolored look as men scooped large heaps of them and threw them into burlap sacks.

Aethel reached the other end of the room and pushed through another door. This one opened into a long, dimly lit hallway. At the end of it he reached one more portal and hesitated. He gently rapped on the wooden planks and heard a meek voice call out.

"Enter."

The palace usher did so, entering an office similar to the Grand Admiral's, though much smaller and without a grand view of the ocean. Shelves of books lined the edges. A simple desk sat in the center cluttered with open books and half-written papers. Lingering next to one of the bookshelves, a long, pointed finger hovering just over the spines searching for the right tome to pick, was a man dressed in a long silk robe the color of the sky. A cloak of magenta wrapped around his shoulders falling down to touch where his calves would have been. A large hood hung limply down the man's back, which would have covered his bald head. Leaning against the bookcase next to the man was a tall wooden staff, a red orb glowing at the end. A sense of power emanated from him.

"My lord Jorgon," Aethel inclined his head respectfully before speaking. "I am here to report that the rumored lords and ladies from the plains have arrived."

Jorgon's glowing eyes flashed brightly as he continued to peruse book titles. "Yes, I sensed their presence. However, there is something . . . amiss with the energies of some of their party. I cannot place my finger on what it is yet, but I suspect some sort of ruse."

"What would you have me do?"

The energy-wielder found the book he was looking for and eagerly plucked it from the shelf, flipping through its pages rapidly as he made his way back to his desk.

"I will not risk our work here being interrupted," he said

softly. "But I also cannot risk exposing our operation quite yet. For now, we will keep an eye on them. If they wish to explore the city, let them, but have someone watching them at all times. Do not let them wander down paths they should not be. If they prove to be a problem, I will have to handle it myself. Do you understand?"

Aethel bowed deeply. "Of course, my lord."

"Be sure to give them every deference in the meantime," Jorgon continued, though his mind was clearly now focused on the contents of the tome he had chosen. "It is also possible that they are truly lords of the plains, in which case, to risk exposing your role in the palace would do us no good."

"I understand, my lord." Aethel bowed again. "Then, I shall retire for the night."

Jorgon nodded absently, his violet eyes blinking slowly, absorbing knowledge as the palace usher backed away and closed the door behind him.

CHAPTER SIXTEEN

After such a long journey, Salevari would have slept through the whole day in her dark room without a care in the world had the palace's servants not entered and pushed back every single curtain to announce the sun's arrival. Bright light filled her room, startling the viatari awake and instantly blinding her. She raised a hand to cover her bleary eyes, blinking rapidly, slightly confused.

"Good morning, my lady," one of the servants, an older woman, curtsied. "Is there anything we might bring you to start your morning?"

Salevari groaned and fell back onto soft pillows.

"Nothing," she said. "Is it late?"

"The sun has only just risen." The servant answered, then curtsied again and followed her fellows out of the room. Salevari stayed where she was for a few more minutes before finally forcing herself out of bed.

The comforts of Halding Port's palace could not be overstated. Even as Salevari entered the bathing room, perpetually filled with a nice layer of steam, to wash her face, her thoughts lingered on the gloriously hot bath she had taken last night. How the water had comforted her skin, soothed her muscles. The steam provided a nice weight of heat that was not overbearing, like a blanket. She could live like this for the rest of her days and never tire of it.

She shook her head. These comforts were nothing more than a temporary gift to enjoy while they carried out their mission. Once they were done with Halding Port they would be back in the field, in the mud, sweating with labor, their time here only a memory to cherish.

Putting some purpose into her steps now that she was fully awake, Salevari burst into the living room trying to keep the temptation for another hot bath in the back of her mind. Simon was lounging in one of the couches, holding a pillow and seemingly lost in his own thoughts. Drathanar and Aniria sat huddled together facing the windows, watching the sun push itself higher over the horizon. Zael was nowhere to be seen, presumably still in his room. Salevari thought Tera was sleeping in as well until the human wanderer burst into the suite from the outside hall. In her hands she carried several live chickens by the neck and a small crate filled with live quails. She carried herself forward with an air of accomplishment.

"Breakfast!" She called.

They gathered in the suite's dining room and took their place at the table. Tera let the chickens run loose, which the viatari quickly caught. They then snacked on the quail, losing enough of their human illusion to have their teeth revert to fangs, which they then sank into the animals' bodies. As they consumed the life-energies from their prey, the chickens and quails shuddered and shriveled as if they had been left out in the desert sun. Simon and Tera, having seen the viatari way of eating many times before, ate their own breakfast, which the staff had brought earlier, without missing a beat.

"Where did you get these?" Salevari asked, licking her lips as she finished the last of the quail. "I can't imagine the palace has many animals running around freely."

"None at all, dear," Tera responded, swallowing a final bite of bacon and washing it down with a dark, thick liquid. Coffee. Salevari had been told it filled the humans with energy like animals did for the viatari. "I had to nab these from the kitchen."

"Did you ask for them?" Simon asked,

Tera shook her head, "I left a note. Told them Aniria has a special way she likes her birds prepared that only I know."

Simon put down his fork and knife and crossed his fingers bringing them to his face as if this act would help contain whatever impulsive reaction he might give.

After a few minutes, he finally spoke, "In a place like this, they likely keep strict count of their inventory. Otherwise, the workers would take what they wanted whenever they could. You may get away with it this time, but you should be more careful in the future. We don't want to give away any hint that our viatari friends are not who they say they are and stealing *live* food from the kitchens will bring questions that we do not want to answer."

"Simon is right," Salevari bit her lip, wishing she could breathe the life-energies she had taken back into the avians. "I appreciate the gesture, but we cannot eat like this again. If we are to convince everyone here that we are human, we must eat like them. I'm sure there are plenty of rats in the city for us to hunt during the night."

Aniria sighed, the mention of rats sitting like a heavy ball of disappointment in her stomach. She grabbed the last remaining chicken which squawked desperately in protest and sunk her fangs into its neck. Quivering, the bird dried out like the others and soon joined their carcasses in the corner.

Tera pursed her lips but couldn't think of anything to counter Simon's point. "I'll get rid of the evidence, then. Though, I think you give the elites here too much credit. They're too rich and drunk on their own lavish lives to care much about anything."

"That may be," Simon responded, leaning back in his chair as he enjoyed his own cup of coffee. "But it's not the elites I'm worried about, or the Grand Admiral. It's the staff. They care about their jobs, for one reason or another, and they will do their utmost to ensure they're done well. But enough of that—" he shifted forward, his body wound tight like a spring. "We have a busy day ahead of us and we should discuss what we intend to do with it."

"Well, Aniria and I will be with the Grand Admiral," Salevari shrugged, not thrilled with the prospect. She would have to rely on Tera's training on how to politely reject nobles to get her through the day. "He said he would give us a tour of the city, but I doubt we'll learn much. Someone like him will likely only show us the good parts and boast of all the things Halding Port has to offer."

"I agree," Simon nodded. "So I think it best that some of us venture into the city proper and interact with the common folk."

"They won't speak to us if we're dressed like nobles and guards." Zael pointed out.

"Which is why we will leave the palace as we are, then find a place to change clothes so that we can better blend in."

"Who will go, then?"

"It should be you three, don't you think?" Salevari suggested, pointing out Simon, Zael, and Drathanar. "You'll have a higher chance of earning trust and getting people to talk than any of us would, since humans seem to think that women are nothing more than items for display."

Simon cracked a smile. "The humans here certainly seem to think that. You're right, though. We would be best suited for this task."

"What do I do, then?" Tera asked. "I wasn't invited to join the Grand Admiral."

"You were able to find your way to the kitchen and back without getting yourself lost," Salevari shrugged. "That's more than any of us could do in this vast maze of a palace. Perhaps you can glean something from the staff here. I'm sure no one would question a lady-in-waiting asking for gossip to share with her lady."

Tera considered this for a moment, then nodded, her eyes flaring with pleasure. "And in doing that I can also get an idea of what life in the palace is really like. That could be interesting."

"Then, we all have our tasks," Simon lifted himself from his seat. "Zael, Drathanar, let's prepare. We should leave immediately so we can spend as much of the day among the commonfolk as possible. I'm sure there's much to see."

The two viatari stood and made their way out of the dining room. Before Simon followed them, he glanced over his shoulder at Salevari.

"Don't be too quick to dismiss the Grand Admiral. He might try to win you over with honeyed words, but there's still much you can learn from him. In his boasting, he may let slip something we can use as leverage when the time comes to negotiate. Stay focused and ask questions."

Salevari nodded. Simon was right. She couldn't let her

personal distaste for the Grand Admiral get in the way of her purpose here. She and Aniria had been warned how little they would be able to do themselves when it came to completing their task, but there were still ways to serve. This was one of them.

"We don't have to meet Fradrick until noon," Aniria leaned forward eagerly. "What do we do until then?"

Salevari thought about that, watching Tera gather every last chicken and quail carcass into her arms so that she could take them somewhere discreet for disposal. She stood and moved for the door, her body gravitating toward something large and soft that she had been so rudely stolen from this morning.

"Do what you want, Aniria. I'm going back to bed."

With another few hours tucked under her belt, Salevari finally felt fully rested. She stretched, reaching her hands skyward and clenching her eyes shut in pleasure as she and Aniria walked out of the palace and into the sprawling courtyard.

Standing in the middle of the path halfway between the palace and the surrounding wall was Fradrick. He wore a simple black shirt, trousers, and a long green jacket that reached his calves with gold trim along the flaps and feathery epaulets. On his head sat an old tricorne full of tears and holes.

"Afternoon, my ladies," Fradrick bowed low as the two viatari approached. His eyes roved over each one, taking in the stylish dresses Simon had made for them like they were a painting to be studied. "You're looking as radiant as the sea on a calm day."

"Thank you, Grand Admiral," Salevari and Aniria curtsied, offering their hands. "You . . . are quite dashing yourself."

Fradrick chuckled and took their hands, stopping short

when he saw Salevari's were gloved with fine white silk that reached all the way up her arm and under the sleeves of her dress. The smile on his face cracked for just a moment, but he recovered quickly and placed his kiss. Now it was Salevari's turn to smile.

"I believe I told your husband to call me Fradrick. You should do the same. Now, let's be off! Lots to see in me wonderful city."

Offering his arm for each lady to hold, he led them out of the courtyard and into the city proper. They turned left, following a road to the sea. Salevari was surprised to see that the cobblestone street they tread on was incredibly clean, as if each stone had been individually washed. Shopkeepers stood outside their stores, sweeping mindlessly, offering a smile and a friendly wave as the trio passed.

In fact, everyone was waving as they passed. A quiet discomfort ran down her spine as she realized these people were being friendly, too friendly. And too willing to be seen as such. Flowers were offered to her and Aniria as well as free samples of fruit.

The ladies who bore baskets full of the sweet treats beamed as the viatari took them. Salevari noticed their clothes were well-cared for and a much better quality than she remembered seeing when they had arrived here the other day.

"You must excuse their enthusiasm," Fradrick almost hummed the words. "They are honored to have my guests walk down their street."

Salevari pursed her lips. She was sure this honor he spoke of had been forced onto them. What had the man done to ensure the people here behaved and kept their area clean and tidy and false? She was sure if she pulled her arm free and ducked away, made her way through the nearest alley and into a neighboring street, she would find a much more realistic picture of what life in Halding Port was like. Serania had told her enough from her own adventures here to know that this was not natural.

Minutes passed with them walking under a constant, but never overwhelming, barrage of faux friendliness from passers-by before they found themselves on the docks. It was a large stretch of wooden posts, planks, and a vast number of slips holding vessels of varying sizes. Crowds of sailors kept busy cursing into the wind, mooring incoming boats and ships, and carrying crates and bags full of supplies, trade goods, and other materials from one location to another. Seagulls drifted in lazy circles overhead or cried incessantly from the tall yard-arms of Halding Port's fleet.

Salevari took in the fleet. They were an impressive sight, exactly how the statues in the palace courtyard portrayed them. Tall masts reached for the sky, sending spear-like shadows across the docks and into the city. Sails were bundled neatly along their booms. Ropes traversed across several parts of each ship, intersecting and connecting with other lines to form a complicated system of rigging that she could never hope to understand. Marines and sailors kept busy cleaning weaponry or swabbing decks while men in long leather jackets with bronze embroidery along the edges, marking them as captains, stood cockily at the helm hollering orders.

"Feast your eyes, ladies," Fradrick said with no small sense of pride. His chest puffed out and he let out a long breath as if he'd been holding it in. A yearning entered his eyes that had not been there before. "The jewel of our city. I won't tell you our exact numbers, mind you, but we have all classes of war-ships from frigates to sloops to carracks. Many different fleet groups, all of varying sizes, all deployed in different parts of the Southern Seas, keeping our fishermen, sailors, and trade routes safe. The one you see here is the fourth fleet, me own."

"Your own?" Aniria repeated.

"Aye," the yearning in Fradrick's eyes transformed into a fire. "I used to sail with them in me younger days. By the waves do I miss those times. Now it's just the desk and papers and letters and . . . bah!" He shook his head, taking a moment to compose himself and shifting his hat. "No matter, I'll not bore you. I bore meself talking about the Admiralty. Anyway, our fleet are armed with top-of-the-line ballistae with plenty of ammunition, both bolts and stones, in the hold. Plus, our marines are excellent shots with bows and slings."

Salevari glanced over at Aniria and knew they'd had the same thought. Once Fradrick took them aboard the nearest frigate and had the sailors demonstrate the effectiveness of their weaponry, she felt a sense of confirmation. While it was interesting to watch these ballistae launch projectiles across the water for several hundred feet at a time, they were nothing compared to dwarven cannons.

Cannons had been given to the viatari and installed throughout Aleganthia's wall to great effect. They had proven detrimental in alleviating the siege that city had undergone almost a year ago. They could prove just as useful to the humans here, improving their fleet's firepower by leaps and bounds. It was a risky idea, giving them such a dangerous weapon, but this wasn't the time to think cautiously solely based on the fact that they were dealing with humans. So long as they used cannons against The Turned One's forces, she was sure the dwarves wouldn't object too fiercely to the prospect of sharing their technology.

She tucked the thought away. If she needed it when the time came to negotiate, she would bring it back.

After spending an hour giving the viatari an extensive tour of most of the fleet that was docked, as well as pointing out and admiring the extensive seawall protecting the docks from any direct attack or invasion, Fradrick led them back into the city, heading for the surrounding wall. He approached a set of stairs leading up onto the ramparts. The guards stationed at the foot of the steps saluted as he walked past.

"Are we allowed to come up with you? I would think the wall would be off limits to civilians." Salevari asked sheepishly. She cringed inwardly. Perhaps she was laying it on a bit too thick. But the Grand Admiral didn't seem to notice.

He guffawed and threw his arms over the guards. They didn't move. "Normally you'd be right. But you're with me today, and as Grand Admiral I can go wherever I please with whomever I want. Isn't that right, boys?"

The two guards yelled in unison, "Aye, sir!"

Once they were on the ramparts, Salevari leaned against the battlements, taking in the view. Miles upon miles of coastal plain stretched out before them all the way to the horizon. As they walked along the wall, passing guards on patrol and more ballistae emplacements, the swamplands west of Halding Port also came into view. Small villages and towns dotted the land, all connected by winding roads which joined together at a central point to lead here.

"It's breathtaking." she said sincerely.

"Aye, it is," Fradrick stood stiffly next to her, his coat flapping in the wind, his hat stubbornly staying on his head.

Their eyes met. Salevari could see the desire in his own, could see his heartbeat quicken by watching the artery in his neck pulse. She turned away, pretending to blush. If this was how she had to play her game, she would play it. Aniria pretended not to notice, amusement flickering on her lips.

Fradrick cleared his throat. "With our high walls we can see any enemy coming our way for miles, sometimes days, before they're close enough to lay siege."

"I can hardly believe anyone would dare lay siege to this place," Aniria commented.

"Aye, it hasn't happened for a century. And even then, it was only a coalition of small towns nestled just past the southern tip of the Silent Mountains. Needless to say, their siege didn't last long. Or so the histories say."

They remained a moment longer on the wall, enjoying the breeze and the silence from being up so high and away from the city. Finally, they made their way back down. Fradrick led them into a museum filled to the brim with old, rusted weapons, old manuscripts, maps and scrolls, and a myriad of oil paintings, sculptures, and artistic vases that depicted various points of Halding Port's history.

They spent a couple hours meandering their way through the collection. Fradrick told of the fierce war between the humans and the vashi. The viatari nodded along, feigning shock or horror where it mattered. The story he told was not too different from Tera's version, though with some clear human bias. Salevari couldn't help but think that the vashi might object to some of the claims the Grand Admiral made regarding their bravery and honesty.

Finishing his story, he began to ask them questions of their own home and what life was like in the plains. Salevari and Aniria responded with the well-rehearsed script Simon had drilled into them. They gave only vague details of Halshire, its people, its customs, and mentioned the darimun and viatari, which elicited an interested exclamation from their host.

"Ah, the viatari. We've heard of them. Can't say we've dealt with them hardly at all being this far south, though. I know your people must hate them, but I must say I'm more curious about them than anything. I'd love to meet one someday."

For a moment, Salevari imagined what sort of reaction she might procure if she dispelled her human illusion right then and there. With a shake of her head, she discarded the temptation.

When noon came, Fradrick brought them to a restaurant situated in a quieter part of the city. Intoxicating aromas of spices and cooking meats and freshly poured wine met their noses as they entered. A platter of boiled seafood was put before them as they took their seats at a table overlooking the ocean. The food was widely varied. Many of these creatures Salevari had never seen before. Some came in shells, large and small. Fish were layered on top of each other in the center, steam slowly rising. Red spider-looking beasts that Fradrick called "crabs" and another variation called "lobster" sat with soulless eyes, staring accusingly at them. The whole thing was decorated with greenery and some fruit, though Salevari suspected that part was rarely ever eaten.

They dug in.

Salevari's eyes closed involuntarily as the sweet taste of delicate meat exploded on her tongue. Aniria groaned with pleasure when she slurped a succulent piece of crab leg. It was an exquisite meal, made all the more frustrating because it did nothing to sate the viatari's hunger even after eating their share. Still, Salevari couldn't say she regretted it. She didn't look forward to hunting rats later that night as she stared wistfully toward the ocean.

When they finished, Fradrick led them outside the wall and onto a private beach, reserved solely for members of the palace. The elites. Salevari saw some of them walking along the sandy shore. Others swam and played in the waves. Still others were waist-deep in the water, staring into the vast sea, a fishing rod gripped tightly in their hands.

"Aha!" Fradrick cried, clapping his hands with delight. "They managed to set it up in time." He pointed out a small canopy set up over two chairs that leaned out at a wide angle. A tall fishing rod leaned against one of them and in between was a bucket of ice, two bottles of wine protruding from it. Empty glasses stood to the side.

"Come" Fradrick almost pushed the viatari forward as he guided them into their shaded seats. He uncorked one of the bottles and poured a glass, handing one to each of them. Then, with a small salute and a happy grin, he grabbed the fishing pole and eagerly bounded for the roaring waves, tearing his coat off as he went and letting it fly behind him.

Salevari glanced at Aniria, then at her drink, then called for the Grand Admiral, "Fradrick, what exactly are we supposed to do here?"

"Just relax!" He yelled back, jumping over waves as they came. He went deeper into the water, finally finding a good spot, cast his line, and let the waves bob him up and down as he reeled it back in.

The viatari shrugged, leaned back in their seats, took off their high-heeled shoes, clinked glasses and sipped their wine. It was a good vintage.

"What do you think about the day so far?" Salevari asked, refilling her glass.

Aniria shrugged, a disinterested frown on her face. "It's obvious he's manufactured this day to bring out the best of this place. We'll learn nothing about the problems this city may be facing from our adventures today."

"We have a potential bargaining chip though, at least."

"Were you thinking cannons, too?"

Salevari scoffed. "How could I not? The answer is so obvious. And not just for their ships, their wall too. We could present a vision of Halding Port becoming completely impregnable."

Aniria cracked a smile. "Isn't it already?"

"Perhaps not against the darinsha."

"Then we're back to our original problem. If we can't figure out what the real issue is here or how to fix it, we'll have nothing to offer the humans except cannons—which they'll never get without becoming firm allies with us beforehand."

They uncorked the second bottle of wine and began to pour.

"Maybe we should just ask him outright," Salevari wondered out loud.

Bright laughter mixed with the ocean breeze. "I wish you luck, then." Aniria waved as Fradrick returned to them, his trousers soaked. "I get the feeling he's not the type of man who easily talks about his problems."

Fradrick picked his coat up off the beach and slapped the sand from it, tossing it over his shoulder as he reached the canopy. He scooped some ice water from the bucket and ran it through his hair and face.

"Ah!" he sighed. "Nothing better after a hot day in the sun. Shall I call for more wine?"

"Actually, Fradrick," Salevari swirled what little wine remained in her glass as if she were bored. "We wanted to ask you something about Halding Port that's been bothering us since we arrived."

Concern flickered onto the Grand Admiral's chiseled face. He set down his fishing pole and sat on the edge of Salevari's seat, his large hands only inches away from her bare feet. She was immensely aware of how little movement he'd have to make to touch her.

"What troubles you?"

"When we arrived, the people here looked about ready to riot, and it seemed to be because of our presence."

"They were wild," Aniria added, putting a slight tremor in her voice. "Guards had to get involved to quell the crowds."

"I guess what we want to know," Salevari continued. "Is what is going on here that could cause such a fuss? Surely rumors of lords and ladies from the plains can't be that important to the common folk."

It was a bit vaguer than Salevari would have liked but enough of her question was there to reel in a decent answer. By the haunted look dominating their host's features, he thought so too. "I heard the report from me guards. I must apologize that you and your family had to go through such an ordeal. I've no doubt it was frightening."

"But *why* did it happen?" Salevari leaned forward, and in doing so, brushed her toes against the edge of his hands. He registered the touch, his body briefly turning rigid before he slowly shook his head.

"No offense, my lady, but I wish not to speak of me work at a time like this. It does me no good." He looked out toward the sun. Hours yet remained of its bright light. "I think it's about time to return to the palace. Perhaps we can have dinner and speak of lighter topics. I have many more questions about the plains."

He stood to leave. Salevari turned her gaze to Aniria who only shrugged as if to say, "I told you so." Jumping from their seats, they gathered their shoes from the sand and ran after the Grand Admiral, electing to make the journey back barefoot.

Upon returning to the palace, Fradrick bid them farewell

and made his way up to his office, saying he had a few reports and letters to look over before dinner. His footfalls were heavy with melancholy with each step up the grand stairway. Aethel appeared from one of the adjoining hallways and offered to lead the viatari back to their room, which they accepted gratefully.

Back inside their suite, they stripped off their restrictive fabrics, throwing them haphazardly onto the couch. Simon would yell later about how much he had worked on them, but right now the only thing they could think of was comfort. Aniria found a nightgown in her closet and quickly put it on, lounging on the couch within minutes and dozing in the realm of dreams.

Simon, Zael, and Drathanar had not yet returned from their own adventure in the city, though Tera had. There would be time later to share details of their days and compare notes together, but that didn't stop Salevari from asking her how the day had gone.

"Nothing to report. The staff here are tight-lipped. Couldn't get a thing out of them even if I tried to cut it out with my blades." The human wanderer said with a scowl as she flicked a dagger into the opposing wall. She stood to retrieve it, her shoulders hunched, muttering with each step, "First Victria, then the chickens, and now I can't get any bloody information. . . ."

Salevari's heart went out to the human wanderer. But she knew better than to offer words of encouragement when someone was brooding. More often than not, they sounded false and they were the last thing people wanted to hear. No, she thought, better to let her brood for now, vent her frustrations out with her daggers, then tackle the subject in the morning.

With a shrug and nothing to do but wait for the men to

return, Salevari decided to indulge once more in something she had been thinking about since that morning. She slipped off her undergarments and glided into the hot, steaming pool that dominated their bathing room. She let out a content sigh and leaned back against the stone edge, allowing her limbs to float freely.

Staring at the ceiling, her mind was awhirl with thoughts and possibilities. Though much of what she thought was focused on the mystery that was this place, part of her dwelled on the day's events in a different manner.

She'd had *fun* today. She realized this with a start. She couldn't remember the last time she'd been able to relax and unwind with not a care in the world. Her life for the past several centuries had been nothing but leading her people in Dalyr through each day, fulfilling her duty, defending them, overcoming challenge after challenge. She'd forgotten what a day of leisure felt like.

She laughed, the echo of her voice laughing back at her. She looked around on the off chance Aniria had gotten off the couch to join her. But she was alone, and she was glad of it. Because she couldn't wipe off this damned happy grin.

CHAPTER SEVENTEEN

The guards made no fuss when Simon and his viatari companions told them they wanted to go out and see what Halding Port's bars and taverns had to offer. One of them even made their own recommendations on which establishments had the best drinks and which had the best food. The iron-wrought gates swung open. Simon thanked the guards, and the trio filed out without a second glance.

They went down a few streets before ducking into a dark alleyway. Simon pulled out a bulging sack he had hidden under his noble's cloak and distributed a change of clothes to Zael and Drathanar, leaving his own for last.

These clothes, while still higher quality than most could afford, were much less flashy and more in the northern style of the plains; a simple brown tunic tucked into loose trousers made of wool and soft boots lined with rabbit's fur. For a brief moment, Simon felt like his old self, back when he was *actually* the chief of Halshire.

"Where will we go first?" Drathanar asked as they finished folding their previous outfits carefully. Simon stuffed them into the bag and swung it over his shoulder.

"First," he said, peeking out of the alleyway to make sure no one was around to watch them come out. He beckoned for the others to follow and in one swift motion pushed out of the shadows and into the adjacent street, walking down it as if he'd been there all along. "We need to go to the markets. Merchants always get carried away with spreading rumors and they aren't quiet about it. We could learn something from them."

"We should actually visit the taverns as well like we said we would," Zael suggested. "I find humans talk much more freely over a drink in a dimly lit room than anywhere else."

"Yes, you would have experience with that, wouldn't you?" Simon grimaced, remembering the terrible human rebellion he had been forced to help the viatari quell months ago. Zael had been instrumental in infiltrating the ranks of the dissenters to keep Salevari informed of their movements. He had remained a shadow among them up to the end. Even Simon hadn't realized his true role until the night the dissenters had been dealt with in one fell swoop.

"We'll visit the taverns as well, then. We'll need someplace to eat when the time comes, anyway."

The markets were a cacophony of yelling, fighting, and insults. The whole of Market Way was lined with stands, each one selling different wares. Some sold weapons, well-crafted swords and axes that were "forged by the dwarves themselves," which Simon highly doubted. Others sold fresh fruit right next to piles of fish that had been caught only that morning. Still others called for passersby to come inspect their mounds of multi-colored spices that they had out for display in wooden bowls. There were money changers, traders of all sorts, vendors of exotic pets, cooks preparing simple but savory meals as the orders came in, performers stalking through the narrow streets, trying to catch the eye of anyone they passed. It was chaos. And the smells were bewildering.

Simon had to cover his nose as he passed a few stalls, their wares either too pungent or too sharp. The viatari behind him fared no better.

"Stick close to me," he shouted as a crowd of consumers shoved past him to get to a stall selling talismans and other trinkets labeled as "magical." "We don't want to get separated here."

There were too many people on this street. Simon found himself jostled or pushed to the side by a stranger far too often, even as he did his best to avoid the more crowded areas. As they walked, their interest gravitated toward a merchant who had just finished setting up his stand, piled high with round, flat loaves of bread.

"Bread for sale!" the merchant called out loudly. "Two silver pieces for half a loaf!"

"That's outrageous!" A man yelled out even as he bought two loaves. He wasn't the only one. A frenzy developed as people rushed desperately toward the bread merchant. A crazed look entered their eyes. Fear was in the merchant's even as a thin layer of greed remained—enough for him to stand his ground as he sold his wares. Within minutes, the stand was empty. The merchant's pockets bulged. He whistled a happy tune as he took down his shop. The crowd dispersed, returning to their previous roaming state, looking for their next purchase.

Glancing back at his companions, Simon could recognize their discomfort. He couldn't blame them. What they had just witnessed was as bizarre to him as it would be to anyone. Nothing like this madness had ever occurred in the markets in his town.

They continued on, brushing past a few passersby too closely and earning several foul names as their reward. Zael took whatever abuse was thrown their way in stride, though he stared down the offending humans as if memorizing their features for later. Drathanar, however, looked ready to erupt. He glared at everyone they passed. To his benefit, this convinced others to steer clear of him, as the Dalyran general was not small in stature. Still, Simon would rather not risk inciting a fight in such a narrow, crowded space. Such encounters easily evolved into full-blown riots. He pulled into a gap between two stalls selling food, guiding his companions out of the ever-shifting current of people.

"We won't discover anything here," he admitted breathlessly. "This market is unlike any I've ever known. There are far too many people and all of them talking at once. We'll never hear any rumors the merchants might be sharing with each other."

"I agree," Zael scowled, eyeing a particularly large man who seemed to have bumped into the viatari one too many times. "Besides, if we stay any longer, Drathanar might lose his temper."

"Speak for yourself," Drathanar spat. "I see you studying everyone you pass. You would hunt them later in the day."

Zael shrugged. "There are far fewer witnesses at night. Who knows what really happens during those tired hours?"

"Enough," Simon said sternly. "We're leaving this place and going to one of the taverns the guards recommended. It's as good a place as any to start. We can grab a couple drinks while we're at it and cool our heads."

They all agreed and maneuvered their way through the crowds as efficiently as they could until they finally stumbled out of Market Way and found themselves on a far less populated side of the city. Here there were proper shops that sold simple materials like flowers or building materials as well as numerous bait and fishing shops.

After asking for directions to *The Rosy Pirate*, they went on, turning down several streets before finally finding themselves in front of a swinging wooden sign overhead with a skull and bones laying on a bed of roses.

They swung the door open with a loud creak and stepped in. Simon nodded in satisfaction. Like all taverns, this one was dimly lit. Barmaids navigated their way between tables carrying trays of food or tankards filled to the brim with drink. There were only a few patrons here today, it still being the morning, but that was enough. It only took one loudmouth for secrets to spill.

Zael and Drathanar found a table near the corner while Simon approached the bar to buy them all drinks.

"I don't suppose you have any wine?" Simon asked, aware of the viatari's preference.

The bartender shrugged. "Just a few cheap vintages. Our ale is a much better quality."

"I'll have an ale. Two glasses of wine for my friends over there—in fact, I'll take the bottle."

He tossed a silver coin which the bartender deftly caught.

"Like a meal with your drinks?" the man asked over his shoulder as he poured. "Got a fine fish head stew going in the back."

"Not quite yet," Simon had to force his face to remain neutral. The idea of a fish head stew was as unappetizing to him as going out into a field and grazing with the livestock. "We'll probably be here a while."

The bartender nodded and slid a tankard full of ale and two empty glasses along with a bottle of wine across the bar.

"Be seeing you, then."

Simon inclined his head, gathered the drinks into his arms, and returned to his companions. As they sipped their glasses, they watched the patrons within go about their business. A few looked to be fishermen, sharing stories of their early morning adventures. A couple of guards sat at another table, speaking darkly to each other in low voices. This piqued Simon's interest. If there was anyone who might know about a problem in the city, it would be them. He wondered what approach he might take to get them to talk, then realized he might not have to do that. Next to their table hung a large wooden board with a plethora of individual sheets of paper tacked onto it, like a message board.

"Stay here," he said. "I'm going to check on something."

The viatari shrugged as he got up and continued savoring their wine. Simon walked past the guards nonchalantly, his eyes fixed to the board but his ears searching for their voices. He could barely hear their lowered tones, too little to make out what they were actually saying.

As he tried to listen, his eyes perused the contents spread out before him. There were a few wanted posters, a few leaflets announcing lost pets and rewards for their return, and a few job advertisements. Along with them, scattered randomly across the board, were a peculiar set of messages. Simon picked one off. It appeared to be handwritten, the lettering scrawled hastily, as if the author wanted it to be unrecognizable. It read:

Who are the elites?
What is their purpose?
Salmon swim upriver, never down. Is it because they cannot, or they know nothing else?
Whispers of bread. Grains of truth hidden. Sickness comes from

falsehood.
Procured a pretty penny from the salmon upriver lately?
Do you feel the maws of a bear looming over you?
Feel its hot breath in your face?
Walls all around. Salmon and bears entrapped, nowhere for either to go.
Ask questions.
Awaken, and break bread.
—P

"Can we help you, sir?"

Simon turned to see the two guards glaring up at him suspiciously. It was clear he had overstayed his welcome, though in truth he had not meant to. While he initially had been trying to eavesdrop, the message he had plucked from the board intrigued him so much he had forgotten his original task. So it was no issue for him to feign ignorance as he waved the sheet of paper before them.

"What is this?"

The guards glanced at the sloppy scrawl and frowned with disapproval. "You must not be from around here if you don't know about the thurn posts."

"I'm not. This is my first time here. I'm from the plains, so we don't have anything like this." Simon couldn't keep the excitement out of his voice. He also didn't fully understand it. Something about this paper was eliciting such a response from him.

"If you're a visitor then you need not worry about it," the other guard replied bitterly, bringing his heavy tankard to his lips. It was clear their distaste for these anonymous posts ran deep, though Simon couldn't guess why yet.

"I see," said the human chief thoughtfully, catching the eye of the bartender who had been watching his interaction with the guards. "I'll be on my way then. Apologies for disturbing you, gentlemen. I thank you for keeping the streets safe."

The guards grunted and turned away to resume their whispered conversation, now with some extra energy. Simon made a mental note of their reaction and, paper still in hand, forged a path toward the bartender. He slapped it down on the bar. The man didn't flinch, nor did he look at the paper, but kept his gaze steadily on Simon while he took a faded rag to a dirty glass.

"Can you tell me what this is?"

"What's it to you, stranger?"

Simon shrugged. "I'm a curious man."

The bartender sighed and put away the half-cleaned glass before picking up the page and skimming through the words. "What did the guards tell you?"

"That they were just some silly anonymous posts I shouldn't take too seriously."

"Perhaps you shouldn't," the bartender sounded tired. "These posts have been showing up randomly throughout the city for the last year or two. Always the same type of questions, always the same format, and never a consistent posting time. The people read them, they ask the same questions. People make guesses as to what the cryptic messages mean but no one has any solid answers, even though many claim they do."

"What is that final letter? I've never seen it before."

"Few have," the bartender nodded knowingly. "The 'Þ' is an old rune we used to use in our writing centuries ago. It's long been out of use. It's called the 'thurn,' so the ones who follow these messages and devote themselves to deciphering their meaning call them thurn posts."

Simon's heart quickened. Something about what the bartender was saying was resonating with other events he'd witnessed in the city. If there was one thing he knew, it was how to use words as a means to get what he wanted out of people, whether that was through inspiration, intimidation, or flat-out deception. There was something of that quality in this message, but he needed to read more of them to be sure.

"Is there any special meaning to this rune? Why does the author use it as their signature?"

The bartender let out a long, tired sigh. "Lots of theories on that one. The most prevalent thought is that the rune was often used as a substitute for the word 'protector' in the old days. And so whoever is writing these posts is announcing themselves as a protector of this city."

Simon's face twitched. Whoever was behind this, they knew their history. They understood symbolism. They were clever.

"Where can I find more of these?"

Scoffing, the bartender spread his arms out wide. "Everywhere. They're posted in every square and plaza, not to mention the taverns and inns. If you're talking about new posts, though, you'll have to go to the main plaza at the center of town. Thurn posts always get put up there first, for whatever reason."

Simon slapped the bar with his hand and pushed forward another silver coin. "Thank you for the information, my friend."

A grunt was all he got for an answer.

He turned to leave, but before he could take a step another question pushed itself to the forefront of his mind. He glanced over his shoulder at the bartender.

"One more question. Do you believe in what's in these posts?"

The bartender's eyes hardened as he answered, "Once. But I've been burned too many times by false hope to fall for them again; no matter how good the promises they make may sound."

Simon nodded and made his way back to his companions who were deep in their own conversation. They looked up at him, frowning.

"We will discover nothing by sitting here," Drathanar declared. "We're wasting our time."

"As I told you," Zael's jaw clenched. "This type of work takes time. We cannot force results, but we have to be willing to wait for as long as it takes for an opportunity to present itself. That is what it means to be subtle." He raised his glass to finish its contents and muttered, "Not that you'd understand the meaning of the word."

Drathanar glared. "I am a warrior. I don't slink about in the shadows to get what I want."

"Well, we're not here to bash in heads either," Simon clapped both of them on the shoulder and leaned in so that he was eye-level with them. A year ago he would never have imagined himself in this position. Not just that he was so close to a pair of viatari and actively working with them, but also that he was having to settle disputes between them.

"As it happens, I've discovered some information that I think points us in the right direction." He presented the leaf of paper he had plucked from the message board.

The two viatari looked it over, then back at him with the same incredulous expression. "What is this nonsense?"

"That is an example of the power of the written word, my friends," Simon took the page back and read through it again, his eyes shining with admiration. "Messages like this have been popping up all over the city for the past couple years apparently. They have some sort of grip on the populace here, the bartender all but confirmed it for me. We go now to find more of these so-called thurn posts and see what we can glean from them."

Without waiting for them to agree, Simon left *The Rosy Pirate*. The two viatari were quick to follow, their small disagreement a thing of the past as they continued to look through the thurn post to try and decipher it. They might have initially thought it was a disordered mess of words, but Simon clearly believed there was something deeper behind it and they were willing to trust his instinct.

They made their way toward the city's center, which opened up into a grand plaza. Stalls lined the edges selling goods, freshly cooked foods, and clothing. A multi-tiered fountain sat in the middle of the square, spitting water from its center which then fell over the edge into the next tier until it hit the main pool at the bottom. People sat around the font, resting or observing others around them as they went about their day-to-day activities.

Situated beside the decorative structure was a square pillar that rose up ten feet from the ground. On each side of it was a wooden board plastered onto the stone face. Each board was covered in individual leaves of paper. Simon made a beeline for them.

He glanced through a few until he found another thurn post, which read:

When was Halding Port established?
Who was it taken from?
Who are they?
Horses bear bags of grain from the plains, praise the waves when you see them come through our gates.
The Grand Admiral casts his net but catches only minnows.
What feeds on minnows?

Ask questions.
Awaken, and break bread.
— Þ

"This one makes even less sense," Drathanar muttered.

Simon's eyes widened as he read the post. He choked back a laugh and shook his head. Whoever was behind this, he couldn't help but admire their work.

"It's not meant to all make sense or for each line to relate to the others of the same post. But the ones you should be focusing on are in the middle. Whoever is posting these knew we would be coming far before anyone else did. That's why the people went berserk when they saw us pass through the gates as lords and ladies of the plains. This Thurn character told them we would be some sort of sign."

"How do you know they foretold our arrival and didn't just get lucky with a wild guess?" Zael asked.

Simon cocked his head. "It would be a pretty wild guess, don't you think? No, whoever is doing this, I don't think he's some hooligan doing it for fun. This person knows what they're doing, and they have an efficient way of staying informed with current events. The only question now is what's their motive."

"That may be your only question, but I'm still confused as to *why* this "Thurn" is even wasting their time making these posts." Drathanar folded his arms and shook his head, tossing away a different page he had plucked from the message board, letting it blow away with the wind.

"Isn't it obvious?" Simon took a moment to observe the people around him. They were all living their normal lives, but there was a subtle tension in the air. People spoke just a bit too loudly, a bit too quickly. They glanced around furtively, their body language all wrong. These people were waiting for something, ready to pounce on that something like a trap. But it was one that would never spring.

"These messages do a good job at giving people a false sense of hope. You've seen how the elites live. Now you've seen how the regular folk live. Many here are probably struggling to get by. A lot of these posts have to do with bread and grain and sickness. I suspect there's something wrong with the food supply that the people are aware of but that the elites aren't doing anything about. That would explain why the market was a madhouse today, too, especially around the food stalls. Did you notice how expensive bread was and how outraged the people who had to buy it were?"

The viatari listened intently, even Drathanar, though doubts still swam behind his narrowed eyes.

"With these messages the author is portraying themselves as some protector of the commonfolk from the elites. They're creating division without being obvious about it. They're presenting a problem and then presenting themselves as the solution to maintain the status quo of life. The people here are aware of something nefarious happening behind the scenes because of these posts, but they'll never lift a finger to help themselves because they believe whoever is behind this is doing the fighting for them."

"And so whatever's really going on continues unnoticed and unchallenged," Zael finished.

"Exactly."

"Then who's the author?" Drathanar asked. "Perhaps it's the elites who wish to keep these people under their control to avoid any unrest that would come with a famine."

"Or do you believe these messages are being spread by a third party with their own motivations and goals?" Zael asked, taking another page from the board and looking through it with newfound respect.

"That's the question," Simon sighed, running a hand through his hair. He was excited. He couldn't help it. The diabolical genius behind these messages mirrored his own when he led his people against the viatari and followed them into the Forbidden Lands, where they were eventually destroyed by the Creature's demons.

Whoever was writing these messages didn't really care about the people. It was possible the elites of Halding Port were behind this mass deception like Drathanar suggested, but even the city's guards seemed to think these were just the works of some miscreant fool. Then again, city guards weren't always privy to the machinations of those they worked for, so that theory couldn't truly be discounted yet. However, it was just as likely there was another party behind this, as Zael thought. If that were the case, what was their motivation? Subduing the people like this could surely only benefit Halding Port's elites.

Simon's thoughts were interrupted as a dirty man in rags who smelled strongly of fish approached them. A toothy grin flashed as his eyes gravitated to the papers they held in their hands.

"Nice to be out of bed, ain't it, brother," the man said in a soft voice. He cackled. "Ah, the floods are nigh!"

"What flood?" Simon asked.

The man regarded him with amusement. "Fresh blood, eh? New followers of Thurn? You'll see eventually. It's all truth. The floods will come in waves of green like the days of old to wash away all the corruption and evil staining this heathen city. Then, we'll all be free."

Another cackle, followed by a sickening cough. "You wanna

hear my two cents, these thurn posts have been such a blessing. They've exposed the corruption of our rulers the likes of which I never could have imagined beforehand. Their day of judgment will come."

"What corruption have these posts exposed, exactly?" Simon asked.

"Well," the beggar thought for a moment. "They have money, they live large while the rest of us roll in the dirt. They do nothing about our food issues—"

"Why are there food issues here?" Zael asked. "Your city is right next to the sea, you have an abundance of fish right at your door."

The beggar guffawed and scratched his scraggly beard. "Plainsmen, eh? How little you know. Just 'cause we catch the fish don't mean we get to eat 'em. That's what I'm saying! It's all about the corruption, and Thurn is the one to thank for exposing it. If you really want to learn more about it, I suggest you listen to the man they call *the interpreter*. He comes by almost every day to read new thurn posts and tell people what they mean. Genius, that man is!"

Simon tossed a few copper coins the beggar's way which he caught skillfully. He thanked them with a wave of his ratty cap and skipped away toward another group of people who he began pestering.

"Crazy fool," Drathanar muttered.

"Crazy perhaps," Simon agreed. "But he's helped us figure out our next move."

The viatari general shot him a curious look.

Smirking, Simon flipped another coin into the air and caught it as he meandered toward the merchants set up at the far end of the plaza. "We wait for this 'interpreter' to show up and we hear what he has to say."

They spent the remaining hours of the day inspecting the wares of various merchants. There were countless objects of interest but neither Simon nor the viatari had any real desire to buy anything. The merchants quickly caught on to this and lost interest in their presence, though they stopped short of chasing them off for loitering.

Finally, as the sun began its descent and shadows grew long, Simon noticed a lone man walking purposefully toward the message boards, a few leaflets in hand. He hammered one page on each side of the square pillar then made his way to a section of the square where others dressed similarly to him were waiting. They all wore simple black robes with a silver sash tied around their waist. A basic podium—nothing more than a large crate—had been set up which the man stepped onto.

Simon caught the attention of his companions and together they joined the gathering crowd as the man prepared for whatever performance he had in store for them.

"Citizens of Halding Port," the man's voice boomed for all to hear. "I, known to many of you as the interpreter, come with another message from Thurn."

The crowd cheered. Some muttered anxiously. There were a few guards keeping watch over them from a distance. They all shared the same dark expression.

"His latest post reads as such: 'Wherein does power lie? How does the lion sleep at night? What about the kraken? Grains of sand along the beach, countless except to those with a trained eye. You saw the riders yesterday. What is the main agricultural product of the plains? Will the fish jump into our nets when bread comes stale and molded? The vigilant man lives. Ask questions. Awaken, and break bread. Thurn."

The interpreter allowed for a moment of silence so the

message had some time to digest in the minds of those gathered. Simon grinned. Whoever was writing these things had confirmed their arrival, then. Perhaps he or she had been there at the gates when they rode through. Perhaps word had reached them from somewhere else. Either way, Thurn had been quick to use the event as a means of legitimizing their messages. It was a clever ploy.

"The words of Thurn are always up for interpretation," the interpreter's voice broke the silence like shattering glass. "But it's clear to me the focus for this one remains on our food shortage crisis. How long now since our last shipment of grain was received from our trade partners? Wheat is the main agricultural product of the plainsman. Thurn wishes for us to focus on this issue."

Murmurs among the crowd. A few worried looks crossed.

"Without bread we cannot eat. You know as well as I that the elites hoard all of our labor in their palace. They eat the fruits of the sea while we are left to fight for the last loaf of stale bread."

Vigorous nodding from the crowd. Simon dwelled on this last point. He had noticed people fighting for bread and grain in the markets earlier that day but had initially dismissed it as part of the raucous behavior of the market culture here. But bread wasn't the only food available to the people in this city. Even in this plaza, several stalls were established that sold fried meats, fried fish and an assortment of grilled and steamed vegetables. Yet no one seemed to think of these. Their sole idea of food was fixated on the idea of bread and the lack thereof.

"My friends," the interpreter's tone softened. "I cannot give you all the answers tonight. I must ponder on Thurn's message myself. You know well how much time and effort it takes to unravel the crumbs he leaves us."

He. So Thurn was a male, and this interpreter seemed to know that. Or he was just assuming. Either way, Simon tucked away that piece of information for later in case it proved relevant.

"I will return tomorrow, hopefully with more answers. Until then, remain awake. Awaken those closest to you. Ask questions. Make them see that this world they live in, our society, is a farce. The day of the floods will come, just as Thurn promised, and with those purifying waters will the impurities we suffer through in our daily lives wash away. Until then, my friends, live your lives as best you can. The fight goes on whether you see it or not."

With that, the interpreter stepped off his podium and departed, disappearing into one of the nearby alleys.

Zael let out a low, impressed whistle. "He's in on it."

"I think so, too." Simon said. "Though we can't prove that yet."

"Did anything he say matter?" Drathanar asked. "If it did, I couldn't tell you what."

"It did matter," Simon answered confidently. He turned and made his way out of the plaza, heading back for the palace. His companions followed. "The key here is food. Food can control a city, and something serious has gone wrong with Halding Port's supply. We have to find out what that is and why it's happened and how it connects with The Turned One—because I would bet you everything I have that she's involved in this somehow. There are still many questions that need to be answered, but that interpreter has at least given us one valuable nugget of information."

"We now know the underlying problem with Halding Port," Zael finished.

"Exactly. We figure out how to solve it, how to tie it to The Turned One, and we provide a great service to the Grand Admiral. We now have exactly what Salevari wanted. The perfect bargaining chip."

CHAPTER EIGHTEEN

Night fell before Drathanar, Simon and Zael returned to their suite. The palace servants had been busy scurrying through the whole building, lighting candles and chandeliers, installing torches, and doing everything they could to ensure the palace remained well-lit without the sun's assistance.

Salevari turned to greet them as they entered, but their attention wasn't on her. Their eyes gravitated to the next room over where large platters of fruit, fish, and some well-cooked steaks had been placed along the table. The savory aromas wafted through the whole room, snaking into their flaring nostrils and causing their stomachs to growl menacingly.

"Go and eat," Salevari ordered. "We will have time to discuss your day after. Zael, Drathanar, Aniria and I have already gone hunting. There are some rats in your rooms if you wish to consume them."

They all nodded. Salevari let them eat in peace, watching water bubble down the fountain in the middle of their living room. Once they'd had their fill, they gathered together, pensive looks on their faces. The feeling in the air was as taut as a bow string.

Salevari stood and poured herself a glass of wine. "I'll start," she said, letting the red spirit loosen her tongue. "We learned more from the Grand Admiral than I expected. And we were right to believe he wouldn't show us anything within the city that might tarnish its reputation."

"I take it you had a nice day then?" Simon leaned back on a couch and crossed his arms as he grumbled.

"We did, as a matter of fact," Salevari replied evenly. "And that's the point. The Grand Admiral went out of his way to show us the good parts of the city. He may have even incentivized some of the commonfolk to be on their best behavior on the off chance they ran into us during or after his tour. If we weren't certain there was something deeply wrong with this place before, we are now."

Zael scoffed, shaking his head slowly. "You have no idea."

"Quiet," Drathanar seethed, taking a seat next to Aniria, who suddenly had an interest in the fireplace opposite them. "Let the Chancellor finish her story."

"Thank you, Drath. As I was saying, we weren't able to learn much from the man himself. When we asked him about our arrival and why the people here would have been on the verge of a riot like they were, he refused to provide an answer. His demeanor completely changed. Before he had been as playful and exuberant as a little boy. And after . . . he just looked tired."

"We already knew something was going on here," Simon shrugged. "That's the whole reason we're here, so that we can thwart whatever plot The Turned One has concocted and present it as our gift to the Grand Admiral."

"Yes, but now we also know that Halding Port's leadership has some awareness of this problem. We also know that whatever it is, it's being kept secret from anyone who doesn't need to know."

"Well it's a good thing we discovered what the issue is then," the human chief drawled. He sat forward and recounted their day in the city, from the state of living for the common folk to discovering the thurn posts and then finally focusing on the interpreter himself.

Salevari thought long and hard once Simon had finished. "You say you believe this is some campaign to keep the people of this city subdued?"

"That's what it appears to be," Simon nodded. "The messaging is cleverly worded to reveal a problem that most people here probably suspected to begin with. Instead of inciting the populace to rise up and actually enact change, however, these posts make it seem like others are doing the fighting for them on their behalf. They just don't know it because the fighting is taking place in the shadows. It's all very subtle. If the average person believes they don't have to do anything to free themselves from whatever form of captivity they're under because someone else is doing it for them, they won't lift a finger."

"What about this interpreter?"

"He's clearly in on the operation, though how deeply I cannot say. We'll have to observe him in the coming days if we wish to learn more."

"And you think The Turned One's agents are behind this campaign?" Salevari asked.

Simon shrugged. "She must have some hand in this, but that's the part that remains unknown. It could be The Turned One directly influencing events here or she could be working through Halding Port's own leadership. The point of Thurn is to keep the civilian populace in check. I would need to determine motives for each party to see who benefits more from the final result before I could make any guesses."

Zael stood up and began pacing, lines creased his face as his mind tried to put the pieces together. "If the leadership is behind this, then is it in our best interest to ally ourselves with them? If they'll do this to their own people, they can't be counted on to help the vashi, who they have a history of hating."

"If the leadership is behind this," Aniria said, her gaze finally turning away from the dancing flames. Her face was flushed as if she'd been sitting close to the fire this whole time. "Then that means The Turned One has something worse planned for this place or Halding Port is already in her pocket. Either way, it spells bad news for us, though I suppose we'll still have to at least try to thwart whatever scheme she has in play."

"Aniria's right," Salevari said soberly. "Though if there was something worse than what we've already discovered surely there would be signs."

"I can't say anything since I was in the palace all day, but perhaps we just don't have all the pieces we need yet," Tera suggested absently as she cleaned her daggers. "We know about this thurn campaign, we know it focuses heavily on some food supply issue this place is supposedly undergoing, we know that the messages are laced with strange symbolism of disease and danger, presumably to make the believers dwell on fear. How does this all connect?"

They all looked at each other, but none of them had a solid answer.

"We can't expect to discover it all so soon," Salevari finally said, swallowing back the frustration she felt growing in the pit of her stomach. "We should follow this lead, though. Keep observing this interpreter. Find out where he lives, how he obtains these messages, who he works for."

Zael nodded. "I can do that."

"We should also follow up on the Grand Admiral," the Chancellor continued. "I don't think he's the one behind this. He seems, if anything, more preoccupied with the fact that it's even happening. But he could also be playing his cards close to his chest. We barely know the man. His highly energetic, enthusiastic persona might just be a facade."

She nodded to herself. There was more work to be done but that was to be expected. Even so, she thought they were making remarkable progress. She looked at Tera.

"How was your day?"

"Uneventful, as I mentioned before," Tera drawled, taking out a whetstone to sharpen her daggers. A coarse grinding sound filled the room as she moved her blade up and down its surface. "The staff here are a tight-lipped bunch. Couldn't coax a damn thing out of them. The elites I happened to encounter through the halls were just as silent but that was because they barely gave me the time of day. I must appear too much like a servant to them."

"Tough day," Simon commented, picking at his teeth with his fingers.

The ghost of a smile flittered on Tera's face as she continued, "Though, there was a message I received from one of the butlers before you all returned. The Grand Admiral will be throwing his feast for us next week. Which means the Admiral's Ball is also next week."

Simon lurched forward, nearly jumping off the couch. A dark shadow passed over his eyes. "Which means—"

"You're going to have to teach Aniria and Salevari how to dance." Tera finished, letting out a bright burst of laughter.

"Dance?" The two viatari shared an apprehensive look. "Dance with whom?"

"Well, you will presumably dance with me, seeing as I'm supposed to be your husband," Simon replied with an annoyed groan. "Aniria will no doubt have a line of young men waiting their turn to ask for her hand."

Zael continued pacing. Drathanar frowned. Aniria crossed her arms. "I don't suppose I have a choice in this."

Simon grimaced. "You do not. We may be from the plains, but even nobles from our part of the world should know how to interact at a social event."

"It can't be too hard, can it?" Salevari asked. "It's just . . . a movement of the feet. Like combat training."

The humans shook their heads in synchronized amusement, grins of pity stretching their lips.

"On top of everything else we have to do," Simon sighed in defeat. "This is going to be a busy week. We'll need all the rest we can get. Is there anything else we must discuss?"

"There is, actually," Salevari pursed her lips. She disliked revealing her ignorance, even if she couldn't help not knowing every aspect of human culture. Dancing had been mentioned during their lessons in Donsea, but there hadn't been any demonstrations. The viatari in Dalyr didn't dance. There were more important things to do, like survive. She didn't know about those in Aleganthia, but judging from Aniria's face, they were in the same boat.

"While we didn't discover much about Halding Port's internal struggles, we did discover a valuable bargaining chip we have at our disposal when the time comes to negotiate with the Grand Admiral."

"Oh, and what can we offer Halding Port on top of saving their city from whatever The Turned One has planned for them?" Simon cocked his head.

"Cannons."

A sharp look came from the humans. "Cannons?"

Salevari nodded, wetting her tongue with another sip of wine. "The city's defenses and fleet are impressive, but their weaponry is rudimentary compared to what the dwarves have. If we share the technology and upgrade their defenses as a show of good faith, that alone could be enough to bring them to our side."

"Or, once they have their cannons and truly become a force to be reckoned with, they decide to dishonor our agreement. Even if they don't join The Turned One outright, they would become a wild card that we could not afford. What if they use their new power to fully subjugate the vashi?" Tera argued.

"Exactly," Simon seethed, rising from the couch. "Besides, you never offered this sort of assistance to my people when you were trying to bring us to your side."

"The humans of the plains hated us for centuries," Salevari said calmly, swirling her drink and watching some of it stick to the glass. "The humans of the coast claim to have no such prejudice. Befriending your people required a different strategy. Besides, your towns were being overrun by darimun. Cannons would have made no difference."

"So you would trust these humans not to turn their new weapons against you as soon as they could?"

"Not right at this moment," Salevari shrugged. "That's why we must continue observing them, studying them, so that we might learn what their true motivations are and how we can play them to our advantage. If we find that we can trust them, then our offer of cannons can come into play. But in the meantime, this is something we should be mentally preparing ourselves to offer."

Silence enveloped the room, broken only by Tera as she asked, "Do you think the dwarves would give up such a technology?"

"They did with Aleganthia."

"The dwarves and viatari had long been friends."

"Times have changed. The situation demands it."

Simon shook his head and threw his hands up in disgust as he took back his seat.

The Chancellor's eyes softened. She understood his frustration, as petty as it might be. He and the other humans of the plains had proven themselves as staunch allies for months now. To him it might seem like a slap in the face that she would offer other humans such a powerful gift when, at most, his people had only been given an approving clap on the back. But this was no time to be petty. In the end, the plainsmen had been given a new home in Aleganthia, and *that* city was protected by cannons.

"Believe me when I say I understand your feelings on this, Simon," Salevari said. "While I have no personal qualms about the idea, I won't allow my opinion to be the sole reason we carry it out. I'll send a message to Felix and Serania and ask for their thoughts. I'll send one to King Dunkell as well. There's still plenty of time before we even need to make this offer."

After a long moment, Simon finally nodded, and the tension in the room evaporated.

"Good," the Dalyran Chancellor smiled pleasantly. "Then, if that's all anyone has to say on the matter—"

Zael stopped his pacing and tensed up. His gaze shot toward the door leading out into the palace hallway. He strode quickly forward and ripped it open. There was a yelp and a shuffling of feet.

"Get back here!" the viatari captain shouted as he gave chase down the hall.

Simon quickly leapt from the couch, following him and shouting, "Wait, Zael, come back!"

But Zael had already disappeared around the corner. Simon groaned, then followed. Drathanar moved to do the same but stopped mid-stride when Salevari help up a hand.

"Wait," she said sternly. "Two will be enough to catch him, especially with Zael leading the way."

"You think he intends to catch him?" Drathanar asked with a frown. "I fear he might kill him."

"No, he knows the importance of our mission. Whoever that was, they just got caught spying on us. We need to capture him so we can learn the reason for his presence. Then, if we like the answer, we can find out who he works for and then, if we're lucky, we'll have more pieces for this puzzle we find ourselves trying to solve."

Tera studied her. "You seem awfully relaxed considering what just happened. That human probably knows now that you're all viatari. He'll tell his masters."

"I expected our enemies to send spies against us. It's only natural. They would want to learn about these plains nobles who no one has ever heard of."

"Well then, let's hope Zael can catch him."

Salevari downed the rest of her wine and set down her glass, crossing her legs as she sunk deeper into the couch and closed her eyes. "I have no doubt that he will. Unless our enemies are craftier than we give them credit for, there's no chance they manage to shake Zael when he's on the hunt."

"Zael, stop where you are!" Simon yelled breathlessly, finally catching up to the viatari as he stood waiting in the middle of the courtyard just outside the palace.

The viatari captain glared over his shoulder with a scowl. "Why are you telling me to stop? He's going to get away."

Simon pointed at the guards standing beside the wrought-iron gates. "You can't just go around running at your full speed like a viatari here," he whispered harshly. "If you're going to give chase, you have to maintain your humanness."

"You want me to run slower?"

"Will that be a problem?" Simon raised an eyebrow. "I'd be surprised if you tell me you can't catch that eavesdropper without your extraordinary speed."

Zael scoffed. "I'll catch him, even if I could only walk. Are you coming?"

Simon nodded and the two set off. They passed the guards, who hadn't seen anyone suspicious come in or out of the gate.

"He must have climbed a portion of the wall, then." Simon ventured.

"Doesn't matter," Zael replied, pushing past the gates and making his way through the city streets, now alive with stumbling drunks and other locals enjoying their free time as they pleased. "I can sense his life-energies still. They smell strongly of fear." He pointed down a dark alleyway. "He went that way."

They ran down the alley onto another street. Simon let Zael take the lead, keeping his eyes open to their surroundings while the viatari kept searching for signs of their quarry.

As they continued their chase, the crowds around them thinned and the streets darkened as public lighting via torches and braziers became scarce. Eventually, they came across complete silence and darkness as Zael continued leading them to the outer edge of the city. The only thing providing any light for them to see with was the moon overhead.

"What did the man look like?" Simon whispered as they ran down yet another alleyway. The path they were on was worn and old and led to a large graveyard.

"I didn't see his face," was the murmured reply. "He had a mask on."

"How will you know you have the right man, then?"

The viatari spared a moment to regard his human companion. "I told you, I can sense their life-energies. It leaves a stench in its wake wherever he goes."

"So that's how you're tracking him?" Simon shook his head in amazement. "I didn't know your people could track their foes like bloodhounds."

A rare chuckle. "Not all of us can. This is a fairly unique ability I have."

Their path led to a large, empty park full of trees and benches burdened with creeping vines. A trail snaked through the patch of woods, forming a wide circle that eventually led back to where they now stood.

"He's here somewhere." Zael said softly, sniffing the air. "He's using the wildlife within these woods to mask his scent. Smart. I can't pinpoint where he's hiding." He indicated the trail splitting in two directions before them. "I'm going to follow the path on the right. You go the other way and we'll meet on the other side. With any luck, one of us will run into our man. Are you armed?"

Simon pulled out a curved dagger from his sleeve. Zael nodded.

"See you on the other side."

They went their separate ways. Simon took his time going down his part of the path. His senses weren't as sharp as the viatari's. He was sure Zael had no trouble seeing in this darkness. While the moon's light helped him, there were still too many dark patches that his vision couldn't penetrate.

It was the same with his hearing. Crickets chirped wherever he went. He heard the crack of branches off to his right but couldn't tell what had caused the noise. The soft call of owls mixed in with everything, occasionally making him jump.

Still, he pushed forward. Simon was a capable fighter. If the man they were chasing chose to ambush him, he was confident in his ability to defend himself.

There was the crack of a branch, louder than the ones he'd been hearing before. He tensed, turning around and holding his dagger out in front of him. Strong arms wrapped around his chest, pinning his own to the side. He yelled and thrashed with his whole body, kicking whoever was attacking him from behind as best he could, hoping to get in a lucky blow.

"Calm down, it's me."

Simon stopped thrashing and felt the pressure around his chest release. He breathed out, then rounded on Zael.

"What are you doing?" he seethed. "Why did you attack me? I thought you could see through life-energies or whatever."

Zael shrugged. "Yours were giving off strong fearful scents just like his were. I realized it was you when I came upon you, though. Otherwise, I would have immobilized you with my attack."

"How thoughtful." Simon frowned and tucked away his dagger. Not for the first time, he was glad he no longer considered the viatari his enemies.

"I'm guessing you saw no sign of him either, then?"

Simon shook his head. "It's a big park. Lots of places to hide."

Zael sniffed the air. "It seems he's given us the slip. His scent is already fading."

"Can't you follow it?"

The viatari shook his head. "I don't think so. If our quarry is smart, which he has already proven himself to be, he'll go back into the crowded parts of the city to mask what remains of his scent. Now that he's evaded us, his sense of fear will quickly die out. That's the only thing that was letting me follow him so easily."

"So, what do we do now?"

"As much as I hate to say it," Zael said bitterly. "We go back to Salevari empty-handed. Drathanar will enjoy this, I'm sure."

Simon sighed and crossed his arms. He looked back across the dark field to the other side of the park where they had started their search. He hoped to see some sign of a shadowy figure slinking away, but there were too many shadows to make any one out. With the trees moving as they were, he counted at least a dozen hooded figures escaping into the city at the same time.

CHAPTER NINETEEN

When Felix's forces returned to camp, the somber mood in the air compelled everyone to maintain silence. There were no discussions about what had just happened, no asking about missing friends, no reliving memories. A watch was set up and everyone else went to sleep. They would deal with the trauma of today tomorrow.

As for Felix, after hearing a report listing early estimates of how many they'd lost, he wheeled his horse straight for the central command tent, dismounted, and disappeared within its confines. He said not a word, nor spared anyone a glance. Thuradin only caught a glimpse of the elder viatari before he hid himself from view. His face had been haunted, on the verge of breaking. The dwarf could only imagine what was running through that ancient mind.

Realizing there would be no progress in the coming days and that the siege had returned to a standstill, Thuradin decided now was as good a time as any to take some leave so that he and Myrna might spend some time together. He brought their request to Serania, who only shook her head in a way that made the dwarf think this was the last thing she cared to have on her mind.

"Take a week," she said dismissively. "It's unlikely you'll come back to find any changes in this camp."

"I thought the same," Thuradin said with a touch of uncertainty. "Still, I thought I'd have ta fight a little more for this request, considering our losses."

"That's for me to worry about," Serania snapped. Her face contorted instantly with regret, and she shook her head again. "I'm sorry, you're not to blame for this disaster. We all must move past this loss in our own way. If that means you need a week away from this place, do what you must. Let me handle the realities of this situation we now find ourselves in. That's what my mother appointed me to do, after all."

Thuradin nodded. He wished he knew how to convey his sympathy and encouragement for her, but he also knew now was not the time for trite platitudes. Instead, the only words that left his lips before he turned and marched off were, "Good luck."

Packing their bags and mounting their rams, the two dwarves set out south until they found a perfect camping ground on the north bank of the River Lunadar. A thin stand of woods surrounded them. They pitched their tents in a small meadow only a few dozen feet from the river itself. The birds sang cheerfully, unaware of the troubles of the world. Squirrels poked their heads out curiously from their homes in the trees. Splashing came from the nearby river as if the fish, aware of their presence, were challenging the pair of dwarves to catch them. It was a challenge Thuradin was all too happy to oblige.

Now, on the sixth day after Felix's disastrous assault on the Three Spires, Thuradin found himself sitting on the bank of the River Lunadar, Myrna only a few feet to his right, rods out and cast and gripped comfortably in their hands. The sun shone brilliantly in a bright blue sky, its heat minimal. A nice breeze would gust past the dwarves every now and then, playfully flapping Thuradin's beard. It had been a week of peaceful leisure, the likes of which he'd rarely enjoyed during his long life.

The first few days had seen their fair share of awkwardness as he and Myrna hadn't had much opportunity to share a meal, much less a full conversation before now. They spoke in short sentences, bluntly, and once whatever topic they grasped onto had been fully exhausted after a few short minutes, they would sit in silence, staring at the coals that told of the fire they'd created the night before.

Those awkward moments were a thing of the past, however. Once they had grown more accustomed with each other, conversation flowed as easily as the river they camped next to. Thuradin was amazed at how simple it was to speak with his daughter. They shared stories about their lives in the Dwarven Kingdom. Thuradin spoke of his time with the royal guard, as well as the campaigns he'd been a part of during the early wars against the burrowers centuries ago. These stories Myrna had never heard before, and she listened with interest. She spoke of her exploits with her own company. She'd been assigned to the tunnel wall separating Tinas Ern from the outside world. It was a relatively quiet assignment but every now and then a grattle would wander into their tunnel which they would then have to dispatch. Aside from tales of the past, they discussed their favorite ales and the intricate balances required to brew them. Thuradin shared with her the recipe his own father had given him centuries ago.

"That is a Stonebeard secret," he said with a proud smile. Myrna's eyes went wide as she studied the list of ingredients he'd written down.

"And ye're giving it ta me?"

"Of course!" Thuradin chuckled. "Ye're a Stonebeard, aren't ye lass?"

The week had gone by quickly, and now with their final day before they had to return to camp upon them, Thuradin was loathe to watch the sun's progress through the sky.

They spent several hours of the morning fishing in their usual spot, but after a week of doing this, the fish had caught on to the tantalizing bait that magically appeared in their waters every day and stayed away. With no fresh catches to supplement their food stores, Thuradin roasted several squirrels he had snared the other day for their lunch. The smell of roasting meat quickly filled the meadow, and the dwarves ate with gusto, picking the small bones clean.

After lunch, they spent a few hours sparring, as they had much of the week. Thuradin had always known his daughter was a capable warrior, having seen her in action himself. Fighting her, however, gave him a whole new appreciation for her skills. They used sturdy wooden sticks they'd found in the woods rather than their actual weapons, which still hurt enough to leave welts if one of them became a little too overzealous with their attacks.

Myrna's skill with a buckler was impressive. With minimal movements, her protected left hand always managed to be in position to block his attacks, even finding its way past his own guard at times. She would charge him, buckler first, forcing him back. Then, with his balance off, she would swing her stick at his face, feint, then bring the weapon around toward his knees. If Thuradin hadn't been such an experienced warrior himself, the move would have easily led to his losing the match. As it was, he simply jumped over the attack, rolling to Myrna's flank where he was able to unleash a flurry of swings with his own two sticks.

They continued like this for hours, Thuradin giving pointers whenever he got past Myrna's defenses and laying on praise when she did the same to him. Finally, panting hard, sweaty, and with fresh welts forming, they dropped their practice weapons and took turns bathing in the cold river.

With night approaching, Thuradin roasted the rest of the squirrels and a fish he had been fortunate enough to snag with his bare hands during his dip in the river. They ate in relative silence, staring at the fire. They didn't voice it, but neither wanted the week to end, to return to the trials of their time. But they knew they had to. Duty commanded it.

"I hated ye."

The words had been said so softly, Thuradin wasn't sure he'd actually heard anything to begin with.

"What's that lass? Ye want some more fish?" A quick look told him her appetite was long gone.

"I hated ye," she said again, more forcefully.

Thuradin sat silently for a time, stoking the fire with a long stick.

"I know, lass."

"I hated ye because, growing up, it felt like ye had abandoned mum and me. Left us for the 'grand adventure' in Dun'Burell. That's what she always called it."

Thuradin said nothing. This was a conversation he'd known they would have eventually. It was inevitable. He had thought, with his exile in the Dwarven Kingdom lifted, they might have had it in a more familiar setting, but one thing had led to another and that opportunity had never come. Now it was here, and he knew better than to interrupt his daughter from releasing these pent-up feelings.

"Ye know," Myrna's green eyes reflected the flickering flames before her like glowing emeralds as she stared into them. "The last thing she told me before she passed was ta nae hold it against ye. Ta lend ye my support." Her gaze switched over to him. There was only the barest hint of an accusation in it, but it was quickly overshadowed by the general sense of confusion she felt. "She said yer call ta duty was more important than what we might have wanted for ourselves. Then she died, and her body now lies in the Halls of Stone."

Thuradin closed his eyes, remembering Agata. Her smile. Her cheery laugh like the sound of bells echoing in a cave. His heart twisted.

"For the longest time I blamed ye for her death because I felt yer so-called duty had been the cause of it, since it had taken ye away from us. Ye weren't there ta help her when she needed it most. And then when ye killed King Ronorim and everyone in the Kingdom whispered yer name along with the word 'traitor,' I didn't know what ta believe."

"I understand, lass," Thuradin said softly. "Ye need nae say more."

"But I do," she retorted forcefully. "I thought ye had forsaken duty, that ye never knew what it was ta begin with. Which is why when I chose ta become a warrior, I did so with the sole purpose of restoring the honor of our name by showing everyone what real duty was. But after witnessing the realities of this world, seeing the enemies we face here, and learning the truth behind all yer actions, I know now that I never knew what the word was myself. But ye always did, and I felt ashamed for how I had judged ye.

"I understand now why ye did everything ye've done from the beginning. And I wish ta follow in yer footsteps. Perhaps that's the real reason I followed the warrior's path. Some part of me must have known—or, at least, hoped for—the truth behind ye ta be something for me ta look up ta. Ta live up ta."

"And ye do well as ye are," Thuradin responded warmly. "Ye were right ta be angry with me, I did nae give ye the attention ye deserved when ye were a child and that's a mistake I see clearly now. I only regret it took me getting so old ta see it. But the past is done with. We cannae dwell on it, or it'll keep us trapped there ta our dying breath. I could nae be prouder of seeing the lass ye've become. And I know yer mother would feel the same."

Myrna nodded but clenched her jaw. She looked like she wanted to say more but was unsure if she should.

Dipping her head, she sighed, defeated. "I don't know *what* it is that I've become. I understand now, being duty-bound myself, what ye had ta go through when I was a child, the choices ye had ta make for our king and Kingdom. And I gladly make the same choices. But I have an easier time of it right now because I have no family that I could return ta. My only family, more often than nae, is right beside me on the battlefield. If I had a husband, had time ta bear children, I fear I would nae be able ta live up ta the same level of duty that ye did."

Thuradin eyed the last skewered squirrel dripping grease onto his lap and set it aside, his own appetite a distant memory. "What is it ye're asking, child?"

"I guess . . . I want ta know if it's impossible. Is it impossible for us ta have families and children ta nurture for the future and at the same time fulfill the duty we're honor-bound ta uphold when called upon?"

Crackling flames filled the night as Thuradin mulled over the question. Even the crickets and other night creatures quieted down so they could listen in on the answer.

"Duty is difficult," he said gruffly. "Duty is sacrifice, and when ye choose ta put it above all else, ye cannae second-guess it. Our job is nae ta win honor for ourselves or our name. It's ta protect those around us and our way of life—in this case, ta protect the world from those who would destroy it. That's why duty must be fulfilled, because ta neglect it puts everything ye know and love at risk.

"For me, though my heart yearned ta remain by yer side and yer mother's, I would nae dare risk yer safety for what we perceived at the time ta be a major threat ta our existence within the mountains. It's nae impossible . . . but it's certainly difficult to have a family and a calling ta protect others at the same time."

"How can it be done, then?" Myrna asked with a strained voice. Her brows furrowed. She looked desperate for an answer, as if it was the one thing that would keep her from drowning in this quagmire of doubt that tormented her.

But Thuradin shook his head. "Sadly, lass, that's an answer I cannae give. As ye pointed out fairly, I failed in maintaining my own family and fulfilling my duty at the same time. I couldn't balance the two. But I know it can be done. Others do it all the time and are no less honorable."

"Did ye know that would be a problem when ye and mum married?"

A frown played on Thuradin's lips, "I suspected."

"Then why get married at all?"

"Lass, even though we're blessed with long life—at least, compared ta humans—time is nae guaranteed ta us. When it comes ta love, ye must grasp it when the chance arises, for the chance doesn't come often for anyone. When I met yer mother I was only a guard under my father's command in Dun'Burell, but I knew instantly that she was the one for me. When love is true and destined, yer heart will know. . . . It's difficult ta describe the feeling, but it's almost an instinct."

"But ye never got ta enjoy the family ye helped create," Myrna said in a choked whisper.

Thuradin nodded sadly. "Aye, lass, and that's the sacrifice duty sometimes calls for. I cannae say I like it, but that's the truth of the matter. And I'll carry that regret with me ta my grave."

"Then, I shall never marry," Myrna said resolutely. "All I know is how ta fight and war and service, and I refuse ta make the same mistakes ye did."

Smiling kindly, Thuradin corrected her, "It was nae a mistake, daughter of mine. *Ye* were nae a mistake. If I were presented with the choice again, I'd make the same one. As I said, when love presents itself, ye cannae help but hold onto it. Ye're still young, child. There's still time for ye ta grow tired of wars and fighting, ta have yer desires change from grasping a sword ta grasping the small hand of yer child. There's time for ye ta find love. And when ye do find it, ye'll know. I think ye'll discover it'll be difficult then for ye ta forsake it."

Firewood burned through, collapsing into a heap of coals and ashes, sending hot sparks flying.

"It's late," Thuradin grunted, stoking the fire, though it appeared there would be no reviving it. "We have a full day's ride ahead of us tomorrow. We should get some sleep."

He stood up and made his way to his tent. Before he could lift the flap to enter, however, Myrna's voice called once more for his attention.

"Father," she said, looking at him with a warm smile that he had so rarely seen. The heat he felt from it was akin to the bed of coals that only recently had been protecting him from the chilly night air. "Thank ye for this week. I enjoyed my time with ye."

Thuradin beamed and ducked into his tent, murmuring, "As did I, my child, as did I."

The next day they knocked down their tents, tied their belongings to their mounts, and after a quick breakfast of eggs which they found in a nearby nest, began their long ride back to camp.

Though it took all day, Thuradin didn't feel any worse for wear by the time they reached their destination. Dusk had fallen, yet looking out across the sea of tents and the large number of warriors milling about aimlessly, he could tell nothing had changed since their departure, just as Serania had said it wouldn't.

"I must check in with my legion," Myrna said, guiding her ram onto a separate path.

"Go on, then," Thuradin nodded. "I'll see ye tomorrow."

He watched her ride off until he could no longer see her bouncing black hair. Then he dismounted and led his own ram to the stables, where he handed the reins off to one of the hands working there.

Yawning, he trudged through countless crisscrossing paths toward the dwarven grid, ready for a full night's sleep. He wasn't sure what would come tomorrow, but he was certain there was work to be done and he wanted to be as well-rested as he could for it. But first, he thought eagerly, perhaps there was enough time for a bowl of tobacco.

Entering his tent, he threw his bags onto his cot and dug through them, looking for his pipe and tobacco pouch. It wasn't until after he pulled them out, that he noticed a shadow move in the corner opposite him.

"Why 'ello there, commander."

Thuradin cursed. "Damn yer beard, Morteth. I swear ta Nythirim, if ye sneak inta my tent in the middle of the night again I'll drive my axes inta yer skull even after I realize it's ye."

The assassin laughed and stepped out from the shadows, letting his dark cloak flow out behind him. "Always a pleasure ta speak with ye, tha' it is."

Grumbling, Thuradin packed his pipe bowl vigorously with clumps of dried tobacco, spilling a fair amount. "Why are ye here now?"

"Commander, don' tell me ye forgot!"

"Forgot what?"

A devilish ambition entered the assassin's words, "The fate of Hork Anvilgar."

Thuradin froze, his fingers shaking off bits of tobacco from the clump he'd just pinched out his bag. He looked sharply at Morteth.

"What have ye done?"

Morteth shrugged, taking a seat on Thuradin's cot. "Nothin' yet. I just though' I'd come and discuss the plan I've devised for 'is most unfortunate passing." He cocked his head. "Nae havin' second thoughts, are we?"

Thuradin was about to say yes, of course he was, when an odd feeling crept over him. His mind felt muddled, the only thing it could focus on being images of Lyrie's tear-stained face, Hork's bruised, brutish hand. A fearful flinch. His initial hesitation converted into hot anger, and he resumed packing his pipe a little more forcefully.

"No."

"I'm 'appy ta hear tha'."

"Tell me yer plan."

"Well," Morteth jumped up excitedly, clapping his hands

as he began to pace in the small space. "As ye've assigned yer rival in love ta spend the remainin' years o' this world pushin' up flowers—"

"He's nae my—"

"—As ye say, commander, as ye say. Since ye've so deviously assigned me ta guide our esteemed Hork ta a much be'er life, but 'ave nae the stomach for the realities o' me line o' work, I 'ad ta do a fair bit of thinkin' ta come up with a suitable plan that'll complete the job and allow ye ta sleep at night."

Thuradin raised his eyes to the ceiling. "How long is this going ta take?"

Morteth ignored him and continued. "Jobs like this are tricky. Ye see, we want ta take out the target, but we don' want ta leave a scene tha' might make others question wha' really 'appened. Tha' immediately takes out methods involvin' blades or poisons. Poisons especially, since they can be so messy, as I'm sure ye remember."

An image of King Thelm Ironaxe lying on the floor of his room, his son Ronorim holding him as a constant flow of bubbling froth leaked from his mouth, blocking his airways, came to Thuradin's mind. It was one of his greatest shames that he had failed in protecting the king. Morteth was the one who had brought that particular shame to him.

"I remember," he growled.

"The next thing I had ta consider was the timing. I think it best this task take place durin' the wee night hours. Less of a chance that yer lassie walks in on me doin' the deed that way. Wouldn' want tha', now would we?"

Thuradin glowered silently. Morteth took the silence as acceptance and went on with his explanation, enjoying the taste of every word that passed his lips.

"Aye, we don' want the poor lass traumatized by 'er

'usband's early passin', so nighttime provides the best opportunity ta carry this out. However, the only issue with tha' is I'm nae sure if Lyrie sleeps in the same bed as 'er honorable 'usband or if she sleeps on the floor—or even in the same tent, for tha' matter—but I need ta make sure she's nae there when the time comes. That's where ye step in."

"Me?" Thuradin asked incredulously. "I'll nae take part in any of this business."

Morteth studied him for a moment, then smirked. "Ye already did when ye gave me the go ahead, commander. Besides, I only need ye for a distraction. Durin' the night, ye'll call Lyrie from 'er tent. Tell 'er ye wish ta speak in private, tell 'er wha'ever ye need ta but get 'er out and away from the tent. Then, while ye two are 'aving a lovely little chat, I'll make me move. I'll be in an' out in a matter of minutes, so that's how long ye must keep 'er talkin'," he hesitated, suddenly unsure. "Ye can 'old a conversation for a few minutes, can't ye?"

"How will ye do it?"

Grabbing a pillow, Morteth brought it to his face and mimed suffocating. Thuradin cringed. It was such a ludicrous way for a dwarf to die. It was almost comical. But nothing was truly comical about this situation.

"Really?" he asked. "A pillow? Ye're going ta suffocate him with a bloody pillow?"

Morteth shrugged. "'Tis a viable method, believe it or nae. It does the trick an' afterward, there's no sign tha' any foul play occurred, even if there's a struggle. Ta anyone else, it'll look like the wonderful dwarf known as Hork 'as passed away in 'is sleep."

Thuradin considered this with some alarm. He couldn't *believe* he was actually considering this course of action. Everything Morteth told him sounded well thought out. If it worked, then Hork would be out of the picture and then . . . and then what?

Lyrie would be free. But another part of him asked, *free for what?* Thuradin's brows furrowed. *She'd be free ta do as she likes without fear of her husband's hand.*

He nodded. That answer satisfied him enough, though the other side of him bringing forth these questions still didn't seem pleased.

"Well, commander?" Morteth asked confidently. He already knew what the answer would be. Thuradin hated to admit it, but he was right to be so confident. This had to be done.

"I'll provide the distraction. When do ye intend on doing it?"

"Tomorrow night," Morteth turned, his cloak flaring behind him as he said the chilling words. He left the tent, disappearing quickly into the shadows. Thuradin watched him go, his gaze slowly sinking to the pipe he still held in his hands. The idea of smoking no longer sounded appealing. Sighing, he put it away and collapsed onto his cot, hoping sleep would take him quickly. But he knew better. He was in for a long night of endless doubts, thoughts, and two sides of a mind waging war against itself.

CHAPTER TWENTY

Only one thought dominated Thuradin's mind the next day: Morteth's big plan. He imagined how it might happen, then replayed these images over and over in his head, feeling more distressed with each repetition. He was distracted, absent from the present, and those around him noticed.

"Are ye alright, Thuradin?" Borim asked with some concern as he watched his friend spill another spoonful of porridge onto the table. "The table doesn't need ta eat, ye know."

"Nae hungry," Thuradin murmured as he scooped up another spoonful of the gruel. Borim raised an eyebrow but said nothing else.

Several tables across from them sat Hork and Lyrie. Thuradin had been watching them all morning, observing their movements, watching their every action together. Today had been a rather mild morning in terms of Hork's behavior. For the most part, he'd ignored his wife, who'd been following him around camp dutifully and quietly. Now they sat together, both eating the same porridge he was, though Lyrie looked to be taking her time with hers.

His mind was a frazzled mess. Even so, Thuradin was determined to do his part in making what he had planned with Morteth a reality. Part of that plan involved leading Lyrie away from her tent on the pretext that he wanted to talk. But first he had to tell her he wanted to do so without Hork knowing. And so, he kept his distance, waiting for an opportunity to present itself. As he waited, another part of him continued to wonder why he was going through so much trouble, encouraging him to abandon this path before it truly was too late. But Thuradin tuned those thoughts out. He couldn't afford distractions.

With a grunt, Hork stood and took his bowl back into line for a second helping. Lyrie watched him go, and once he was far enough, let out a long breath, closing her eyes as if holding onto this single moment of peace and solitude with the hope that it would never end. Sadly, Thuradin couldn't let her have this. His opportunity had come.

Without mentioning anything to Borim, he stood and made his way over to Lyrie, gently putting his hand on her shoulder to let her know of his presence. She jumped and jerked her head around to see who had grabbed her. Upon seeing Thuradin she sighed in relief, though she remained on edge. Her eyes shot over to her husband in line, no doubt wondering if he would notice what was going on.

"I need ta speak with ye," Thuradin said firmly.

"Thuradin," Lyrie began. "I cannae—"

"Please, Lyrie. It's important. And it's a matter that must be discussed privately."

After a moment's thought, she finally nodded. "Alright, but it better be important. What is it?"

"Nae here," Thuradin whispered, keeping his eyes on Hork who was nearing the front of the line. Any minute, he would turn to head back to his seat and would see Thuradin speaking with his wife. Who knew what would happen after that within the privacy of a tent? Thuradin couldn't be the cause of that. "Nae now. Tonight. Meet me by the outcropping near the camp perimeter. The one that overlooks the Three Spires."

Understanding his urgency, Lyrie nodded and turned back to her porridge. Thuradin quickly returned to his own seat. Borim raised an eyebrow, concerned, after he turned to see who he'd been talking to.

"I hope ye're nae planning on stirring up trouble," was all he said.

Thuradin chuckled feebly as he shook his head but could say nothing in response. He feared his voice might betray him. He'd accomplished his goal for the day. Now all that was left was to wait for nightfall and Morteth would handle the rest. Until then, the long hours of the day loomed ahead.

Though it was well into the night, Thuradin was as wide awake as ever. His heart hammered incessantly. His mind spun dizzily as he continuously went over what was about to happen. The other part of him, the dissenting part, desperately tried to inject another dose of regret in a final effort to make him call off Morteth, but to little effect. The fact was he *did* feel regret for what he was allowing to happen, what he was participating in, but he also knew this was for the greater good. This was to help a long-time friend who so stubbornly refused to seek help herself.

Well, he thought, some things didn't need to be asked for. He watched the moon sitting high above on a dark throne of stars. It was full tonight, and its bright light draped over the surrounding landscape like a soft, white dress. Even the ominous Three Spires didn't seem so hostile.

Footsteps came from behind.

Thuradin didn't turn to see who it was. He already knew. And he knew what her arrival here meant. His heart sank as the reality of what was happening in the dwarven grid clicked. But it was only for a moment.

Lyrie didn't say anything as she sat down next to him, following his lead and gazing out at the pretty landscape before them. After a few minutes of this, she cleared her throat. The night was wearing on.

"What is it ye wanted ta speak ta me about, Thuradin? Ye said it was important."

"Aye," Thuradin said, his voice choking. "I'm just . . . trying ta think of how I should pose this question."

Lyrie looked at him curiously. He faced her. A soft breeze played with a few individual strands of blonde hair that hadn't been gathered and secured in her tight bun. Her eyes shone brightly under the moonlight and none of the uncertainties or fears that accompanied her when she was with Hork clouded her face. She was beautiful. Thuradin had always known this. But tonight he recognized it in a different way. His heart skipped and he berated himself. He also sent a curse Morteth's way for putting this idea of how he saw Lyrie in his head in the first place.

"I wanted ta ask," he finally said, turning away from her. He needed to focus on the conversation. It would do no good if their talk ended too soon. "What happened ta Hork?"

Lyrie winced. "What do ye mean?"

"Don't hide it from me," Thuradin said with some sternness. He wouldn't let her pretend. Not tonight. He wanted her to acknowledge what was really happening, if only so he could know that he wasn't making overreaching assumptions. "I can see the blemishes on ye from his hand. I can see yer whole demeanor change from the brave lass I know ta some helpless, docile thing when ye're near him. I'm nae the only one, either."

Her eyes were wide, terrified globes. Her breaths came in ragged gasps as she turned away. She brought her hands to her head and clenched her eyes shut as if trying to squeeze out some horrid memory.

"I remember how Hork used ta be," Thuradin continued in a softer voice. He put his hand on her shoulder for comfort and felt some tension release. "We used ta all be good friends, us three. So I want ta know what happened? What changed him?"

"Damn it, Thuradin," tears welled up in Lyrie's eyes, but she refused to let them fall. "Ye're right. Ye're right about all of it, though I don't want ta admit it."

He sat silently as she took a moment to compose herself. Once she regained control of her breathing, a familiar fierceness crept in, mixing with unfallen tears.

"It's true he was nae always this way. Ye remember him from the old days. But then ye must also remember what others would always say about us, about *him.* They'd always compare him ta ye. Probably because of how well we got along, but they'd mention things like how much better off I'd be with a dwarf like ye than someone like Hork."

Thuradin remembered. He'd always detested those remarks made by ruthless gossips and tried to stop them where he could. Surely Hork knew that. Surely he wasn't being pinned with the blame for those whispers.

"It got ta the point where he began ta grow paranoid that I would truly go behind his back and do something . . . dishonorable with ye," heat rose in Lyrie's face but she was determined to finish her story, so she pushed on. "I tried ta convince him that was madness, tried ta remind him that he was the one I loved. But he wouldn't listen. He dwelt on this paranoia. It ate at him. It was made all the worse because of how much he looked up ta ye, Thuradin."

"Me?" Thuradin balked at that. Hork looked up to him? Even back in the old days, he would have never expected such admiration.

"Oh aye," Lyrie laughed lightly, but it was short-lived. She brought her knees to her chest and rested her chin on them dejectedly. "Perhaps I should have been the one who was paranoid that he'd run off with ye, the way he used ta speak of ye sometimes."

She cracked a smile. Thuradin did not.

"Kidding, Thuradin," she sighed, shaking her head. "Anyway, this darkness within him grew by the day and led ta him leaning too heavily inta his drink and other . . . abuses. It turned him inta what he is today. Physically and emotionally."

An owl called from above and swooped down, grabbing a scurrying mouse only a few feet from where they sat. The rodent squeaked desperately from the owl's talons as it was spirited away. Thuradin watched this happen with dispassionate interest, his thoughts dwelling on another similar scene that was surely happening this very moment. He imagined the struggle. The sense of surprise he would feel, followed by the helplessness in knowing he couldn't fight back. Breaths would come with more difficulty as the seconds passed, a soft but heavy object dashing any hope for one more fresh lungful.

"Thuradin?"

Thuradin shook his head, shattering the scene. "Sorry. Been a long day. I find myself dozing off more often now than before."

She stared at him for a moment before answering, "I suppose so."

"Anyway," he wanted to bring the focus of the conversation back to her. "If ye saw Hork changing as ye did this whole time why are ye putting up with it? Why nae leave it all behind?"

"I made an oath, Thuradin," Lyrie said firmly. It was almost a reprimand, a reminder of what dwarven marriage was. As if Thuradin had forgotten. "I swore ta love him until our dying days. It's more painful than ye can imagine ta watch someone ye love with all yer heart decay inta someone ye hardly recognize. But I still love him because I know who he can be. That's why I stay with him. That way, when he finally grabs hold of his senses and comes back, I'll be able ta say proudly that I was a part of that, that I fulfilled my oath."

"Ye still love him?"

"Of course I do."

"Ye truly believe he'll come back from who he is now?"

A pause. In a soft voice, Lyrie answered, "I have ta hold onta that hope. I have ta believe that our love is strong enough ta weather any tribulation."

Thuradin shook his head, kicking a nearby pebble off the overlook and watching it fall to the field below. "Ye're an admirable lass, Lyrie."

She shrugged. "It's nae an easy task I've set upon myself. He hits me, as ye've guessed. He yells at me, hurls words at me like daggers. But I still love him, and I won't let him push me away. That's what love is ta me."

With each word said, Thuradin felt himself sinking a little more into the dark hole he had dug himself. They had been speaking for half an hour now. If Morteth was as quick as he claimed to be, his job was done. The deed was done. There was no turning back now. And now was exactly when Thuradin wished he could call the whole thing off.

"I know why ye're asking me these things," Lyrie mentioned, her gaze fixated on the moon as it slowly rose, carving its way through the black ink. "It's funny. I don't think those remarks people made about us would have bothered him so much if there hadn't been an echo of truth in them."

They looked at each other, moonlight filtering through the small gap of space between them. Thuradin felt his breath catch. Lyrie punched his arm, a sly grin playing on her lips.

"Come now, Thuradin. Don't tell me ye never noticed my feelings. I noticed yers."

"Ye're saying—"

"Aye."

"Since when?"

"All along."

"Then why. . . ?" Thuradin was lost for words. His mind spun now more than ever. He felt his imagination getting carried away. Perhaps Morteth *had* had a point after all.

Lyrie sighed, her shoulders drooping. "We were nae fated, Thuradin. We never had the right moment. Ye already had Agata when we met. Then I found Hork before she passed. It wasn't meant ta be. But I couldn't help feeling how I did and I know ye couldn't either. Still, that's another reason why I must hope that I can help Hork return ta who he was. I fear I'm partly ta blame for his transformation."

"That's unfair ta yerself."

"Perhaps. But it's how I feel."

Lyrie yawned, then pushed herself onto her feet. She looked down at him.

"I appreciate yer concern for my situation, Thuradin, but know that ye cannae get involved. It'll only make things worse."

She turned to leave. Thuradin shot his arm out behind him

and grabbed her by the hand, stopping her in her tracks.

"Tell me," he said, a hint of desperation following his words. "Tell me outright. If yer situation was unsustainable, if it became too much ta bear, would ye ask for help. Would ye truly?"

Lyrie stared at him, her mouth hanging open in surprise. Then came a sad smile. She squeezed his hand and let go. His arm fell to the side, the part of his hand that had held hers still prickling with warmth.

"If it came down ta such a case," she said slowly, like she was thinking of the answer as she spoke it into existence. "Ye would be the first one I asked ta help me."

Without another word she turned and disappeared into the line of tents.

Thuradin sat back down on the outcrop. He couldn't think, couldn't focus. He was only supposed to have served as a distraction, but he'd learned much from that conversation. And now . . . now with what he knew, a single thought dominated his mind.

What have I done?

The next morning a piercing scream woke the camp.

Thuradin jumped out of his cot, bewildered, confused, not fully awake yet. Another scream. It was animalistic, desperate, terrible.

Was the camp under attack?

Grabbing his axes, he rushed outside, running to where the sound was originating from. Other dwarves were following his example, all with the same alarmed expression. It soon became apparent where the screaming was coming from. Thuradin's feet turned to lead as he slowed to a stop. Others continued rushing past him.

Hork and Lyrie's tent stood before him. Inside was a cacophony of noise, all drowned out by that one blood-curdling scream.

Knowing what he was about to witness, Thuradin forced himself forward until he was standing just outside the tent. The screams broke down into a mournful, high-pitched wail. He opened the flap and stepped inside, pushing past a few other dwarves who were standing by the entrance.

Inside, lying on his cot on his back was Hork Anvilgar. Still, pale, with half of his body already turned to stone from *entombment*. Kneeling beside him, her face buried into his stiff body, was Lyrie. Her normally tight bun was undone. Her blonde locks fell all over the place as if a storm had taken control of each individual strand. Her eyes were puffy and red. Her cheeks were glossy with tears. Her voice was hoarse, but still she wailed.

A few more dwarves rushed into the tent, pushing past everybody. They made their way to Lyrie, tentatively gripping her shoulders. They were Enurg'en. Thuradin could tell by the robes they wore and the layers of stone necklaces around their necks, marking them as dedicated servants of Nythirim.

"Lass, ye need ta move away now," one of them said gently.

"Aye, we're going ta do what we can ta slow his entombment so we can move him back ta the Dwarven Kingdom."

Lyrie nodded, still crying but allowing herself to be pulled away. The Enurg'en took position on either side of Hork's body and began chanting, one hand hovering over the earth while the other hovered over the body.

Thuradin felt hollow, as if his heart had been ripped out but he was still somehow allowed to live without it. He knew now, without a shadow of a doubt, that what he'd allowed Morteth to do, what *he* had done, had been a mistake. A fatal mistake. He shook his head barely managing to keep from letting loose a slew of curses against himself. He could do that later. How could he have ever thought this was a good idea?

As several dwarves volunteered their services to help carry out Hork's body while the Enurg'en continued chanting, Lyrie looked around the room. Her eyes widened as if she just now realized how many dwarves she'd summoned here with her wails. They fell on Thuradin.

"*You*," she whispered, a shaking finger pointing directly at him.

The word struck him like a hammer. He wanted to leave, to run and avoid the accusation he knew was about to be lobbed at him, but he was frozen in place.

"Ye killed him."

Everyone's eyes turned his way, disapproving and suspicious, a lasting symptom of his former banishment. He felt the pressure from their gazes. He felt exposed. So exposed.

He responded with the first thing that came to mind. It was dishonest, dishonorable. But he couldn't bring himself to speak the truth because he himself couldn't understand how he'd condoned such a thing.

"I did no such thing. How could I have? Why would I have?"

"Because of what we spoke about last night. Because you saw what Hork was doing ta me and ye took it on yerself ta be the solution, didn't ye?" Lyrie shot back, venom in her voice.

"That's ridiculous," Thuradin grasped around, trying to think of a way out of this. "And ye just said yerself. We were together last night talking. How could I have done it?"

"Ye hired someone ta do the deed, then," Lyrie seethed. "But the blame still falls on ye."

"Lyrie, come now. . . ." Everyone's gaze remained on him. They accused him. They were right to, but he suspected they would have accused him even if he truly had been innocent. He squirmed under the scrutiny of so many of his peers. "How do ye know he didn't die naturally? He looks peaceful enough ta me. If he hadn't already started entombment, I would've thought he was just asleep."

But Lyrie shook her head, a sob escaping her lips as she said, "Hork doesn't sleep on his back." She screamed in fury and tore at her hair.

The surrounding dwarves looked at Thuradin with even more disgust as if that revelation alone was proof enough that he must be involved with this crime. He looked at each of them, desperate to convey his remorse; or, at least, his confusion. His eyes found Myrna's, who had joined the forming crowd. She stared back at him like he was a stranger. Shaking her head, she turned and left, marching back to where she had come from. She'd heard enough.

Thuradin tried one more time to make a desperate plea, reaching out for Lyrie and grabbing her hand as he had last night. She stood stock still but didn't pull away. Perhaps that was a good sign.

"Please, lass, ye must believe me when I say that Hork was once my friend. I wouldn't hurt him, much less kill him."

Lyrie turned slowly with a manic expression, on the verge of breaking down.

"Ye lie," she whispered, her voice cracking. She looked down at her hand, still enclosed in his and yanked it free. She lunged forward, taking Thuradin by surprise and shoving him hard, knocking him to the ground. She stood over him, a dark shadow hiding her features. "Is this what ye expected, Thuradin?"

"I don't—"

"Did ye expect ta come in here once I discovered my husband had been murdered and just sweep me off my feet?"

Thuradin sputtered, trying to spit out a denial but nothing intelligible came out. That seemed to be answer enough for her. She turned and joined the dwarves carrying Hork's body, helping them lift him out of their tent.

Before she left, she called out to him once more, "Leave, Thuradin. Leave me with my husband."

Even after she was gone, everyone else remained where they were, their eyes never leaving the disgraced dwarf before them. Thuradin figured he should at least be grateful that Hork was disliked by so many others in the dwarven camp, otherwise they might have attacked him themselves to carry out an honorable vengeance, even if all they had was a suspicion that he was involved. As it was, they left him alone. For now. Thuradin wondered if it would be better if they hadn't.

Pushing himself up, he left the tent, not wanting to be the center of attention anymore. He had a lot to figure out. First and foremost, why he had hired Morteth to do this. It was completely dishonorable, an act he had been resisting now for months in his own head. Every time, it had been ousted with little effort, until recently. What had changed? Surely, it wasn't him. The idea of condoning the assassination now appalled him as much as any time before. He found the mental fog he'd been enduring since he came back to camp had dissipated somewhat, but not completely. His thoughts were a little clearer, now. Clear enough for him to wallow in regret.

As he trudged back to his tent, hoping to escape into its confines for the day so he didn't have to endure the judgment of the whole siege camp, his eyes were drawn to the Three Spires in the distance. They loomed overhead like a dark crown. An ominous aura seemed to surround them, but they were just rocks. His dwarven intuition told him there should be nothing inherently evil about the mountains themselves. But now, he couldn't trust himself to know anything. He buried his face in his hands and wished he could disappear.

CHAPTER TWENTY-ONE

Time was a loose construct within the dark cave Victria and her companions were being held prisoner. How many days had passed? How many weeks? Had it been months already? Victria couldn't begin to guess. All she knew was that she was exhausted. Her mind felt dull. Her limbs ached from their constant restraints. Her body stank. More prevalent than anything else, however, were the pangs of hunger she felt.

Their caretakers fed them enough to keep them alive, but only just. Even a single plump rat would have been sufficient to reinvigorate them. As it was, all they were given were sickly creatures minutes away from dying naturally and bugs. Lots of bugs. They had life-energies like anything else, so the viatari were able to feed on them. But theirs were worse than the sickly critters. They left a sour taste in the mouth and did little to nourish them. Their bodies often felt weaker than before when they were forced to eat them.

However much time had passed, they hadn't been left alone for much of it. Gar'Gir was a constant shadow among them, carrying out his experiments and jotting down notes on his old, stained journal. Often, he would come into the cavern while they slept, rudely rousing the viatari from their slumber. Rest was a rare luxury, but even when they did have it, it was always brief and troubled.

Victria didn't have nightmares, instead her dreams were sweet. She often saw herself back home in Aleganthia, watching everyone go about their day from the high balconies of the keep. She would dream of Felix, of Thuradin, of Tera, but their faces faded with each subsequent vision. Every time she woke, an intense yearning bordering on physical pain pierced her chest and crept along her whole body. Tears would form. She didn't know which state of being was worse, to sleep and dream or stay awake and witness the day's tortures.

For now, she was awake in her living nightmare.

Screams and pained gasps filled the cavern. Natiari was strapped to the metal table. Sweat ran down her body as she writhed. Gar'Gir observed her with an amused interest. He reached over and took her pulse as another spasm took hold.

"Mmm," he said, his voice carrying. "These brainwyrms are proving effective at knocking down mental defenses." He took out his journal and a well of ink, dipped his quill, and wrote a few notes.

Victria bared her fangs and jerked her arm toward her with as much strength as she could muster. As always, the chain digging into her blistered wrists remained taut. She'd tried to snap free from her bonds like this a hundred times and a hundred times received no reward.

That wouldn't keep her from trying. New surges of determination always seemed to run through her when she was forced to watch her friends suffer, even when she didn't understand the type of pain Natiari was going through at the moment. As of yet, she hadn't been subject to this new "brainwyrm treatment" that Gar'Gir had spent hours explaining to them. She didn't remember much of what he'd said, but she did know that these new wyrms targeted their minds.

Gone were the days when Gar'Gir gleefully studied the limits of physical pain their bodies could withstand. Now he had moved on to observing the intricacies of mental anguish. Whatever he was doing, it seemed to be yielding results.

Gar'Gir limped to where Natiari's head struggled, streams of blood and sweat running down her forehead. Her eyes were closed but fluttered under her lids rapidly like she was dreaming. The burrower put both hands around her temples and Natiari's writhing stopped. Her eyes popped open and she took in a long, shuddering breath.

"Tell me," Gar'Gir spoke urgently, shaking the viatari's head to force her focus on him. "What do you remember? Quickly, before the images fade."

Natiari choked back a sob, "I saw, . . ."

"Yes?" The burrower's eye bulged with excitement.

But her mouth snapped shut along with her eyes and she shook her head. Gar'Gir let out a disappointed sigh but quickly recovered.

"No matter," he shrugged. He retrieved a jar of drain-wyrms and applied one to Natiari's forehead before undoing her bonds.

Victria wasn't sure that the parasite was necessary anymore. Of all of them, Natiari appeared to be the one worst affected by their captivity. Her skin had turned a sickly, pallid color. Her strength was long gone. She rarely spoke, even when they were free of Gar'Gir's stifling presence. She watched their tormentor throw her friend over his shoulder like a sack of grain and carry her to her section of the cavern. He rechained her arms and legs with practiced hands and let her go. Her head lolled to the side. She was already unconscious.

Beside her, Madira whimpered.

Gar'Gir's mad gaze flashed excitedly, drawn to the sound.

"The experiments must continue," he said with a rotten grin as he limped over. "When one can go no further, another must take their place."

He reached out to undo Madira's chains even as she tried to shrink away.

"Stop!" Victria cried out, heat in her voice. Tears rushed down her dirt-caked face. She couldn't hold them back. Nor did she allow herself to feel the smothering weight of embarrassment because of them. She bared her fangs at the burrower and jerked her arms one after the other, trying to break her chains but to no avail. "Don't touch her!"

Gar'Gir froze, watching her display of defiance. His excitement grew. Shuddering with anticipation, he gleefully turned away from Madira and limped over to Victria.

"Yes, the defiant one," he dropped his face down to her level and brought it close. She tried snapping at it, hoping to snag some part of him so she could drain his life-energies, but his reflexes were too fast for her.

His hacking laughter filled the cavern. "You *are* a feisty one. I know you only wish to protect your friend over there but . . . yes, perhaps you are right." He applied a second drainwyrm to Victria's forehead. She was the only one who still required two to make her docile enough to move. She felt her chains come undone but couldn't feel much else.

"You haven't undergone the brainwyrm treatment yet, my dear, have you?" He shook his head, clicking his tongue. "We must change that. It will be good to see the effects of that wonderful tool on a *fresh* specimen. Yes. Yes. I am so glad you spoke up and volunteered. *Yes!* This will be an excellent experience, I can already tell."

Stumbling, Victria could do nothing but follow along as Gar'Gir's strong arms dragged her from her corner of the cavern to the table. He splayed her onto it and expertly secured her limbs so that she couldn't move. The haze instantly lifted from her mind as the burrower removed both drainwyrms.

There was a moment of intense clarity within her mind. A small burst of energy flowed back into her limbs. Perhaps if she could just . . . but then Gar'Gir's visage returned and dominated her vision, his face close to hers again and any thought she might have had about resisting or escaping was forgotten. A long, skinny black worm wriggled between his fingers.

"The brainwyrm," Gar'Gir declared in awe. "Do you remember what I told you about what it does, my dear?"

Trembling, but unable to control it, Victria shook her head.

"Ah, no matter," He shrugged, taking the brainwyrm out of her line of sight. She felt something tickle against her ear. "You'll experience it soon enough. I, for one, can't wait to discuss these results with you." He grinned, a mad glint in his eye. "Sweet dreams."

A sharp drilling sensation pierced her ear. Victria tensed up and yelled, trying to force her arms from their bonds as the brainwyrm squirmed deeper into her ear canal. Finally, the pain passed beyond her ear and her mind went completely numb. She gasped. Her eyes drooped of their own accord. She tried to lift her head, but it felt as heavy as a mountain. Unable to fight it anymore, her eyes closed completely.

When next they opened, she found herself in a familiar room. Beams of sunlight streamed in through tall, arching windows. Victria sat up, gasping. Her heart pounded as she looked around with growing confusion. She was back in her room. But how was she here? The last thing she remembered was being chained up in the dark caves of the Three Spires . . . and that terrible, vile face. But those dark images were fading fast from her memory, as if they had only been a terrible dream.

She brought a hand to her face. Her cheeks felt warm and flush, but her skin was clean. Her hair was smooth and silky, a brilliant sheen of silver. She touched her forehead but couldn't feel any sort of blemish or scar from wyrms latching on.

Had it really only been a dream?

Victria tossed away the bedsheets and lifted herself out of bed. She felt her usual strength. There was no hint that she'd been held captive in a dark cave for who knows how long. She went to her bedroom mirror and saw her reflection. Looking back at her was the same person she'd always seen before, though her face was now riddled with confusion.

A stutter of energy originating from her stomach distracted her. She was hungry. Ravenous. Marching to her food pantry, she pulled the door open and stared. Inside were cages of chickens, small pigs, a few reptiles, and a large number of smaller critters, exactly as it had been the last time she remembered being back home.

Without dwelling too much on it, she took a couple of chickens and several squirrels and devoured them, leaving a pile of dried husks in her wake. Energy coursed through her body, refreshing her. She let out a sigh of relief and smiled, but there was still just a single worm of doubt that what she was experiencing wasn't real, was somehow being manipulated.

Still, if that was the case, she didn't know how to stop it. Her only option, then, was to learn more about where and when she was and discover what was really happening, and perhaps how to escape it if need be. She opened the door leading into the keep's main hallway and stepped out.

Several viatari were carrying out their daily tasks; dusting surfaces, beating dust out of the drapes hanging from each window, sweeping the floors. Victria walked past them, greeting them as they noticed her. So far, everything seemed normal. She didn't know why she was letting this small doubt consume her still. The terrible images of her chained up in a cave and her friends being tortured were almost forgotten by now. If she found one of them, confirmed that these memories were indeed only a nightmare she'd had, perhaps then she could let herself fully relax.

She strode with purpose through the keep's hallways, catching glimpses of the city below. Seeing the bright, white walls of Aleganthia in the distance brought a smile to her face. She made her way up and down several flights of stairs, passing between floors in her search for a familiar face.

Finally, just as she was about to go down to the first floor and leave the keep entirely so she could search the city itself, she stumbled into her favorite dwarf, one who had come to be such a dear friend. Thuradin Stonebeard was walking her way, his gray, braided beard flapping back and forth with each step.

"Morning, lass," he called out to her. He stopped short when he saw the look on her face. "Are ye feeling alright? Ye look like ye've just seen a ghost."

Victria let out a shaky breath. The moment she'd seen him her nightmare had come back to her. She remembered the moment of her capture. She remembered watching Thuradin disappear in the underground pools as the vashi he clung to liquefacted out, leaving her and her friends alone and trapped. She reached out and gripped him by the shoulders, doing her best to keep her voice calm.

"Thuradin, what day is it?"

The dwarf eyed her curiously. "It's Thursday, lass."

"Thursday, when?"

He shook his head. "I don't know what ye mean."

"Have we gone to the Three Spires yet?"

Now Thuradin really let his worry show. He reached up to her forehead, feeling her cheeks. "Are ye feeling sick, lass? Why are ye asking me these things?"

"I just need an answer," she responded softly.

Thuradin opened his mouth like he wanted to ask more. A moment passed, then he shrugged.

"Our scouts are still searching for a good spot ta set up a siege camp, but we haven't set out for the Three Spires yet, in case ye didn't notice. We're all still here."

Victria grabbed hold of this piece of information and picked it apart. If her time in the caves *had* been a dream, then everything she saw from this moment on to her capture had only been her imagination. Months of time had passed, and all of it imagined? Could that really be possible?

She took a step back and leaned against the wall. Her heart was still hammering away, enough to steal her breath for a moment. She knew Thuradin was staring at her with concern, but she ignored him. She needed to figure this out.

"Lass, I think ye should go see someone about this. I've never seen ye this way and we need ye in top shape if we're—"

But she wasn't listening anymore, because she had just seen someone she thought she would never see again. What little breath she had left her completely. Her feet moved by their volition as she passed Thuradin and made her way for the end of the hall where Felix was walking. The shape of his name left her lips, though her voice caught in her throat.

Felix moved out of sight into the next hallway and Victria

started to run. There was something familiar about what was happening here that still bothered her. It was as if this were her second time reliving this day. She cast the thought aside.

There was only room for one thing in her mind right now. If there was one lesson she had learned from her terrible dream the night before it was to not put off what she could do that day. There was no guarantee that they would all return from the Three Spires. If something were to happen . . . well, she didn't want the bitter taste of regret to follow her as it had in that nightmare.

"Felix!" she called out once she had him in her sights again.

The elder viatari's back straightened, his head perked up as if he had been snapped out of some long-winded thought. He was in the middle of turning to face her when she launched into him, wrapping her arms around him and burying her head into his chest.

"Victria?" he stammered, looking down at her in utter shock.

She looked up into his eyes, her own fierce and determined. She would not let him go. She refused to let this chance slip away. She needed to tell him what was in her heart.

"I love you, Felix," she said. Hard as she tried to resist them, nerves still caused her voice to quiver, but she pushed on. "I love you. I've loved you for as long as I can remember."

"What–I–"

Without waiting for him to say anything else, she leaned in, her lips locking with his. Felix's body stiffened for a moment but then relaxed and she felt his arms wrap around her body. She could feel his breath on her cheek as they stayed like that. A smile of sheer joy played on her lips. It was a moment of pure exhilaration, the likes of which she'd never experienced and only imagined.

Then, her smile faded.

Felix's arms fell abruptly from her body. He leaned his full weight against her. His lips, which had been warm and comforting, turned cold and still like stone. A different sensation from the soft caresses they'd been giving her took shape. Like something was crawling into her mouth.

Separating from him, she saw a stream of white maggots burst out and fall from his lips. They squirmed in midair as they fell and wriggled away once they hit the floor. She desperately spat out the few that had been transferred to her, gagging as she realized what had happened. But what *had* happened? There were a range of feelings whirling inside her in that moment but only one held dominance. Absolute confusion.

"Felix, what is this?" she screamed.

Turning to him, she could see his face was ashen. His eyes had turned black and he stared ahead as if he saw nothing. Now, without her weight to hold him up, he stumbled forward a few steps and fell. Victria caught him, turning him urgently onto his back and touching her hands to his forehead.

He was hot. Burning. Steam drifted from him at a steady pace.

"Victria?" he called out to her, his voice raspy.

Tears burned the corners of her eyes as she recognized what this was. This was the same corrupting sickness Felix had been infected with when he drank the black water from the north. Water that had been corrupted by The Turned One.

But how could he be sick again? He'd received the antidote already.

Unsure of what to do, she held onto him tightly, caressing his short-cropped hair while doing her best to keep from breaking down.

He needed help. She needed to get him that help.

Tearing her gaze away from her love to call for it, she froze. Before her stood a burrower in a long white robe. His single eye shone with intelligence and a predator's grin revealed blackened teeth.

Instantly, Victria felt as if the floor around her was collapsing, that she was falling. She knew now what this was. *This* was the dream; or rather, a memory of an opportunity she'd had to share her feelings with Felix. In the actual event, however, her nerves had gotten the best of her and Felix had walked away none the wiser. She remembered watching his back shrink away.

This . . . Felix lying on her knees, slipping away faster than she would have believed possible. Their kiss. None of that had happened in reality. This wasn't real, but somehow her tormentor had manipulated her memory enough to make her believe that it was, had manipulated the events within the memory itself. Had he been watching her this whole time?

"So, this is what keeps your hope alive," Gar'Gir nudged Felix's gasping body with his foot. He chuckled. "Your source of strength. How pathetic."

"What is this?" Victria whispered in horror. Her eyes were drawn back to Felix. As terrible a sight as he was, it was still better to look at him than at the grotesque being standing over her.

"The brainwyrm," Gar'Gir said smugly. "I told you its effects already, but you clearly didn't listen. It lets me see through your memories, bending them as I will, corrupting them. By doing this we get to witness a special kind of mental pain. After all, what happens to the mind when it no longer bears any memory of what made life worthwhile for the subject? Does it continue on in pain? Does it die? I'm eager to find out."

Felix gasped. His body convulsed, then he was still. His chest was still. Victria let the tears fall. Though she knew what she saw was false, her body and mind couldn't help but react as if it were real. As if her love's death had truly come to pass.

"This isn't real," she seethed through gritted fangs. "I'm still in the cave."

Gar'Gir nodded sagely. "Very good, viatari. But that doesn't make what you're experiencing any less real."

She stared up at him. Her red eyes narrowed in fury. "I will kill you, even if it takes my last breath, monster."

He leaned in close and stroked her cheek with a long, gnarled finger.

She flinched.

"Ah, but the experiment is only beginning," he chuckled with glee. "Come, let's see what other memories we can corrupt."

CHAPTER TWENTY-TWO

Victria awoke with a jerk of her body. She breathed in deeply as a wave of nausea filtered from her head down to her toes. Her skin prickled and she felt the need to scratch her arms and legs vigorously. She looked around.

Trees surrounded her. Tall, familiar trees that reached high into the sky, their green-leafed arms stretching out toward each other in a continuous canopy that swayed peacefully and synchronously as the wind commanded. A breeze played with some loose strands of her hair, guiding them into her dry mouth, which she promptly spit out.

Instantly, an image of her spitting out maggots flashed through her mind. She put a hand over her mouth as if she might be sick and pushed herself onto her knees, but nothing came out other than a weak whimper. Her eyes took in her surroundings, wide and frantic.

The breeze brought with it the earthy scents of home. A heavy weight of unease perched upon her shoulders. Her instincts told her something about what she was seeing was wrong. She tried to remember her dream, but only garbled fragments came forth.

She had thought her dream was real . . . and then it wasn't . . . and then it was again. She took her hand from her mouth and stared at it. She picked up one of the numerous leaves that cluttered the forest floor and felt its brittle body. It bent easily as her fingers played along the edges. She put it to her lips. Bitter, dry. Just as she remembered.

She was somewhere in the forest surrounding Aleganthia.

Why had she fallen asleep here? And why couldn't she remember what she'd been doing before she decided to lie down on a bed of leaves?

The sound of rustling from behind brought her to attention. She turned, her heart quickening, and jumped to her feet, lowering herself into a fighting position. More rustling. The foliage was too thick for her to see through it, so she waited in anticipation for whatever was making the noise to come out.

She didn't know what to expect out of the dense wall of undergrowth and trees, but when she saw Felix step into the small clearing a load of weight lifted off her.

Conflicted feelings took turns piercing her heart. She was so glad to see him, as if she thought she might never get to again. Even so, she kept her guard up. Felix shouldn't be here. But of course he should, they were home in their forest, where they had been for so many centuries.

You've fallen for this once before.

The fleeting thought made Victria's uneasiness return. An image of Felix wasting away in Aleganthia's keep took hold, his eyes black and unseeing. But as quickly as it came, it left, and was immediately forgotten.

"Nice nap?" Felix asked, a quizzical smile playing on his lips. His eyebrows arched in concern. "You do not look well."

Victria shook her head resting her hands on her knees.

"Bad dreams, I think. I feel drained."

The elder viatari nodded sagely. "It is not as restful as you might think sleeping in this forest. I did try to warn you."

They stood there for several minutes while Victria recuperated her strength. Finally, taking a deep breath, she relaxed and took in her oldest friend, staring deep into his eyes. They were the same deep red that she remembered, the same ancient feel behind them. Her heart stuttered.

"Shall we continue our hunt?" Felix asked, reaching out for her hand as if to lead her forward. She took it.

That was it. A hunt. That was why they were out in the forest. Felix had asked her that morning if she would join him in stalking a large elk he had observed from the wall the other day. They would feast on it together before the sun set and then return to Aleganthia. Another day perfectly spent.

"I'm surprised you let me nap while we were hunting," Victria huffed, taking her hand back from Felix once they were back on the elk's trail. Her mind lingered on the weathered feel of his palm, the strength of his fingers. "I hope the elk didn't gain too much of a lead on us."

Felix shrugged, his eyes fixated on the forest floor as he followed barely perceptible signs of the beast's movements.

"The forest may be large but there are only so many places such an animal can go. We will find him no matter how long we delay, I think. Besides," he looked back at her and winked. "You looked like you needed the rest. Rough night?"

Victria laughed hollowly. "You have no idea."

But when she tried to think of what she'd done the night before that had worn her out so much, her mind came up blank. She tried harder to recall the past day's events, just as a red-speckled bird flew in a strange, low arc from one tree branch to another all while producing three sharp chirps.

"I knew that bird was going to do that," she said, her tongue dry and heavy in her mouth. There was something wrong about how familiar the avian's movement was. Like she had seen it before, but only once. A unique movement that could never be reproduced. Except in a dream. Or a memory. She felt time slow down as she looked at the trees around her with a growing awareness.

"Birds do that all the time," Felix stated, confused.

Victria shook her head. "Not like that."

He studied her. "Should we go back to the city? Perhaps you are getting sick."

"No, let's keep going," she walked past him, briefly squeezing his arm if only because she wanted to feel how real he could be. "I need to make sure what I'm thinking is correct."

"And what might that be?"

Victria didn't answer.

The two continued making their way through the forest. Felix took back the lead, his focus once more on tracking their quarry. They entered another clearing where sunlight broke through a gap in the trees, brilliantly lighting up a small part of the forest floor.

They looked up. Clouds floated high over the gap. Felix chuckled as he pointed one of them out.

"Maybe it is the angle, but that one—"

"Looks like a dwarf," Victria finished in a monotone voice.

He glanced her way, eyebrows raised. "Yes. How did you know I was going to say that? Was it that obvious?"

"No," Victria sighed, looking away from the bright sky and moving on. Though the leaves and grass around her were all so vibrantly green and even the tree bark seemed to glimmer like bronze, everything she saw was taking on a dim hue.

"I just remember you telling me that before."

"How–?"

Victria whirled around, marched back to Felix, grabbed his face and firmly planted her lips on his. He grunted in surprise but didn't push away. She stayed on him like that for some time, relishing the moment, wishing it was real, hoping it was real. She was almost certain now that it wasn't.

She pulled away. He gasped, looking down at her with a new sense of wonder.

"Victria, I–"

"You're not real, my love," she said softly, stroking his cheek.

A pause. Felix cracked a smile and chuckled. Taking her hands in his, this time much more purposefully, he said, "Not real? If that was not real, I do not know what is."

Victria shook her head and began to walk away again, calling back to him, "No, sadly, you do not."

They pushed on. Felix awkwardly stole glances at her every now and then, whereas she kept her gaze forward. Her mind was working overtime. She was beginning to realize she remembered this day. In reality, she and Felix had gone on a hunt just like this before. She hadn't napped. But there had been three events of note.

One was the red bird. It had swooped low beside them and called out so erratically that it had caught both of their attention. Victria had remembered it ever since. Their second stop had played out exactly as she just experienced. Felix had commented on the clouds. One of them had looked like a dwarf, which had been noteworthy to her because this day took place when the dwarves were still isolated within the Silent Mountains. And their third stop . . . was yet to come. But it would be the final proof for her that this present reality was not, in fact, real.

Once she established that, then she would have to discover *why* it wasn't real. Already, more fragments of the dream she'd had during her nap were returning. She had woken up confused in that dream as well but the reason behind that evaded her.

A hand on her shoulder snapped her out of her thoughts. She blinked and turned to look at Felix. He held out a squirrel.

"Eat," he said gently. "You need something to replenish your energy. Perhaps that is why you feel like you are not yourself today."

She stared at the squirrel squirming in Felix's hand, chattering away as if pleading for its life.

This was it. This was the third memorable stop. During their trek, Felix had taken a moment to swipe a couple of squirrels from a nearby tree. They had shared them, consuming their life-energies together before continuing their journey. Felix had even said something similar about keeping up their strength.

She let out a shuddering breath, tears forming. Her voice cracked, "Oh, Felix."

Felix slowly lowered the squirrel and let it go. It scampered away, jabbering triumphantly as it quickly climbed a tree and disappeared behind a gnarled knot.

"You knew I would offer you the squirrel."

Victria nodded, her tears finally too heavy to keep in.

"But I let it go just now."

"It doesn't change what happened," she choked out.

He took her into his arms, squeezing firmly as he whispered, "But I am real. I remember all of our times together. I remember finding you in the woods. I remember fighting beside you. Fighting the darimun, the Creature. I remember it all. I am *real*."

Victria sniffled but said nothing. She just wanted to be held, wanted to close her eyes and fall asleep in Felix's arms, relishing in the feel of his chin on the top of her head. Maybe if she did that she would find herself waking up in her own bed. Felix would come in with a knowing smile, telling her that he had told her it was all real. He would tell her that the familiar feeling she'd had all day was just a fluke.

But she knew that wasn't what would happen, she knew that any minute now, something terrible would occur in this memory, just as it had in the one she was in prior to this. She remembered everything now. Images of Gar'Gir standing over her as she held Felix's lifeless body resurfaced. Along with them came images of herself chained against the stone wall of a dark cavern.

"Surely what is happening right now is not something you remember."

Victria shook her head, "No, but that's because I must have changed something when I kissed you."

She felt his smile. "You mean you did not kiss me before? Too nervous?"

A laugh escaped her lips, and then she gasped. She pulled away from him, his own good humor instantly fading. She looked at him wide-eyed.

"What is it?"

"I *changed* the memory," she whispered.

Felix shrugged. "That is assuming this is a memory to begin with, which I would still prefer to think it is not."

Victria didn't respond, her mind working frantically. She began pacing as her thoughts came together.

"I changed the memory by doing something I wouldn't have done back then. But only *after* I realized what I was seeing wasn't real."

"But you did not know this was not real until I offered you the squirrel."

"I suspected. And that seems to be enough to allow me to make such changes. And if I can manipulate things here . . . then maybe I can escape too."

Victria would never know how Felix might have responded. As soon as she came to this conclusion, a crash sounded from nearby.

The two viatari turned toward the sound and saw the giant elk they'd been hunting step out from behind a tree. It was a large and magnificent beast. Its antlers arced high into the air, branching off into several clusters of lethal points. Its fur shone a brilliant amber as rays of sunlight hit it. It snorted angrily at them, shaking its head.

Felix took a cautious step toward it, then the elk stumbled.

It let loose a terrible cry as its eyes transformed into a dull yellow. Its body morphed and broke and grew in size several times over. Its once-amber fur turned a dull shade of purple and black. A purple aura seemed to emanate from the beast like a perpetually cascading mist. It roared. Felix took a step back in shock.

"A darim," he whispered. "The Creature has returned."

Victria blinked. This hadn't happened in her original memory, either. Was this a result of her meddling or were different memories merging together?

The giant darim lowered its sprawling crown and pawed the earth with its sharp hooves. It snorted again, letting loose gusts of purple mist. Felix put an arm out, pushing Victria back.

"Stay back," he warned, his gaze never leaving the darim. "This is a big one. I am not sure we could take him on ourselves even if we fought together. We will have to lose him in the forest and make our way back to Aleganthia, where we can get some help."

"That's not going to stop it from charging at us right now," Victria pointed out.

The darim charged, closing the distance between them in seconds. The two viatari jumped away to either side of the beast. The elk didn't stop until it hit a tree, cracking through its thick trunk and felling it with one swipe. It roared as the tree groaned and crashed onto the forest floor.

Getting up quickly, Felix drew his dirk and tried to slice through the darim's legs, if only to buy them time, but the blade could only make a shallow cut. Victria attacked on the other side, plunging her own weapon deep into the darim's ribs. The beast roared and swung its head wildly, catching her as she tried to pull back and sending her flying.

Wind rushed out of her as her back connected with the hard surface of a tree trunk. She slid down and collapsed onto her side, trying to take in a breath but finding it difficult to do so. Her regenerative abilities kicked in. She could already feel warmth spreading across her back as her shattered ribs repaired themselves. Within a minute, she was able to breathe normally again.

She tried to stand but stumbled and could do nothing but watch Felix as he used his extraordinary speed to keep the darim at bay. He was masterful with his dirk, but he'd been correct in his earlier assumption. This foe was too powerful for them to take on by conventional means. It would take several viatari fighting together to do it. As it was, Felix was proving to be more of a nuisance than a threat.

The darim roared fiercely and thrashed its head in all directions, forcing Felix to jump back.

"Victria!" He called out, keeping his blade between him

and the darim. "Tell me when you are fully healed and we will make a break for it back to Aleganthia. I am sure we can outrun it."

Victria was about to call out that she was ready when she stopped herself and remembered. None of this was real. This was just a memory. She felt pain, felt exhaustion as if it were real but if she were to die . . . what then? Would she wake up back on the metal table with Gar'Gir's gruesome face hovering over hers? If she died here would she simply not wake up at all?

She looked once at Felix, taking him in; his calm features, his short-cropped hair, his ancient red eyes. She wanted to see him again, the real him. If she could escape from this nightmare, maybe she could escape from her own imprisonment as well. And if she died here with what she was about to do? Well . . . at least she had tried.

She stood and slowly made her way around to stand next to Felix. The darim watched her progress. Once she had placed herself between them, she turned and flashed the elder viatari a final smile.

"I will see you again," she said. "I promise."

She dropped her weapon and spread her arms out, walking toward the darim.

"Victria, come back!" Felix yelled. He continued to yell, waving his arms frantically, trying to force the darim's attention onto him. He rushed forward to attack, but the beast blocked him easily with its antlers. A single swing of its head forced him back once more. Felix did everything he could to keep Victria from doing what she was doing.

Everything, except pulling her back himself.

The darim watched her curiously as she approached, eventually standing close enough that she could pet its snout if she wanted to. She could smell its acrid breath as it puffed out more gusts of purple mist. She stared into its yellow eyes, waiting for it to realize this was no trick. Waiting for it to attack.

Rearing back, the elk-darim roared one final time and swung its head straight for Victria. Closing her eyes, she tensed. But the blow never came.

She opened her eyes and saw the darim frozen mid-swing. Turning around, she saw Felix was frozen as well, his mouth open in a soundless scream as he reached out for her.

"You think you are clever."

It was a familiar voice. One that normally sent shivers up Victria's spine. But this time, upon hearing it, she felt a thrilling rush. A strong grip on her arm whirled her around and she came face to face with Gar'Gir. She stared defiantly at him. Victorious.

He grunted. "You are the first, I think, to detect the brainwyrm's machinations while embedded so deeply in your own memories. You're supposed to forget your previous experience entirely when you wake up in a new memory, though it stays locked away in your subconscious—hence, the mental anguish of this experiment. It only ends when *I* take the subject out of the realm of memories. But somehow, you were able to deduce that you were in one on your own. And so quickly, too. How did you do it?"

Victria shrugged. "I would think you could figure that out with your so-called intelligence."

Gar'Gir snarled. "Whatever the case, we're done here. I will discover my answers in due time."

"Why did you keep the darim from killing me? What happens if I die?" Victria asked. She hated having to converse with this burrower as if they were actually on an intellectual journey together, but she needed answers. If she knew what was behind death's door in these memories, perhaps it could bring her one step closer to figuring out how to escape from them; or at least how to better weather the storm she and her companions were in.

The burrower's jaw clenched.

"You don't know," Victria realized.

"No," Gar'Gir admitted. "But it doesn't matter. I will learn the answer eventually. Death here either means escape from the brainwyrm, which most likely means it dies in your head, or it means death in the real world. Either way, don't think death will be your escape from me. We will learn the answer to all things—in due time."

Victria grinned, an idea forming. Perhaps she had found her method for defying her captor. If she and the others could thwart Gar'Gir's experiments in this way, then it might lead him into making a mistake out of frustration or anger. And that could grant them their opportunity to escape.

"Your thoughts are too easy to read," Gar'Gir sneered. "Don't think you will interfere with my experiments so easily. It's only a matter of time before you too are unable to tell the difference between reality and memory."

Victria presented both of her hands to Gar'Gir and in a mocking tone said, "Take me back to my cell, then."

The burrower laughed, a harsh sound that devolved into a sickly hacking. "Ah, viatari, we are not done here yet. Please, observe."

Gar'Gir snapped his fingers and Victria found that she had been transported a few feet away from where she had been standing. Turning to her right, she could see the side of the elk-darim still in position to smash her into oblivion with its horns. Felix stood farther off to the side, still frozen in horror.

Now, however, nothing stood in between them.

"But there's no point in—" Victria began to say, but another snap of the fingers from Gar'Gir forced her words to die in her throat.

Instantly, Felix fell to his knees, weeping as he believed Victria was about to meet a gruesome end. Instead, he looked up in confusion when he realized she was no longer there. In her place was a massive darim charging full speed at him. Even with his extraordinary speed, there was nothing he could do to avoid the attack.

He tried to leap to the side but the darim caught his leg with its terrible jaws and pulled him back, tackling him to the ground. His screams filled the forest with something Victria had never once heard come from his mouth. Fear.

The darim clamped down on his midsection, tearing into flesh as the elder viatari tried to crawl away. Incensed by its prey's refusal to die, the Creature's minion launched itself up into the air and crashed back to earth, Felix underfoot.

Victria heard bones break. She could no longer hear Felix's cries of pain, but she felt them with every stomp of the darim's hooves. Finally, she turned away, unable to watch as the darim decided to run back and forth, trampling the limp body beneath it over and over as if for sport.

She knew none of this was real, knew the Felix here was just part of her memory. He had not died this day. He was still out there thinking of some way to save her. She knew this. But the pain she felt from witnessing such a gruesome death, especially of one she had always loved, was too much. She fell to her knees, a sob escaping her lips.

Gar'Gir leaned over her, chuckling as, once more in control, he said, "Now, we are done."

CHAPTER TWENTY-THREE

Salevari was surprised when Zael and Simon returned without their quarry. Even with Zael holding himself back by maintaining his human disguise, she would have expected success. Clearly, they had underestimated their enemy. It wasn't a mistake she often made. She would have to take care not to make it twice.

But as there were no other clues pertaining to their eavesdropper, there was nothing they could do to pursue the matter. Zael spent all day every day the following week venturing out into the city in search of more information about Thurn. He was certain there was a connection between them and their eavesdropper. Salevari wasn't so sure. For all she knew, whoever had been at their door had just as much chance of being a staff member within the palace who overhead part of their conversation and got spooked when confronted by Zael's sudden appearance. Whatever the case, the fact remained that they had no way of finding out who it was without some stroke of luck befalling them. So Salevari kept herself busy by focusing on more trifling matters.

Like learning how to dance.

All of the furniture within their spacious living room was pushed against the wall. There was nothing they could do about the fountain in the middle but that was to Tera's liking.

"The way the elites dance in Halding Port involves constant movement in a wide circle, so this will just make our practice sessions more realistic," she said as she clapped her hands in an even, consistent tempo.

The days were long and tiresome. Dancing like a noblewoman involved tiny, precise steps all while rotating and orbiting the center of the dance floor. Salevari's posture had to be perfectly straight with each movement, her head held high. Her hands always clasped to Simon, one in his own hand and one on his shoulder. And while she knew there was no deeper meaning behind it, she couldn't help but focus on that one hand of his resting against her hip.

He had noticed this discomfort on their first day together when her lips pressed together tightly upon his touch. They stayed still like that for a moment. A smirk edged its way across his face.

"It's all for appearances, remember," he said in a bored tone. "I don't intend to bed you once the night is done."

Her eyes flashed. "That's good," she responded, stepping in closer and draping her arm around his neck as she brought her lips close to his ear, "because I would *break* you."

Simon remained silent after that.

They practiced for hours each day, their legs stiff and bodies dripping in sweat after their sessions. By the middle of the week, Salevari's body began to move on its own.

"Let's hope you can move that easily when there are others around and actual music for you to follow," Tera commented.

Aniria didn't have as easy a time. Partnering with Drathanar, who also didn't know how to dance, the two swung in wild circles around their suite. They dared not look at each other as they did so, for fear of what one might see in the other's eyes.

Salevari noticed them as she nimbly twirled under Simon's guiding hand. "You'll never impress all the young elites who will undoubtedly ask for your hand that way, Aniria."

The young viatari scoffed, a scowl reappearing as she stepped on Drathanar's toes. "I don't intend on dancing with any humans. Or at all, for that matter. I will reject each and every one who asks."

Simon chuckled, murmuring, "Oh, how the young men of this city will fawn over her, each one desiring to be remembered as the one who won her over."

Salevari couldn't help but agree.

After that exchange, Drathanar moved with much more ease, even trying to spin Aniria in place as Simon had done.

When they were not dancing, Salevari and Aniria were trying on dresses. Again.

"The dresses we made in Donsea won't do," Simon explained as he brought a measuring tape across Salevari's hip and ankles. "Since we're from the plains, I think we can get by without having to wear what the noblewomen here wear. But still, I'll have to make something much flashier for this event."

"What's wrong with the dresses they wear here?" Salevari asked.

Tera guffawed and stood up, lifting her arms around her own hips and forming a wide curve. "Theirs are held up by a wooden cage underneath in order to make their waists look bigger than they actually are. Very clunky. You two would hate it."

The viatari shared a look. They already hated this, but if Simon believed he could produce something better, they would have to put their faith in him.

While the human chief was busy pouring his energies into creating party dresses with the leftover material he had brought from Donsea, Tera oversaw their continued education.

They sat at a table, Tera pacing behind them.

"Backs straight," she chirped, slapping Aniria's arm lightly with a thin ruler. Aniria groaned but complied, holding her head up as high as it would go. Her face was an open book, but it worked in her favor. Salevari thought she had the appearance of a highborn human looking down on a gathering of peasants before her gates.

"Now, what you see before you is the cutlery that is used in any fine dining situation such as the one you are about to find yourselves in," Tera explained, pointing out the variously sized spoons, forks, and knives laid out on either side of an empty plate. "There will be several courses during this meal. With each course, you will use a separate set of cutlery. You start on the outside and work your way in. Easy?"

The viatari nodded, though Salevari couldn't help but think how silly this all was. Why did the humans here make such a pretense about eating food? So many rules and importance laid on a single fork or knife. Ridiculous.

"When you eat, you must appear dainty. Take small bites, chew with your mouths closed. Of course, since you are supposed to be from the plains, I'm sure those around you will not mind too much if you aren't the perfect porcelain doll they've bred their own women to be. All the same, try not to eat with your hands."

"In fact, don't eat at all," Aniria muttered.

Tera leaned down with a fixed smile. "What was that, dear?"

"It's not like their food will do anything for us," the viatari sputtered angrily. "What's the point in participating in these ridiculous, rule-infested traditions?"

"The point," Tera stood back up and resumed her pacing, her finger pointing skyward like a schoolteacher before an impatient child. "Is the conversations. Between courses, those around you will want to talk. You two will be especially popular since you're the special guests. This will be our best opportunity to learn more about what's happening here from the elites' perspective."

"It will be a chance for us to learn if the Grand Admiral himself is in some way tied to Thurn as well," Salevari added.

"Let's not get ahead of ourselves," Tera cautioned, tapping her shoulders with the ruler. "Back straight. It'll be better if you use dinner to build rapport. Learn what you can about the city if you can do it subtly; but ask too many direct questions too soon, and you'll scare off anyone who otherwise might have let something slip. Tongues will be looser during the dance, after a few drinks have been had."

And so their lessons continued. Tera showed them a book with intricate drawings, outlining the different foods they might encounter during the feast and how to eat them. She taught them other methods of greeting strangers other than a curtsy, such as presenting their hand for a kiss for the men or kissing the air next to both cheeks when they greeted women.

The lessons were extensive and exhausting, which made Salevari all the more grateful when she could end each day with a lavish bath. She wasn't sure she would have been able to endure the grueling week without them.

Finally, on the morning of the feast, Simon finished their dresses. He had the viatari try them on, standing on a pedestal in front of a mirror while he and Tera took final measurements so he could hem the ends as needed.

Salevari gasped when she saw herself. Her dress was a deep blue and seemed to shimmer near her shins, as if so many stars reflected the light around them. A single strap of silk snaked its way over her left shoulder while the other was almost bare. Still, even on that side, an impressive pattern of thin, scrunched lace connected to the thicker fabrics, giving the appearance of light blue flowers having been pinned upon her right shoulder.

She shifted her body and saw that the dress wrapped around her figure perfectly. Too perfectly. Silk hugged her waist tightly, restricting any flexibility she might have had with her legs. It wouldn't be enough to keep her from walking or dancing, considering the tiny movements she was expected to make, but if there arose a need to fight. . . .

Looking up, Simon noticed the forming frown.

"Come now," he said. "You weren't planning on throwing any kicks at this party, were you?"

"We don't know if the leadership here is behind Thurn or that eavesdropper that escaped you and Zael a week ago. If they end up being the culprits, these dresses put me and Aniria in a bad position. We'll be surrounded by enemies with no way to fight for ourselves."

Simon shrugged. "That's what Zael and Drathanar are here for. They should be enough by themselves to at least buy us time to escape if we need to."

"I will protect you, my lady." Drathanar said, standing across the other side of the room, his eyes averted.

"Zael will not be at this party," Salevari countered. "In case you didn't notice, he's taken to going out into the city every day until the late hours of night."

"Well, you have me," Simon said with finality. "This dress may be a little restrictive, but like Tera said before, you would have hated wearing what the other women will be wearing. You can thank me later."

He stood up, putting away his tape measurer and snapping shut the little notebook he'd been writing numbers down in.

"I'm done taking measurements from both of you. You can undress and get back into your regular clothes. I'll have these adjustments made before the feast begins this evening."

Turning, he left the room at a brisk pace. Tera drifted behind Salevari, helping her off the pedestal and then out of her dress.

"Drathanar," she called out without looking up from her work. "Help Aniria with her own dress, will you?"

The Dalyran general blinked heavily, his voice hoarse as he asked, "You wish for me to undress her?"

Aniria's face turned as red as the shining fabrics wrapped around her lithe frame. "I think if you just undo the straps on my back, I can handle the rest," she said meekly.

Drathanar hesitated, gulping for some excuse to get out of the room. In the end, his eyes hardened with determination. He stepped up behind Aniria and gently began undoing her straps. His eyes stayed focused on the thin strands of fabric and leather cords, not once lifting the slight amount they needed to take in the bare skin of her exposed neck and shoulders. Aniria's eyes were cast to the side wall, her hands clasped together in front of her.

Neither dared look at the mirror before them.

Zael leaned against a bare section of stone wall in Halding Port's central plaza. Around him, stalls were alive and bustling, their owners calling out incessantly to passersby as they tried to sell their goods. The day was hot, save for the moving shadows produced by a fleet of full clouds slowly drifting across the sky. People ate. Some drank. An incessant hum of noise hung in the air.

And Zael observed it all.

This was the seventh day he had come here with the hopes of catching one of the thurn posters in action. Unlike his companions, he was positive there was a third party behind Thurn. After all, if the leadership had been involved like Salevari and the others still suspected, they would have been outed as viatari by now, since the eavesdropper, once escaping him, would have made a beeline to the Grand Admiral to make his report.

A scowl marked Zael's face as he remembered that night. He still couldn't believe that whoever it was had escaped him. A quick shake of the head allowed him to refocus. Now was not the time to dwell on past mistakes. With so many people in the plaza, a follower of Thurn could make his way through without anyone noticing. He had to keep his eyes sharp.

Unfortunately, each day so far had produced zero results. There hadn't been a new development since he was here with Simon and Drathanar a week ago. The buzz from the latest post had already died down among the general public. He still heard whispered mentions and some discussion from those passing him but not nearly as much as earlier in the week. If there was a time for a new post to appear, it had to be soon. Especially if whoever was behind it wanted to keep these people on a hook like Simon thought they did.

His goal originally was to catch the interpreter, but as the day grew late, Zael became restless enough that if anyone posted something related to Thurn he was ready to track them down no matter how low on the operational chain they were. If they were involved with movement, chances were good that anyone he caught would know the whereabouts of the interpreter. Once he found the interpreter . . . well, he had his own way of extracting information. Salevari might not approve, but since he was the only one making any real headway here, he felt she would eventually come around to his way of thinking.

Evening came and Zael still hadn't budged from his spot. Many of the stall keepers around him were packing up their wares and disassembling their stalls, tying each piece together and lugging them onto carts where they could haul them back home. They shot him a few peeved looks but said nothing. That was fine with him.

The plaza was thinning out. As more people left to go home or patronize the city's bars and taverns, the energized atmosphere died down, and silence grew along with long shadows of buildings watching over the empty space. Zael found himself enveloped by one of these shadows.

Eventually, he was the only one left in the plaza. The only sound filling the air was that of the fountain's churning water. The viatari captain stood where he was for another hour, the last rays of sunlight disappearing.

Finally, as complete darkness took hold, a lone figure made his way to the square pillar at the center of the plaza. The viatari's eyes followed his every move. Why would someone post something at a time like this, when there was no one around to read it? He suspected he knew the answer to that question.

The man hammered a single sheet of paper onto all four boards and promptly left. Zael watched him go, making a mental note of which street he took before he jumped out of the shadows and ran for the pillar to read what had been posted.

His heart leapt. As he had guessed, the man had been a follower of Thurn. This new flier presented a message as confusing and nonsensical as every other one Zael had read.

When does the tide turn?
A feast of plenty for those least deserving,
A perfect time to make our name.
Sharks circle in dark waters.
What type of shark is most aggressive?
The time for floodwaters comes soon.
The tide will wash away the filth.
Those undeserving will find the waters unforgiving.
They will be washed away.
Ask questions.
Awaken, and break bread.
- Þ

He shook his head at the nonsensical writing and ran down the same street as the man who had posted it. His heart pounded in his ears and his limbs quivered as they anticipated the chase ahead.

It was night. Darkness covered every corner and alleyway. Those still out and about were merry with drink and company; they would not be paying attention to their surroundings. He reveled in this sense of freedom. As far as he was concerned, he had no restrictions, and he intended to use every method at his disposal to accomplish his goals. This time, his prey would not escape.

CHAPTER TWENTY-FOUR

Zael held nothing back as he rushed through winding streets and dark alleyways. Salty wind whipped his hair back and stung his eyes as he ran, but he pushed on. With the blanket of night covering him, and without Simon hounding him from behind, it was only a matter of time before he found his quarry.

There were few others he passed as he ran, most of them having already turned in for the night; their slumped bodies and empty tankards a testament to the revelry they'd endured. Because of this, finding the path of his prey was easy.

Hunting in the city was not like hunting in the forest. There were no trails to follow, no broken branches that told tales of passage, no shallow footprints on damp earth. Here, Zael had to rely on his sense of hearing and his own knowledge of the city's many streets and where they led more so than his ability to sniff out someone's life-energies.

For the past week, upon returning to his room every night, he had spent hours studying maps of Halding Port. He knew where this street led to, where someone might go if they followed the next one over. He knew, after that, the road ended in a T-section. And after that, he had a fifty-fifty chance of choosing the right direction.

He planned on catching his target before he had to make that choice.

The human's footsteps reverberated in the still night. He had chosen a path far from any establishments providing nightly entertainment and so no one was around to mask his presence. Zael, on the other hand, tread lightly, climbing expertly over the side of buildings and launching himself onto the roofs so that he could approach from a better, more unexpected angle.

Within minutes, he spotted his prey. The man wore a simple, hooded black robe. It did well to hide him in the shadows covering the streets, but Zael's keen eyes could make out his unbothered movements easily enough.

The viatari stopped in his tracks for a moment and crouched where he was, observing the man's path as he formulated a plan.

More likely than not, this was just a simple grunt in the grand scheme of things. He was also Zael's first and best chance at finding out where the interpreter might be. There was no question, he had to capture the human alive. And he knew how to do it without being seen. Just ahead of where his target was about to cross was a long, dark alleyway that cut through the side buildings and deposited any travelers brave enough to traverse it onto a wider, brighter street that led straight to the docks.

Zael quickly moved into position, jumping from roof to roof until he stood directly above where the alley's shadowed entrance was. He waited. The man below was only a few paces away from where he needed to be and still remained unaware of the danger awaiting him. As far as he was concerned, this was just another night where he had done his job well. He even began whistling a merry tune.

Jumping off the roof and landing deftly behind him, Zael lunged at the man, clamping one hand over his mouth while presenting a dagger with the other and pressing it against his back. The man grunted but otherwise didn't move, feeling the cold steel poking through his cloak.

Zael dragged him back several paces into the shadowed alley before he removed his hands, whirled the man around and pushed him against the wall.

"P-please, sir!" he said. "I have no money for you to steal. You waste your time!"

"I'm no petty thief," was Zael's cold reply. "What are you called?"

The man looked up at him, eyes wide and full of terror. His face was remarkably pale, even though the moon was hidden by clouds tonight.

"G-Gabon." He finally managed to spit out.

"Well, Gabon," Zael crouched down so that they were eye-level and twirled the dagger between his fingers. The man's eyes followed the blade's movement. He whimpered. "I've got a problem. You see, I'm looking for someone. Someone in your little organization. I'm sure you've heard of him. People call him 'the interpreter.'"

Gabon's focus shifted from the dagger to Zael. His terror drained away, a neutral mask taking place.

Oh, very good, Zael thought. *They've been trained on what to do if they're captured.*

"I know nothing about him," Gabon stated. His voice was confident, rang true. For all the viatari knew, it could be true. But he wasn't about to trust the first words that came out of a stranger's mouth.

"You will take me to him."

"I don't know him."

"You know him. Someone is giving you those papers to post in the city, and you're not the only one. You all dress the same, so someone must be supplying you with uniforms. And the best part," a smile spread like a corrupting plague on Zael's face, "is I can tell you've been trained for this exact scenario. Someone gave you that training."

The man said nothing, but Zael could sense a small air of uncertainty settle over the human as he shifted in place.

"I know about your little organization. I know all of you involved with this Thurn character are connected in some way. You may be a grunt in the ranks, but even you would have a superior to report to and I suspect the interpreter must be that man."

"I don't know what organization you're talking about."

"Be silent!" Zael punched the wall only inches from where the man's head rested, cracking it. The man heard the cracks, turned to see them himself. A note of panic entered his voice.

"That's solid stone. How did you. . . ?"

The cold smile returned. "You were probably trained by this interpreter or others on how to behave in case you were captured. How to resist interrogation, maybe even torture. But I doubt you were prepared for this."

His body shimmered. The blond hair and gray eyes of his human illusion melted away into his more comfortable silver and red. Fangs replaced the flat human teeth he'd been burdened with. He bared them hungrily.

Gabon watched in horrified awe. His body trembled and curled together as if trying to present a smaller target would increase his odds of survival.

"I'm sure they never taught you how to resist a viatari," Zael finished, pressing his dagger to the man's throat. "I must say,

I've grown tired of feeding on rats and it's been centuries since I fed on a human."

"I-I-"

A soft shush came from the viatari as he brought a finger to his lips. "Not another word unless it's the answer I want. You will take me to the interpreter."

Gabon shook his head vigorously, his mask cracking and falling apart. "I can't—I don't know where he lives!"

Zael frowned. "Wrong answer."

He grabbed the human's left wrist and squeezed. Bones shattered. Gabon screamed, but no one heard him. They were alone in this dark alley, just as Zael had intended.

He let go and towered over his quarry as the man hunched over in pain, nursing his broken wrist with his remaining good hand.

"Do not make me ask again."

Tears streaming down his face, Gabon nodded, a soft sob escaping his lips. Zael patted him consolingly.

"Good man," the viatari nodded. "You may yet walk out of this with your life, forcing me to continue subsisting on your city's disgusting rodents."

After giving him some time to get over his broken wrist, Zael lifted Gabon onto his feet and pushed him forward. He was led through several streets that only days before he would have never recognized. As they entered each one, however, he made a mental map of his path in case he needed to find his way to the interpreter again in the future. Though, he doubted his main target would have much of a future, save for growing flowers.

After thirty minutes of being led by a whimpering Gabon, the pair stopped at the end of another alleyway, just before they entered the proper road. Gabon nodded toward the large residential building directly across from them.

"He's in there," he said glumly. "Third floor. Room 317, I think."

"Who does he answer to?"

"I dunno. You'll have to ask him yourself."

Zael moved as if he were reaching for the man's other wrist. Gabon squirmed away screaming, "I swear! I don't know anything else about him!"

The viatari chuckled, lifting his arms in a placating manner. "Alright, I believe you. Keep your voice down."

"So, is that it?" Gabon asked tentatively. "Will you let me go?"

Zael made a grand show of considering the option before breaking the news.

"Not quite. I can't have you wandering off to your organization's headquarters and warning them about me. That would make this whole night pointless, I think."

The human dropped his head in defeat. "You're going to kill me?" But then his head popped right back up, fear bringing a tremor to his voice. "You're not going to eat me, are you?"

Shaking his head, Zael scoffed. "I'm not going to eat you. Human life-energies don't match well with our appetites, which is why we make it a point not to hunt your race."

The man let out an audible sigh of relief.

"But I still can't let you go."

Without warning, he let loose a flurry of punches, aiming for vital points such as the throat and heart, knocking Gabon into the adjacent stone wall. The human slid down hard onto the cobblestone alleyway, blood streaming from his nose and ears. He lay there unconscious, his breathing ragged.

Dragging him into a sitting position, Zael leaned him against the alley wall. Then, he sat and watched as Gabon's breathing slowed, grew shallow, and finally came no more.

He patted the dead man's leg and stood up, summoning forth his human guise. Salevari would scold him for this if she found out, he had no doubt. Still, he couldn't risk leaving loose ends tonight. There was too much at risk on this hot trail where he had found himself.

"Thank you for the information."

Turning to the residential building Gabon had pointed out, Zael made his way inside, climbing the worn, wooden steps that led to the higher floors until he found himself on the third.

He looked around. The floor was carpeted but dirty, littered with stains from spilled drinks and some that looked like old, dried blood. The line of doors on either end of the hallway were grimy, rust covering several hinges. The air was stagnant and heavy with the stench of mildew.

Every sense of his was on high alert as Zael pushed his way forward looking for room 317. This would be a perfect place for an ambush, he thought.

But as he crept along, no doors swung open suddenly, no traps were sprung, and he found the room he was looking for without issue.

Looking around once more to ensure he was alone, he put his ear against the door, hoping to hear something interesting before he made a move. All that met his ears, though, was the shuffling of feet on the other side.

Not wanting to waste any more of the night, he kicked the door down and rushed in.

A yelp came from another room deeper in the apartment. Zael made his way through the next open doorway and found himself in a kitchen with a single bearded man staring at him, wide-eyed. The man held a knife. Zael settled into a fighting stance, but the man had other plans.

He turned the knife toward his own belly and brought it in. Were it not for the viatari's speed and quick reflexes, the man would have gutted himself in his own kitchen, staining the cracked white tiles with blood and offal. As it was, Zael grabbed his wrist just inches before the blade plunged into flesh.

The two stared at each other, struggling for control. The human brought his other hand around and tried putting more force behind his initial effort, but Zael was ready for it. He batted the arm away and reached for the knife itself, grabbing it by the blade. He wrenched it away and threw it across the room, droplets of blood following the movement. Then, he struck the man sharply on the nose.

Blood spurted from the spot and the human cried out, grabbing his broken face as he stumbled backward. Zael swept his feet out from under him and put a foot against his chest, pinning him to the floor. He leaned over with a triumphant leer.

"Hello there, mister interpreter," he said, his voice low and menacing. "I have some questions for you, but I'm afraid you'll have to wait to hear them."

The interpreter's eyes bulged. He groaned in anger, kicking his feet in a futile effort to escape.

Grabbing him by the neck, Zael dragged him back to the living room and threw him on the single couch that furnished it. He found a few cords of decent rope and tied the man's hands and feet together.

"If you're with the Grand Admiral's intelligence," the interpreter growled. "I'll have your job for this. I have rights, even in this putrid city. You can't just–agh!"

Zael stuffed the interpreter's mouth with a dirty pair of socks that had been lying on the floor and then went to work.

As the interpreter continued a series of muffled grunts telling off the viatari, Zael went through each room searching meticulously for some clue that might point him to his next goal. He dug through shelves, opened cabinets, even went through stores of rotten food looking for something. Anything.

He had hoped that with his sudden intrusion he might have caught the interpreter off guard in such a way that something might be left out in the open. If there was something, however, it was well-hidden or already destroyed. That left little room for him to figure out his next course of action.

On the verge of giving up as he swiped behind the frame of the last of a series of cheap paintings, Zael peered into a nearby wastebin and found scraps of paper with charred edges. He picked them out, turning them over.

It was impossible to get the full message from the surviving fragments but there was no doubt in his mind that these were the remains of a letter. From these scraps, he could decipher three words written in a sloppy script: "tunnels," "graveyard," and "grain storage." He brought the pieces of charred paper back to the living room where he presented them to the interpreter.

"What is this?" he asked, ripping the socks out of the man's mouth.

The human's face blanched. "I don't know what you're talking about."

"I've already broken your nose," Zael responded in a calm voice. "I can break more of you. Much more."

"You think pain scares me?"

"Who gives you Thurn's messages to interpret?" the viatari asked, grabbing a chair and settling down into it. He grabbed the man's hand, taking care to separate his fingers. "Who tells you how to interpret it?"

"Thurn's posts and the meaning behind them are obvious to anyone with the ability to think."

Zael grabbed the man's pinky and pulled. A loud pop filled the room, followed by howls of pain. For good measure, he did the same to the ring finger.

"What is this graveyard?" the viatari asked, switching gears. "Is it the headquarters of your organization?"

"I would never tell a non-believer!" The man spat in the viatari's face. Zael wiped the mixture of saliva and blood off slowly. He considered changing back into his viatari form to enhance his intimidation tactics but thought better of it. There was still plenty of time to obtain what he needed to know through subtler ways.

"So, your organization is a religion then?"

The man scoffed, averting his gaze. "Religion is a joke."

"Is Thurn real?"

"Of course he's real. Who do you think creates the papers I interpret?"

Zael shrugged. "You could be writing them yourself."

Laughter. Another pop. Then, screaming.

"You bastard!"

"You have seven more fingers," Zael said business-like. "Then I have to move on to your toes. Tell me, why did those papers mention grain storages? Is your organization involved with the production of bread?"

Behind Zael a tall candle sputtered three times in quick succession. A slow, mad cackle crept out of the interpreter's throat. Zael pulled on his index finger, but no howls of pain followed.

"It must be a funny joke you've thought of," he mused.

The man's laughter died down, his face shining as if he was the one victorious in this exchange.

"You're too late," he shouted euphorically.

"Too late for what?"

"All those questions and you've yet to ask me the most important one!"

"Which is?"

Another chortle, then, "The Grand Admiral's assassination."

Zael froze. With some effort, he managed to keep his face neutral even as his mind blanked. There was clearly more to learn, and he had to act like he was in charge of this interrogation. Even so, he could feel his control slipping away like the tide.

"You plan to assassinate the Grand Admiral?"

The interpreter nodded enthusiastically.

"And why are you telling me this so freely?"

"Because there's nothing you can do to stop it!" the man shouted gleefully. He giggled. "The strike will occur during their wretched dance tonight. Once the Grand Admiral is gone, there'll be no reason for anyone else to ignore us. Everyone will see that Thurn's words were true. Long has he foretold of our Grand Admiral's demise."

Zael thought about this for a moment. Sadly, the human was right. There was no way for him to make it back to the palace before the dance started. He wouldn't be able to relay this critical information to Salevari and the others. But, he decided, that was no real reason for worry. If an attempt was made on the Grand Admiral's life tonight, he was confident his companions would be able to react in time to stop it.

So long as they kept their guard up.

He stood and wandered over to the window, making a show of looking through it, as if reflecting.

"You're right," he finally said. "There's no way I can make it back in time to warn them."

The interpreter snickered and began to hum. His legs kicked up and down as if he were having the grandest time.

"But I have friends looking out for the Grand Admiral," the viatari shrugged, turning his attention back to his prisoner. "And they are more than capable of protecting him. There's no one better. So," he sat back down on the couch next to the interpreter, grabbing his hand again and pulled out his thumb.

A scream of agony.

"The thumb always hurts the worst," Zael observed. "And you still have one more. Since my friends and your friends will be busy with each other tonight, I think we should do the same. After all, we still have much of the night ahead of us. Plenty of time for you to answer *all* my questions."

It was the promise of a painful night. One Zael fully intended to carry out, even if he didn't get all of the answers he wanted. He only hoped, while he was busy with this, that his faith in his companions was not misplaced.

Salevari and Aniria walked with trepidation as Aethel led them through the palace halls toward a night full of unknowns. They had prepared for this event, trained extensively in the art of human entertainment and memorized books full of tedious information pertaining to human existence. All so they might not raise any suspicion among the elites here that they were, in fact, not human.

Salevari walked arm in arm with Simon by her side, who wore a remarkably simple tunic of light brown leathers with lines of gold threaded into it, shaped into mesmerizing patterns. A thick belt with a square-cut sapphire in the center helped bring the outfit together and around his shoulders hung a thick, woolen cloak with dark fur lined around the edges.

He caught her staring.

"What?"

She shrugged. "Nothing. I just thought you looked rather plain next to me."

Simon stifled a laugh, "Perhaps, but I like to think of it as a matter of us plainsmen wanting to show off the beauty of our ladies rather than keeping the attention on ourselves."

Her lips twitched as Aethel opened a large set of doors leading into the dining hall designated to hold tonight's affair. She glanced at Aniria beside her, then at Drathanar and Tera who trailed behind. They all nodded. They were ready.

"Let's give them a show."

A wave of conversation, the clinking of glasses, and many boisterous greetings met their ears all at once as the doors opened. They entered a giant room with a ceiling carved to look like waves rippling across its surface. The wood was even stained a dull blue, giving them a realistic appearance. Voices echoed across the spacious hall.

Along the walls hung several giant portraits of serious men, all wearing the same armor with the same crest around the chestplate, that of an anchor hanging from a round shield. For one wall, there were no portraits. Instead, a single continuous pane of glass made up this section of the room, allowing for an unobstructed view of the docks, the sea wall, and everything that lay beyond, bathing in the dying light of a setting sun.

"May I present," Aethel announced in a loud voice. "The lords and ladies of the plains!"

All eyes turned to the newcomers. Salevari felt their stares, could see their curiosity manifest in whispered exchanges and subtle glances. The women in particular ogled her, hiding their mouths with flamboyantly decorated paper fans as they whispered their opinions to each other. She had no doubt as to what thoughts they held. Jealousy and disapproval swam through their narrowed eyes like a well-lit sign for all to read. She kept her head high as Simon led her in.

A repeating, resounding boom filled the room as Fradrick surged through the crowd, clapping with great pleasure. He bent down and kissed the hands of Aniria and Salevari—lingering a moment too long with hers—as he murmured, "You look radiant tonight." He clasped Simon's arm, staring unabashedly into his eyes. Then, he turned to face his other guests and yelled in a boisterous voice, "Now with our final guests having arrived, let us take our seats and feast!"

Footsteps replaced conversation as each party found their spot along the long wooden table that stretched across the middle of the room, of which Fradrick sat at its head. Aethel guided Salevari and Simon toward the center of the table with Aniria sitting directly across from them. He then directed Drathanar and Tera to stay near the wall with the rest of the guards and servants, of which there were many.

Once they were all seated, a host of servers filed out of the side doors carrying large platters laden with a variety of foods. These were placed along the center of the table, all within reaching distance for anyone to pick at. Salevari saw everything was hand-sized, a one-bite morsel. There were some shellfish she remembered seeing in the restaurant Fradrick had taken them too, like the shrimp, and there were new ones she had never laid eyes on.

Guests clapped with delight. Salevari reached out to take some food from the platter nearest her when she noticed no one else was moving. She took back her hand and looked around curiously.

Fradrick stood with a somber expression as he raised his

hands. Everyone else did the same.

Together, they chanted, "May the waves bless our shores with its fruits, may the storms clear quickly under the light of the rising sun, may the fish remain plentiful, may wind ever fill our sails, may our enemies tremble at our might, and may we never forget our gratitude for all the blessings we have been given."

With the last word a moment of silence followed. Then, Fradrick lifted a goblet high into the air.

"A toast to our guests from the plains! Aniria, Salevari, Simon, you are most welcome here. We are eager to hear all about our brothers from the north. May our friendship only deepen from this day forth."

The elites cheered and drank from their goblets. Salevari sipped from hers and licked her lips in surprise. The wine, at least, was delicious.

Like a bubble, the silence that had conquered the room only moments before now burst as conversation once more erupted around them, this time accompanied with music. A small band set up in the corner of the hall, composed of a harp, a few stringed instruments, and several made of reeds that their players blew into. No one paid them any mind. Everyone was too preoccupied by the food before them. Arms shot out from every direction, grabbing what they could.

Salevari's plate ended up as an assortment of strange looking shellfish. A few stared soullessly up at her, their shelled bodies plump and red. Others were nothing more than a slab of slick meat laying on an open shell. Unsure what this one was, she asked the elite next to her, an older man with a soft voice.

"Ah," he said with a knowing grin. "You wouldn't know what that is now, would you? That is an oyster, my lady. A delectable treat if I may say so."

"How do I eat it?" Salevari asked.

The man took an oyster from the central platters and showed her. "You hold the shell to your lips like so, then you suck hard and the meat should fly in." He demonstrated.

"I prefer them raw, but some like to sprinkle a lemon wedge over the meat to give it some flavor. Best to eat it quickly, though, and forget the fact that the creature is still alive as you devour it."

"This thing is alive?"

"As I said," the old man nodded sagely. "Best to forget."

An idea formed in her head. Salevari threw the oyster back, feeling its slimy body play against her tongue. With great control, she allowed her fangs to come forth, piercing the meat with them. She sucked out what little life-energies there were and swallowed what remained. A small burst of energy ran through her veins and she sighed appreciatively. It wasn't much, but perhaps they didn't have to go through the whole night on an empty stomach.

She turned to tell Aniria about the oysters but found her viatari companion embroiled in a conversation with a young man, his luscious brown hair pulled back in a ponytail. He leaned in close from his chair, wearing a confident smile as he spoke of whatever was on his mind. His words might as well have been carried away by the wind for all the good it did him. Aniria remained stoic and unimpressed as she stared blankly ahead, daintily taking food from her plate and putting it in her mouth. Small bites, just as Tera had taught them.

After some time, a new wave of servers flooded into the room, carrying smaller plates covered with a silver dome. They were placed in front of each guest. Once the last plate was set down, the servers removed the domes in one synchronous movement and retreated back the way they came.

The food before Salevari was small and pretty. She had no idea what it was but the fragrant aromas rising from it made her mouth water. She grabbed hold of a fork and picked off a piece of the delicate meat. The moment it touched her tongue, she froze. A soft groan of ecstatic pleasure yearned to escape her lips as she chewed through the delicious array of savory flavors. Her dish was cleaned in seconds. With the experience over, she couldn't help but feel a lingering sadness about it, both because she had finished her meal and because it had done nothing to actually sate her hunger. She reached for another oyster.

But that was only the first course, and each following one proved more impressive than the last.

As the feast went on, Salevari tried striking up conversation with some of the other elites seated around her. None of them were interesting. None truly answered any questions she lay before them. In fact, they all wanted to know more about her instead; what life was like in the plains, what her role as a chief's wife was, what luxuries she had or didn't have.

She answered their questions as best she could, remembering everything Simon had told her about his people's way of life, but once she'd done so the elites lost interest in her and talked amongst themselves. The only one who seemed able to hold a conversation was the old man seated next to her, who she discovered was named Aegal. But even he had his moments where he simply lapsed into silence.

"Do these feasts happen often?" she had asked at one point between courses.

Aegal smacked his lips appreciatively as his eyes closed. No doubt he was reminiscing about what he had only just finished eating. "Every month as far back as I can remember. Everyone here would riot if the food stopped coming. We all enjoy the marvels the kitchens here are able to produce too much. And it's never the same! That's the amazing part."

"That's a lot of food to go through, I would think. I can't imagine it all gets eaten."

The old man wheezed with laughter. "Oh no, there are plenty of people here who's goal it is to complete every course of the night. Most fail. They underestimate how filling they are, despite their small size."

"And what happens to the waste?"

"Gets thrown out, I suppose." Aegal shrugged, then reached for a small crab which he promptly began to disassemble.

"Do the common folk get the scraps then?" Salevari asked, mimicking surprise.

Another wheeze. "Oh no. That would be madness! No, I believe all the waste is dumped into the ocean. Most of it came from there, anyway, so it seems only right that whatever we don't consume gets sent back home."

Salevari's expression soured even as the delicious smells of their next course curled beneath her nose. "I hear there's a food shortage crisis within the city. Don't you think it would help the people if whatever wasn't eaten here was given to them?"

"Hmm," Aegal thought for a moment as he sucked on a crab claw. Then, in a dreamy voice he said, "Not my place to say. I only focus on the here and now." And with that, all of his focus narrowed onto the plate before him, his eyes darkening with desire.

The conversation ended there and Salevari was left feeling like she had been struck. She finished her next course numbly, barely registering the succulent texture of the fish as it melted in her mouth.

But as the courses continued, her conversation with Aegal soon fell by the wayside of her concerns. The food was all that mattered to anyone, that much had quickly become obvious. She understood now why it was all anyone talked about. By the time the final course was finished, she was left satisfied beyond measure and impressed by the culinary expertise of humans. They had created works of art for both the eyes and the tongue that she could never hope to reproduce.

As the last plate was taken away from the table, another volley of clapping exploded through the room. Fradrick stood, eagerness manifesting under his bristling mustache. "Now that we've had our fill, let us make our way to the next room for the dance, shall we?"

CHAPTER TWENTY-FIVE

Fradrick led the way. The elites eagerly pushed their chairs back and got up to follow, a few doing so slowly while holding their stomachs in discomfort.

Salevari and Aniria shared a distressed glance, but there was no stopping this river of events they had jumped into. Just like they had with the feast and the awkward conversations and the incessant questions they'd been bombarded with, they would endure this next part.

Once more hooking her arm around Simon's, Salevari walked toward the wide entryway at the end of the hall. She had thought the room holding the feast had been grandiose, but even it paled in comparison to the ballroom.

The ceiling was several stories tall. Three large chandeliers hung from thick iron chains. Hundreds of candles flickered in place, providing a dim light that spread evenly. The white marble floor beneath them gleamed as if recently polished. It stretched long and wide, bare except for one long table sitting along the far wall.

On this table sat an assortment of colorful and skillfully

crafted deserts as well as some more savory appetizers. It was manned by at least a dozen servers, several of whom watched the elites filter in with a hunger in their eyes. It was here that drinks were had as well.

A line formed with guests eagerly awaiting their turn to fill their goblets with wine or ale or, for the sailors in the party, something much stronger.

Crowded on a stage against one side of the room was another band. The musicians who had been playing during dinner took their seats among them. This orchestra was many lines deep, composed of a variety of instruments, many of which were unfamiliar to Salevari. They played the same somber note in unison as they prepared for their performance.

Guests continued pouring in and once everyone had taken what they wanted from the refreshment table, they gathered around the edges of the room, creating a spacious circle in the center where those who wished to could dance. A hush fell over the crowd as Fradrick strode confidently into the circle, his leather coat flapping with each step.

He scanned the room with a hungry grin. Salevari's skin prickled. She had a feeling she knew who he was looking for. Her suspicions were confirmed when they locked eyes. His grin broadened. He approached, bowed low, and offered his hand.

"If I may," he glanced at Simon, who nodded. "For this first dance, I would be honored if you would join me, Lady Salevari."

Salevari shot Simon a look, a plea for help, but all he did was cock his head to the side, encouraging her to go along with it. She grimaced, though she understood the importance of this moment. A dance with the Grand Admiral was the perfect opportunity for them to speak. They'd be close enough to hear each other's words while the music drowned them out for everyone else.

Sighing inwardly, she took Fradrick's hand, letting his massive palm envelop hers and lead her out onto the dance floor. He swung her in front of him, grabbing her waist and holding her other hand with expert control. She assumed her own position, her mind awhirl and nerves awakening as the reality of what was about to happen came upon her. All eyes were on them. She hoped Tera's and Simon's lessons stuck or she was about to make a fool of herself.

They stood like that for a minute as the band shifted into position. The conductor readied his baton. The pair stared into each other's eyes, his eager and enjoying the moment, hers determined and focused.

The music began. It was a slow melody with a happy feel behind it. The multitude of different instruments produced a sound that blended wonderfully and filled the room with a serene ambience.

Together, Fradrick and Salevari began their dance. Her feet moved on their own, following the pace that he set. They twirled slowly, methodically, as onlookers stared. She paid them no mind. Her focus was solely centered on what her body was doing. She could hardly hear the music.

The Grand Admiral pushed her out gently and held her hand high over her head, using his fingers to guide her as she spun in place, him orbiting her like the moon. He pulled her back in. She felt a smile creep onto her face that was not of her own making. It felt like an exciting bolt of lightning was coursing through her limbs as they flowed gracefully across the floor.

"I hope the feast was enjoyable," Fradrick said, his face alive with energy.

"Everything was delicious," she responded, and meant it. "I have never experienced anything quite like it. I must say your people have a knack for creating art on a plate."

If she didn't know any better, she might have thought the Grand Admiral was blushing. "I would have spared no expense or talent to ensure an impressive display be had for our special guests."

They danced in silence. Fradrick looked like he wanted to say more but required more courage to broach the subject. Finally, his reservoir filled enough for him to push the words out.

"I said it before, but I'll say it again, you are an absolute beauty to behold. I knew from the minute I first laid me eyes on you that you were someone special."

Salevari smiled, hoping her lips weren't too tight. If he only knew. "Why, Fradrick, do you always speak to married women this way?"

He threw his head back and laughed, tossing her out for another series of spins. "I don't," he admitted. "But for you, I'd fight a plains chief."

She raised an eyebrow, "Not a good way to deepen friendships, I think."

The Grand Admiral shrugged, but he said no more on the matter. He had made his admiration heard, not that Salevari hadn't suspected it from the beginning.

The song swelled, hinting that a grand finale was fast approaching.

A thought came to Salevari as they whirled within the open space, allowing her to take in the servers standing behind the refreshment table. They were watching her like everyone else, but something in their eyes. . . . A chill ran through her along with a foreboding feeling she couldn't shake.

"This ball only happens once a year, right?"

Fradrick nodded. "It's a special event that we host to commemorate our victory against the vashi."

"Lots of important people here tonight, then."

Again, the Grand Admiral nodded.

"I hope there's enough security to keep us all safe."

He shot her a quizzical look. "Of course, my lady. I have me guards posted throughout the room. No one would dare harm us here. Why do you ask?"

The music came to an end. Everyone clapped with gusto, both for the musicians and for the pair standing in the center of the room.

Salevari took a step back and curtsied, her lips a thin, unreadable line. "It must be my imagination. Thank you for the dance, Grand Admiral."

Fradrick bowed, though his face plainly stated his desire for them to continue their conversation.

Making her way back to Simon, she looked again toward the refreshment table and decided she needed a drink. She pulled him by the arm and led him to the line, Aniria following in their wake.

"Where is Drathanar?" Salevari asked.

"As a guard, I imagine they have him posted somewhere among the crowd," was Simon's easy reply.

"Here," a voice came to them from their left. Snaking his way through a few couples who were on their way to the center of the room to dance, he reached their place in line. His eyes remained on the crowd, scanning constantly. He murmured, "There are too many people here for my liking."

"Did Fradrick mention anything interesting?" Simon asked.

Salevari shook her head. "I didn't have the chance to ask. But while we were dancing I got a bad feeling, like someone with nefarious intent was watching us."

Eyebrows raised, Simon asked, "Does your bad feeling tell you who might be bearing this ill will?"

She motioned toward the servers.

"Not all of them," she clarified. "But a few sent off warnings in my mind as we entered the ballroom, and again while I was dancing. This feeling I have is strong, and I've learned to always trust my gut."

Simon thought for a moment. "Tera is working with them as Aniria's personal assistant. If we let her know, she can keep an eye on them."

"I will do that," Drathanar disappeared into the crowd hovering by the refreshment table before anyone else could volunteer.

As he left, a young man approached Aniria, who crossed her arms when she saw him. Salevari recognized him as the one who had been trying to speak to her all throughout the feast—or, at least, he had been speaking without caring much if she listened.

He bowed low, offering his hand for Aniria to take. She peered first at it, then defiantly into his eyes.

"I will not take no for an answer," he smirked. "I wish only for one dance. If you deny me, I will hound you for the remainder of the night until you grant me this honor."

Aniria flared her eyes at Salevari in exasperation, but she restrained herself from any fiery remarks. If the young man was good on his word, she would have to deal with him for hours on end. That was something she would rather not have to waste her energy on. With a defeated sigh, but making the displeasure plain on her face for all to see, she took his hand and allowed him to lead her out onto the dance floor.

Drathanar promptly returned, watching them go with a

steely expression. "Who is he?"

"Some young elitist who has his eyes on Aniria, it seems," Simon chuckled. "Will you go rescue her?"

The Dalyran general scowled, placing a hand on the hilt of his sword. "It's not my place."

After waiting a few more minutes, they finally got their drinks and moved for an empty gap along the wall where no one would bother them. Their solitude was short-lived and rudely broken, however, by a boisterous laugh.

"My friends!" Fradrick called out as he marched their way, a full tankard in his hands, its contents spilling onto the floor. He swung his arms around the shoulders of both Salevari and Simon, leaning into them for support. It quickly became apparent that this was not his first drink of the night.

"I hope you're enjoying yourshelves," he slurred.

"It's quite a remarkable party," Salevari was tempted to shove his arm off, but she allowed it to stay for now. If she lured him in close enough, perhaps she could pry him for some of the answers she needed. She remembered Tera's words about building rapport, however, and quickly changed tactics.

"Simon, you should have heard the Grand Admiral on the dance floor earlier. Apparently, he does not think too highly about marriage."

Simon raised an eyebrow but played along. "Not flirting with my wife again, were you?"

Barking laughter assaulted their ears. "Your wife loves to pick a fight doesn't she? Not to worry, chief. Been married once meself. I know how precious a lady who's shworn herself to you and you to her can be." His tone softened as old memories resurfaced. "Mine died years ago in the plague."

Salevari winced. Despite his grating personality, her heart went out to him. "I'm so sorry, Fradrick, I didn't know."

But the Grand Admiral vigorously shook his head. "No, no, don't you be shorry. There was nothing to be done about it. It was fate, I shuppose. I'm alright. I've had me time to mourn." A nostalgic smile returned to his face. "In the end, we had our good times together, she and I, but I still have a love out there that I can live for."

"And who might that be?" Simon asked.

A faraway look took hold of Fradrick as he said with deep passion, "The sea. She's always been me first love anyhow. By the waves do I miss her. What I wouldn't give to just sail away for a month or two and let her take me where she willed."

His eyes found Drathanar's still figure. The Dalyran general was taut as a spring watching Aniria spin around on the white marble, her red dress flowing despite her stiff movements as the young elite who had her hand kept her body close to his.

"You there, guard," Fradrick called out. He pushed himself off of Salevari and Simon and went to lean on Drathanar, who leered at him with displeasure.

"How can I help you, Grand Admiral?"

"You can't help me," he responded. "But you look like you need shome advice and I want to give it to you becaushe you're young. I wish someone had told me when I was your age. Sho now I'll do you the favor."

Drathanar raised a skeptical eyebrow.

"If ever in life you find something or shomeone you wish to protect and hold and cherish, you must do all you can to make it happen." The Grand Admiral swayed in place, but Drathanar caught him, his skeptical look quickly evaporating. He now hung onto every word.

"There can be no heshitation or second thoughts when it comes to securing what you want in life," he continued after taking a heavy swig from his tankard. "You must be shteadfast in your desire to shail forward. Grab the rudder with all your might and even should a rogue wave come surging your way, you shail through it. There can be no obstacle too great, 'cept your own shelf-doubt." He emphasized the last words, jabbing the viatari in the chest.

Drathanar stood in stunned silence. "I must continue forward through all obstacles, even myself," he repeated softly.

Fradrick clapped him hard on the back, happily exclaiming, "That'sh right!"

"Excuse me."

The Dalyran general walked off, making a beeline for Aniria. He pried the young human away from her and took her hands. She looked up in surprise. The young elite recovered quickly from the shock and stormed back ready to fight, but a single deathly glare from the viatari and he cowered away. A smile played on Aniria's lips as Drathanar, still holding her hand, now took her waist and led her across the floor. Lights sparkled in her eyes like stars as she stared into him.

Salevari chuckled. She approached Fradrick and gripped his shoulder. "I must say, that was some surprisingly good advice."

He shrugged. "Just our job as elders to teach the youth so they don't repeat the mistakes we made."

"Then there's something we should discuss in an effort to avoid a different sort of mistake from being made."

Fradrick raised an eyebrow, "Oh, and what might that be?"

"Thurn."

"What's that?" He leaned in, cupping a hand to his ears.

"We must discuss Thurn, Fradrick," Salevari yelled. She would not be denied.

But the Grand Admiral only shook his head, pointing at the orchestra.

"Music's too loud," he yelled, keeping his eyes averted. "I must greet me other guests anyway. We'll speak again." And with that he was gone, disappearing quickly into the crowd.

"Now what do you make of that?" Simon asked, finishing his drink.

The Chancellor did the same. "He clearly doesn't want to talk about it. But I don't think it's because he's behind it. That would be too obvious."

"If it makes you feel better, I don't believe he's behind Thurn, either. I think Zael may have been on to something with his third-party theory."

"Maybe," Salevari's brows furrowed as she took a moment to think, trying to piece the puzzle together. "But then why won't he talk about it?"

"Either he doesn't take the situation seriously or he doesn't like serious conversations. Considering he just shared with us the tale of his dead wife so easily, I think it's the former." Simon walked into Salevari's line of sight and bowed, offering his hand.

She studied it, arching her eyebrows in disbelief.

"Perhaps some distraction will help us find the key to this puzzle. Besides," he sneered. "We have to make some kind of show to prove that we're a married couple."

She sniffed and took his hand. "How far will you go, I wonder, for appearance's sake? I hope you don't plan to kiss me tonight."

"Please," he spun her into position, and they began stepping in rhythmic succession, following the crowd as they went. "I would never dare bring my lips so close to your fangs. I value my life too much."

She chuckled and allowed him to lead her through the orbiting mass of sweating bodies. She would never admit it out loud, but she found that she enjoyed this thing called dancing. She enjoyed the music. It invigorated her, made her *want* to dance. And the feeling she got when she spun, she never wanted it to leave.

As she danced, she spared a few glances to observe those around her. Laughter abounded as old married couples, newlyweds, and nervous, newly formed alliances all glided in sync to the melodic tune. Faces passed quickly in the dim, flickering light of the room, but two faces in particular were frozen in place.

A smile strained against the limits of Salevari's face as she witnessed Drathanar and Aniria pressed against each other, still against the world around them, their lips locked tightly together.

The image quickly disappeared as she was led away, the space between them overtaken by other dancers. She had to fight the urge to lean her head against Simon's chest. With everything going on in the moment, thoughts of her husband were running rampant in her mind. How she would have loved for him to be here, dancing with her. How they would have laughed.

The music ended. They all clapped. A shout pierced the din drawing everyone's attention.

One of the servers ran headlong into the crowd. Salevari saw a flash of metal and then the server yelped, throwing his hands up in the air as he fell forward, a dagger protruding from his back. In his own hands he held a sleek blade that glinted dangerously under the chandeliers. Tera jumped over the refreshment table and ran to the man she'd felled, finishing him off by running another dagger through his heart, even as he tried to crawl away.

He wasn't the only one causing a commotion. Screams

scattered across the crowd as three more waiters jumped over the refreshment table. They each pulled out a similarly sleek blade from their sleeves and made a mad dash in the same direction. Salevari followed their path and instantly knew what was happening.

Fradrick watched the waiters coming at him with confusion. A cutlass was strapped to his waist, waiting for him to pull it out but he remained frozen, stunned.

A few guards materialized from within the crowd and captured one of the servers, snapping his blade arm as he struggled against them.

Another of the waiters was stopped by Aniria as he ran by her. She grabbed him by the throat before he could pass and slammed him into the ground. The man groaned, the last sound he would ever make as Drathanar grimly drew his saber and brought it down on the waiter's neck.

The last assailant rushed forward wildly.

Finally, his wits returning, Fradrick reached for his cutlass, but he was far too late. The waiter slipped behind the Grand Admiral, grabbing him by the neck. He lifted his blade high in the air, ready to plunge it into his target's heart but that was as far as he got.

Salevari jumped from the crowd, tearing at the length of her dress to free her legs as she leapt at the attacker, tearing him off Fradrick's back and throwing him against the far wall. The assassin groaned as he hit it and fell to the floor. He struggled to stand. Salevari promptly walked over to where he lay and stomped on his neck, a resounding crack echoing across the room.

Silence abounded as all eyes fell on Salevari and her companions. Fradrick stared as well, breathing hard, his hand over his heart, his cutlass finally in hand.

"What is the meaning of this?" he roared.

But no one answered. He looked to Salevari for one and as the memory of how she had saved him returned, an understanding passed between them.

"These assassins were part of Thurn," Tera called out. "Check behind their ears. They'll all have the same tattoo, I wager."

Salevari checked behind the ear of the man she'd killed. Sure enough, a prominent "Þ" in thick black ink stared back at her. Fradrick inspected the man himself, shaking his head in disgust.

"There's no hiding from it now," Salevari brought his attention back to her. "We must discuss Thurn before they become too big of a problem to handle."

Nostrils flaring, Fradrick grumbled as he sheathed his blade, but nodded.

"We'll discuss this," he motioned toward the dead bodies that his guards were now collecting and then at Salevari and her companions. "*All* of this. I want to hear everything. First thing tomorrow, in me office. Aethel will escort you."

The eyes of every guest were still frozen on the wild scene they had just witnessed. Fradrick turned to them, unable to hide his fury and embarrassment.

"This ball is over," he declared. "Return to your suites. Lieutenant, double the guards. I want everyone here protected with every resource we have until we find the culprits behind this hideous act.

"Aye, sir!" One of the guards saluted and ran off.

Fradrick was quick to follow. He stormed through the stunned crowd, his broad shoulders stooped in anger, his hands clenched into beefy fists. As Salevari watched him go, she couldn't help but think, there would be a heavy price to pay for whoever it was that had enraged the Grand Admiral of Halding Port.

CHAPTER TWENTY-SIX

The sun had barely risen when Aethel woke them by knocking on their individual doors, calling them out by name. He stood silently outside in the hallway as he gave them time to get dressed. Once they were all ready, he bid for them to follow him, and he led them through the palace's many halls as he had when they first arrived.

As they approached Fradrick's study, Aethel hesitated and turned to them, saying softly, "The Grand Admiral has had a hard night of it. He's tired and in a foul mood the likes of which I've rarely seen. I urge you, try not to upset him further. Be mindful of your words. When he's done with you, I'll be right outside to take you back."

"Thank you, Aethel," Salevari said as the usher knocked on the door.

A gruff voice came from the other side, "Come in."

The heavy doors swung open and they stepped through.

Aethel bowed as he announced their arrival, "The lords and ladies of the plains as well as their guards and lady-in-waiting, as you asked, sire."

Fradrick looked up from the scroll he'd been reading, concern heavy on his face. His eyes were dark and sagging. His brow was creased like old paper. He leaned heavily with one arm on his desk while the other held up his reading material, more of its kind stacked high all around him.

His room was no worse for wear. The bookshelves that had once been so neat and organized now had gaping holes in them as books and scrolls had been ripped out. Those that proved useful remained on the Grand Admiral's wide desk. The others had been unceremoniously cast aside.

It was clear the Grand Admiral had been up all night reading. Salevari guessed he was catching up on any and all reports he could find about the movement that plagued his city.

"Close the doors, Aethel, if you would."

A soft click from behind, and they were alone.

"Now," Fradrick eyed them warily, leaning back in his chair and crossing his fingers over his broad chest. His normally good humor was a thing of the past. "Before we begin any kind of conversation I would be remiss if I did not thank you all for saving me last night from that dastardly attempt on me life. Believe me, I am grateful."

"Of course, we were only lucky—" Simon began to say, but Fradrick cut him off with a lifted finger.

"That said," he continued. "I find meself in a troubling position. You see, I no longer believe you to be who you claim you are."

Silence. The viatari dared not even share a glance for fear such a move might confirm the Grand Admiral's suspicions.

Simon cleared his throat, "I'm sorry, I must admit my confusion."

"What is your confusion?"

"It sounds like you're accusing us of something. What has

given you this idea that we're not from the plains?"

"Ah," a grim smile crept under his lavish mustache as he wagged a finger. "That's not what I said. I said I don't believe you are who you say you are—that is, lords and ladies of the plains. And you are clearly not, despite how you dress. No noble or elite or lord I know would have jumped into the fray as you did. No, most would have hidden, trembling in a corner as they wet themselves in their fine silk."

"Perhaps you underestimate the character of the highborn plainsman," Simon said in a low voice. "We are not the same as the fat elites who hide within this grand building."

"No, indeed," the Grand Admiral mused. "And perhaps you're right. Perhaps stopping assassins is just another day in the life of a plainsman noble. But me gut tells me otherwise. Now," Fradrick pushed himself out of his desk and walked around to the front, leaning back on it as he crossed his arms and studied them. "I will ask only once. Who are you, really?"

Simon opened his mouth to respond but a hand on his shoulder from Salevari stopped him. Their eyes met and an understanding passed between them. She glanced back at her viatari companions.

"There's no better time than now."

They nodded. Together, their bodies shimmered. Their human guises fell away to reveal silver hair, red eyes, and long, sharp fangs.

To his credit, Fradrick hardly blinked as he witnessed their transformation. Instead, he whistled softly, shaking his head in disbelief. Not a trace of fear crossed his features, though he didn't look too eager to take Salevari's hand and plant a kiss anymore.

"The viatari in the flesh," he murmured. "And I had only ever heard stories."

Salevari shrugged. "I can't speak to the truth of whatever you've heard, but we're real enough."

Raising a bushy eyebrow, he asked, "I see everyone's hair has turned silver but yours, my lady. Why is that?"

"Personal preference."

That earned a chuckle, but Fradrick's face quickly returned to its solemn state. "What brings your kind to Halding Port?"

"Now, that's the real question." For the next half hour, Salevari talked. She told an intricate tale of the acolytes and those they corrupted, about their war which had dragged into its destructive clutches the viatari, humans of the plains, burrowers, dwarves, and vashi. She spoke of the siege around the Three Spires. She shared the horrors and dangers that The Turned One and the Creature posed on Azar. Finally, she explained the real reason it had been deemed necessary to send a delegation to the humans of the coast.

"We learned that the vashi are under threat of invasion by the darinsha, a similar but much more hostile race from the northern waters. The vashi Supreme Overseer, Avmoshir, told us that their defenses were insufficient to counter the enemy, even if he were to pull all the forces he's lent us for our siege in the north. We cannot afford to lose the vashi as an ally and so—"

"And so you came here to find reinforcements to help repel this invasion," Fradrick finished. He gave a hefty sigh as he turned to face the window, staring at the ocean that stretched out before his city as if he could already see the battles that would rage there. "Strange that you believed the best way for me to lend you our fleet was to present me with a netful of lies."

"That was not our intent," Salevari shook her head. "It was necessary for us to come disguised so that we might get a good understanding of this city's culture and leadership before we began any sort of attempt at negotiation."

Fradrick whirled to face them, rugged anger in his voice. "We have no prejudices against your kind like the plainsmen do, viatari. You had no right to slink through our streets like spies at your own whim."

The Chancellor shrugged. "We had no way of knowing how the people here felt. We had no choice in that regard. Past experience required us to be cautious."

"And as you can see," Simon added. "Us plainsmen no longer fight against the viatari as before. We have joined them in their fight against the corrupted acolytes."

"And you?" Fradrick's hard gaze landed on Tera, who cocked an eyebrow.

"I'm just a wanderer," she shrugged easily. "I hold no allegiance to any particular race or region."

The Grand Admiral was silent for a moment as he thought things through. "It's quite a tale to believe," he finally said, much of his anger dissipating.

Salevari's eyes softened. She understood his hesitancy to believe. Even she wished most days that she was in some sick nightmare and that none of what was transpiring was really happening. But that wasn't reality.

"It's all true."

The Grand Admiral nodded slowly. Deflated, he walked back around his desk and sank into his chair, letting out a long, heavy breath of air. His fingers drummed on the wooden surface.

"You said you came to negotiate," he finally said. "What's your offer?"

Salevari stepped forward and placed her hands on the Grand Admiral's desk, leaning down so their eyes were level.

"We need Halding Port's fleet to reinforce the vashi. We need you to keep their waters safe. You don't have to send any forces to join us in the north, but we welcome any support you might give."

"Quite a tall ask," Fradrick murmured, his eyes half-closed and distant. "I'm sure I've told you before how much we hate the vashi. And they hate us with equal measure."

"We're not asking you to be their friends," Salevari insisted. "We're asking you to work with them not just for the sake of the Southern Seas, but your own coastline. The vashi may hate you, but they've left your people alone for centuries so long as your fishermen don't cross into their waters. Do you think the darinsha will be so restrained once they've wiped out their rivals?"

"I think if we leave them alone to do as they please, they might. What business would they have with us?"

"The darinsha have sworn themselves to The Turned One," Salevari said, a slight note of exasperation entering her voice.

"Seems to me that's more of a reason not to provoke this 'Turned One.' If we don't fight her, she'll have no reason to attack us."

This brought a scoff from the viatari. "Her goal is to envelop all of Azar into a state of chaos. All of it. That includes Halding Port. She's already attacking you and you don't even know it."

The Grand Admiral cocked his head. "How so? I've not read any reports detailing an attack on me city."

"She's behind Thurn."

Distress popped onto Fradrick's face briefly at the mention of the name, but he quickly regained his composure. Clearing his throat, he took a breath.

"Very well, let's say I believe your premise and that it is in

Halding Port's interest to aid the vashi. Let's even pretend I can convince the city to get behind this effort willingly. So far, all I've heard is a list of demands. What would you give in return?"

"For starters," Salevari grinned, a gleam in her eyes. "We can take out this Thurn organization that's been a thorn in your side for the last two years."

Bushy eyebrows shot up at that. "And why would you do that?"

"Call it a show of good faith. In getting rid of them we can safeguard you from any future attacks they may have planned and prove to you that whether you join our cause or not, The Turned One has her sights on your city."

Another pause as Fradrick considered the proposal. "You truly believe this 'Turned One' is behind Thurn?"

Salevari nodded. "I have no doubt she has her hand in this."

Letting loose another great puff of air, Fradrick grunted, "Well, if you can prove it and get rid of them at the same time, this city would certainly owe you a debt. But how will you find them? My own intelligence network has been unable to track down any sort of headquarters or ringleader."

The Dalyran Chancellor cracked a smile as she motioned for Zael to join her. "We have not been idle. Zael here took it upon himself to follow a hunch he had, and it led him straight to a man they called 'the interpreter.' From him, we obtained some valuable information that I think points us in the right direction."

Fradrick shifted his gaze, waiting for an explanation.

"The man I spoke with had a tattoo on his leg of a gravestone with a particular symbol: a cross with skulls hanging off the arms. There was also the remains of a letter in his wastebin. The letter was too far gone to salvage any kind of complete message but there were still a few words I could decipher. One of them had to do with a graveyard. I suspect the headquarters may be underground or you would have found it already. The entrance may be in a cemetery, though which one it is has yet to be uncovered."

The Grand Admiral's eyes widened at the mention of the tattoo, "That symbol is used by the diggers at Origin Graveyard. It's Halding Port's oldest. The fact he had it inked on his skin means he worked there and was likely a man of some import among the diggers."

"Then we'll need to scout that area to discover where the entrance to these tunnels might be," Salevari said with confidence. "Once we find it, you can be sure we'll finish this business with them, and you'll never hear the mention of 'Thurn' again."

Fradrick nodded, a heavy weight coming off his shoulders. "What else can your alliance offer?"

Zael sneered. "You need more?"

Shrugging, the Grand Admiral replied, "You're the one that said taking down this organization would be a gesture of good faith. Which means you must have something else that can actually benefit us in the long run. I want to know what it is."

If Salevari could have avoided her second offer she would have, but Fradrick had seen right through her. She would have to lay it all out and hope the dice fell in her favor. She doubted he would be foolish enough to decline their help when he so clearly needed it. But a small worm of doubt wriggled within her mind.

"I have yet to receive word from the dwarven king stating he will agree to it, but I have a feeling he will. When you took us out to see your city I was impressed by your defensive capabilities and the strength of your fleet. But you stand to make both stronger."

"How?"

"The dwarves possess a technology that they've already shared with the viatari. It's a contraption that shoots fire and stone with such power it can knock down entire sections of trees with one shot. It's called a cannon. If you were to install them to your walls and fleet, it would increase your firepower in ways even I can't imagine. Halding Port would truly be impregnable."

Fradrick leaned back in his chair. "It's a nice promise, but alas, only a promise. What if the dwarven king refuses to share his cannons with us?"

"I do not believe he will," she narrowed her eyes. "After all, there's no reason not to make one's friends stronger in the face of a threat that could swallow the world."

The Grand Admiral nodded. "Very well, I'll consider this alliance. I'll need to know more of these 'darinsha' and the threat they truly pose if I'm to convince the elites to fall in line with this course of action, however."

"Aren't you the Grand Admiral?" Salevari scowled. "Why does it matter what they think? All they do is eat and sleep like fat pigs, anyway."

A boisterous laugh filled the room. Fradrick wiped away a tear once he finally settled down. "Ah, my lady, that may be, and I may have a great weight of authority in this place, but the elites control the purse strings. Without them, I'm left in the water without a sail. They'll need to agree with helping the vashi if I'm to promise anything. That's why I told you it was a tall ask.

"I'm a reasonable man. I can see the threat. I can swallow

me pride to protect me city and the waters we fish, even if it requires fighting alongside a sworn enemy. But our elites aren't like that. That's why I say the more information you can give me, the better chance I'll have of convincing them."

The viatari's scowl converted into a grimace. "Even we don't know much. We've only just learned of their existence. What the vashi's Supreme Overseer told us was that they are a powerful, warlike race. The vashi defeated them long ago, but it nearly destroyed them to do so. In terms of what they're like, I understand they're similar in many ways to the vashi themselves."

Fradrick rolled his shoulders as he stood, though he stayed behind his desk. "Well, it's a start. I do believe we have the beginnings of an agreement."

The two leaders stared at each other, a final reading to make sure nothing that needed to be said was left unsaid. Fradrick presented his hand.

"Take care of Thurn, and your good will is established. I'll do all I can to move forward with this proposal. If you get those cannons into the deal, all the better. And when the time comes that Halding Port's fleet must set out to sea, I'll personally take command of the flagship."

Salevari glanced at the hand, then back up at Fradrick. The time for talking was done. Now was the time to ensure all the promises she'd made weren't just empty words. It was another chance to show the mettle of the viatari. She would gain Halding Port as an ally, no matter what it took.

She took his large hand. They squeezed.

"Firm grip," Fradrick grunted.

Salevari smiled. "I could break your hand."

He laughed as they released each other. "I believe it."

Sitting back down, he sighed. "Go, do what you must in

my city. I'll send some officers from my intelligence division to your quarters to share any information they might have on Thurn that you don't already have. Know that I'll keep secret the fact that you are viatari. Obviously, you must maintain your human appearances once you leave this office. When Thurn is taken care of and the time is right, you can reveal your true selves to the elites. I'm sure that'll help lend credibility to the tale I must tell them."

The viatari nodded and shimmered once more as they took on their human guises. Again, the Grand Admiral shook his head, this time in admiration.

"And when we have some peace and quiet," he grunted, putting his feet on his desk and shutting his eyes as he leaned back. "I would love to learn more of your people. If we are to be friends, I think it is only right."

Salevari glanced over her shoulder as she placed a hand on the doors leading out to the hallway. "I look forward to that time, Fradrick."

Pushing against the heavy oak, the viatari, Simon, and Tera exited the Grand Admiral's office. They soon found themselves back in Aethel's calming presence and followed him back to their rooms, leaving the Grand Admiral to sleep in peace.

CHAPTER TWENTY-SEVEN

Thuradin saw his wife and immediately knew he was dreaming.

She was as beautiful as he remembered with luscious brown hair that fell gracefully past her shoulders in a waterfall braid. Her voice was light and cheerful when she spoke to him. They sat together on a section of rocky cliffs overlooking the gigantic caverns of Dun'Burell, their feet hanging precariously over the edge. They were laughing, their hands meeting in the middle.

"How I've missed ye, lass," Thuradin murmured.

Agata shot him an incredulous look. "So, it only takes dying ta finally catch the attention of the great Thuradin Stonebeard."

He made a face. "Ye know I never wanted ta leave ye . . . I had no choice—"

"And still he cannae take a joke even when I toss it straight at his face."

They shared a warm look, then beheld the many clusters of stalagmites and stalactites before them, giving the cavern an appearance of the maw of some ferocious predator frozen in time.

"I know this is a dream."

"What gave it away," Agata chuckled. "The fact that I'm here?"

Thuradin dropped his head into his hands. As good as it was to see his wife, even if only in a dream, the problems of his waking self still tormented him.

"I don't know what ta do," he said hoarsely. "I've made a terrible mistake, and I don't know how I can ever make amends. I don't even know how I made such an error in judgment ta begin with."

Agata regarded him with pity, but there remained warmth in her eyes. "My husband, ye're the strongest, most loyal, and most dutiful dwarf I've ever known. I know ye always strive for what's honorable. I know, in the end, ye always make the right choice. Ye never shy away from sacrifice, from duty. That's just the type of dwarf ye are."

Thuradin sniffed and turned to look at her, but her image was fading. Her voice was barely audible as she whispered, "Hold on ta who ye are."

He blinked, and found himself lying on his cot, the remnants of tears sliding down quickly as if trying to escape his notice. Hanging off his fingers was a half-filled tankard of stale ale. He groaned and lifted himself up into a sitting position, cradling his pounding head for a moment.

Pushing himself to his feet, he stumbled across his tent to the small basin on the other side. He splashed some water onto his face, sputtering as its cold touch helped chase away the effects of last night's drink. Leaning over the basin, breathing heavily, he took a moment to gather himself.

For the millionth time, Thuradin reflected on what he'd had Morteth do. Unsurprisingly, since that fateful night, there'd been no sign of the dwarven assassin. He was certain that Morteth was mounted up with all his belongings riding as fast and as far away from the Three Spires as he could get. With any luck, he would never hear from that wretch again.

That's just the type of dwarf ye are.

Agata's words jumped back to the forefront of his mind. They were from a dream, but they rang true. Only, they shouldn't have. How could he be the dwarf she had described when he had approved—assisted, even—in such a heinous act? Nothing about him made sense anymore. But he knew he couldn't let the subject remain as it was and fester. He'd wasted enough days wallowing in misery. He had to explain himself to somebody, anybody.

And he knew who to start with.

Borim had told him weeks ago that King Dunkell was planning a visit to the siege camp as a way of boosting morale for the dwarves. Luckily for Thuradin, the king had chosen this week to come, arriving only yesterday.

Confident in his course of action, he strode out of his tent and stomped through the crowded paths straight for where he knew Dunkell and the royal entourage had pitched their tents.

Before long, a large, wide tent with numerous banners of the royal insignia—a black, double-bladed axe—fluttering in the wind filled his vision. Royal guards formed a perimeter around it, their hard eyes and thick, heavy armor discouraging anyone from testing them. They studied Thuradin as he approached.

"I'm here ta see the king," he announced.

"No one sees King Dunkell without his invitation," one of the guards stationed in front of the entrance growled.

"I thought he came here ta see *us*," Thuradin countered. He wished he still had the authority he used to have as commander of the royal guard, but those days had long since passed.

"He came ta see *real* dwarves, perhaps," the guard replied, spitting on the ground before Thuradin. "That would nae include yerself."

The tent flap moved to the side and a stout, black-haired dwarf with a neatly trimmed beard stepped out. An intricate golden crown with a large ruby in its center sat on his head. King Dunkell saw Thuradin, saw the guards, and immediately understood the situation.

"Now, Harrek, Thuradin has been pardoned for whatever vile act ye still seem ta take issue against him for. I will see him as I've seen all my other subjects."

"My king," the guard slammed his plated fist against his chest in salute as he inclined his head. "With respect, his very presence is an insult ta our kind."

Dunkell narrowed his eyes, his voice dropping dangerously low. "That would be something for me ta decide, young Harrek."

Harrek's face turned a shade of scarlet. Grimacing, he stepped to the side. The King led Thuradin to one of the rear chambers where they might have a little more privacy from the staff carrying out their duties nearby.

"Thuradin, my friend, it's good ta see ye. I wondered if ye might show up at some point."

They gripped each other's shoulders affectionately. Dunkell looked him over once, his pity plainly visible.

"I take it ye've already heard, then." Thuradin sighed, reading the expression on his king's face as easily as he could a scroll. News traveled fast in camp. He shouldn't have been surprised that this particular story would have already reached the King's ears. Especially when many saw the assassination as an affront to dwarvish cultural norms.

Dunkell nodded somberly. "I have. Is it true? Did ye

actually have a hand in this assassination?"

Thuradin hesitated, but decided honesty was his best course forward and nodded. If there was anyone in the whole Dwarven Kingdom who might be a little sympathetic to what he'd done, it would be Dunkell. After all, he had used the same assassin to put a target on his own father's back.

"I did."

"I cannae judge ye, as ye well know, for reasons I'd rather nae state in case curious ears are about. I must say, however, how shocked I am by this."

"I don't know why I did it," Thuradin admitted almost pleadingly. "Ye know it goes against everything I stand for ta go against an enemy—any enemy—in such an underhanded manner."

Dunkell nodded slowly. He made his way to a small table in the corner where there sat several steins and a tapped cask. He poured amber liquid into two of them, offering one to Thuradin. Thuradin declined, pointing at his own head and grimacing. The King shrugged and chugged the first drink, cradling the second.

"It's true that what happened goes against what many might think of the great Thuradin Stonebeard. But what of it? The fact of the matter is ye *did* do it." He took another sip of ale, smacking his lips. "Tell me, why have ye come ta me?"

Thuradin shook his head. "Ta be honest, I'm nae entirely sure."

A knowing grin sprouted on Dunkell's face as he wagged a finger. "Ah, but ye do know. Ye probably came ta try and explain yerself ta me, ta see if I had any insight on the matter that could settle yer actions and the type of dwarf ye believe yerself ta be, thus helping ye feel better."

Thuradin shrugged. "Perhaps."

Shaking his head, Dunkell finished his second drink and tossed the stein aside. "I sympathize with ye, my friend, but the fact of the matter is what ye did was a dishonorable thing. I've already heard requests by other high-ranking dwarves that I should have yer exile reinstated–something I do nae intend on doing, so ye know," he said quickly as Thuradin shot him an alarmed look.

"But all the same," the King continued. "Yer actions have created a terrible tension within our own camp. I have enough ta deal with in the Silent Mountains. I don't need problems arising out of my forces here. I cannae be in two places at once ta handle them."

Heat rising to his face, Thuradin shook his head in exasperation. His thoughts became muddled as he spat out, "Hork was an abuser. He hit his own wife with nae a care–I saw it with my own eyes! I couldn't allow such a sorry excuse of a dwarf ta continue on like that. What I did, I did ta free her. Surely ye have some understanding of that type of choice. Think of what ye would have done ta yer brother had I nae been in the tunnel that day ta do it for ye."

Dunkell took a minute to respond, his voice hushed when he did, "Committing a terrible crime for the good of the people is different from doing it for one person. One is more selfish. I'll let ye decide which is which. My advice, Thuradin," a heavy hand fell on his shoulder, followed by an uncomfortable squeeze. "Go find Lyrie. Gain her forgiveness somehow. It'll be the first step in healing this rift I feel forming. If she can find it in her heart ta forgive ye, others should have no issue doing the same."

With that, Thuradin found himself excused and escorted out of the tent.

He muttered to himself as he stomped away. His heart felt

cold in his chest, lurching reluctantly against his ribcage with every step he took. He raised his eyes to the clear blue sky above. A pair of hawks flew high overhead. Whatever heat he had felt during his conversation with the King dissipated gradually as he watched them circle each other. Perhaps Dunkell was right. Perhaps what he needed to do was try once more to explain things to Lyrie and ask—no, beg for her forgiveness.

Whether she would listen. . . .

He made his way to her tent and found that she was not there. Asking around, he learned that she was on duty patrolling the camp's perimeter. Not wanting to waste time looking for her in what was a rather expansive perimeter, he went to a taskmaster to ask for her specific whereabouts. The human he spoke with determined her approximate location for him after consulting a series of maps and lists. With a quick thanks, he turned and set out in that direction as quickly as his feet would take him.

In no time he reached the stand of trees the taskmaster had pointed out on a map. Lyrie would be around here somewhere on patrol, but Thuradin had to be careful when tracking her. The last thing he needed was to find himself the subject of an ambush because she and her patrol thought they were being snuck up on by some enemy.

Luckily for him, it didn't take long before he noticed movement out of his peripherals. Turning to look, he saw a line of dwarves marching just a few dozen feet ahead to his right. He called out to them.

"Lyrie Swordmeist!"

The patrol halted and turned toward his voice. A few drew their weapons. One of them took off their helmet, revealing a tight bun of blonde hair. Even from this distance Thuradin could see the disgust on her face. Clearly, she'd recognized his voice.

She took a few steps away from her patrol then waited for him to come to her. He approached with some trepidation. Now that he was here, he wasn't sure what to say. He felt a simple "I'm sorry" would be woefully inadequate.

"What do ye want, Thuradin?" Lyrie barked after a minute passed without him saying anything. "As ye can see, I'm a bit busy keeping the camp safe."

Thuradin let loose, the words vomiting out of him before he could control himself. "I don't know why I did what I did, Lyrie, ye must believe me. Ye *know* me, ye know I'm nae the type ta stoop ta such a low level. I cannae explain what was going on in my head. Aye, I wanted ta protect ye. I hated seeing what Hork was doing ta ye, and it was only after the deed was done that I realized–"

Lyrie held up a hand, bringing his stream of words to a halt midsentence. She leered at him, her eyes like daggers digging into his own.

"Ye're unbelievable," she shook her head. "I honestly don't know who ye are anymore, Thuradin. I suggest ye return ta camp until it's yer turn ta patrol the perimeter. I don't want ta hear anything else from ye."

Putting on her helmet, she marched back to her patrol and led them deeper into the woods, quickly disappearing from sight.

Thuradin staggered back. He shouldn't have expected much out of this encounter, truth be told, but the reality of this broken friendship–and what could have been–stung him deeply nonetheless.

Eyes downcast, he trudged back the way he came. So blank was his mind, he only realized he was back in camp when the grass underfoot turned into a thin layer of flattened dirt.

"Father."

Thuradin's head snapped up. Myrna stood only a few paces before him. A mixture of confusion, revulsion, and pity adorned her face. Her hand sat loosely on the hilt of her sword.

"Myrna."

The two stared at each other for several minutes, neither saying a word. Finally, she opened her mouth as if to speak, but instead shook her head and turned away.

"Myrna," Thuradin called out again. "Wait!"

Myrna stopped but didn't turn around.

"I don't know what ta say," he confessed shakily. His heart hammered in his ears, drowning out all other sound. "But I'm so sorry if all I've done is disappoint ye. This is nae what I wanted. Ye must believe me."

After a brief pause, still with her back to him, Myrna responded flatly, "I must speak with Serania." She walked away.

Someone could have swung a heavy two-handed war hammer over his head and Thuradin couldn't have felt more crushed than he did now. Tears stung his eyes, but he held them back. He refused to allow himself to be seen in such a miserable state by anyone in this camp. Shaking his head and slapping his face to try and force back some composure, he returned to his tent. There remained at least one other he could see, one more friend who he might explain this all to. One more pillar of support he could lean on.

He slipped through the entrance to Borim's tent and sat heavily on the floor, leaning against the stone basin within. Borim sat up in surprise, regarding him with curiosity.

"I know there's no door," he said. "But usually people knock before they enter."

Despite the jovial nature of the words, they were said with a heaviness that matched the air around them. Thuradin didn't want to recognize it. It was a sign of how this conversation would go, but he had to at least try to see it through. Borim had always been there for him, always understood him. This time could be no different.

"I don't know what ta do," he admitted.

"Aye," Borim said softly, still studying his friend. "Ye've put yerself into a corner, haven't ye?"

"I don't know why I did it." Thuradin tried to explain everything that had led up to his decision. Morteth's temptations. Hork's behavior. His feelings for Lyrie. The brain fog. All of it.

Borim listened without interrupting. His eyes relayed no judgment, but his frown never lifted.

In the end, Thuradin wasn't sure he was able to explain himself well enough, despite trying his best. Borim looked him over for a while longer before responding.

"Thuradin, I've known ye a long time. Ye're my oldest friend and that friendship will never die as far as I'm concerned."

For a moment, Thuradin could almost breathe easier as Borim's words soothed him. But the dwarven warrior wasn't finished.

"However, what ye did was a travesty. It was dishonorable, which is an understatement. I honestly cannae believe that ye were behind it, and yet ye admit it ta me yerself," he shook his head. "I don't know, my friend. I don't know what ye expect me ta say. I don't know how ta help ye. All I can say is that we must each take responsibility for our actions. When the time comes ta reap the rewards—for good or ill—we must accept the consequences."

Thuradin's vision blurred as a strange numbness took hold. Borim was right, of course. He knew it. But it still felt like he didn't understand. By Nythirim, he himself didn't understand. Could he really expect anyone else to?

After several minutes of silence, Thuradin stood and shuffled out of the tent without a word. Borim watched him go.

In a trance, he took the few steps necessary back to his own tent. Upon entering, his eyes were met by his twin axes resting on the nightstand beside his cot. Their serrated edges gleamed sharply. They called to him.

It felt as if the ground were collapsing around him, as if the world were falling apart, as if The Turned One had already won. It was because of his own actions, he knew, but he was now forsaken by everyone he had ever known and loved. He was alone. His chest felt empty, an unfeeling muscle within pumping blood for no apparent reason. There was no light, no heat, just the continuous, mechanical pump.

Tears returned, and this time he let them fall. He stepped forward and grabbed his axes, examining them, admiring their craftsmanship. Their purpose, ever since he had left his home, had been to defend Azar, to protect the world from those who would throw it and all its inhabitants into a perpetual state of chaos. Of destruction. Of desolation.

The same desolation he now felt.

Was there a point in continuing this defense? Was there a point in saving Azar from the forces of the corrupted acolytes if he had no place in it anymore? He would fade away from existence slowly, his life a long tale of infamy because of a single lapse in judgment. Was that really what his legacy would be?

He wiped the tears from his eyes, sniffling hard. Turning, he went back outside with the hope that the brightness of the day might alleviate some of this despair. Instead, his vision filled with the Three Spires looming overhead in the distance.

He gripped his axes tightly, his knuckles turning white. Moving on their own, his feet led him forward until he had once again left camp. With each minute that passed, the Three Spires loomed larger and more prominently.

He could fade away, he thought, or he could leave this world in a blaze of glory. He could leave it with a final account of heroism, an image of the duty-bound dwarf he'd always aspired to be. He ground his teeth, a new resolve forging a path before him. He would be remembered, oh yes, even if the sole reason behind it was a spectacular death.

CHAPTER TWENTY-EIGHT

Dried leaves crunched underfoot as Thuradin hiked his way through a small patch of woods. His axes hung heavily from his belt, slapping against his thighs. Pushing branches aside as he passed, he let them whip back into place without a second thought. His eyes never wavered from their forward path.

He was done thinking. He had decided what he had to do, not just for himself, but for Myrna. As it was, she couldn't carry the Stonebeard name on and hope to live out of the shadow of disgrace he had muddied it with. He had to redeem it, if only so that she could live on with some semblance of respect and honor.

Those were the thoughts that dominated his mind, that kept his feet moving forward one step at a time. Nothing else mattered. Not Azar. Not the friends he was leaving behind. Not even the value of his own life.

So caught up in these thoughts, he didn't hear the sentry hailing him from behind until he felt a hand grip his shoulder and forcibly turn him around.

"I said, halt!" the sentry yelled. Once the dwarf realized who he had stopped a look of confusion crossed his face. On either side of him stood a human and a viatari, their weapons drawn but lowered.

"What are you doing here, Thuradin?" the viatari asked. Thuradin recognized him but couldn't recall his name. His foggy mind churned for a moment, trying to summon it forth. Finally, after a few minutes, it came to him. He had fought with this warrior many times defending Aleganthia.

"Evening, Vandaar," Thuradin said, casting his gaze to the side. "Been a while since I've seen ye."

Vandaar Lumeward, once a companion to Borim when he had set out to secure an alliance between Dalyr and Aleganthia, nodded. "I ask again, what are you doing here? You're not scheduled for patrol in this area."

"I'm going ta the mountains," Thuradin answered, tapping the axes hanging off his belt.

The dwarven sentry guffawed. "By yerself? Are ye mad?"

"Perhaps," Thuradin glanced over his shoulder, looking at the path he wanted to take. He should just turn and walk away. These guards didn't truly care what his intentions were, especially the dwarf. They were just doing their jobs, and he had no time to waste humoring them. The longer he stayed, the more he feared he might think himself out of this course of action.

"If ye'll excuse me, lads," he turned and continued on his way.

"I will have to report this rash decision," Vandaar warned. "Serania will not be pleased."

"Do what ye must," Thuradin called back. He didn't care. As far as he was concerned, whoever Serania sent after him would only come along to collect his body anyway.

The sentries watched him go until he disappeared in the trees.

Now that he was alone again, a steel-like resolve returned where the sentries' distraction had weakened it. His lips fell into a stubborn line. His fingers twitched. He had perhaps an hour's march before he arrived at the base of the Three Spires.

An hour to mull over what he was doing and what he would do when he got there.

An hour to dwell over all the mistakes of his life, using the fire from those failures as fuel to keep his feet moving.

An hour to feel the breeze caress his face as he continued stomping through the undergrowth.

Serania paced, her hands behind her back, frustrated, annoyed.

Ever since Felix's failed assault on the Three Spires, he had kept himself locked away in the command tent. Nobody saw him. Not even Serania was permitted to enter. The guards stationed out front made it absolutely clear what orders they'd been given and they, being the loyal warriors they were, refused to disobey.

And so, command fell to her. She didn't mind the authority, nor the responsibility. It was how it had come about that set her blood aflame with ire.

All her life she had known Felix as the most level-headed viatari to ever walk Azar. In many ways, she had aspired to possess the same level of mental fortitude. But what she was witnessing now was alien to her. This insufferable, stubborn, foolish version of her uncle was not the same one she knew. There was no excuse for it, even with the extenuating circumstance of Victria's capture.

If anything, he should have been performing at his best in

order to secure her release. That's what she would do if she were in his situation. At least, that's what she believed.

Before her, observing her with their erratic tendrils, sat the four acolytes. They had convened days ago to discuss the ramifications of the loss they had suffered, and to try and give birth to new strategies that might help them meet their goals but to no avail. Short of sitting in these foothills for an indefinite amount of time and maintaining their siege, no good had come from their discussions.

"We should be grateful that Felix's assault didn't cost us the siege," Serania spat out not for the first time.

The First One's ancient voice filled the tent, "We must be patient. Time may yet provide us another opportunity so long as we keep our corrupted siblings contained."

"There's no guarantee that we *can* keep them contained!" she shot back. "Yes, we can keep their armies from pushing through and running rampart across Azar, but a small group could easily slip by us under cover of night. I've had to redeploy several garrisons and outposts south of us to bolster our forces here so we could maintain our perimeter, but now there lies no safety net past that."

"Is there no one else we can call on for aid?" Scorpus scoffed, the sound like a splash in the ocean. "I never realized the resources of your cause were so limited."

Serania leered at the acolyte from the Throne of the Deep, her least favorite. If anyone had asked her, she would have said it was more trouble than he was worth having him here.

"We viatari are stretched thin. Any reserves that remain are in Aleganthia and Dalyr. The rest of us are here fighting and dying. The humans are in the same boat. And as you very well know, the dwarves and burrowers can't send anymore help our way until they've sorted out their own problems at home. Need I remind you why we can't call upon the vashi as well?"

"I know well the threats we face," Scorpus drawled. "But I still find our current situation to be woefully suboptimal. At this rate, our dear brother and sister need only send wave after wave of their minions to pound against our lines until we finally break and the world is theirs."

Serania let loose a haughty breath but said nothing. As much as she hated to admit it, the acolyte was correct. But there was no solution to this problem that she could see, and if he had one, he wasn't sharing it.

"There is something else we must address," Veliris piped up in his soft voice. His tendrils writhed, several of them shooting out to mix with those of his brothers. "Have you sensed it as well?"

A moment of silence fell as flashes of light burst between the acolytes' tendrils. Serania stopped her pacing and watched with a growing sense of distress. What new problem could these troublesome beings bring before her now?

"Disturbing," The First One finally murmured.

"Unfortunate," Faenerus agreed.

Scorpus snickered. "Perhaps they need not send their minions against us, after all."

"What is it?" Serania asked, dread knotting together in her stomach.

"We have detected a wave of corruptive energy wash over this camp, undoubtably from our sister," The First One answered. His tendrils pulsed rapidly with light like a heartbeat. "You must send out a message to everyone here that they must continue to do all they can to control their emotions and feelings. They must maintain a sound mind and emotional fortitude. Perhaps implementing a regimen of meditation in the mornings will help produce a standard for everyone."

Serania shook her head, confused. She pinched the bridge of her nose to stop the dull ache that was giving birth behind her eyes. "I don't understand. Why is this suddenly a priority?"

White tendrils squirmed before her. "Do you not know? I explained to Felix weeks ago of the capabilities our sister had with us being so close to her and told him to warn the camp and how to counter her influence. He did not share this knowledge?"

"Felix never said anything to me," Serania groaned, rubbing her temples. "Or to anyone, for that matter. What do you mean we need to counter her influence?"

The answer was not one she wanted to hear.

"One of our sister's abilities is to manipulate the emotions and thoughts of any person," The First One explained. "If that person dwells too often on the negative, allows darkness to enter their heart, they become all the more susceptible to her whispers. The worst part is they don't even realize what is happening. She can control their choices, their actions, and all the while they believe these things come of their own free will."

"It is how she so easily implants herself in a society and slowly molds it into the subservient state she desires," Faenerus added.

This sounded eerily familiar to Serania, as if she had witnessed something like this happening already. With his next few words, The First One confirmed her suspicions.

"I believe, sadly, that she has already taken root in several hearts within this camp."

"Felix," she breathed, her eye widening.

The acolyte's tendrils nodded. "He isn't the only one, either. This last pulse we detected was strong. Strong enough for us to track its target, as if she wanted us to know who she had grabbed hold of."

"Can't you do anything to stop it?" Serania asked incredulously. "We've been here for months!

"We have been," was the answer. "However, we are too close to her area of influence, and our camp is stretched over too large an area. My power is enough to nullify much of hers, enough so she does not corrupt you on the spot, but I cannot negate her entirely. That is why it was so important for everyone in this camp to do their part."

"Is this true?"

Serania turned to see who had entered the tent. Myrna's bright green eyes were wide, a sense of horror behind them as she beheld the acolytes.

"Is it true?" The dwarf repeated. "Those who are affected cannae act of their own accord even if they think they are?"

"It is true, little one," Faenerus rumbled.

"Myrna," Serania said, confused. "What brings you here?"

Her voice came back timid, scared. "I came ta discuss my father, but when I approached the tent I heard what was being discussed and . . . I fear I've made a terrible mistake."

"What do you mean?"

Just then the tent flap was pushed back and another figure entered.

"Vandaar," Serania blinked with surprise. "What are you doing here? Aren't you on patrol?" Her heart faltered as a sudden thought came to her. "Has there been a breach in the perimeter?"

"Not at all," the viatari said smoothly. "But I came to deliver some other news that I thought you should know."

He glanced at the dwarf and hesitated, unsure if he should continue. Serania motioned for him to do so.

"Our patrol encountered Thuradin Stonebeard walking out of camp. He was making his way for the Three Spires armed only with his axes. When we asked him his intentions, he would not say outright, but I inferred it was not beneficial to his well-being. He would not turn back and so I came to report his strange behavior."

The only sound within the tent was Myrna's ragged breathing.

"I must go," she choked out. "I need a ram."

She rushed out. Serania watched her go with alarm. If The Turned One had manipulated Thuradin into throwing away his life so recklessly, how long before she manipulated Felix into doing something similar. She swallowed hard, striving to keep her whirling thoughts in check.

"Thank you, Vandaar," she said with some difficulty. "You may return to your post."

The viatari bowed and left the tent, leaving her alone with the acolytes once more. A plethora of panicked thoughts hit her all at once, coming at her like a raging whirlwind.

"Is there a way to free those who have fallen into her grasp?" she asked after a few minutes had passed.

"If they are brought to me, I can purge whatever taint my sister has polluted them with, just as I did to the black waters of the north," The First One said. "But that should only be for the worst cases. For many, simply exercising mental and emotional restraint will be enough to expel her influence."

Serania nodded. If anyone warranted having the acolyte purge them, it would be Felix. She suspected he was too far gone to throw off The Turned One's whispers on his own. She knew now what her immediate priority was.

Sitting in these foothills and waiting for their enemy to grow bored enough to die on their own was no longer an option. If they continued as they were, The Turned One would pick them off one by one over time until the entire army deserted. If they wanted to end this conflict, they needed Felix—and they needed him to be of sound mind. Whatever hold the corrupted acolyte had over him, she needed to break it.

Before Thuradin towered the Three Spires in all their malevolence. He sat within a pair of bushes just on the edge of the tree line. The only thing between him and the mountain path directly across from him, his future, his end, was a small field of patchy earth.

He unhooked his axes and lay them across his knees as he crouched, studying the area. Despite what he was doing, he wasn't so foolish as to charge in blindly. If he wanted to die an honorable, glorious death, he had to take as many of these corrupted foes as he could. He had to approach this situation with a vision in mind.

His eyes scanned the path ahead, looking for any sign of the enemy, searching for movement. If The Turned One had any patrols or sentries stationed here, they had made themselves scarce. A few corrupted burrowers lumbered up the path toward the first switchback, but that was it.

Surely, once he came out of hiding and approached the path himself, enemies would pour forth as they had during their previous battles. His lonely presence would be too easy a target for them to ignore.

Breathing deeply and with great control, he closed his eyes and visualized what he was about to do.

As if from above, he saw himself stand and push his way through the bushes, walking confidently toward the mountain path. He began hiking up the trail, his axes held before him.

Within a few steps, the enemy made their appearance. He saw the twisted faces of burrowers and humans corrupted by The Turned One's essence. He also saw a few darimun scattered among them.

The battle began.

He let loose a war cry, the loudest and fiercest he had ever made, for it would be his last. Charging the enemy, he swung his axes in a mad frenzy. His opponents were taken aback initially by his fury, unable to keep him from laying waste to the first few foes he met. But they quickly recovered.

And they did not fight with honor.

They crowded him, encircling him so he couldn't escape. He didn't care. He continued swinging his axes with abandon, his limbs given unlimited energy by a final burst of adrenaline. He felt something hard strike his back but his chestpiece held, absorbing the worst of the blow. He spun around and brought his blades down onto the head of whomever had struck him. Yelling angrily, he ripped them back out.

More blows rained against his back and legs. His plate armor was strong and thick, but there was only so much it could protect him from. His knees buckled. A blade found a gap in his chestpiece and slid its way into his side. Hot blood seeped through, dripping down his legs.

Thuradin kept fighting, felling foe after foe.

A large axe swung for his head. He ducked but didn't see the second swing. The heavy blade cleaved his chestplate in two and sank deep into his chest. He gasped for breath, the initial pain numbing instantly as his vision darkened. His legs gave out completely and he sprawled onto his back. More blades pierced his armor and body. Breathing became difficult. Blood pooled beneath him. The last thing he saw was another axe swinging for his head.

Thuradin opened his eyes. He let out the breath he'd been holding. His heart hammered relentlessly against his ribcage as if in protest of what he was about to do. His skin prickled and turned cold. Doubt slid into his mind. Did he truly want to go through with this? Was this his only option?

The faces of all those he loved returned to him. In his mind, he reached out one last time. Then, he remembered their words, their pity, their rejections. He bowed his head. There was no one left. This *was* his only option.

With a fierce look, he stood and prepared to step out of the bushes, ready to turn what he had visualized into reality.

The sound of rustling came from behind.

Quickly, he turned, axes held before him. Had the enemy detected him and made a move to attack from behind? This venture would do no good if he was ambushed and killed in the woods like a fool. He waited, ready to swing at whatever came out from the trees.

The bleat of a ram reached his ears and he relaxed. He lowered his weapons as a gray, shaggy beast with large curving horns burst through the trees, sliding to a stop right next to him. Its rider hopped down and tackled him to the ground.

"Da!"

Thuradin froze as Myrna held onto him, shuddering with a series of sobs.

"I'm sorry, da."

Thuradin's arms found enough life in them to wrap around his daughter as she continued weeping into his shoulder. Clarity returned. His heart lurched. Tears welled up in his own eyes. He couldn't remember the last time she had called him "Da."

"What are ye doing here?" He choked out gruffly.

"I'm sorry," she repeated. She sniffled, pushing herself up

and lifting him with her. Her eyes were red and puffy as she stared into him, gripping his face. "I never should have doubted ye."

Thuradin's eyes gravitated to the floor. He couldn't look at her without feeling a burning sense of shame eating at him from the inside.

"I did a revolting thing, something that cannae be forgiven. I must make amends, if only for yer sake. This way, you may live on with the Stonebeard name with some vestige of honor."

She slapped him, following it up with another desperate hug.

"Ye fool!" she cried. "What ye were about ta do would have done nothing ta restore yer honor. All ye would have done is leave me alone in this world, picking up the pieces ye left behind."

Thuradin's brows furrowed. He hadn't thought of it that way.

"Besides," she continued. "What ye did wasn't yer fault."

Now he scoffed, breaking out of her hold and turning away. "Of course it was my fault. I may nae have committed the act, but I allowed it ta happen. I helped it happen."

"Ye had no control over what ye were doing," Myrna pleaded. "Believe me, I heard it from the acolytes themselves. They can explain it better than I can, but none of this is yer fault. Please, da, come back ta camp with me."

Thuradin's eyes softened. "I appreciate yer effort, dear daughter, but I assure ye I'm in control of myself. I've done what I've done. I must take responsibility for it."

Myrna shook her head vigorously. "I know how Hork made ye feel. Ye were already a mess of confusion and anger and whatever else he made ye feel. The Turned One took advantage of that and manipulated ye inta making choices ye would never have made otherwise. Please," she grabbed his hand and brought it to her lips, her voice now just a whisper. "Come back for me. Let them prove ye wrong."

Conflict raged within Thuradin. There was hope glowing in his heart now at the thought that his daughter's words might hold some truth. But another part of him maintained a festering pool of doubt. He'd failed in this life, he had to atone for that failure. He took in his daughter and her grief-stricken face. An image of Agata forced its way back into his mind and he remembered her words from his dream.

Hold on ta who ye are.

Finally nodding, he took her hands in his. "Very well." Her eyes shot up, hope rekindling under a layer of unshed tears. "Take me back."

CHAPTER TWENTY-NINE

They rode together on the ram Myrna brought, taking their time on the journey back to camp. Neither spoke as they rode through the rolling foothills, but they rested in each other's company; each one grateful to still have it.

There was no fanfare upon their return—not that Thuradin had expected any. There did, however, seem to be some interest. All eyes were glued to him as they paraded through the camp pathways toward the acolytes' tent. It wasn't just dwarves who stared, either. Humans, viatari, vashi, and burrowers all came out in droves watching them come through.

Thuradin shifted uncomfortably in the saddle. "I know I'm a rather controversial figure now, but why has such a crowd gathered ta see our arrival?"

Myrna shrugged. "My guess is that word has spread about The First One's warning. They've heard what The Turned One is capable of and that ye were sadly one of her victims. I suppose they're here ta see what that might look like."

"Hmph," Thuradin grunted, forcing himself to keep from acknowledging the gawking bystanders. "I don't feel any different. I doubt I look any different."

"Let's wait for when ye're before the acolytes before ye make that judgment. Only they can see inside yer soul."

They were met by a mount handler to whom they passed off the reins. They continued on foot. Before long they arrived to the acolytes' tent. Upon entering, both dwarves stopped in their tracks in complete surprise.

Not only were the acolytes waiting for them inside, but a great crowd had gathered within, all of whom turned their gaze toward the pair. There were representatives from each faction present, but there were only two faces Thuradin saw that he cared about. Near the front stood Garadin and Lyrie, both observing him with a combination of bitterness and pity. It was Garadin who approached first.

"Serania has told us that yer actions lately have been a result of The Turned One having twisted yer mind ta her will without yer knowing," he explained. "I find that rather convenient."

"As do I," Lyrie crossed her arms, taking a stand next to Garadin. "But if it turns out ta be true, . . ." she hesitated, her eyes falling to the floor. "Well, let's just see what's what first."

Thuradin stood there, the faint hope he'd felt before returning. But he dared not nurture it. After all, even he wasn't sure if this whole business with The Turned One was legitimate.

"I'm only here because Myrna insisted I return," Thuradin said in answer. "I cannae say that I believe in this wild claim myself. But I will subject myself ta whatever end this may bring."

"You need not worry in that regard," now Serania stepped forward, sympathy heavy on her words. "This claim comes from The First One himself. Go, stand before him so he may purge you of this corruption." She raised her voice, so all could hear. "Let all bear witness to this cleansing, so none may continue to claim that blame should be put on the shoulders of this dwarf, who I know to be honorable, for any past transgressions."

Thuradin turned a shade of red as he was led forward, avoiding eye-contact with everyone. He was grateful for what Serania and Myrna were doing to clear his name—though he thought they were laying it on a bit thick.

As he approached the acolyte, a sense of calm and peace covered him like a warm blanket.

"Thuradin Stonebeard," The First One murmured. "We meet again."

Thuradin stood where he was with some trepidation. The last time he had dealt with this primeval being had been during the Siege of Garon. At the time, he'd had information that might have prevented Aleganthia from being sacked by the Creature, but The First One, not wanting the siege to be broken off prematurely and his sister allowed to escape, had put the dwarf to sleep. In the end, Thuradin hadn't been able to tell Felix this vital information and Aleganthia had burned. But that was some time ago, back when the ancient being had only just joined the war against his corrupted siblings. Perhaps this time he could trust the acolyte.

"What do I do, acolyte?"

"You need only stand there," The First One answered. One of his white, translucent tendrils approached the dwarf's head. "I shall use my powers to draw out this corruption from you like poison from a wound and then I shall obliterate it."

The tendril placed itself gently on his forehead and Thuradin felt a surge of energy course through his veins like he'd been struck by lightning. He kept his footing, but his body visibly shook, drawing murmurs from the gathered crowd.

Slowly, The First One pulled back his tendril. Attached was a squirming essence of black haze. It was like looking at a small storm cloud. The thing squirmed in place, agitated, trying to escape. As soon as it ripped away from Thuradin completely, a clarity entered the dwarf's mind unlike any he'd felt in weeks. The dull fog that, even during his best moments, had always been present, disappeared.

Gasps came from all around as the black essence continued to squirm in the acolyte's grip.

"Clever little thing," he mused. A moment later, there was a flash of blinding light, the crackling sound of something burning, a pungent odor, and a high-pitched wail. Thuradin had to shield his eyes along with everyone else to avoid being blinded. By the time they were able to look again, no evidence remained of the black shade.

"The cleansing is complete." The First One's tendrils swayed peacefully from his golden artifact, like nothing had happened.

Thuradin looked at his hands and closed them into fists. So, what Myrna told him had been true.

"You must now take great care to maintain your mental fortitude," the acolyte continued, drawing the dwarf's attention. "My sister may try to reinsert herself into your mind. She hates to lose what she has spent effort and time obtaining. She may target you specifically. Do not allow yourself to dwell on any sort of negativity; instead, keep your mind still. Do you understand?"

He nodded, turning to face the crowd, all of whom now looked at him with newfound sympathy, many with amazement. Lyrie burst into tears and threw her arms around him.

"It wasn't yer f-fault," she sobbed. "As soon as I saw that t-thing I knew—"

Thuradin returned her embrace, patting her back comfortingly. "Ye were right ta blame me. Now with my mind cleared, I feel ashamed ta no end that I ever thought such an action was ever the right one. I still say there's no excuse for it, no matter how muddled my mind may have been."

She pulled away, looking sternly into his eyes. "I cannae hold ye ta blame when ye weren't yerself. If ye must have forgiveness, then take it—know that I forgive ye. Now don't ye dare continue ta put his death on yer shoulders." Again, she let her head fall into his chest and wept. She wept for her husband, for her friend. Her tears were rivulets of sorrow for what had been swept away into the past, and joy for what brightness remained for the future. Thuradin let her spill it all out.

Once she was done and regained enough of her composure to back away sheepishly, her eyes glued to the ground as she continued sniffling, Garadin stepped forward with an outstretched arm.

Thuradin took it.

"Perhaps I've misjudged ye after all this time," Garadin said gruffly, his grip tight. "While I still hold qualms about some of yer actions from the past, I'm ready ta leave it there and move forward. For the good of Azar. What say ye, cousin?"

Thuradin smiled broadly, unable to contain his elation.

"For the good of our family," he said. "Let us never part in anger again."

The gathered spectators cheered, the scene before them beyond anyone's ability to observe with indifference.

Penetrating the din of clapping and cheering, The First One's voice rang out. "As heartwarming as this is for us all, we must bring our focus back to the issue at hand. There remains one other who requires my cleansing touch."

Serania nodded. "The acolyte is correct. We must wake Felix from the same evil."

"Can we convince him ta come here?" Thuradin asked.

"That will not be necessary," The First One replied firmly. "I will go to him myself."

Everyone moved aside and formed a path. Several viatari and humans stepped forward, grabbing a litter from the back of the tent and fastening the acolyte to it. While they did this, others went outside to find a good spot where they could watch the whole ordeal. Thuradin, Lyrie, and Garadin found themselves following the crowd as they marched together to the command tent.

After several minutes of waiting, The First One emerged from his tent, strapped to a litter and carried by the same viatari and humans who had secured him to it. They trod along the narrow path created by the gathered crowd toward their destination.

"You may not pass," the guard stationed in front of the command tent said sternly as Serania approached.

"I will no longer play this game," she responded, an edge to her voice. "You either let us through to see Felix, or you let the world fall into chaos at the hands of our enemy. I do not exaggerate. You decide."

The guard looked uncertain as he stammered, "B-but my orders–"

Serania got right in his face, her lips inches away from his ears as she harshly whispered, "Take a walk."

For a moment, the two viatari eyed each other. The guard's gaze faltered. He turned and walked away out of sight.

"It will do no good for so many to see their commander in

the state that he's in," The First One said pointedly just before his carriers brought him inside the tent. "Thuradin, Serania, you two may enter. The rest must wait out here."

Garadin nodded. "The acolyte is right. Go on, Thuradin. Myrna, Lyrie, and I will hold back the crowds."

After squeezing his daughter's hand reassuringly, Thuradin followed Serania inside.

The interior was a mess. Maps and banners that had been hanging along the walls were now strewn across the floor. The table in the center was split in half, a cluttered mess of papers, ripped scrolls, and battered books piled up in the middle. On the other end of the tent, near the water basin, lay Felix on his back, the crook of his arm covering his eyes. It was dark in here. The small braziers that normally lit the space had long since run out of fuel. The only light now came from the acolyte's pulsing, white tendrils; but even that only created a faint glow that did not reach far into the darkness.

"You may set me down here," the acolyte said softly to his carriers. "Then you may go."

His carriers did as they were told, the viatari stealing a concerned glance behind them before they left.

"Felix," Serania whispered, coming to his side and placing her hands on his chest. "You must come back from this. The First One will bring you back."

"There is nothing to come back from," came Felix's pained reply. His voice was raw, weak, unfamiliar to Thuradin's ears. Had he been this unrecognizable as well?

"Fear not child of Arokun," The First One's tendrils extended across the room, bringing their soft glow with them, surrounding and cradling the elder viatari's body. They hovered just over his skin, as if examining him. "My sister has gotten the better of you once again. She has infected your mind in the most subtle way. Your feelings are not your own, Felix Draka, but I will make you whole again. Once I purge you of her essence, you will see the truth in my words."

Felix scoffed and shook his head but made no move to stop what was happening.

A tendril made contact with his forehead and, as with Thuradin, brought forth a hazy, writhing black haze as it slowly pulled away. This essence was darker than the one pulled out of Thuradin's head and much larger, but The First One kept his grip.

A flash of light filled the room. The sound of burning flames. A scream. Then darkness returned.

Thuradin looked hopefully in Felix's direction, expecting to find the elder viatari back on his feet, an amazed expression on his face. But he remained where he was, as he was. A sad sigh escaped him.

"My troubled heart persists," he said faintly. "I feel no energy in my limbs. My will to continue is gone."

"Unexpected," The First One murmured.

"What does this mean?" Serania demanded.

"It means that while my sister may have amplified the darkness within him somewhat, the intensity of that darkness is his alone."

"How do we snap him out of it, then?"

"The only remedy to darkness is light, and light can come in many forms—not least of which is the sturdy bridge of feeling."

Serania glowered murderously at the acolyte. Before she could say anything she might regret, Thuradin stepped in. "We have no time for riddles, First One, speak plainly."

"You must speak with him," the acolyte sighed. "Remind him of who he truly is. Sadly, I am no use in this endeavor."

Bringing her gaze back to Felix, a softness entering her eye, Serania called out, "Felix, you cannot remain like this."

No response.

She pushed on, "Many are still relying on you, including me. We cannot hope to pull through this struggle without you."

"You cannot pull through this struggle *with* me, either," he responded.

"So you've had one loss," Serania struggled to control her voice, keeping notes of frustration from barging in. "Think of all the victories you've had before then. Everyone here admires your leadership, requires your leadership. They need you. And they're not the only ones." She hesitated, as if wondering if she should broach the subject. "*She* still needs you, too."

Felix stiffened. "I failed her."

"She's still waiting for you to save her," Serania insisted. "But you can't do it like this. She needs you to come back. How much time has she spent in those mountains because you've been wallowing away?"

"The lass is right," Thuradin chimed in, stepping up to Felix's side. "Victria yet lives. Had they killed her, they would have sent her head in a box by now ta further devastate ye. There's still time ta keep that from becoming a reality."

Felix moved his arm away, revealing wounded eyes, deep red pools overflowing with despair. But within them a hint of recognition grabbed hold of the dwarf's words. Their eyes met.

"She is still alive," he repeated, saying the words as if he was tasting how they felt on his lips.

"Aye," Thuradin nodded. "And ye're the only hope she has ta remain that way."

A moment passed where they all remained as they were, the words just spoken hanging in the stale air around them, absorbing into the viatari's skin. Finally, he lifted himself into a seated position and regarded them both.

"I . . . feel weak, as if freshly born with legs unused to carrying my own weight."

Thuradin grinned. "Then ye need nae carry this weight by yerself. Lean on us for support and we'll help ye along the way."

Felix nodded gratefully and turned to Serania. "Can it not be done without me?"

She shook her head. "That's the wrong question. She's not expecting us to save her. She's expecting *you.*"

Fire rekindled in Felix as he took in her words, nodding along to each one. "I apologize, Serania, for leaving you alone to handle my mess."

Serania shrugged, a relieved smile marking her face in the dark.

Shakily, he brought himself to his feet, his attention turning to the acolyte across from him. "Where do we stand?"

"Where we did before," The First One answered. "We have the numbers to maintain our siege, but as Serania has pointed out repeatedly to me and my brothers, we cannot hope to contain her in the Three Spires forever. Eventually, she will find a way to slip out and find the Purity Scepter. Once she has that in her possession, we will find ourselves greatly disadvantaged in this war."

Thuradin's brows furrowed. "What is this 'Purity Scepter'?"

A tendril quickly shot out, latching onto his forehead and transmitting an image of a strange rod. As quickly as the image came, it left, leaving the dwarf with the vague feeling that he'd been shown something familiar, something he'd seen before. He thought hard, trying to remember as the conversation around him continued.

Another series of images ran through his mind of the day they raided the Three Spires in search of Veliris. He remembered the vast storage rooms pocketed throughout the Spires' tunnel system. His mind's eye brought him back to the room full of gems and gold and . . . that strange rod he couldn't help but be drawn toward.

The connection struck him, bringing forth a spirited shout. "I've seen that rod before!"

The conversation around him died. The air grew heavy as they all took in what had just been uttered.

"What did you say?" Serania asked breathlessly.

"When we raided the Three Spires ta save yer brother," Thuradin explained, pointing at the acolyte. "We searched many rooms within their tunnel system. Within one of them was the rod ye just showed me. It was stored among a plethora of precious metals and gems, which made me believe it was just another trinket."

"You are saying my sister already has the Purity Scepter in her possession?" The First One asked in a somber tone.

"The rod I saw matches what ye just showed me."

There was a moment's hesitation, then, "I must search your memories, if you will permit me."

The First One didn't waste time waiting for an answer. A tendril shot out, reconnecting with Thuradin's forehead. It felt like someone was spinning him in fast circles as the acolyte did his work. After a few minutes, the tendril detached and the acolyte let loose a loud, gurgling cry.

"I have been too lax in my efforts against her," he lamented, his voice no longer bearing its normal cadence of peaceful serenity. "Time and again she has proven herself to be one step ahead of us." He turned his attention back to the viatari. "We can no longer wait here. Maintaining this siege is not a viable option. We must take the fight to her and hope we can wrest control of the Purity Scepter before it's too late."

"But we have already tried that course of action," Felix objected. "There is no way to penetrate their defenses."

"You must find a way. For if we cannot do it, and my sister escapes, I fear our odds of victory in this war may slip away with her."

Felix grimaced at the harsh reality presented to him but eventually nodded. He began to pace and think. His eyes roved over the various maps on the ground, scanning each one, searching for inspiration. Finally, they landed on one that depicted a closer look at the mountains surrounding the Three Spires, one that depicted the hot springs they had found weeks ago. He stood frozen, staring at it for several minutes, barely breathing.

"There is one way," he declared. "It may be our only way."

Concern clouded Serania's visage as she asked, "What is it?"

"We do exactly what we did when we raided the Three Spires the first time, except the opposite way."

They all took a moment to try and share Felix's vision. It did not come easily.

"Explain," The First One demanded.

Excitement entered Felix's voice as he laid out his plan, something Thuradin hadn't heard in a while. He was confident in what he was putting forth and that was reassuring.

"The issue with our last assault was that the enemy could see our movements clearly, making us easy to counter," Felix spoke rapidly, his mouth struggling to keep up with his mind as he paced ever faster. "What if we sent our main force up the mountains to attack the hot springs? Once we take them, we can infiltrate the Spires with our vashi and bypass all the traps the enemy has waiting for us on the mountain pass. At the same time, we have a small fraction of our forces go up the main path and enter through the front entrance. With the battle focused on the hot springs, there should only be minimal resistance. If we can get in from the hot springs and the front entrance at the same time, we can trap them in their own tunnel system. Then, it's only a matter of fighting it out."

"The hot springs are too heavily defended," Serania countered. "It would take too long to reach them, and we would be more vulnerable the longer we stay in the area. Those waters lie in a deep vale. Hills all around. Once inside, anyone could approach us unopposed and we'd never know it until it's too late. Besides, we don't have enough vashi to liquefact all of our forces at once into the Spires if The Turned One has her servants waiting for us on the other side."

Felix raised a finger, a confident, knowing smile on his face. "Ah, but she does not know that we do not have enough vashi. The trek up the mountains to reach the hot springs is arduous. She will not expect us to send our full force that way. We can send scouts ahead of us to find the best path up, but if we move carefully. she will not know we are upon her until we are charging into the vale. Once we take the springs and begin liquefacting our forces into the Spires, we need only hold out long enough for our smaller force to attack them from behind. In those confined tunnels, a pincer attack like this will prove devastating."

"It seems to be a good plan," The First One said thoughtfully. "And unless you can think of any other, Serania, it is the one we must pursue. Time is of the essence. We do not have days to deliberate."

Serania scowled but eventually nodded. "Very well, if you're confident about this, Felix—"

"I am."

"Then this is the course we will take. I'll inform the commanders and officers to get their forces ready for a morning march."

"Have them ready by nightfall."

"Nightfall?"

"Darkness will provide us the cover we need to ensure our enemy has no chance of seeing our movements for as long as possible. I will pick out those I want with me for the frontal assault."

Serania blinked. "You?"

Felix nodded, his face deadly serious. "Me. I will lead the smaller force up the mountain path."

"But the risks—"

"I will not sit idly by this time and watch those who follow me go to their deaths. I will lead them personally and, with any luck, we will make it up that path and through the entrance in one piece."

Serania clearly didn't approve but knew better than to say anything. This would likely be their last chance to gain any sort of victory against their enemies. Anything short of conquering the Three Spires would mean an end to their siege as well. She doubted they would have the numbers to maintain it afterwards. If this was to be their final effort here, she couldn't blame him for wanting to lead it from the front. She would have done the same in his position. She nodded.

"So be it."

CHAPTER THIRTY

Victria couldn't think, couldn't focus. Her thoughts were scattered like so many broken pieces. Time remained elusive. Her stomach was an empty void. Her eyes passed blearily over the metal table before her for the millionth time as she took in her friends.

They were in bad shape.

While she couldn't count the days, so much time had passed under torment they no longer felt pain in their limbs as they sat chained to the wall for hours on end. Their heads lolled to the side, greasy hair covering their faces as they tried to snatch sleep in this rare moment of solitude from their tormentor.

Though they were all in a decrepit state, Natiari suffered the worst. Her skin sagged from her face. Her eyes drooped, always half-closed these days. Her cracked lips bled from lack of water. She barely spoke anymore even when they were alone.

Seeing her like this, Victria couldn't help but feel anger run through her, going all the way to her toes. Of them all, she was the only one still with the most spirit. And Gar'Gir knew it. Perhaps that's why he toyed with her more than the others, offering a slew of lies about what was happening outside the mountains.

The burrower talked about raids their forces had made on the siege camp, bragging about how many had died. He spoke of their friends being killed, devoured by darimun. His latest lie dealt with a supposed assault on the Three Spires itself, though Victria couldn't tell how long ago it had been since she heard that piece of news. She only remembered he had shared it right before putting her through another session with the brainwyrm.

"Your hero," he had said, observing the skinny, black wyrm wriggling between his fingers with affection. She glared at him, despite the apprehension she felt from what was about to happen. "The viatari you so hope will rescue you. He took his forces and tried to take these mountains, you know."

She hadn't responded, but her mind had raced. Any initial jubilation from the news was quickly stifled however when she realized the assault must have failed, because Gar'Gir was here, and smiling.

"Yes, quite the battle. I watched it unfold from one of the higher caves. Your people were decimated. They were lucky to escape with as many as they did. I wonder if he'll try again, or if he finally realizes how hopeless your situation is."

She lay her head back on the table, fighting back the urge to spit up bile. Gar'Gir leaned in and applied the brainwyrm.

He's lying, she had thought, before she was spirited away into the realm of memories.

Now, she wondered if he truly had been lying, or if there was some truth in his words. She still believed Felix would save them—she *needed* to believe it—but they'd been here so long . . . doubts were beginning to creep in. And she wasn't alone in having them.

"He's not coming, Victria," Tessa said sadly, her gaze fixated on a single small rock protruding from the floor in front of her. "We don't have much time left here."

Victria's head jerked. She hadn't realized her friends had stirred. She wondered how long they'd been observing her, reading the thoughts that were plain on her face.

"Don't say that!" she hissed. Her voice echoed. They sat up rigidly, eyes turning to the door across from them, hoping it hadn't been enough to draw their tormentor's attention. Minutes passed and they remained alone. They all sighed in relief.

Victria lowered her voice. "He will come. He has to."

"He can't come," Madira chimed in weakly. "The enemy is too great for him to break through. You heard what the burrower said."

"He lies!"

"Maybe," Tessa coughed. "Or maybe he's telling the truth. Victria, please," they locked eyes, both desperate, both full of fear. "We have to consider the possibility that no one is coming. We have to think of how we might escape ourselves."

"There is no escape," Natiari mumbled so softly she could barely be heard. She groaned as she forced her head up and to the side to see her companions. Ghosts swam behind her dull, red eyes. "We will die here."

"No, Natiari, you can't give in—"

But her friend was already not listening, her head listing forward limply as if she had fallen back asleep.

Victria bit her lip, turning her attention back to Tessa. She hated what they had become, been forced to endure, hated how they all were barely clinging to life. She hated this cave, the chains binding her, the table before her. She closed her eyes and relented. Perhaps Tessa was right. If they wanted to escape, they had to do it themselves and they needed to do it while they still had enough strength to pull it off.

"Alright," she finally said. "We'll escape. How do we do it?"

The question hung in the air, heavy and taunting. Minutes passed with no answer between them. Defeated, Tessa and Madira hung their heads.

"I will think of something," Victria encouraged them. "Just don't give up, please. I need you all to stay with me."

The smallest nods were all she got for an answer. She could work with that. She racked her brain, trying to remember as much as she could about their time here and what she had observed about the burrower who tormented them.

She had undergone several brainwyrm "treatments" since her first one and had become skilled at breaking out of her memories by her own will, much to Gar'Gir's displeasure. She was the only one able to. Tessa and Madira struggled and suffered painfully during their sessions. Natiari always teetered on the edge of insanity. Perhaps her resilience to that particular wyrm was the key to their escape. If she could only think of how best to implement it.

She thought harder, focusing on Gar'Gir himself. She tried to remember exactly how he went about his experiments with them. The burrower was an ordered individual. He always did things exactly the same way every time, as if it was required to produce the best results.

Before he unchained them, he always placed an extra drainwyrm on their heads to weaken their resolve. Lately, once he had them strapped to the table, he would bring over the brainwyrms first. With surgical precision, he would apply one wyrm and remove the other. The viatari would be asleep before they could try anything. As they slept he always turned back to the shelves on the far end of the cavern to put away the drainwyrm in the jar where it belonged.

An idea formed, a sharp ray of light piercing the clouds of fog that suffocated her. There was a chance, but she had to be able to take advantage of it. First, she needed to make sure the way she remembered Gar'Gir doing things was indeed correct.

She opened her mouth to share this new idea with her friends, but just then footsteps reverberated from the tunnel leading into their prison. She shut her mouth. She would share details later. For now, they all needed to mentally prepare for what was to come.

The ugly visage of Gar'Gir melted out of the shadows, a sardonic grin fixed on his lips. He clapped his hands as he approached the chained viatari, observing each one.

Victria glowered at him.

"Ooo!" the burrower exclaimed, chuckling. "The spirit in this one never dies. Always so exciting!"

He moved on to Tessa, then Madira, grunting dismissively at both of them. Then, he stopped before Natiari, who didn't bother to raise her head. He crouched, grabbing her chin and jerking it up so her eyes were forced to meet his.

She gasped for breath, baring her fangs at him weakly. His grin broadened and he moved to undo her chains.

"At last!" He rasped, excitement laced in each word he spoke. "At last we shall have results."

"What results?" Victria demanded. She pulled against her chains, though she knew how futile it was. She was worried for Natiari. She wasn't sure how much more her friend could take, especially if their tormentor had another brainwyrm session planned. The illusions had proven too much for her to handle. Gar'Gir knew this. He had to.

The burrower looked her way, his eyes narrowing eagerly. "Why, isn't it obvious?" He lifted Natiari, throwing her arm over his shoulder as he carried her slowly to the metal table. "We're about to see one of your kind reach their limits."

Madira struggled against her chains with a sudden burst of fury.

"No!" she cried, straining against her bonds. "Take me, I still have more to give!"

Gar'Gir stopped where he was and turned his head, regarding her coldly. "Your eagerness is noted, viatari. But you need not make such a scene. Each one of you will have your turn. You have my word."

Madira's face fell. Whatever fighting spirit had possessed her evaporated instantly. All she could do was watch as the burrower turned back toward the table to take another step.

And tripped.

Victria wasn't sure how it happened, didn't see what he had tripped on. All she saw was his crippled body lurch forward suddenly as if thrown. Natiari crumpled to the floor, rolling away from him by several feet. There, she lay unmoving.

"Go!" Victria cried, wishing she could lift her friend up herself and give her the push she needed. "Run, Natiari. Get out of here!"

But she could barely move. Even if she hadn't had a drainwyrm attached, she was in no state to do more than exist. Natiari's arms shook violently under her weight as she tried to lift herself up. Her head sagged like a sack of stones. The best she could do was crawl—slowly.

It wasn't enough.

As if he had all the time in the world, Gar'Gir lifted himself from the stone floor and limped over to where Natiari continued to struggle for movement. He stared down at her, cackling as her limbs finally gave out and she collapsed, her breaths coming in ragged gasps.

He kicked her onto her back and picked her back up, dragging her the rest of the way to the table. With no care for gentleness, he threw her onto it, strapping her arms and legs into their leather bonds. He removed the drainwyrm that had been attached to her forehead and immediately placed a brainwyrm by her ear. The wyrm slithered in and Natiari's head fell to the side as she entered her own realm of corrupted memories.

Victria observed all of this carefully, making mental notes on how long each task took.

Still cackling, the burrower limped back toward the rock shelves and put the drainwyrm in a jar with hundreds of its own kind. Satisfied, he grunted and returned to the table, leaning over the helpless viatari. He watched with glee as her face twisted, nightmares invading her mind.

A few minutes passed with no further changes and finally Gar'Gir grew bored.

"It is time to move this experiment along," he declared. "Time to really test the capabilities of this wyrm."

He retrieved another brainwyrm and applied it to Natiari's ear. She squirmed, her body struggling against its bonds. Her face twisted further, desperation leaking from every pore.

"Another."

Natiari whimpered, wincing in pain. Her fists clenched hard enough for her nails to cut into her palms. A thin trail of blood ran down, dripping onto the stone floor. The others could do nothing but watch in horror.

Gar'Gir chuckled, clapping his hands. "Wonderful! Another!"

A scream erupted from Natiari's lips. Her body shook violently, every muscle and nerve trembling. Madira turned away, tears running clean trails down her dirty face.

The burrower watched with fascination as his subject continued to convulse. Almost without thinking, he applied another brainwyrm.

The convulsions intensified. Blood burst from Natiari's eyes and nose, streaming down her face. Yellow bile driveled from her gaping mouth. Her screams turned silent as her body arched upward, staying like that for several seconds before finally collapsing back onto the table with a heavy *thud.*

There Natiari lay, limp, her chest unmoving. Lifeless. Her head fell to the side, her red eyes half open and dull, staring directly at Victria.

Time seemed to stop as Victria stared back, her mind unable to register what she was seeing. The horrors of the past several minutes replayed in her head over and over. Natiari's final scream still echoed in the cavern. She couldn't feel her own heart beating. Couldn't hear Tessa and Madira next to her wailing their fury at Gar'Gir as he lifted his hands triumphantly into the air. The only thing that penetrated her numb mind were the three words he said.

"Results, at last!"

Hatred filled her. Unfamiliar, but hot and powerful. She wanted this burrower to feel pain, wanted to watch him suffer. And she wanted it to be done by her hands.

Her body trembled. She felt a wetness on her cheeks, felt her face scrunch uncontrollably as she joined the lament. Her breaths came rapid and harsh.

Her friend was gone. How many long centuries had they lived this life together? Every memory she'd ever had with

Natiari standing by her side flashed through her mind at once.

And now she was gone.

After jotting down a few notes in his journal, Gar'Gir undid Natiari's straps and pushed her unceremoniously over the side of the table. Her body hit the floor hard. But this didn't bother the burrower whatsoever as he made his way around, humming a jubilant tune, and grabbed her by the arm. With little effort, he dragged her back to her place against the wall, leaving her in a heap.

Turning to the remaining, grieving viatari, Gar'Gir sized them up once more, then shook his head. Madira shrunk away while Tessa and Victria wished he would come closer. Close enough to bite into his face.

"Ah, I cannot wait any longer," his voice was euphoric. "I must compare these notes with the others." He limped away, journal in hand.

Before he disappeared into the shadows, he called back to them, "Do not fret, my beloved specimens, I will return to continue where we left off. After all, what is an experiment worth if I cannot duplicate results?"

And with that, he was gone.

Whatever tension held the viatari together as they faced their oppressor faded with him. Their bodies slumped and each wept alone.

Through her tears, Victria could see Natiari's still form lying on the other side of the cavern. She yelled in frustration, pangs of guilt stabbing into her. This was *her* fault. Her friend was dead because of *her.*

She was the one who had suggested they surrender in the hopes of Felix rescuing them. She was the one who had told them to trust her. And they had, only for this to be the result.

She wished now that they hadn't surrendered. Natiari had

been right. It would have been better for them to die fighting. At least that way, they would have been together in death as they were in life.

She shook her head. She couldn't allow herself to wallow over this line of thinking. Her tears dried. Anger returned, fueling her and filling her with energy despite her hunger.

Tessa and Madira were still alive. The desire to escape and save her remaining friends consumed her mind, honed it. She could no longer wait for Felix. They would escape. They would find their own way out of these wretched mountains. They would survive. And she would make sure of it. Even if it cost her life.

CHAPTER THIRTY-ONE

"Let's go over what we know," Salevari leaned over the dining table in their suite. Simon and Zael stood next to her while Aniria, Drathanar, and Tera sat comfortably on the cushioned chairs they'd brought in from the living room for this meeting.

Spread out across the table were reports from the Grand Admiral's intelligence officers. They'd brought her anything and everything to do with Thurn. Thick folders filled with reports spanning back more than two years sat open for her to peruse. Within them were copies of every single post made by Thurn since the beginning. Hundreds. All of them gibberish, as far as she was concerned. There was no coherent message between most of the posts, but there were some reoccurring themes. One of them she found interesting.

"So many of these posts mention a food shortage or allude to images of grain and other bread-related concepts. What do we know of this rumored food shortage?"

"Rumored?" Simon repeated with a raised eyebrow.

"Yes, rumored," Salevari said sternly. "The elites here don't know anything about it. When I brought it up at the feast, all I got for a reply was awkward silence and a few odd looks—as if I didn't know what I was talking about."

"Well, of course they're not going to say anything," Simon shot back. "They're living in luxury. They have those extravagant feasts every month! Do you really expect them to care about the plight of the commoners?"

"That's exactly my point," Salevari shook her head, running her fingers through her hair. "The elites here are *always* having these feasts. Longer than Thurn has been around. That means, as repulsive as they are, they aren't the reason for this city's ailments. So that begs the question, why did the food shortage begin hand in hand with the thurn posts?"

This brought a pause from the plains chief as he thought the logic through.

"You raise a fair point," he conceded. "But I can tell you I saw the realities of this food shortage first-hand. Prices for bread are outrageous. The markets are as dangerous as the wilderness."

Salevari nodded absently, scanning through more of Thurn's messages as she absorbed his words. "So, we can deduce that someone is intercepting and stealing whatever food shipments normally get imported into Halding Port. That someone is likely the culprit behind Thurn. The fact that this issue only started with their appearance is too much of a coincidence."

"But why would they steal the city's food supply?" Zael asked, leafing through a few posts himself, as if they might hold the answer to the mystery before them. "What would they gain from it? Where could they even hide two years' worth of food?"

"I think the answer to that last one will be revealed when we find their headquarters," Salevari answered, her eyes roving back and forth repeatedly over the same few lines scrawled across the paper she was holding. "As for your other questions . . . a lot of these proclamations also mention disease and sickness quite a bit, don't they?"

Tera shrugged, lying comfortably across the arms of a cushioned chair. A half-full bowl of cherries sat on her stomach, her fingers absently twirling a stem between them. "Dramatic effect, don't you think? Easy to scare people into submission if you keep them thinking that a deadly plague is just around the corner."

"No," Salevari said slowly, thoughtfully. "There must be more to it than that. Disease is mentioned repeatedly almost as much as the subject of bread is."

"Maybe they're putting something into the bread that they've stolen and plan to redistribute it once they have enough ready." Drathanar suggested.

"Sounds like something The Turned One would orchestrate," Aniria agreed as she leaned easily into the Dalyran general.

But Salevari was still shaking her head. "How would they suddenly redistribute two years' worth of contaminated bread into the entire city? It would be too obvious if all of a sudden, crates upon crates of flour and other foodstuffs appeared on everyone's doorstep."

There was a pause as they all tried to imagine how it could be done.

"It could be done by sea," Tera said after some thought.

Everyone's eyes turned to her. "What do you mean?"

The human wanderer sat up, suddenly alert. "Sea caravans lose shipments all the time. Some get lost forever, others eventually turn up much later down the line. Whether by the misguidance of an inexperienced captain or unfortunate storms throwing trading cogs off course, these things happen. When a lost trade ship suddenly reappears, no questions are ever asked. The dockmasters are happy enough to just receive whatever trade goods are presented so they don't have to mark it as a loss on their ledgers."

"So, if The Turned One has procured some trade ships and loads them up with the stolen–and now, infected–foodstuffs–"

"–It wouldn't happen overnight. Two years' worth of trade is still a lot to bring in via ship. But they could inject it into the city without anyone suspecting a thing. The people would rejoice with this sudden wave of good fortune. They wouldn't hesitate to dive into the supplies; their hunger is too great at this point." Tera finished the scenario, the cherry stem she'd been playing with falling through her fingers.

It was a diabolical plot, Salevari thought, and so clever. Looking at Simon, she could tell he was thinking the same. He shook his head, letting out a heavy breath.

"This all sounds plausible," he said. "But what does our enemy gain by massacring the people here with a plague? Even if she's successful, the leadership here, as dimwitted as they are, will survive. I doubt they would partake in those supplies since they have plenty as it is within the palace."

"The Turned One doesn't deal with simple poisons that lead to death," Aniria said darkly, her face hardening as she spoke. "She contaminates with her corruptive essence." She shot a look at Salevari, and the gravity of the situation fell on both their shoulders at the same time. "She plans on corrupting this whole city to her side. The plague is her essence."

"And once she does that," Salevari finished weakly. "There will be no helping the vashi when the darinsha invade."

The air in the room was stifling as the revelation sunk in.

Their whole war for Azar might hinge on whether they could prevent this plot from being carried out.

Zael sighed, letting the sheets he'd been going through fall back onto the table. "Assuming we're right about this, we'll need to gather some evidence whenever we find their headquarters. Otherwise, it's just speculation as far as the Grand Admiral is concerned."

"I agree," Salevari pushed away the thick folders of conspiracy and unrolled a detailed map of the city. She traced a route with her finger from the palace to Origin Graveyard. "Right now, he just thinks Thurn is a nuisance trying to rile the populace up against their government. They're only dissenters, hence the lack of urgency to deal with the problem. Once he sees the truth, if we can bring the evidence we need before him, there'll be no denying that what we told him *is* the truth. It'll be the final nail needed to seal this alliance between our peoples."

They all nodded in agreement.

"Good," the Chancellor allowed a pleased smile to wipe away the lines of worry that had been marking her face. "Then, let's go over our approach one more time so we're all on the same page."

Later that day, Salevari found herself sitting at a table in a dark corner of a seaside tavern with Zael and Simon. She and Zael cradled glasses half-full with wine while Simon sat empty-handed, a scowl on his face.

"We have no business drinking before our task."

Zael sneered. "One glass won't dull our senses. Besides, the viatari have a higher tolerance to alcohol than you humans."

Simon crossed his arms, looking away. "That may be, but

I still don't think it's wise."

"You know we must spend some time here while the others make their way to their destination, Simon," Salevari said soothingly, sipping from her glass. "We might as well enjoy ourselves while we wait. It would look odd if none of us ordered anything."

The human chief said nothing and the viatari were left to enjoy their drinks in silence.

Their plan of approach was simple enough. They had split their group in two, leaving the palace at different times and heading into different parts of the city. There was no telling if eyes were following their every move, so they had to do their best to appear nonchalant and purposeless as the day progressed.

While Salevari and her two companions were seated at the tavern, by all appearances enjoying the view of the ocean from the tavern's open-air patio, Drathanar, Aniria, and Tera had gone to the markets. The two parties would spend a few hours enjoying their day. Or, at least, going through the motions. Once enough time had passed that any tail they might have would find themselves a bit too relaxed, they would make their move.

First, Drathanar and his party would slip away in the markets, taking the alleyways and backroads toward Origin Graveyard. Once they arrived, they would loiter around the gravestones, as if visiting some long-lost friend. At the designated hour, Salevari and her party would do the same, taking a different route. This way, their intentions would be more difficult to decipher than if they had all marched directly to the graveyard as one compact unit.

Hopefully, once all was said and done, their arrival to the graveyard would be largely unnoticed, and their enemy would be none the wiser to their intentions.

"It's time," Salevari murmured, noticing the sun's progress. She and Zael finished their wine and got up to leave. Simon, still with a scowl, tossed a coin to the bartender.

They took the long, scenic road to the graveyard, one that followed the outer edges of the city. They strolled leisurely, enjoying the day's warmth.

Old stone buildings covered with vines flanked either side of their path as they went along. The sun's rays hit these vines perfectly, amplifying their color and making them appear bright green. Only a few passersby were on the road, creating a calm, quiet atmosphere for them to take in.

They passed through several smaller plazas, each one containing various murals depicting a wide scope of topics. Some told stories of the humans' war with the vashi, stone walls painted vividly with the brutal horrors of a war at sea. Others were much gentler, showing off beautiful landscapes that should have been alien to the denizens of this city. Great mountains and forests rose up in vivid colors along the buildings they passed. Salevari thought she recognized some of the regions the artists had rendered.

After an hour of enjoying the city and meandering through a small park decorated with groomed bushes and plots of bright, colorful flowers, they found themselves standing outside a dilapidated wooden fence sealing Origin Graveyard off from the rest of Halding Port.

"Stay on guard," Salevari said. She walked through the entrance, following the path inward as rows upon rows of headstones rose up around her. Her companions followed. They kept quiet, doing their best to portray themselves as solemn visitors.

Far to their left, towering over the regular graves, was a large mausoleum. Three figures stood before it, staring at it. Salevari recognized them instantly and made her way over.

"What a coincidence seeing you here," Tera commented with a sly grin once she noticed who had joined them.

The Dalyran Chancellor nodded her head toward the mausoleum, noting the cracked stones. "Who's is that?"

Zael shrugged and leaned in to inspect a sign posted at the entrance. "Some elite family, I'd imagine. I don't recognize the name."

"No matter," Salevari glanced around to make sure they were alone. As far as she could tell, they were. She'd had no sense of a tail during their walk here and she didn't feel that there were any eyes on them now.

"Let's go inside. We'll hide here until the sun sets, then begin our search."

"We're going to hide in there?" Simon asked with some alarm.

The viatari raised an eyebrow. "Is that a problem?"

Simon scoffed, though he couldn't mask his displeasure completely. "Not if you don't mind disturbing the dead."

They descended into the crypt.

"I'm surprised there weren't any guards posted and that the doors were unlocked," Aniria commented as they entered the lowest level. To the sides of the walls were several rectangular openings cut into the stone. Within these spaces sat coffins of marble, oak, and one made of pure gold.

"This place definitely belongs to some elite family," Zael muttered.

"Is there a chance of someone finding us down here?" Salevari asked. She'd noticed the same thing as Aniria and thought it odd.

"Unlikely," Tera shrugged, inspecting the golden coffin

with some interest.

"We would only be found by those insane enough to do what we're doing," Simon explained. "Perhaps it's not the same in Halding Port, but the dead are sacred to us plainsmen. Being here, . . ." he took in the numerous coffins around him and shivered. "It's not natural."

"Death is not such a taboo here as it is in the plains," Tera called back. "But I say that if no one has come down here to steal this golden coffin for however long it's been here, it's unlikely we're to be discovered."

Salevari nodded, accepting the logic. "Then, we wait. When night falls, we search each and every grave out there for some sign of a hidden lair."

"Why would it be a grave that marks the entrance and not some random tree or plot of earth?" Aniria asked.

"Because of the interpreter," Zael answered. He moved to a corner of the crypt and sat back against the wall, closing his eyes. "His tattoo marked him as a worker here. I think we can surmise that means at least some of the other workers are also involved with Thurn."

"So?"

Zael scoffed and shook his head. "Think. If the workers here are part of the organization, it follows that they likely provided the means for hiding whatever underground headquarters we are meant to find. The gravediggers would be the only ones allowed to interact with the graves here. It's a perfect way to keep the entrance hidden from curious eyes."

Salevari nodded. "Zael is correct. That's why it's important not to neglect even the most weathered headstone. If one of us finds something promising, we'll regroup before moving on to the next phase of our plan. If nothing shows promise, then we'll have to come back another day and watch the surrounding area until someone from Thurn enters or leaves their headquarters."

"Until then," Tera turned away from the golden coffin and followed Zael's example. "We should rest. We'll need all our energy and focus for tonight. Who wants the first watch?"

"I'm not tired," Drathanar said. "I will watch the exit and rouse you when night falls."

"Stay in the shadows," Salevari cautioned.

The Dalyran general nodded and walked away, leaving them to pick out any space they could find some comfort to rest in. Soon, they were all leaning against the crypt walls or lying spread out on the floor. All of them rested easy, except for Simon, whose eyes continuously shifted between each individual coffin keeping them company.

Hours passed in deathly silence. They all managed to find some sleep, even if it was only for a little while. When the time came, Drathanar returned, shaking everyone's shoulder until they were all awake, eager to carry out their task. Simon jerked awake with a yelp.

"Quiet," Salevari hissed, creeping her way toward the stairs leading back to the outside world. "While we're out there, watch for guards. Fradrick told me they patrol here sometimes to make sure there aren't any graverobbers. Stick to the shadows."

"I thought we had free rein with what we were doing," Aniria pouted.

"The guards don't know that."

One by one, they filed out of the crypt, each going a different direction. Salevari hurried over to the far edge of the graveyard on the south side, planning on working her way in back to the center as she inspected each gravestone.

Shadows were plentiful here, making it easy for her to remain hidden as she pushed against each marker or searched through patches of grass in the hopes of finding some hidden latch. There was no moon tonight to guide them, which was for the better. They didn't need to read which stone belonged to whom, and the added darkness only helped hide them from the marauding patrols.

There were thousands of graves to check. Salevari was under no illusion that this would be a quick and easy process. In fact, she figured it would take all night. Even so, after inspecting the first half dozen rows, she felt herself growing irritated from the lack of results.

How well could someone hide the entrance to a secret headquarters in a graveyard anyway?

As she thought this, soft voices came from behind her to her right. She glanced over her shoulder and saw a couple of guards following the trail only a short distance from her, two glowing lanterns held aloft.

Quickly, she ducked between a pair of tall headstones, peeking between them to keep her eyes on the potential threat.

The guards were oblivious to her existence, their eyes following the tall line of trees looming over the trail they walked. Their voices quivered as they spoke of lighter topics. Though, conversations about which ladies of the night were being featured on the streets presently didn't seem to assuage whatever grip this place had on their courage.

Salevari couldn't understand it. Humans feared the dead so much it bordered on the irrational. The viatari, though long-living being, knew death intimately. They welcomed it when it came naturally. For them, it was like falling asleep after a long day. Of course, they also didn't bury their dead, but burned them, leaving no trace behind. In this way, death was but another event in life to experience, rather than hold onto as these humans did with their vast fields littered by the dead.

She turned to lean back against the coarse headstones, waiting for the guards to pass by when she perked up. A sudden change in topic in their conversation suddenly piqued her interest. Their morose words made her skin crawl.

"Did ya hear the report outta the west end?" One of the guards asked.

"I did," the other said. "Strange thing, don'tcha think?"

"Makes no sense to me. One minute those people were fine, the next they're raving mad, attacking anyone they see."

"I heard their eyes turned black. No one could talk reason to 'em, not even their families."

"Damn shame," one guard sighed. "Had to be put down though, nothing else to be done about it, aye?"

"Sadly," the other agreed. "Hopefully it was an isolated incident. Though I heard some officers talking. Could be a new plague starting–"

The humans walked out of earshot before Salevari could hear the rest. She shook her head, knocking it back softly against the headstones behind her. The Turned One was already making her move here. The guards had mentioned black eyes. That could only mean those people had been corrupted by her essence.

She forced her thoughts back to the present before they could run wild. If Tera was correct about how The Turned One would go about reintroducing this poisoned food supply, then this might only be the result of an initial shipment. There could still be plenty left stored in their headquarters, tampered and untampered, waiting to be confiscated. They just had to find where it was.

Not wanting to waste another second, she pushed off the

headstones and continued inspecting the graves around her.

Several more hours passed with no results. Frustration bubbled once more within the Chancellor, threating to boil over. She stood up straight, stretching her back and groaning after another grave proved to be a dud.

Voices again. The telltale sign of flickering lights from lanterns bobbed in the distance. Salevari dove behind the next row of graves, sliding into the one at the end. She felt it give way slightly and froze. She was laying right next to the path the guards would walk across, she realized, but there was no time to move elsewhere. She stayed where she was, frozen, hoping the guards would be inattentive in their duties, focused more on their own fear of being in this place.

Her hopes were met. The guards never broke stride as they continued down their route, their lanterns as good as wooden swords. Clearly, those stationed to patrol Origin Graveyard didn't care for their task, desiring to be on their way as soon as they could.

Salevari watched them go. Once they were far enough away, she lifted herself back into a crouching position, wiping away some loose dirt from her side.

She glanced at the grave that had given way when she landed against it. It was fresh, judging by the loose patch of dirt that lay before the headstone. She put her hands on the weathered marker and pushed. With little effort, the headstone gave way, lifting a patch of earth along with it. A hole appeared, with a narrow set of stairs leading down into a dark void.

Her heart jumped in triumph. This was it.

Looking toward the guards to make sure they hadn't glanced back at the worst possible moment, she carefully brought the gravestone back down until the earth that had been raised was once more flush with the rest of the plot.

Drawing her sword, she thrust it into the ground right behind the headstone so she could find it again more easily. She hated the idea of being without her weapon, but the threat was below them, not above. She would have her blade in her hand again when she needed it most.

Taking a final note of her surroundings, she turned and ran across the graveyard in search of her companions. It took the better part of an hour to find them all. Once they were gathered, she led them back to the fresh grave where she had left her sword.

They traveled carefully, taking care to shrink into the shadows when they noticed patrols approaching. It would do no good to be caught now when they were so close to reaching their goal.

Finally, Salevari saw her sword sticking out of the ground right where she'd left it and rushed forward, grabbing the hilt and ripping it out of the earth. She sheathed the blade, patting it affectionately.

"You're sure this is it?" Simon whispered skeptically. "It looks like half the graves I've seen tonight."

Salevari pushed against the headstone, once more tearing up the surrounding earth and revealing the dark hole beneath. Eager grins popped onto everyone's face. Simon raised his hands in defeat.

"Let's not waste any more time," the Chancellor whispered. "Everyone in."

They took the stairs one by one. Once Tera dropped down, Salevari followed as the last member. A thick cord of rope hung from the patch of earth connected to the headstone. Pulling on it, the contraption swung back into place, covering the secret entrance and thrusting them all into darkness.

CHAPTER THIRTY-TWO

Once Salevari pushed her way to the front, she led them all downstairs. It was pitch-black and unnaturally silent in the cramped space. They moved slowly, having no way of knowing how far down they had to go before encountering something. Their hands stayed glued along the surrounding walls, relying solely on their sense of touch to guide them forward.

"Agh!" Salevari winced as she bumped headfirst into a solid surface. Reaching forward, she felt around and realized she'd run into a wooden door. Her hands groped where she thought a knob or handle might be. Something metal met her fingers and they wrapped around it. She twisted, and the door gave way, depositing the viatari and humans into a more spacious set of tunnels.

These were not so dark. A few torches lined the stone walls, spread out evenly. They were still alone, thankfully. Salevari hadn't taken the time to think of what they might be stumbling into when she had pushed against the door.

Taking care to keep their steps soft, they crept forward. Salevari drew her sword and unclasped the small buckler she had hanging from her belt. The tunnel they were in was a straight path, leading to a single door. Her heart quickened at the thought of what might be behind it.

Once they were near enough, she put an ear against its wooden planks. Shuffling feet, grunts from physical exertion, and soft-spoken conversations sounded from the other side. Turning back to her companions, she nodded. Whispering, she reminded everyone of the plan one last time.

"We go in quickly. Tera, Simon, you stay by the door and keep anyone from escaping. As far as we know, this is the only way out. Once the rest of us finish clearing whatever lies before us, come forward and start seeing what we can gather and take back as evidence."

Tera and Simon nodded.

"Are we going for the kill?" Zael asked.

Salevari considered. "Incapacitate the first few we face so we can have some prisoners to question. The rest must die. Don't hold back. They've chosen to be here, they must face the consequences. Revert to your original forms. Let them know from whom they met their fate."

The viatari nodded and, grinning viciously, shimmered back into their natural forms. Salevari took a breath to steady herself as she did the same. She reached for the door, twisting its handle, and pushed through.

They rushed into a circular room with numerous tunnels leading in various directions. They were met by a large crowd of humans. Many were in the process of moving hefty wooden crates from one room to another. A few desks were stationed against the walls, clerks seated behind them keeping track of the goings-on within. As one, they looked up from what they were doing.

Their eyes were black. Those who were still moving shuffled

about as if they didn't have full control of their bodies, like they were in a trance. Salevari had seen humans in this state before but only when fighting against The Turned One's forces.

Any misgivings she might have had about what they were doing here evaporated in an instant. She reached the nearest human she could and brought her buckler down against his neck. The man crumpled and she moved on, doing the same to several others before the rest realized what was happening. Unfortunately, it didn't take long for them to register the fact that they were under attack.

In unison, they yelled and rushed the viatari. They bore no weapons, save for what few hammers and crowbars were lying around that they could get their hands on. The viatari were vastly outnumbered, but their opponents didn't stand a chance. Salevari weaved through the crowd, striking left and right first with only her buckler, then her sword once she decided she had incapacitated enough of them.

Blood ran underfoot, filling the cracks between stones as The Turned One's slaves fell by the dozen, their cries often cut short by a swift strike of the blade.

Within minutes, the fight was over. Salevari's eyes roved through the whole room, making sure there were no other foes to face. Satisfied, she pointed her sword, glistening red under the torch light, at the tunnels leading to other parts of the underground.

"Each one of you, pick a tunnel and follow it to its end. Wipe out anyone you encounter. When you reach the end, come back and go down another until we've explored each and every one of them. Then, we'll go through that last one directly across from us together."

"Why are you leaving that one for last?" Drathanar asked,

wiping his sabers with the sleeve of one of the men he'd killed.

"I have a feeling . . . I can't describe it. I just feel that none of us should wander through that door alone."

With no one raising any protest, they continued their work. It was a bloody affair. More corrupted humans hid within these tunnels, as Salevari had suspected. They were left leaning heavily against the wall as she passed. Deep cuts and punctures stained their shirts red with blood, her blade waving with wild precision back and forth within the narrow space.

More crates were stacked within these tunnels. Salevari noticed they each had the same symbol on them, that of ears of grain. Their theory that the stolen food shipments were being kept here appeared to be correct, then. Though, she knew this wouldn't be everything that had been stolen over the past two years. How much was missing? How much was already en route for delivery to Halding Port's docks?

She shook her head. These questions would have to come later. Right now, the task at hand demanded all her attention, and she could not relent.

Each viatari cleared three separate tunnel wings before meeting back in the central room. Their blades ran wet with blood. They panted from exertion, sweat making their skin glisten. Still, their job here wasn't done. There remained one more door for them to explore.

"Tera, Simon," Salevari called as she moved for the portal that, for reasons she couldn't explain, filled her with dread. "I think we've cleared them all. Come on out and start figuring out what we can take back to the Grand Admiral as evidence."

Without waiting for a response, she pushed through the door, her viatari companions following close behind. They found themselves in another tunnel, empty save for the torches burning against the stone wall. This one was much like the first, a long straight path forward that led to a single, simple wooden door.

The viatari advanced with caution, their weapons at the ready. They might appear to be alone, but for all they knew, the walls could give way at any moment to reveal hidden pockets filled with enemies just waiting to surround them.

Salevari's gaze remained locked on the door ahead. Her dread grew with every step she took. Something was drawing her forward, some unfamiliar presence that she could sense. It was as if the air itself gave off a tainted aroma.

She hesitated before reaching for the handle. Looking back at her companions, she warned, "Stay on guard. This feeling I have about what lies ahead has only grown stronger. Something about what we are going to face is not natural."

They all nodded. Everyone could sense the tainted air, but that wouldn't stop them from completing their task here. They steeled themselves, ready for whatever might come.

Kicking the door down, Salevari rushed into a square office. Shelves of books lined the walls and a simple desk stood in the center. Sitting behind this desk was a lone man.

He was strangely clad, as far as the Chancellor was concerned. She had never met any human dressed in long, silk robes like this one, its sky-blue color giving off a dull sheen against the torchlight.

The man was hunched over his desk, quill in hand, in the middle of writing a long letter when they entered. He continued his work even as the viatari spread out along the room, their blades never wavering away from him.

For a minute they stayed like that, watching him as he wrote while he continued to make a show of not noticing their presence. Only after finishing his letter, folding it, and stuffing it inside an envelope which he secured with hot wax and a seal, did he look up, expressionless. His eyes glowed with swirling layers of violet energy, replacing his natural orbs.

"Ah, the viatari," he said in a meek voice. "You have finally arrived."

"You're the leader of this organization," Salevari stated. There was no question in her mind. This man was unlike the others, uncorrupted, yet working alongside them. That could only mean he was the head of this plot—a willing agent of The Turned One. "You're Thurn."

"You are correct," the man said with the ghost of a smile. "Though 'Thurn' is such an ugly name. I was forced to take it on for obvious reasons of anonymity. As that is no longer required, you may call me by my true name, Jorgon."

"You would introduce yourself to us?" Drathanar's eyes narrowed.

Jorgon shrugged, clasping his hands in front of him as if he were about to give a lecture from his desk. "I think it only fair you know who I am, seeing as I will be the one to kill you."

Salevari stepped forward, bringing the point of her sword only inches from the left side of Jorgon's face. He didn't flinch.

"Surrender," she said, her voice low and threatening. "You may yet walk away from The Turned One's yoke with your life."

With a soft chuckle, the human grabbed a staff that had been leaning against his desk and stood up. He turned his face only enough that he might make eye contact with Salevari. Her hands felt damp with sweat as she took in his visage.

"You mistake me. I am no mere pawn, Chancellor of Dalyr. I joined my master willingly. She is one I gladly serve to help bring this world back under its natural state, one of chaos."

"Surrender!" Salevari shouted. "Share your delusions with

someone who cares. I will not offer you this chance again."

Jorgon scoffed, shaking his head and clicking his tongue in disappointment. "Don't be preposterous. To surrender now would mean I have allowed an outside force to assert control over my being. As my body is now a vessel for chaos energy, that would be quite impossible."

"So be it."

Salevari swung her sword, aiming for Jorgon's neck. She would make quick work of him, if only to keep him from yammering on. Her blade passed through its intended target, but no cut appeared. The momentum from her swing forced her forward, throwing her off balance. It was as if her attack hadn't met a single ounce of resistance that flesh and bone would have offered. Her mouth opened in shock as the image of Jorgon faded away.

"I offer my congratulations," his cold voice came from behind her, whispering into her ear. "You have officially made yourselves a problem for me. As such, I shall deal with you myself."

A sudden force pushed against Salevari's back, like she'd been hit by a dwarven battering ram. Her body flew across the small office, slamming into the wall of books opposite her. She felt the air in her lungs rush out. She groaned as she slid to the floor, but quickly pushed herself back up, ignoring the dull ache in her ribs.

Across from her stood Jorgon, an outstretched hand falling back to his side. He turned and regarded the other viatari. "I must admit, you discovered my operation and found our headquarters much quicker than I thought possible. It seems I underestimated you in that regard. But no matter. Once I've dealt with you and the two humans poking around in the other room, I will be able to resume my operations and bring this terrible city under the rightful control of my master."

Baring her fangs, Aniria rushed forward, her dirk held close to her chest and pointed toward Jorgon, aimed at his heart. But like Salevari, she passed harmlessly through the human's image as it flickered once more and disappeared.

Aniria stumbled and tried to regain her footing so she could turn around, but it was too late. As quickly as the human had disappeared, he reappeared—right behind her.

Casually, he raised his right hand and let loose a blast of purple-white energy that shot toward Aniria like a beam, hitting her back and burning through her leather armor. She screamed, falling to the ground and writhing as the energy dissipated. Acrid smoke rose from her back as well as the stench of burning flesh. Jorgon observed her with interest.

"I must say, your resilience is impressive. Most would have disintegrated immediately had they taken a direct hit like that."

Drathanar roared in rage and charged the robed man, swinging his sabers wildly. Despite his incredible speed, Jorgon matched it with every step; ducking, stepping to the side, and parrying with his staff at just the right moments to avoid the viatari's lethal blades. A confident smirk hung from his lips the whole time.

"Not just your resilience then, your speed as well!" He observed, ducking low to avoid a wide swing from the viatari. "Your race is truly a marvel. I'm almost tempted to let you hit me just so I can experience first-hand your legendary strength. What a shame you've decided to fight against my master instead of with her."

Drathanar kept swinging, growing more frustrated with each attack that missed. His blades bit into bookshelves, cut deeply into the desk Jorgon had been sitting behind, but couldn't find the soft flesh of this chaos-wielding human.

After several minutes of this, Drathanar relented and stepped back, breathing hard as he tried to think of a different approach. His eyes flicked over to Aniria, taking in her charred skin, her face clenched in pain. She whimpered, her eyes shut tight. Rage took hold once more, drowning out any sensible thinking.

"I sense the chaotic energies oozing from your pores, viatari," Jorgon murmured with pleasure. He inhaled deeply and sighed. "Delicious how they change the air. But you have so many tendrils surrounding you right now, you must feel so *tired!*"

He snapped his fingers.

Instantly, Drathanar's eyes rolled back, and he collapsed in a limp heap. Were it not for his chest still moving, Salevari would have thought he had died on the spot. She glared at her opponent, slowly shuffling her way around to his side. Zael did the same on the opposite end.

"What are you?" she asked. "I've never seen or heard anyone from any race wield such power as you do."

Jorgon bowed, as if accepting a compliment. "Indeed you have not. I'm the only one in all of Azar who can do it. What you've just seen is the raw power of chaos energy."

"I thought you said chaos can't be controlled. How is it that you wield it?"

Jorgon nodded understandingly. "A common misconception. I don't wield chaos energy like you wield that sword of yours. Rather, I am its vessel. It flows within my entire being. All I merely do is channel what exists around me and the energy does the rest. I admit, it is difficult to explain to those who are still only flesh and blood."

Zael lunged just as he finished his explanation. But like

Aniria, he found himself passing through a shimmering image, his dirk now aiming for Salevari's heart. His eyes widened as he realized what just happened.

Reacting quickly, Salevari deflected the incoming blade with her buckler, shoving Zael into the adjacent bookshelf as she did so, saving him from sharing Aniria's fate as a purple-white beam shot out between them. The air around them crackled, burning with energy.

Rushing forward, she charged, swinging her sword in measured strokes. She hoped to find a weakness in her opponent's footing, his stance, anything at all to give her the edge she needed to win if only for a second. But just like with Drathanar, Jorgon always seemed to be one step ahead, dodging her attacks with ease.

She wondered how this was possible. It wasn't that he was as fast as her, he was still limited by his human body. Instead, it was as if he could read her movements as easily as one of the books lining the shelves around them, allowing him to anticipate her every move. She thought back to what he'd told Drathanar before her general had been taken out of the fight.

The human had claimed there was chaos energy swirling around the viatari, as if he could see it. As if he could read it. If chaos energy was everywhere, in everyone, perhaps it was able to tell him what she would do before she did it.

If that was the case. . . .

She shot both her sword and buckler out simultaneously in an awkward attack without a second thought. To do so in a real battle would have meant certain death as she abandoned any guard she might have had against an enemy's counter-attack. In this case however, it allowed her to land her first blow against Jorgon as he leaned away from her sword only to find his face meeting the full force of her buckler.

Now it was Jorgon who flew across the small office, slamming into the bookshelves. He grunted, blinking rapidly. He brought a finger to his nose and came back with a small stain of blood.

"So, you do bleed," Salevari grinned. "It appears you still have some flesh and blood in you."

Jorgon's glowing orbs flared.

Zael took his place next to Salevari.

"Keep your attacks random," she instructed. "Don't think, and we might come out of this alive."

Jorgon took a deep breath. Slowly, the scowl on his face reworked itself into a pained smile. "I must say, your strength is as impressive as the legends say. It was quite a telling experience to endure firsthand—and certainly not one I shall be repeating."

The viatari stepped forward, swinging their weapons in a haphazard fashion, doing what they could to put as little thought into their movements as possible. Jorgon danced backward to evade their attacks, but he was starting to struggle now. Beads of sweat formed on his creased brow as he concentrated on their approaches.

When his evasive movements proved insufficient, his image would shimmer as it had several times already, reappearing behind them. Knowing this trick, however, the viatari were quick to react. They jumped in opposite directions, narrowly avoiding the beam of energy that always came from behind before regrouping and going back on the offensive.

After some time fighting like this, Jorgon clapped his hands together and a ball of energy erupted from his body, pushing the viatari back like they'd been met with a forceful gust of wind. They landed in a heap, their strength suddenly drained. Their limbs felt like lead. Their minds wandered in fields of fog.

"Enough of this," he gasped, trying to catch his breath and wiping sweat from his brow. He regarded the viatari with a strange sense of pride. "It seems you've come to understand one of the basic principles of chaos energy. I must say, you are quick learners. I would be proud to call you students of mine, if either of you were willing to follow this path of enlightenment."

The viatari struggled to find their feet while Jorgon leaned heavily on his staff. Whatever effect he had cast on them had affected him as well.

"I think we must consider this altercation a draw. I've not had to use chaos in that manner before and it has drained me. Again, it seems I've underestimated your abilities. Make no mistake, there shall not be a third time."

He turned as if to walk out of the room, nothing standing between him and the tunnel leading to the exit.

"Wait!" Salevari called out, finally finding enough strength to stumble forward, her arm shakily holding her sword out. "You won't escape."

Jorgon paused and looked over his shoulder to regard her one last time.

"I have a pressing matter to attend to. I'm sure we'll see each other again soon. Until that time, viatari."

Then, he raised his hand as if reaching for something and from his fingertips emitted a blinding light that filled the small room. Salevari covered her eyes, wincing from the sudden luminosity. The next second, the light was gone and her eyes refocused. But it was too late. The energy-wielder named Jorgon was gone.

Perhaps it was because he was no longer in the room with them or perhaps whatever curse he had cast on them had faded with time, but strength flooded back into her limbs.

"Look after the others," she ordered Zael as he also lifted himself back onto his feet. "I will chase him down."

She rushed through the tunnel and burst back into the circular room. There she found Simon and Tera still inspecting the bodies and the wooden crates scattered throughout.

"What's happened?" Tera asked incredulously. "It sounded like quite the battle in there."

"Another time," Salevari snapped. "Did either of you see where he went?"

The two humans shared a look.

"Where who went?" Simon asked.

"Jorgon! The human I was fighting. Glowing eyes, dressed in a silk robe, you couldn't have missed him. He should have only just ran through here."

Tera shook her head. "No one has come through here."

Salevari let out a long, defeated sigh as she staggered back into the adjacent stone wall. Her legs crumpled beneath her as all the adrenaline left her at once.

So, he had escaped. Clearly, the energy-wielder had some method of teleportation similar to the acolytes, which meant he could be anywhere, roaming freely, plotting his next move.

And a man that powerful . . . she shuddered to think what someone like that could do.

CHAPTER THIRTY-THREE

There was no time to dwell on what couldn't be controlled.

Pushing herself off the wall, Salevari stumbled forward, her legs still shaky. She took in the scene around her, the blank stares of the dead meeting her wherever she looked.

"Tera," she called, sheathing her sword and clipping her buckler back onto her belt. "Go back to the palace and alert the Grand Admiral about what's happened here. I'm sure he'll send his intelligence officers to investigate the scene themselves. Lead them back here."

"I thought we wanted to bring the evidence of this place to him ourselves."

But the Chancellor shook her head. "Fradrick needs to understand how big this operation was. He'll still have room for skepticism if all we bring back are a couple crates of grain and a few severed heads. He needs to hear about this place from his own men."

Tera nodded and left the room, disappearing down the tunnel that led back to the outside world.

"And me?" Simon asked.

"You need to find the source of The Turned One's corruption," Salevari said, turning back to the office where her fellow viatari remained. "There will be a box here somewhere filled with vials or flasks holding a thick black liquid. You'll feel the pressure of evil on your shoulders like a physical weight when you find it. Felix told me about it once. It was what the corrupted burrowers were using to corrupt the waters of the north before we found it and captured it. Find that, and we have undeniable evidence that The Turned One was involved in this whole thing."

"Don't we already know that?"

"*We* know it," Salevari said with some exasperation. "Fradrick does not, and I cannot leave him with a shadow of a doubt. Find it and come get me when you do."

Simon grunted. "And where are you off to?"

She raised her hand in a small, dismissive wave as a response. She still felt incredibly drained as she retraced her steps down the long tunnel back to Jorgon's office. The battle had taken much out of her, though she didn't care to admit it. The chaos energy their opponent wielded seemed to leech its power from everyone and everything in the vicinity. It certainly had with the viatari. Her stomach rumbled. She needed energy. The thought of scampering squirrels or the platters of flopping fish Thomas always fed them back in Donsea left her mouth watering.

Upon reentering the office, she found Drathanar had woken up from his stupor. He leaned heavily against the bookshelf, his other hand pressing against his temples as he clenched his eyes shut. Aniria remained on the floor, unconscious, her exposed back being examined by Zael. Salevari joined him.

The stench of singed flesh still lingered. A circle of black char was imprinted across Aniria's back where the energy beam had hit her. Within that spot, the skin and muscle underneath looked to have been eaten away, exposing some bone.

"No human healer will be able to mend this," Zael murmured.

Salevari agreed. It was a dreadful wound. Worse, it was one caused by unnatural energies.

"We'll have to hope that her regenerative abilities can do the job, despite the nature of her injury," she said.

"I think they will. Though, it's likely to be a slow recovery."

Salevari patted Zael on the shoulder, then went over to Drathanar to check on him.

"Are you alright?"

The Dalyran general grunted, wincing. "My head feels as if it has been split open by a dwarven axe."

"Do you remember what happened?"

He nodded, his eyes narrowing. "That cursed human said something about chaos energies surrounding me and snapped his fingers. When he did that there was an immense pressure that squeezed my head until I heard a pop. The next thing I know I'm waking up on the floor with Zael looking down at me." He tried to take a step forward, then thought better of it. "Enough about me. How is Aniria?"

"She'll be fine," Salevari reassured him. "She's badly wounded, but she lives and her regenerative abilities should heal her eventually."

Worry left the Dalyran general's face once he heard the news. "That's . . . encouraging," he forced out through gritted teeth.

"Rest easy, my general," Salevari eased him back to the floor so he could lie down. "When we return to the palace I'll have you meet with the human healers to see what they can do about your head."

"Thank you, Chancellor. I apologize for failing to kill that human. Did you get him?"

A scowl hung from her lips. "You have nothing to apologize for, my brave general. But no, I also failed to kill the human. He escaped. Time will tell if we must face him again."

"Next time he won't escape my blades so easily."

Salevari chuckled and patted him on the head encouragingly. As she stood up, Simon entered the room. He took in the scene before him, eyebrows arching up when he saw two of the four viatari lying on the ground incapacitated.

"What is it, Simon?"

His eyes met hers and she instantly knew he'd been successful in his search.

"You found it?"

The human chief nodded. "You should also know that the Grand Admiral's men are already here. They're in the central room, inspecting the dead. Apparently, they had their eyes on this place all night just to see what became of us."

"Good," she nodded with approval. "Less time wasted. Take me where you found it. I must secure it before they find it for themselves."

Simon led the way. When they entered the central room, the intelligence officers within glanced up to see who had joined them. A few jumped back in shock when they noticed Salevari's red eyes and sharp fangs.

"Evening, gentlemen," she said matter-of-factly. "Carry on with your work."

After a brief hesitation, they did just that. Clearly, Fradrick had been true to his word, even going so far as to keep his entire intelligence network in the dark regarding their true identity.

Simon led her down one of the side passages, one filled with many twists and turns. Passing through a large holding room filled with stacked wooden crates and bodies of the slain, they entered another long series of tunnels until they finally came upon a narrow, square room at the end.

Opening the door, a small, wooden chest lay before them. They glanced at each other.

"I checked it already," Simon said before she could ask. "This is what we're looking for."

Not wanting to leave anything to chance, Salevari bent down and opened it herself. An overwhelming aura of malice assaulted her like the stench of a corpse. Inside were rows upon rows of glass vials, less than half of them still full of a viscous black liquid.

The essence of The Turned One. They had found it.

She closed the lid, taking a moment to let the air around them settle back to a calmer state.

"We've got what we came for," she finally said. "We'll take a couple crates of food with us as proof of the food shortage as well as the plot The Turned One had planned for this city. We'll also take these vials. My guess is that most of what's here has already been contaminated. Did you find any documents of significance?"

"A few thurn posts tucked away in the pockets of the slain and some inventory lists. Nothing special." Simon shrugged.

"I'm sure anything vital would have been in Jorgon's office," the Chancellor pursed her lips. "I doubt he left anything behind that he didn't want us to read when he escaped."

"We should still check."

Salevari grabbed the small chest and tucked it under her arm. "We will. We can do a quick search while we pick up the others, then we return to the palace and report what we found to Fradrick. It's time to make him choose a side."

They turned and began making their way back.

"What of the intelligence officers?" Simon asked.

"Ignore them," Salevari answered. Her mind had only one focus now. She'd completed her part of the bargain, now she had to make sure Fradrick upheld his end. "They can carry out whatever investigation they wish, but we're the ones who will present the facts to the Grand Admiral. Besides," she added with a small smile. "I wouldn't want to interrupt their work when they're busy cleaning up our mess."

The sun had only just sent its first rays to stir the city when they were met in the palace by a cohort of healers who shoved their way forward to take Drathanar and Aniria under their wing. They spared only a moment to recover from the shock of coming face to face with a party of viatari before taking the two injured ones away from the main lobby to the hospital wing, chattering diligently as they observed their wounds. A man with a quill and journal jotted down notes as quickly as he could, trailing behind the rest.

Salevari, Zael, Simon, and Tera remained where they were at the foot of the grand staircase, Zael carrying two heavy crates of foodstuffs while Salevari clutched the small chest of The Turned One's essence under her arm. Eventually, they began looking around. Someone was missing; someone who always appeared out of the shadows to greet them at a moment's notice, as if he always knew when they needed him.

"Where's Aethel?" Salevari asked a nearby guards.

The guard stiffened as she approached, the grip on his polearm tightening, "The Grand Admiral's usher has been detained on suspicion of treason."

This forced Salevari to take a step back. "Treason?"

"Aye."

"What treason did he commit?"

"My apologies, but for that answer you'll have to ask the Grand Admiral. A butler will be along shortly to lead you and your fellows to his office." The guard said the last with a hint of finality. The conversation was over.

Salevari nodded, accepting his words and returned to her companions. Moments later, an elderly man in a black suit approached them, bowing low.

"Greetings," he said softly. "If you will please follow me, I will take you to see the Grand Admiral."

Without waiting, the butler spun around and began climbing the grand staircase. They followed, and soon found themselves outside of the massive oak doors they had become so familiar with.

"Come in," Fradrick's voice carried through the thick planks as the butler finished knocking. Salevari and her companions were ushered in. Fradrick regarded them, his bristling mustache twitching under his nose.

"What have you got for me?"

Zael stepped forward and placed the two crates he'd been carrying on the Grand Admiral's desk, scattering piles of paper in the process.

Fradrick grumbled, "That'll take me ages to reorganize."

"Your city has been dealing with a food shortage for two years, Fradrick," Salevari stated firmly. "You and the elites didn't believe this. Perhaps you didn't know. But the evidence of this is before you. Thurn has been intercepting your trade routes and stealing your peoples' food. Here are two crates we found in their headquarters that we brought as proof. Your intelligence officers can confirm that there are hundreds more lying in storage within those underground tunnels."

Fradrick stared at the two crates, deep lines of worry cutting into his brow. He got up, drawing a large knife he had attached to his belt. Slipping the blade between the cracks of each crate, he popped the lids. One was filled with regular grain, a golden sheen coming off it. The other contained the same thing, though its color was tinged with layers of green and black specks. It was barely perceptible, except to those who were paying attention.

"What's wrong with this batch, then?" Fradrick pointed at the discolored granules.

"It's been contaminated by the essence of The Turned One," Salevari stepped forward and placed the small chest she'd been carrying before the Grand Admiral. He raised an eyebrow, looking at her skeptically. "Anyone who eats it now will fall under her influence. They'll be lost. You know this to be true. I know there are already reports of people in your city going mad, attacking others, their eyes black and devoid of all reason."

The Grand Admiral frowned. "How did—"

"Your guards talk too much when they're on patrol in the graveyard," she shrugged. "Anyway, that's not important. What is important is what I've placed before you. If you want proof that what I've been telling you is the truth, open the chest. Inside you'll see what they used to taint your city's food supply, how they planned to corrupt you all to become slaves of The Turned One."

Silence hung between them as the two stared at each other. Finally, Fradrick's gaze fell to the chest. He reached for it, his fingers fumbling with the latches. As he lifted the lid, he gasped, falling back into his chair heavily, his eyes glued to the black vials within.

"Can you feel it?" Salevari breathed. "Can you feel her presence? There's no denying what lies before you."

Fradrick shook his head, defeated, and slammed the lid shut, resecuring the latches. Gingerly, Salevari took the chest back, tucking it under her arm once more.

She tried again, "Do you see now that what I spoke of before is true? The Turned One has Halding Port in her sights whether you wish to be neutral in this war or not. She wants your city."

The Grand Admiral groaned heavily, his eyes rolling up to the ceiling and remaining there, as if he could see through it straight into the heavens.

"I must think on this."

Salevari felt the urge to slam her fists onto his desk, but she restrained herself. Still, her voice came out strained as she asked, "What more is there to consider?"

"Believe it or not, viatari," Fradrick's frown deepened as he met her gaze evenly. He leaned forward, resting his chin on his hand as if in deep contemplation. "I have much more on me plate than what you bring before me. In fact, it's partially your fault that so many issues have been brought up. Yes, you viatari have been a great help to us. You've proven yourselves as friends and I, especially, am grateful to you for discovering the whereabouts of the thurn movement and eradicating them. In doing so, however, you've revealed traitors in our midst. My own usher—"

"Aethel?" Salevari interrupted. "He was one of them?"

Fradrick scowled, his voice bitter. "He served me for decades. My intelligence officers caught him trying to follow you and your friends into the secret entrance you discovered." He cracked a smile when he noticed the viatari's expressions. "Don't look so surprised. My intelligence network is vast and efficient. They report to me by the minute. I knew everything that was going on with you in that graveyard as it happened—at least, while you were above ground. Anyway, the suspicion was enough to warrant a search of his room. In it, we found several thurn posts tucked away in hidden spaces between the stones of his room's walls. In his desk we found correspondence tying him directly to the movement."

Salevari lowered her eyes, accepting the news. Aethel had seemed so unsuspecting. He'd been incredibly helpful to them from the moment they'd arrived. During their stay, she'd grown used to his constant presence within the palace.

"What will you do with him?"

The Grand Admiral waved a hand dismissively, his face twisted in disgust as if he were gnawing on something bitter. "He'll be taken out to sea and cast into the waters. The sharks can have him."

She nodded. It was a gruesome fate, but she had no say in the matter. After all, if Aethel was indeed a traitor, he had brought this fate upon himself.

"I understand the pain that comes from discovering those you thought were friends were in fact enemies, but what I can't understand is why that should stop you from making what should be an obvious decision."

"This decision is anything but obvious," Fradrick replied, rubbing his temples. "Siding with you—with the *vashi*—goes against hundreds of years of our history. It's not something I can force me people to do on a whim. Besides, with this contaminated food being passed around me city, now I have to focus on containing the plague this Turned One has set upon us."

Salevari shook her head, frustration growing by the second. "Whatever contaminated food that's already in the city was only part of an initial shipment. There will be more."

"All the more reason to contain it!" Fradrick slammed his fists on his desk as he shouted. "The docks will have double the watch, inspections will be thorough and strict. I'll not allow any more of me city to fall to this madness."

"Do you believe The Turned One will stop there? If you, by some miracle, discover and intercept every shipment of tainted food her agents send your way, do you think she'll admit defeat and move on? Her only desire is to control you or destroy you. She'll spare none in Azar from her corruption."

"If we have to fight her off ourselves, we will."

This earned a derisive burst of laughter from the Chancellor. "She had an entire operation undermining your leadership, plotting against you for two whole years without you able to do anything about it, and you think you can defeat her on your own?"

Turning in his chair, the Grand Admiral looked out the wide windows of his office toward the sea. A small fleet of ships sailed in the distance, heading for Halding Port. A trade convoy, by the looks of it. His eyes drooped. A wistful sigh escaped his lips.

"What I would give right now to have me only preoccupation be the strength of the wind and the size of the waves," he murmured.

"Fradrick," Salevari pleaded. "We live in a time where we face trials we did not choose. But we have been put where we are because we were meant to face them. If we walk away from this responsibility because we don't like it, or because it's unpopular, or because it's easier, then you neglect the whole reason for your existence. If you're afraid, you're not alone. But only together can we face this fear head-on, knowing that others are around to keep us from drowning."

Fradrick faced them again. Layers of doubt swam like phantoms behind his eyes, but also a certainty that there was only one path forward. Still, an unwillingness to take the first step weighed on him. He wanted to keep arguing, wanted to fight the inevitable. But he knew he couldn't argue forever. And time was not a luxury for them to waste.

"The elites, the admirals," he said in a hollow voice. "They will not listen to this madness. Even with the proof you present, they may not believe that we're under threat. How am I supposed to convince them to side with the vashi, much less aid them in their time of need?"

"What if I could organize a meeting between them and your people?"

Her suggestion was met with skepticism. "And where would we meet? If the vashi came here, they'd be slaughtered in the streets. If we sailed out to meet them, they might drag us to a watery grave."

"I can find a neutral ground," Salevari insisted. "Donsea has already pledged their allegiance, perhaps if we could—"

The doors burst open behind them, followed by a loud *boom* that shook the building. A guard, pale and out of breath, rushed in pointing past the Grand Admiral toward the sea.

"Grand Admiral, sir," he said, a tremor in his voice. "We're under attack, sir!"

Fradrick swiveled in his chair to face the sea once more. The same fleet that had been approaching only a short while ago was now much closer and had their broadsides facing the city. Another *boom* sounded from outside but there was no sign that anything had been fired from the ships.

"Who would dare?" he roared. He turned his sharp gaze at the guard. "Why are we not firing back?"

"T-the ships are out of range, sir," the guard stammered.

"They can hit us somehow but we can't hit them."

"I don't believe it," Fradrick murmured, rising out of his seat and pushing his way around his desk, storming out of his office. Salevari and her companions followed.

His bulking figure swiftly strode through a variety of halls until he burst through a door leading outside. They found themselves walking along the ramparts of a curtain wall connecting the palace to an observation tower rising high over the city. Once inside, they climbed stone steps for several minutes until they reached the top, where they had a commanding view of the entire area surrounding Halding Port. Wind whipped around them forcefully.

A guard stood up quickly and saluted as Fradrick rushed for the railing, leaning nearly half his body out as if that would help him see who was attacking his city more clearly.

"Give me the lens," he ordered.

The guard rifled through a nearby chest and brought out a long, brass spyglass. Fradrick put one end to his eye and pointed the other out towards the ships.

"Ten vessels," he growled. "They look medium-sized. Maybe slightly larger than your average sloop. How is it that they're attacking us from so far away?"

No sooner did he ask this question, than another volley burst from the cluster of vessels. The missiles launched from the sides of each ship, arcing unnaturally in the air with great speed. There was no burst of fire, like from a cannon. If Halding Port's ballistae couldn't fire because the enemy was out of range, then the enemy should also have been dealing with the same issue.

Salevari noticed a strange violet glow emanating from each missile as they fell into the port city. The sound of explosions, crashing wood, and falling stone tore through the air, followed by a chorus of terrified screams.

"Give me that thing," she said to Fradrick, a sudden and dreadful thought entering her mind. He hesitated, not wanting to lose sight of the scene before him, but handed her the spyglass.

She put it against her eye and searched each ship. She could see the crews working. Sailors climbed up the rigging, reloaded heavy scorpion bolts for the next volley, and ran around in general, doing what needed to be done to keep their operation running smoothly.

As interesting as this was to her, she moved on. There was someone specific she was looking for, though she hoped not to see him.

But as her gaze fell on one of the ships anchored near the center of the formation, her hope fizzled out. There he stood in his blue silken robes, magenta cloak flapping in the wind. Glowing orbs stared back at her as if he knew she was watching.

A smile popped onto his otherwise expressionless face as he waved.

"He's here," she breathed, her heart lurching into her throat. Dread filled her not just because she knew how powerful this one man was, but because this time there was nothing she could do to fight him from where she stood. He had free rein to wreak havoc as he willed. And she was helpless.

"It's Jorgon."

CHAPTER THIRTY-FOUR

"Who is this 'Jorgon'?" Fradrick demanded, swiping the spyglass back and jamming it against his eye.

Salevari's lips set in a grim line. "He's the one who organized the thurn movement. We fought him in their headquarters, but we failed to capture him and he escaped. He's unlike any human I've ever encountered. There's something unnatural about him that allows him to control what he calls 'chaos energy.' He's an agent of The Turned One, serving her freely. Beyond that, I don't know much else."

"What is this, then," the Grand Admiral growled. "Some attempt at revenge?"

"You could say that."

"Well, I won't have it! You, private!"

The guard standing to Fradrick's side stiffened like a board, throwing his hand up to his forehead in a crisp salute.

"Sir!"

"I want you to run down to the docks, quick as you can. Tell the captains of the fleet to set out and engage the enemy at once. If you run into any problems send me a bird, and I'll have them rue the day they didn't take the defense of this city more seriously."

The young private rushed away, disappearing quickly down the stairs.

"Why would the fleet not set out on their own right away?" Salevari asked.

"If I knew I'd tell you," was Fradrick's peeved response. "Captains were probably too busy stuffing their gullets with food or drinking themselves to death. Whatever their excuse, if it isn't a good one, there'll be a reckoning should we survive this ordeal."

The next several minutes were spent watching the enemy fleet fire multiple volleys into the city while Fradrick paced, cursing under his breath each time a missile hit. The destruction tearing into Halding Port was terrible. Houses fell. Fires burned. The docks were torn up, debris floating freely within the bay. Luckily, the fleet remained untouched, the city's sea wall absorbing any attacks that might have hit them otherwise.

Though untouched, they also remained anchored where they were.

"Blasted captains, all of them!" Fradrick roared, his face turning red. "Why aren't they moving?"

In answer, a hawk landed along the railings of the observation tower with a rolled-up scroll attached to its leg. Blustering, Fradrick ripped the scroll off, sending the hawk soaring away with an angry screech. He unfurled it, nearly tearing the message down the middle, and read through what was written quickly. His face darkened.

"Apparently my captains are refusing to set sail because they fear the enemy fleet will tear through them the minute they leave the protection of the sea wall." He crumpled the message in a tight fist. "If the enemy outranges our defenses on the sea wall, then they'll likely outrange our fleet as well. Damn them, but my captains are right. They wouldn't stand a chance."

Despite the news, he stood tall, staring defiantly out at the enemy as he mulled things over. Another wave of destruction decided things for him.

"We have to strike back. If we can't engage them with our fleet, we'll board theirs with our faster vessels. They'll be smaller targets, harder to hit since they can better execute evasive maneuvers on a dime."

"I can't say for sure," Salevari cautioned. "But since Jorgon is manipulating the energy around their missiles to strike you from a distance, it's likely he'll be able to manipulate their direction as well. I don't think any amount of evasive maneuver will help anyone escape his sights if that's the case."

"We can't just do nothing!" Fradrick roared. "This is the only plan I have. I'll send three of our frigates with them to provide cover. I doubt this energy-chucker will be able to resist the temptation of smashing a larger target. It might give our boarding craft the time they need to reach their ships. Now—"

He studied his remaining company. "You viatari have already proven yourselves as friends to Halding Port. You've done much, but I must ask of you another favor."

Salevari raised an eyebrow. "Name it."

"Since I scared away that messenger hawk, I need one of you to run down to the docks to deliver my orders to the man in charge down there. His name is Admiral Darill. Tell him I am authorizing him to organize a flotilla of boarding crafts and to have them readied for immediate assault. He'll know what to do. He must also choose three frigates from our docked fleet to escort them."

"Why must we be the ones to give this message?" Salevari

asked, crossing her arms. "Why not call another one of your guards up? I'm sure there are more around somewhere in the palace."

"There's no time to waste," Fradrick responded curtly. "Your race are well-known for their speed. You can get this message to the docks faster than we ever could; and right now, that's what I need."

Salevari considered for a moment. "You realize, if we rush to the docks as we are, it'll be obvious to everyone that the viatari are in your city. You might accept us, but I wonder how your subordinates will handle receiving orders from us."

The Grand Admiral grunted and took off one of the large golden rings he wore on his fingers. He tossed it to her.

"Present this to Darill and there'll be no issue. He'll know that I've sent you directly."

Salevari twirled the ring in her fingers, admiring the detailed anchors etched into the precious band. She tossed it to Zael.

"Go," she said. "See that the message is delivered. Aid them any way you can with their preparations."

Zael inclined his head and departed.

Bowing low, Fradrick placed a fist to his heart. "Thank you, my lady."

Preparations for the assault took hours to organize, made longer by the constant barrage Jorgon's fleet continued to rain down.

Fires raged from the docks to a mile into the city. With the shock and fear of the initial attack having faded away, the townsfolk kept busy forming water brigades on every street as they fought the flames. But there were too many, and more were birthed with each salvo that struck their mark. Smoke bellowed, drifting skyward and creating a thick cloud that made visibility difficult from where they all stood in the observation tower. Still, they caught glimpses of the work being done in what remained of the docks as sailors rushed from end to end, gathering supplies, a force of marines, and ships to carry them.

Now these smaller vessels were gathered together and ready to set out, the first dozen already unmoored and pushed out of their slips. Three frigates, middle-class ships of Halding Port's fleet, slowly drifted into position within the quay as well. Their emblem, a golden anchor with two spears crossing behind it, shone brightly as their numerous sails unfurled. There they sat, waiting for the right moment when they could abandon the protection of the sea wall, which had taken a beating for them.

Fradrick watched this all unfold through the looking glass he had clutched in his hands. Tension turned his shoulders stiff. Another salvo flew from Jorgon's fleet, some missiles hitting the sea wall, forcing sections of it to fall into the waters below, while the rest went into the city, crashing randomly and adding to the fires.

"Now!" he breathed.

The sailors waiting in the bay saw their opportunity. The first few waves of boarding craft quickly sailed past the sea wall and spread out across the open ocean, three frigates evenly positioned among them.

It wasn't long before they were noticed. The enemy fleet turned to face them. A few minutes passed where nothing happened as they readied their next volley. During this time, the assault force tried to close as much distance as they could. But there was no way to reach the enemy before they were ready to fire.

Bolts shot out from their respective ships, the violet glow surrounding them brighter than usual. A few crashed into the smaller boarding crafts, sinking them with one blow and drowning all on board. The majority, however, veered for the frigates. Two of the warships endured the pounding, only suffering superficial damage. The last lost its main sail, a missile hitting it directly in the middle, causing it to crash onto the deck where it brought about more damage. The frigate was quickly left behind as its crew scrambled.

Fradrick groaned but kept watching with bated breath as the gap between the two forces continued to close.

Another volley.

Another frigate was lost, the weight of the attack too much for it to handle this time. It listed portside, gaping holes torn through its hull and sails, turning them into rags. Sailors jumped overboard, swimming away as fast as they could before the ship sunk completely.

The last remaining frigate lurched to one side as it turned sharply, presenting its own weaponry as the smaller crafts continued on their way.

"They're still too far away," the Grand Admiral murmured. "They won't land a single shot."

The frigate unleashed its own salvo against the enemy. A dark line of long, spear-like bolts soared across the gap of open ocean between the frigate and Jorgon's ships, falling well short and splashing harmlessly into the water.

"Tell me, my lady," Fradrick said, his voice soft and layered with tones of defeat. "Would dwarven cannons have been able to hit the enemy from that distance?"

Salevari tried to judge the situation as best as she could, but she was no cannoneer. The best she could do was surmise that if ballistae could *almost* hit the enemy, then cannons certainly would have done so.

"I'm no expert," she said. "But I believe so."

"What if I had cannons on the sea wall?"

"Those I can say with certainty would have been able to hit their targets without issue."

Letting loose a sharp breath, Fradrick tore his gaze away from the battle. "I never thought I'd see the day where this city's defenses proved to be as ineffective as an army of peasants marching on a shield wall armed only with stones."

"Defenses can be improved," Salevari said encouragingly. "And you may yet get the chance to do so. Look, your boarding parties have nearly reached their targets."

"Perhaps with too many losses," he lamented, putting the glass back to this eye so he could watch their progress once more.

The gap between Jorgon's ships and the boarding parties was now small enough that the marines on board were already taking individual shots at the opposing crews with bows, crossbows, and slings. Within another minute or two, they would be able to climb aboard the first few ships and let their swords do the bloody work.

Fradrick searched for the last remaining frigate and let out a strangled cry when he saw that it was torn in half, the bow burning even as it sunk into the water. Crates, barrels, planks of wood, and bodies floated around the wreckage. The marines were on their own now.

Enough boarding crafts survived the approach to board three of the enemy's ships. They threw grappling hooks over the railings and climbed aboard, daggers clenched between their teeth to use in case they had no time to reach for a sword once aboard.

The battle seemed to turn. Though outnumbered, Halding

Port's marines were a well-trained fighting force and easily overwhelmed the crews of the ships they boarded, mainly consisting of ragged looking men who Salevari was sure were under The Turned One's influence already. Jorgon may have had the advantage when he could rely on a ranged attack to keep his foes at bay. But no amount of chaos energy could be used to make a man a better fighter.

A smile slowly lifted on Fradrick's grizzled face as he watched their progress. "Once those ships are taken, my men can sail them into the others and take those in turn until we've captured their entire fleet. We just might survive this ordeal!"

Salevari wished she could share his optimism. The battle looked promising, but if the marines killed all of The Turned One's forces on each ship there would be nothing holding back Jorgon's remaining ones from firing on them.

As the fighting on the boarded vessels began to wind down, it appeared her line of thinking was the more realistic one.

Even as the marines continued fighting the remnants of The Turned One's crews, a giant pillar of purple-white energy enveloped one of the boarded ships. It erupted from the waters like a reverse waterfall, reaching up to the clouds and lasting for several seconds. A roar filled the air that reached all ears across the city. Once the pillar of energy dissipated, there was nothing left of the ship, or those who had been on it. It was as if they had never existed.

Two more pillars rose into the sky, engulfing the other compromised ships. Fradrick paled, cold sweat trickling down his temples. The light from the pillars reflected in his eyes.

As the final burst of destructive energy faded, the seven remaining ships of Jorgon's fleet readjusted themselves to once again face Halding Port and fired a new salvo into the city.

The Grand Admiral's hands began to tremble. Slowly, he

lowered the spyglass. His eyes were wide, unblinking, as if still replaying the devastating scene he had just witnessed.

"All those men. . . ." He choked out. Turning to the viatari, he said in a hoarse voice, "I don't know what to do. I don't—he did that to his own men, too . . . I can't believe it. Halding Port is finished."

"Halding Port is not finished," Salevari grabbed his shoulders staring deep into his eyes. She saw helplessness, defeat, sorrow, but also somewhere in there was the hardened sailor she knew could never shy away from a challenge.

"Remember the rogue wave," she said firmly. His head snapped to attention, lucidity expunging the doubt that had been creeping in. "*This* is the rogue wave. What must you do?"

Another barrage shook the city.

A mad grin popped onto his face. His eyes remained distant, but now they saw themselves at the helm of a ship, fighting the ocean's fury itself instead of the enemy anchored just outside.

"I must sail through it."

He clapped his hands together, rubbing them vigorously as he turned his attention back to the task at hand. "But the question remains, what do we hit them with? Perhaps I can send messenger hawks to the other fleets out on patrol, have them come home and encircle the enemy. Then we could sally forth with our home fleet. We'd lose ships. The city would be devastated. Yes. But we could destroy them, and we could rebuild. . . ."

As he continued muttering to himself this budding plan, Salevari's attention was caught by the ocean itself. Something new was out there, and she had a feeling she knew what it was.

"Give me that." She took the spyglass from Fradrick, who

hardly noticed, and put it back against her eye.

Sure enough, her suspicions proved correct. The water around Jorgon's fleet was churning. She smiled. Luck had come their way. All that remained was to ensure that what was about to happen was witnessed by the right person.

"Fradrick."

The Grand Admiral snapped his head in her direction.

"Tell me, is the smoke in the air deceiving my eyes or is the sea boiling?"

He shot her a quizzical look as he took back the looking glass.

"You're right, but how—by the waves, the vashi have come!"

Even without the magnified view, Salevari could see vashi warriors climbing up the hulls of Jorgon's ships as easily as they would a ladder. They jumped over the railings and made quick work of the crews. More heads popped up from under the sea, watching the battles happening above, ready to join in as needed.

Once a ship was cleared, the vashi would jump off. Large whirlpools then formed under the crewless vessels as vashi waterseers used the power granted to them by Ocaeus to pull them under.

Fradrick laughed in disbelief. "Your friend Jorgon doesn't look too happy." He passed the spyglass back to her.

When she put it to her eye, she saw what he meant. Jorgon stared straight at her, his little smile replaced by a bitter sneer. The next second, a flash of light blinded her. She flinched away from the glass and blinked rapidly until her eyesight returned. When she looked back, Jorgon was gone, and the ship he was on was quickly sinking into the sea.

With the last enemy ship finding its new home on the ocean

floor, the vashi bobbed in the water, their heads moving up and down as waves pushed through them.

"It seems Halding Port has been saved," Salevari noted.

"It has, indeed," Fradrick gulped. "I suppose there's no hiding it now, is there? The Turned One has forced our hand. And there'd be no hand to offer right now were it not for our most hated enemy." He turned to her, still stunned, but with a new conviction in his voice. "If you can arrange it, I will meet with them. Here. Now."

Salevari nodded. "I'll see what I can do."

After a short boat ride to meet the vashi and relay Fradrick's invitation, Salevari found herself standing between Avmoshir, flanked by two personal guards, and the Grand Admiral of Halding Port, who stood alone in his office. The two leaders regarded each other with suspicion.

A few minutes of silence passed like this, until Avmoshir decided to begin the historic encounter. "I must say, despite my people saving yours from certain destruction, it was a difficult journey up here. So many of your guards were ready to strike me down as soon as their eyes fell upon me."

Fradrick shrugged. "Can't blame them, can you? Our peoples have been enemies for centuries, and not everyone witnessed firsthand what happened out there. With time, the truth will be known, but change doesn't happen overnight."

"This is true," Avmoshir conceded.

"Tell me," Fradrick reached for a seat and plopped himself into it. He leaned back, speaking in a cordial but guarded voice. "How is it you discovered that we were under attack so quickly and were able to come to our aid?"

"That would be because of Una, our high priestess," the young vashi answered, dragging over his own chair and setting it across from the Grand Admiral. "She sensed disturbances in the water that reeked of corruption. After sending out a few scouts to investigate, we realized the source was from a fleet of ships filled with servants of The Turned One. It was quickly determined that they were headed your way. Una sent me a message warning me of the situation and I decided to gather our forces to take care of them."

"And why do that? Why help us?"

Avmoshir glanced at Salevari. She nodded encouragingly.

"As I'm sure you've been told, we will soon need protection ourselves. The darinsha could invade our waters at any time. We fought off your enemies as a show of good faith, as a first step in creating friendly ties with you."

"Our history is one of blood," the Grand Admiral stated, stroking his mustache.

"It may be," the Supreme Overseer responded. "But our history doesn't have to define our future. We can break from this path we've traveled down for centuries. As time goes on, as we fight together, perhaps we'll learn more from each other. Perhaps we'll find that we are not the same humans or vashi who fought each other centuries ago."

Fradrick grunted. "A noble sentiment. Well said."

"Don't forget what we've offered as well," Salevari added. "As you just witnessed, your defenses are lacking and The Turned One will seek to destroy you if she cannot control you. The only way to ensure your people's safety is to destroy her and her twisted brother once and for all. The only way we can do that is if you fight with us."

"As you have noted in the past, these old prejudices are hard to kill," Fradrick shook his head but then looked up with a stubborn fire behind him. "But if there is honesty in any man today, they'll admit to themselves that there's more at stake now than maintaining old feuds."

Salevari's eyes lit up. "Then. . . ?"

A rugged chuckle burst from the Grand Admiral's throat as he slammed his fists onto his desk. "To the depths with the elites! I'll take full responsibility for this decision, and I'll convince everyone here of its necessity. My lady, you have our support. Halding Port's fleet is at your disposal."

CHAPTER THIRTY-FIVE

Felix crouched with nearly one hundred warriors—dwarven, viatari, and some human—just within the tree line. Ahead of them, the Three Spires stretched toward the heavens.

Three days had passed since Serania set out with the bulk of their forces up the adjacent mountain range. The camp had been emptied. A path had been discovered by the scouts Felix had sent that provided the best chance for their forces to remain undetected during their trek. Three days was a long time to move such a large army without being seen, but if Serania managed it, they would take the enemy by surprise within the vale.

And that's just what Felix wanted.

There wouldn't be any time for them to organize and form a defensive line by the time Serania arrived. They would be an easy target for the destructive force he intended to unleash upon them, a force that would hopefully give their own fighters an edge in the coming battle. After all, Serania was to begin the fight by unleashing the power of her hidden eye.

Felix was still surprised with himself that he had approved

its use so easily when she had suggested it. But even now, after days of mulling over the decision, it made perfect sense to do so.

Serania's hidden eye was an object veiled in mystery, but one thing about it was blatantly clear. It was a weapon of mass destruction. He had seen it used only a handful of times during his long life, the most recent being during the Siege of Garon. That time, it had largely decided the outcome of the battle, blowing a gaping hole in Garon's citadel and the enemy's forces.

He doubted it would single-handedly give them victory here, but it would serve a purpose. After using her eye, the smoke and noise from its destructive power would be seen and heard for miles around, including from where they sat at the foot of the Three Spires.

It would serve as a signal for them to advance.

He looked in the direction where Serania should be, waiting, imagining a large cloud of dust and smoke rising above the jagged peaks. But the picture before him remained serene. Behind him, an air of restlessness rose like steam.

"She'll get there," Thuradin grunted, as if he could sense the worry infiltrating the elder viatari's thoughts.

"What if she has been ambushed?" Felix wondered in a hushed tone. "What if they were waiting for her on the mountain trail? It is too easy a place to thwart any attacker and we would never know they were in trouble. Why did I not think of that possibility?"

"Do ye think The Turned One would think of something like that?"

"If I would, her commander likely would as well."

Thuradin grunted again. "Serania is strong and smart. If she runs inta any problems, she'll think of a way out of them.

Have faith in her and those who fight with her."

No sooner had he said this, than a dull roar like thunder met their ears. All eyes shifted to the mountains northeast of their position. A thick plume of black smoke rose steadily into the sky.

Thuradin flashed a triumphant grin. "I hate ta say I told ye so."

Felix let out a breath in relief, his nerves settling for what was to come next. There was no telling how many foes remained near the Spires' main entrance. Regardless of their numbers, it would be their job to push through until they reached the tunnels and met up with the main force.

Without a word, he stood up and stepped out from the tree line. The rustling of bushes filled the air as one hundred pairs of boots joined him. Together, they traversed the small field separating them from the mountain pass.

They were met with silence.

A good start, but Felix kept his eyes constantly on the move. He examined every boulder they passed, every crevice in the mountain face as they hiked alongside it. He kept his dirk held before him, ready for a pack of darimun or a company of corrupted burrowers to materialize out of thin air and surround them.

But still they were met with silence, and now they had rounded a number of switchbacks.

It was eerie how still the air was. Not even the wind dared breathe as they progressed to the higher levels. Felix feared each step might be his last, expecting a trap to spring around them. But none came.

By the time they reached the halfway point up the pass, near the exact same spot where their last assault had met with failure, Felix began to feel confused. He kept his composure, kept his sense of caution as he continued the advance, but he couldn't help wondering where the enemy could be.

Yes, he had expected the majority to run off into the mountains to defend against Serania, but surely there had to be some remnant of the enemy guarding this place. The Turned One's new commander, this Drake Thuradin had told him about, could not be so foolish as to have left it completely undefended.

Yet, perhaps this *was* his plan—to throw them into a state of confusion, lure them into a false sense of security, thinking they might make it to the entrance completely unhindered. As they rounded the next switchback, they passed a series of barricades that looked like they'd been forcibly pushed to the side.

So, Felix thought, someone *was* here. The barricades hadn't set themselves up, after all. And yet, the long path before them continued with neither trap nor foe in sight.

They pressed on.

Finally, rounding the final switchback, a new sight met them. Felix tightened the grip on his blade. The air around them grew colder. At the end of the path stood a gaping hole leading into the Three Spires. Leaning against the mouth of this tunnel, half his body concealed in shadow, was a single, short figure.

As they approached, Felix noticed more details. Lying around the stranger were several bodies, still and bloodied. There were burrowers, humans, and a single darim that had been a fox at one time. It was a path of death he had expected to leave himself. But someone had beat him to it. He peered once more at the relaxed figure, pointing the tip of his blade at him.

The figure stepped forward, his arms crossed and a smug

look dominating his features.

"'Bout time ye showed up!" Morteth Shadowmeld shouted, laughing jovially. "I though' I might 'ave ta sleep 'ere for the night!"

"I don't believe it," Thuradin muttered. His body tensed, as if he were preparing to rush forward and greet the dwarven assassin with an axe to the head. Felix held out a hand to stop him, though his gaze remained fixed on Morteth.

"What are you doing here?"

Morteth staggered back, his face dropping into a theatrical state of shock. "Is tha' 'ow ye thank the one who's made yer path up 'ere so easy?"

Felix ignored the theatrics. "You have not been seen since the heinous act you committed against one of your own. It was believed you deserted us or that The Turned One bought you out."

The assassin snorted. A disapproving frown quickly formed. "I may make a livin' in a manner ye deem unbecomin', but I'd ne'er stoop so low as ta serve sommun who's goal is the destruction o' the world where I make me livin'," he raised his arms in exasperation. "I migh' as well stick me daggers inta me black 'eart meself an' be done with it."

"Now that's a plan I can approve of," Thuradin seethed.

Morteth shook his head, clicking his tongue. "Ah, commander, and 'ere I hoped we'd 'ave a much better relationship, given our shared 'istory."

"I will ask again," Felix called out, taking back control of the conversation. "What are you doing here?"

The dwarven assassin walked toward them slowly, his hands half-raised as if he were presenting them the mountain they stood on. He looked around at the surrounding corpses with raised eyebrows. Felix never lowered his weapon.

"I've been busy clearin' the path ahead for ye."

Now it was Felix's turn to look around with a new appreciation as he realized these were the enemies they would have had to face. That is, if Morteth was telling the truth.

"How do we know you are not lying?"

Morteth scoffed. His hands fell casually to the hilts of the daggers hanging off his belt. "Now, why would I lie?"

"Perhaps to hold us over for some trap that The Turned One has planned for us."

Wagging a finger, the assassin shook his head. "Ye disappoint me, viatari. First, I told ye I would ne'er serve her. As ye pointed out already, I like money. There'll be no money in this world if it ends. Second," a mischievous gleam entered his dark eyes. "Don't ye think ye found yer way up 'ere a tad too easily? What, I wonder, ever 'appened ta those funny little traps ye kept runnin' inta last time ye sent us up this mountain?"

Felix raised an eyebrow. "You disarmed them?"

Beaming, Morteth bowed. "Aye."

"You disarmed every single trap on this path *and* slew all the guards on the way up here?"

"I am the best at wha' I do."

Felix lowered his blade, drawing an incredulous look from Thuradin. "If this is true, then we owe you our lives. And I give you my personal thanks. You have saved us a tremendous amount of time."

Morteth waved his hands, chuckling. "Ah, Felix, stop it. I can feel me face turnin' red."

"What do you intend to do now?"

Shrugging, Morteth pointed toward the gaping tunnel behind him. "I've 'ad plenty o' time ta rest waitin' for ye ta catch up. Figure I might as well join ye on wha'ever little quest ye're on."

Felix nodded. "I welcome your expertise." Thuradin's sharp gaze stabbed into the viatari's back. He turned to meet it. "He has proven himself valuable. Only a fool would throw away an ally who could make the difference between success and failure. Remember why we are here today."

A minute passed as Thuradin grappled with the logic of the decision and his own personal honor. Finally, he nodded, though he remained visibly displeased.

Pressing forward, Felix asked, "Have you reconnoitered the tunnel ahead?"

Morteth shook his head, daggers flying into his hands as he turned back toward the gaping mouth before them. "Figured we'd explore it together."

Serania kept low, observing the enemy's position within the vale. Steam from the hot springs drifted slowly upward, producing a thick blanket that made it difficult to see as clearly as she would have liked.

Still, even with that obstacle, she estimated a force of only a few hundred. Burrowers milled about in packs. Humans patrolled between pools of steaming water. The few dozen darinsha, along with their strange crab-like pets that the vashi called kush, soaked in them. There was no alertness about them, no air of urgency, which she thought was strange. It was as if they didn't know or didn't care that they were about to be attacked. She hoped it was the former.

The Turned One should have had lookouts observing their movement. They would have seen Serania's forces climbing the narrow mountain paths heading for the vale. They should have had plenty of time to prepare for the coming battle. But Felix had been correct in his assumptions of the enemy.

Whether it was due to arrogance or a simple oversight, this lack of preparedness would cost them. She'd make sure of that.

She swiveled her head around, studying the surrounding hills. The thought occurred to her that this could be a trap. It would be easy to hide any number of warriors behind these hills, waiting for the right time to rush out. Then again, maybe she was still giving the enemy too much credit.

A different thought gave her pause. It was possible the majority of the enemy's forces were still within the Three Spires, waiting for her to pass through the hot springs into the underground pools, where her forces would be at their most vulnerable. She shook her head. She would think on how to approach that situation when the time came for it. First, they needed to take care of the enemy before them.

A disappointed knot formed in her stomach. Felix had given her permission to use her Eye of the Gods, a hidden gift she had received in the Temple within the Eastern Wald. It was a destructive, wild, powerful weapon. With such a meager target in front of her, it was almost not worth using. Still, she needed to send Felix his signal to advance, and her Eye was the best way to do it.

"Be ready," she warned those immediately around her. The muffled shuffling of armored bodies getting into position briefly filled the air.

A few more minutes passed as she searched for the best spot where she could inflict the most damage. She found it near the center of the vale, where a company of corrupted humans patrolled near a cluster of hot springs, each one filled with several darinsha. She pulled back the strands of hair covering her right eye.

A flash of light burst forth, condensing into a thick beam

of white energy. It rushed forth, crashing into and through the company of humans she had targeted. It tore through the earth, continuing on in a path of utter destruction that left several springs dried up. Enemies disintegrated within seconds of being enveloped, unaware that they had even died.

Letting her hair fall back into place, the beam dissipated. The earth glowed red-hot wherever it had touched. Black smoke rose in great plumes from these areas, racing toward the sky and mixing with the clouds before the breeze caught it and gently brushed it away. Those who had been lucky enough to be outside of the beam's path, stood where they were dumbfounded. One by one, they turned their heads in the direction the attack had come from.

Drawing her sword, Serania stood at full height and pointed it forward.

"Secure the hot springs!"

To her right a chorus of war cries rang through the air as legions of dwarves rushed down into the vale, their heavy weapons raised high and ready to cleave a path forward. Burrowers ran right alongside them, bloodthirst bubbling in their eyes as they bared their flat teeth hungrily for the coming bloodshed. Humans charged from her left, adding their own voices to the din. Serania rushed in, her viatari right behind her, their faces grim but determined. Covering the flanks and the rear were groups of dwarven Enurg'en and vashi waterseers, ready to lend their healing powers wherever they were needed most. Vashi warriors surrounded them as protectors.

It took only seconds for the enemy to realize what was happening. But no amount of time could have prepared them for the wave of death coming their way. They were completely outnumbered. Still, whatever power The Turned One used to compel them forced them together into a single, tight formation. Spears bristled from their front line while those who carried shields covered them.

The two forces met, and Serania entered a world of screams, clashing steel, tearing flesh, and breaking bones. After a few minutes of this, her ears tuned it out and she carried on in a void, aware only of her sword swinging again and again against any who dared approach her.

She moved quickly through the battlefield, fighting as the viatari always did and never staying in one spot for too long. She brought her sword clean through one enemy, then in the next second rushed behind another, thrusting her blade deep into their back.

Despite their formation, the enemy couldn't hold against the sheer weight of the charge presented to them. The dwarves broke through first, their heavy armor lending more weight to their initial impact, sending several enemies flying through the air. Once their lines broke, each corrupted slave fought for their own survival, adrenaline and bloodlust doing what it could to keep them dangerous.

But no amount of ferocity could save them from the full might of their united forces. Within minutes, the last of The Turned One's burrowers fell, leaving only a handful of darinsha and their kush left.

The darinsha fought bravely, their reptilian faces narrowed in a menacing snarl as they used weighted nets to keep a band of dwarves away. Surrounded and wounded, however, they too eventually fell, hissing softly as their blood seeped into the soft earth below.

The kush fought on. Three remained, forming a triangular perimeter. Their large claws were raised and outspread, snapping dangerously at anyone who approached. A few dwarves tried rushing in, avoiding the first few lunges by the beasts and bringing their own weapons down on them, but the kush's armor was too thick and their hammers bounced off. Shocked by this, the dwarves couldn't recover quickly enough to avoid their counterattack. Spiked claws caught two of them, lifting the dwarves high into the air. With a terrible cry, they were cloven in two.

A short standoff ensued where no one else wanted to be the next to try and finish the creatures off. The kush continued clacking their claws threateningly. Finally, Lyrie and Myrna stepped forward with Borim in between, his shield raised and ready.

Roaring a challenge, Borim charged into the creatures, knocking away a kush claw with his shield while he parried another with his hammer. Lyrie and Myrna joined in, jumping on the kush's spiney backs and driving their weapons down into them. Lyrie's sword deflected off the hard surface, but Myrna's found purchase within a crack one of the previous dwarves had made with his hammer. The crustacean let out a high-pitched squeal as she pushed her sword down all the way to the hilt. It stumbled from side to side, then fell forward, green blood gushing from its wound as Myrna jerked her blade out.

A cheer rose from the surrounding spectators. Shrill, angry cries came from the remaining two kush as they turned to face off against the dwarves together. A few viatari took advantage of the distraction and rushed in before they could be noticed. Two hugged the claws shut while a third jumped on top of the kush as the dwarves had, driving their slender dirks deep into its head. With a shudder, the last two kush collapsed, their spiny legs twitching.

Another cheer filled the vale.

Serania let out a relieved breath and took out a rag to wipe her sword before sheathing it.

"Form a perimeter around the hot springs!" she ordered, making her way toward a cluster of the steaming pools that sat undisturbed. "I want patrols on all of the surrounding hills reporting in every thirty minutes. The Turned One could still have her forces hiding out around us. We do *not* want her to catch us off-guard. Vashi, to the pools."

There was a rush of movement as everyone moved into place. Companies were broken up into smaller patrols. Whatever healers weren't assigned to a patrol set up a space where they could treat those still wounded from the recent battle, as well as any who might return from the next one. Warriors who weren't on patrol organized themselves into smaller infiltration parties.

The next part of the plan was simple. Serania had just under one hundred vashi with her who could be used to transport their forces into the underground pools. With that many, she could get three to four hundred of their number into the Three Spires instantly. It wasn't much, certainly not enough to take the mountains by themselves, but it would be sufficient to create a beachhead. So long as they took control of the pools within the Three Spires, they would be able to send in reinforcements and defend against any assault the enemy sent their way.

But first, they had to learn what they were dealing with.

Serania stood at the edge of one of the hot springs and pointed at the nearest vashi. "You, scout ahead. I want to know what we're facing on the other side. Keep a low profile, we don't want to let the enemy know that we've taken the vale yet."

The vashi nodded and was gone in the next instant. Those nearby waited with bated breath, staring at the same spot where he had been for several minutes until he returned, a puzzled frown on his piscine face.

"I do not understand," he hissed. "There are maybe a few hundred enemiesss waiting for usss on the other ssside. They all appear to be lazing about asss well."

Alarms rang in Serania's head. She took a moment to once more glance around at the hills but could only see her own forces patrolling them. From their vantage point they should be able to spot any approaching enemies and they hadn't reported anything yet.

Where was the enemy hiding, then?

If they weren't about to surround her here, then they had to be within the Three Spires. But then why were they not preparing to fend her off?

She shook her head. Whatever the case, their plan was still viable, and that was the important part. Once they secured the pools within the mountain, they could spend whatever time they had left figuring out what was going on.

Besides, Felix was making his own move now. A thought crossed her that perhaps he was facing off against the bulk of the enemy's forces, but she quickly dismissed it. She doubted the corrupted acolyte would be foolish enough to allow the backdoor of her lair to remain so unprotected, especially now that it was clearly under attack. No, there was something else going on, but Serania couldn't put her finger on it.

Her attention shifted to the infiltration groups waiting patiently for her word.

"To your vashi," she ordered.

Three hundred warriors splashed into the surrounding hot springs as each party met up with their assigned vashi and grabbed hold. Serania watched them each disappear as the vashi liquefacted.

Once the last one left, her gaze returned to the surrounding landscape. She couldn't escape the feeling that something was wrong. The Turned One's army was missing, and she needed to know where before it was too late and the knowledge was thrust upon her at the worst possible moment. There was an ambush waiting somewhere, either in the vale or deep within the mountain tunnels. But no matter how often she scanned the surrounding area, hoping to spot some movement, some sign of life, she saw none.

CHAPTER THIRTY-SIX

A distant rumble rocked the dark cavern where the viatari were being held prisoner. Chains rattled, knocking trails of dust off from the ceiling as the mountain shook from whatever disturbance was happening outside.

Victria awoke with a jerk, her eyes fluttering, shifting back and forth as she tried to register what was going on. But as quickly as the rumbling began, it ended, and nothing more seemed to come of it. She turned to Tessa and Madira.

"You felt that, right?"

Her two friends nodded. Victria dared not bring up her far-reaching hope, but her heart couldn't help but race as she wondered if the reason for that rumbling was Felix.

Her gaze swept through the cavern to look for any other sign of an abnormality. They landed on Natiari's still corpse. Her heart, hammering only a second ago, now pained her like it had suddenly stopped. The crack that had been forged there the day she lost her friend expanded, and she deflated.

There was no sense in falling into the same trap of false hope. Her eyes hardened, locking onto the dark tunnel from where their tormenter always entered. No, she remembered, if there was any chance of them getting out it would have to be done by their own hands. That hope, at least, was still tangible.

Based on the half-dozen paltry and half-dead rats they'd been given to feed on, Victria surmised at least a few days had passed since Natiari's death. They hadn't seen Gar'Gir since that day either. No one knew what was keeping him away—not that they were complaining—but they hated the idea of not knowing how long this respite would last. For Victria, the worst part of the wait was practicing patience. She had a plan for their escape now and she was eager to carry it out. But without Gar'Gir, all she could do was sit there and visualize what she would do endlessly while she waited in shackles. It was maddening.

Today, however, her patience paid off. Only minutes after the strange rumbling ended, the crippled burrower emerged from the shadows, limping aggressively toward the viatari. His normally eager face was lined with worry. His eye was hollow and distracted, shifting about with nervous energy as if his thoughts were elsewhere. His mutterings were loud enough to be heard by his prisoners, and he didn't seem to care what they heard.

". . . said they would come for them, but no, wouldn't listen. Now, they've all gone. And only I remain. So close. Enough time for one more experiment, I think. Yes, enough time to duplicate results before they come. Just need to *know*. . . ."

As he spoke, he studied each individual viatari. He lingered on Tessa, but his mind was decided when he stood before Victria.

She remained defiant, angry, her gaze filled with loathing.

She wanted him to know how much she *hated* him, how much pain she would inflict on him when she got the chance. She wanted him to blink when he saw her. And blink he did. His mutterings ceased. A cold, familiar smile spread across his face.

"Yes," he groaned, his words growing with excitement as he worked her chains. "Yes! It's time to break *her*. If results can be duplicated with this stubborn one then there can be no doubt as to the potency. I shall get my answer, then I shall escape."

Roughly, the burrower grabbed Victria by the arm and dragged her over to the table, its metal surface gleaming under the surrounding purple flames. She wished she could free her arm from his grip right then and there, but the two drainwyrms on her forehead did their job too well. She remained powerless against him.

He lifted her and threw her onto the table, securing her limbs with leather straps that were now well worn. In his other hand, he held a long, wriggling black worm. Victria's heart lurched with anxiety. This was it. This was the moment she'd been waiting for. Now she had to hope that her willpower was strong enough for her to follow through with her plan. Tessa and Madira depended on her. They would die if she failed. Images of Natiari's crumpled body came to the forefront of her mind. Anger burned through her veins. Good, she thought. She would let it fuel her. It would keep her from forgetting, from falling too deep into the illusion.

With one swift motion, Gar'Gir peeled off the drainwyrms and brought the brainwyrm to Victria's ear. She felt it slide in and clenched her jaw as it crawled through her ear canal. Her thoughts turned mellow. Darkness clouded her vision. She rolled her head to the side and saw Gar'Gir turn his back to her as he began making his way back to the shelves stocked with his tools of terror. The ghost of a smile flickered on her lips before she blinked.

And found herself facing Felix.

They were in Aleganthia's keep. She looked to her left and right, disoriented, trying to figure out which memory this might be. The sun shone brightly through large windows, warming her face as the beams hit her skin. She took a moment to relish in the feeling. Even if it was a memory, it was a nice change from the constant dampness and darkness she was currently being held in. And it felt so real. . . .

"Victria?"

She refocused on Felix, all thoughts of this being a memory quickly fading. They slipped through her mind like sand through her fingers. She stared into his ancient, red eyes. Why did it feel like she hadn't seen him for such a long time? The threat of tears burned at the corner of her eyes, though she didn't understand why they were there. She reached for his hands. He took hers.

"Are you alright?" he asked.

She nodded, swiping at her eyes. "Yes. I guess I just got lost in thought for a moment."

Felix frowned with some concern. "Based on your reaction, I would say whatever thoughts you were lost in were not pleasant."

Victria laughed lightly. "You know, the funny thing is I can't even remember what distracted me. I'm sorry, what were we talking about just now?"

"Ah," Felix, hesitated. "Well, I wanted to know what your thoughts might be on approaching someone you might have feelings for."

Victria's eyes widened as heat rose to her cheeks. She

gasped, "Where is this coming from?"

Shaking his head quickly, the elder viatari let her hands fall back to her side. "Not for me," he explained. "As you should know, our people approach me all the time for advice in all sorts of matters and many of those subjects happen to be more romantically inclined. Frankly, I have no idea what to say when. . . ."

Victria listened half-heartedly, a small pool of disappointment collecting within. As Felix continued explaining his premise, her thoughts wandered once more. A frown found its way onto her face. Something about the present moment felt wrong. She couldn't shake the feeling. She saw Felix in front of her, talking to her, looking at her, and yet felt that this should not be.

Her gaze drifted as it had before and fell to the end of the hallway where a line of viatari were passing in and out of sight. She didn't recognize any of them, each one with the same generic face. Except for one.

A viatari with a short, silver braid hanging over her shoulder and a confidence in her step that belied her size emerged from one side of the intersecting hallway. It would only take a few steps for her to pass to the other end and out of sight, but for those few seconds, time stood still.

Victria watched Natiari with bated breath. Her chest pulsed with pain as if it had been stabbed, the blade twisting inside. Her gaze latched onto her friend's face hungrily, as if it might be the last time she ever saw it. If she called out, Natiari would hear her, would face her. She would see the light of life in her friend once more, see the soft color in her cheeks, the quiet strength in her eyes.

She shook her head, confused by the bizarre thought. In that instant where the spell was broken, Natiari passed to the other side out of sight and Victria's heart nearly tore in two. She let out a gasp, stopping Felix mid-sentence. His face fell with concern.

"Victria, what is it?"

Images resurfaced in her mind, images she didn't want to believe. She wanted to bury them deep within the chasm of her subconscious, but they would not be put away. Natiari's still body dominated her memory. She relived her last moments, writhing on a sadistic burrower's experimentation table. Screams echoed in her head.

She remembered.

This wasn't real. She stared at Felix, eyes wide and wild. Her plan returned to her. She had to escape, force herself out of this memory. And she knew how she had to do it. Now that she was faced with the real prospect of carrying it out, though, she was having second thoughts. She looked down at Felix's dirk, sheathed and strapped to his waist.

"Victria?" He said her name so soothingly, stepping closer.

"I'm sorry," she whispered. Tears blurred her vision, blurred his face. She let them fall freely. "But you're not real."

She reached for his blade, pulling it out in a single motion and buried it deep into his chest.

Felix gasped, disbelief written all over his visage.

"Vic . . . tria?"

Victria wept, but kept the blade where it was even as her love stumbled backward, falling onto his back. She clambered on top of him, pinning his arms down with her legs, though he made no attempt to get her off. He sputtered for breath. Blood oozed from his wound, spreading across his woolen shirt. A small trickle ran from his lips and down his cheek.

Their eyes never left each other.

Seconds passed. Then minutes. Victria was ready for the

memory to end, but Felix was dying too slowly. He coughed, spitting blood into the air. The shock of what had just happened still too much to allow him to even think about fighting back. Still, this advantage wouldn't last. Victria needed him to die. She needed to escape this memory, needed to return to the present before Gar'Gir came back to her side with more brainwyrms in hand. She needed to do more.

With a painful cry, she pulled the blade out of Felix and brought it back down. Then, again. And again. New stains of red formed along his chest with each plunge. Felix's strangled gasps weakened, but he still lived.

Finally, unable to witness what she was doing anymore, she took the dirk out and stood over the viatari she had loved for as long as she could remember. His eyes followed her as she moved into a position next to his head, his own blade pointed at his neck. *Why?* His eyes questioned her. A single, bloody tear leaked out and slowly trailed its way down.

"It's not real," Victria murmured in a quivering voice. "It's not real . . . It's not real–it's not real–it's not real it'snotreal it's not . . . *real!*"

Closing her eyes, she swung the blade down. There was a sickening thud. Felix's gasping breaths ceased. Tears streamed down Victria's cheeks as she finally let go of the bloodied weapon and collapsed onto her knees, the blade clattering on the floor beside her.

She screamed.

And woke up strapped to a cold metal table, purple flames dancing around the edges of her vision. She felt a draining sensation from her ear, as if a stream of liquid was leaking out. Her senses returned. She focused and took hold of her surroundings.

Gar'Gir still had his back to her. He was putting away the

drainwyrms and reaching for another jar filled to the brim with brainwyrms. Any second now he would turn and see she was awake. She had to act fast.

With the wyrm he had put in her ear now dead and no drainwyrm in place to weaken her, Victria felt a reserve of strength rush through her. It was a shadow of its former self; hunger, fatigue, and trauma having stolen much, but it was enough to break out of her bonds.

Gritting her fangs, she pulled against the leather straps and felt them snap away. There was no time to relish in the moment of freedom, of being able to move her own legs and arms again. She set her sights on her tormenter and with a ferocity she never knew she had, jumped onto his back.

Gar'Gir yelped in surprise as her sudden weight caused him to stumble hard against the shelves. Several jars fell from their spot, shattering against the floor, creating a field of glass for the burrower to step on. He howled in pain as blood pooled under his feet.

Victria held on tightly, refusing to let go. She was weak, and Gar'Gir was surprisingly strong, but she knew she could wear him down. She only needed to incapacitate him . . . then the real work would begin.

She wrapped her arms around his neck, cutting off air. He reached up, trying to pry them away, but anger was her strength. He bucked wildly, trying to throw her, but still she held on. He grunted, gasped, wheezed, did his best to bring in one last gulp of air, but to no avail. Finally, he succumbed, falling to his knees, then onto his face. Victria loosened her hold and checked for a pulse. A cold smile formed when she found it.

Ignoring the scattered shards of glass on the floor, she climbed off Gar'Gir and picked him up, laying him out on the experimentation table. She walked over to where her chains hung loosely from the cavern wall and pulled them off. Silently, she dragged the iron links back toward the table, wrapping them around the unconscious burrower's limbs and neck.

Once he was secure, Victria's thirst for vengeance lifted enough for her to free Tessa and Madira. They gawked at her in awe while she worked on their chains. As the final iron bond fell away, the three viatari collapsed into each other's arms, each one drawing the other two into a desperate hug.

They stayed like that for several minutes, the only sound breaking the silence within their dark prison being the occasional shuddered breath. Finally, pulling away, they stared at each other with the same knowing darkness. They were free now, yes, but there was still something chaining them to this place.

No words were necessary. They made their way to the shelves where all of Gar'Gir's tools of pain stood in all their glory. They each grabbed a jar filled with wyrms of different kinds. Tessa's choice was the skinwyrms which had been the burrower's first tool of torture. Victria grabbed a jar of brainwyrms. Madira chose one that none of them had seen before. Together, they turned to face the burrower and slowly made their way toward him.

By this point, Gar'Gir was awake once more. He watched them approaching in silence. His lips curled in pleasure.

"I have taught you well, viatari. Now you will experience the pleasures I felt as I worked on you. Savor the moment. Relish it. It will stay with you for the remainder of your long lives."

The viatari hesitated, but only briefly. There was no thought behind what they were doing. There was no rationalizing against it. There was only their tormenter lying helpless before them, and the tools they needed for his painful demise in their hands. One more time, they looked at each other, as if confirming this was their best course of action. They all nodded.

Tessa approached first, unscrewing the lid of her jar and holding it out over Gar'Gir's body. The burrower didn't flinch, nor did he struggle against his bonds. He lay there, an eager gleam in his eye. His tongue wet his lips like he could taste what was coming to him.

Flipping the jar over, dozens of skinwyrms poured out. Several of them bounced off the table and fell to the floor where they inched around aimlessly. But most met their target.

Gar'Gir laughed as they crawled over his body. Those laughs turned into strained moans as the skinwyrms buried their fangs deep into his skin, crawling under and digging their way through his body. His jaw clenched, muscles tightened up, but nothing could stop them. Victria watched, mesmerized, as the wyrms, no more than bulges under the skin now, kept on the move, eating whatever flesh they could find. She remembered her own experience with them and shuddered.

Next was Madira, who approached with a small jar of fat, black worms. She opened it. Smoke flowed out, an acrid stench filling the cavern.

"Ah—coalwyrms," Gar'Gir groaned, his eyes rolling. "Never—got—the—chance to try them—on you. What a shame."

Madira turned the jar over, dumping the coalwyrms onto their tormenter. The effect was immediate. Gar'Gir screamed in pain as the wyrms burned straight through his flesh, through his muscle, then through his bone, until they burned through the very table he lay on and fell to the cavern floor, where they continued burning.

The viatari stepped back with some revulsion. Charred holes riddled Gar'Gir's body. No blood poured forth, as the wyrms had cauterized the wounds they'd made, and so he lay there, twitching as skinwyrms continued their dutiful work on what remained. A grin lingered on his face.

"What else—have you brought—for me?" he croaked.

Now Victria stepped forward, holding out her own jar. She looked into Gar'Gir's eye, wanting to relay all of the pain and fear he had put her through one last time, but it was impossible. Even words wouldn't convey the message well enough. Only pain would do it. Pain unto death.

She turned over her jar, spilling out a multitude of brainwyrms over the burrower. At first, there was no effect as they simply inched their way across his body. But as the minutes passed, several of them found their way onto his face and into his large, hairy ears.

Gar'Gir cried out, then laughed, then howled in agony as the wyrms entered his mind. His eyes rolled back. His body convulsed. Bile leaked from his mouth, mixed with blood. Skinwyrms continued shuffling along. More brainwyrms found their way in, many finding access through the burrower's wide nostrils. Gar'Gir flailed, the chains restraining him clinking against the table with every movement he made.

Finally, he let out one last, long scream that bounced off the rocks and delved deep into the viatari's ears where it remained, echoing for the next several minutes. Then, his body fell against the table, limp, bloodied. His eye was wide and blank, but his lips maintained a cruel curve of pleasure.

Victria shook her head, holding back the urge to be sick, and turned away. Numbly, she made her way to Natiari, where she collapsed to her knees. She was soon joined by Tessa and Madira.

Natiari's corpse was beginning to smell. Her skin had turned a sickly green. But that didn't stop Victria from draping her own body over her and letting out the endless wells of emotion she had been holding back since their capture.

She wailed and was soon joined by Tessa and Madira. They knelt there for hours. Their voices turned hoarse, their knees raw and bloodied, their eyes bleary. And still they continued. They wept for the loss of their friend, for the freedom they had just regained, for the pains they'd been forced to endure. For the end of this nightmare they had all suffered.

CHAPTER THIRTY-SEVEN

Within the dark, twisting tunnels of the Three Spires, Felix and his warriors pushed forward at a steady but cautious pace. Though Morteth had worked hard to disarm all the traps on the path leading up here, there was no telling what they might encounter now that they were inside.

So far, their assault had been far too easy for Felix's liking. There had to be something waiting for them, whether that meant new traps sitting deeper within or hidden enemies waiting to come out and ambush them. Then again, another part of him didn't care if there was. Even if he knew what awaited them, he would still push forward with relentless abandon. They had finally infiltrated these impregnable mountains. Victria was within reach. Now that he was here, nothing would keep him from finding her.

A sudden thought struck him, causing him to stumble midstep. What if The Turned One *wanted* him to find her because she was already beyond saving? What if she was already dead? An image flashed through his mind. Her still body lay on a rocky floor before him, her eyes half-closed, her long silver hair in tatters. It was a picture terrible enough to ruin him.

He shook his head. He refused to consider such a hypothetical. Victria was alive, he was sure of it. He needed her to be. Frustrated by this self-inflicted distraction, he tried to still his mind, focusing instead on the task at hand.

Morteth and Thuradin led the way with a small band of dwarves, checking each side passage and clearing the rooms they led to. They searched through empty barracks, empty storage holds, and empty stone closets. They searched thoroughly with each one, not wanting to take the chance that they missed something. The First One had made it clear that, while rescuing Victria might be a priority for Felix, finding the Purity Scepter took precedence. It was somewhere within these tunnels, and if they could take it from The Turned One, that could prove a significant stumbling block to her plans.

Still, while he agreed finding the Purity Scepter was important, Felix thought it was taking too long searching each room as they went. Serania had engaged the enemy hours ago by now and there was no telling how her fight was faring. She could still be fighting for control of the hot springs, or she could already have infiltrated the Three Spires herself and now waited on him to complete their pincer movement on the enemy. Judging by the lack of enemies they were facing right now, he surmised she must be facing some stiff resistance.

"It's strange," Thuradin grumbled as they finished sweeping another storage room that was, like the others, empty. "I would have thought we'd have encountered something by now, but even the storage rooms are devoid of any sign that our enemy has been here."

"Perhaps they used more of their supplies than we expected."

The dwarf grunted doubtfully, motioning for everyone else

to continue on down the tunnel.

"I don't know, Felix. Something is making the hairs of my beard stand up on edge. I don't like how easy this seems."

Felix clapped him on the shoulder, grim but determined. "You are not alone in that feeling, my friend. But we must continue on. There is no turning back when we have come this far."

Thuradin nodded, steeling himself, and the two continued on into the darkness. A few minutes passed where they foll-owed a sparse trail of dim torches along the tunnel wall in silence. But it was soon broken by alarmed shouts from the front.

After shoving his way through, Felix immediately realized the problem. Before them, glaring down with dull yellow eyes, stood a darim. By its appearance, he guessed this one had once been a bear, though now it was several times larger and much more ferocious. A purple aura emanated from it like a thin mist, a sign of the Creature's dominion.

The bear-darim stood on its hind legs, brushing the tunnel ceiling with its head, and roared. The sound reverberated through the stone walls, forcing many within their ranks to drop their weapons and cover their ears. Despite its ferocious nature, the darim didn't charge. It was almost like it had been ordered to stay put and keep whoever approached from passing. Whatever the case, it was an obstacle they had to get through, and Felix had no time to waste.

He drew his blade, crouching into a fighting stance, ready to pounce on the monstrous beast when Thuradin held out an arm to stop him.

"Ye have no room ta fight here, Felix," the dwarf said. "Ye'll have a hard time taking this thing down with yer regular move-ments in such a confined space. Let my people handle this one."

Felix wanted to argue, but Thuradin's words rang true. He took a step back, lowering his blade as the dwarven commander took charge.

"Right, I want fifteen dwarves up front. Five with shields, the rest with heavy weapons. I need two Enurg'en as well ta keep us in the fight. Move it!"

A shuffling of feet filled the tunnel as the dwarves Thuradin called for made their way to the front. Those with shields clustered together to form an iron wall while the rest switched out their regular swords and axes and hammers for the heavier, more formidable two-handed versions.

"Steel yer nerves," Thuradin encouraged them. "I've faced these beasties before. We can take it, but we have ta be smart. The Enurg'en will heal any injuries ye take during the battle, so just try nae ta die in a single blow and ye'll be alright."

He turned to face the bear-darim, twin axes at the ready. "Shields up the center, spread out as ye see fit—ye'll do us no good if it wipes ye out with one swipe of its paws. Ye ten," he motioned to the remaining warriors who had formed up behind the shield wall, their weapons gripped tightly and at the ready. "Split inta groups of five. Take the flanks. Keep yer movements swift. Don't put everything inta yer attacks until we've reached a point where we can deliver the killing blow. We'll take our time weakening this beastie until it cannae move. Then, we go for the kill."

They spread out. The two Enurg'en stayed a few paces behind the shield wall, ready to lend their powers as needed.

The bear-darim snorted and growled, baring its large, yellow fangs.

Felix watched them with a small reserve of concern. He admired their bravery and was impressed with how easily

Thuradin had taken charge. But while he had been correct in observing the limits of the viatari's fighting style, this would be no easy match for the dwarves to undertake either.

With a ferocious war cry, the dwarves charged on all sides. The darim hesitated, unsure of which way it should attack first. That single moment was enough for several dwarves to close the distance. Their axes dug deep into the beast's hide. A furious roar shook the tunnel. The dwarves jumped away just as two large paws swiped at them.

The shield wall rushed forward, those behind the iron slabs banging the fronts with their own weapons, creating a distracting din that caught the darim's attention. It glared at them, rising onto its hind legs once more and then falling forward with its front paws outstretched. The shield bearers dove out of the way, though one didn't jump far enough. A terrible cry gushed out as the full weight of the darim crashed onto the dwarf's legs, crushing them.

The darim loomed over the crippled dwarf, who was trying to crawl away. Enurg'en dug their hands into the earth and began chanting in Ancient Dwarvish, drawing on the life-energies around them to heal their comrade, but their healing wouldn't be quick enough for him to make an escape. A wall of fangs filled the dwarf's vision.

More yelling rang out as the others charged in a second time. Hammers came down on the bear's back paws, shattering claws. Axes bit down once more into its thick hide. Thuradin jumped onto the beast's back, using his axes to gain purchase and began crawling up to its neck.

Overwhelmed by the ferocity of this attack, the darim fell back, twisting its body, trying to shake the strange weight on its back, but Thuradin held tight.

Anger reaching a boiling point, the darim roared and swept

its paws out in all directions, catching a few dwarves off guard and throwing them against the tunnel wall, where they crumpled to the floor and slumped over. The Enurg'en continued their chants, keeping their gazes locked on the enemy before them. Yellow eyes turned their way. The darim sniffed the air, as if it could smell the manipulation of energy around it. It took a heavy step forward, but the Enurg'en didn't flinch.

Then came another dwarven attack.

They ran in yelling, beards flapping behind as they swung their heavy blades with all their might, not caring what they sunk into as long as it was part of the darim's body. Blood poured from many wounds, and the beast stumbled. Its breathing grew labored. Thuradin straddled the darim's neck as if it were a mount and raised his axes high into the air.

"Now!" he shouted.

Every dwarf went in for the killing blow. Those with axes swung for the neck. Thuradin brought his own blades down onto its head, right behind the eyes, digging into its skull. Hammers swung at the beast's maw, pulverizing the bones within. They attacked relentlessly, until the enemy let loose a final, labored breath and was still.

Stumbling back, a few dwarves slipped in the pools of blood that now covered the tunnel floor. They breathed in deeply. Several laughed in relief as they took a moment to admire what they'd done.

Thuradin slid off the dead darim and made his way to the dwarves who had been thrown against the wall. One of the Enurg'en joined him, placing a hand on the rock beside them for more direct healing. After a minute, however, he took his hand back and shook his hand.

"He's slipped away," the healer said sadly. "I felt his life-energies during the battle even after he was struck, but there were too many injuries for us ta heal at once." He felt the rock next to the other fallen dwarf, and after a moment began chanting. The injured warrior groaned.

"The fallen and injured need ta be taken out of the tunnels and back ta camp where they can be given proper care," Thuradin said to Felix.

The elder viatari nodded, "We can spare a few to carry them out. The Enurg'en can go with them, of course. But the rest of us must move on."

Five dwarves were left behind to help the Enurg'en carry their injured and dead back to camp. Those who remained shuffled past the mass of bloodied fur that had once been a ferocious darim. Several humans in the group cast nervous but curious peeks at what they called a demon as they passed.

They followed the tunnels as they had before, seeing no other sign of the enemy's presence. They searched through more rooms but kept coming away with nothing of import. Felix was tempted to give the order that they run headlong through the tunnels until they reached the spot they would reconnect with Serania.

No sooner had he thought this than the sound of fighting met his ears. Everyone stopped in their tracks to listen. There was no mistaking the nature of the noise. Clashing steel and a constant chorus of yells bounced off the stone walls ahead, though it was faint.

"We must be close to the stairwell," Thuradin observed.

"Let us hurry, then," Felix said. "Any rooms we pass on the way can be searched after the battle."

An apprehensive air hugged them as they ran forward. No one voiced their concern, but all thoughts turned to the battle ahead and the sheer number of enemies they must surely face.

Within minutes, they reached a junction in the path. Ahead

of them, the tunnel continued deeper into the mountains. To their right was a set of carved stone steps that led to a lower level.

"This is it," Thuradin breathed, memories of his last venture here flooding back.

Felix looked around in confusion. While the sounds of battle came from the lower level, there remained no sign of the enemy. No sentries. No patrols. He had expected this area, at least, to be filled to the brim with foes, but it was as desolate as the rest of the mountain had been.

"Lead the way, commander," Morteth's jovial voice rang out. "My blades thirst."

Thuradin and Felix shared a look. The same doubts in mind, the same feeling that something was wrong. Still, as they had agreed before, there was no turning back, and Serania wouldn't be pleased if she found out they had kept her waiting.

They descended into the lower cavern and came upon a skirmish, for that was all it was. A few hundred of the enemy's forces stood with their backs to them, holding off a small force of dwarves who had created a shield wall along the edge of the pools.

They kept their heads down behind these shields as the enemy fired arrows and hurled spears, content to sit back behind their own barricades and attack from range.

Despite the unease he felt, Felix raised his blade and brought it down, sending his own warriors forward to crash into the enemy's rear. He didn't know where The Turned One's main force was, but he knew they needed to take care of what was in front of them first if they wanted to reunite with Serania and discuss their next step forward.

The Turned One's slaves turned in shock, their black eyes

expanding when they heard war cries come from behind. Felix's warriors crashed into them, felling several with their first blows.

From the waterline, the dwarves saw their reinforcements attack from behind and cheered, rushing forward themselves just as a large number of vashi liquefacted into the underground pools, more warriors hanging off them. Seeing the battle unfolding before them, they rushed out of the water and added their own weight to the charge.

Together, they cut down the enemy with ease. The corrupted had no chance to defend themselves against such an onslaught and before long, they had all fallen.

Cheering filled the cavern for what appeared to be a decisive victory, but Felix held his tongue. Thuradin, too, didn't look particularly pleased with this outcome. He barked at a few dwarves to watch the stairwell in case more enemies made their way down. Then, he joined Felix to wait for Serania's arrival.

A few more waves of reinforcements came in thanks to the vashi before Serania stumbled her way out of the pools. She took in her surroundings, saw the enemy already dead, noticed their numbers, and scowled.

"I take it by your reaction that you did not face the enemy's full might in the vale." Felix guessed.

She shook her head. "No, there were a few hundred of them, at best. We defeated them quickly, thinking the bulk of their forces must be here waiting for us."

"We encountered a single darim on the way here. Granted, our assassin friend went on his own before us to take care of whatever forces we might have faced on the mountain path. Regardless, the enemy's resistance has been virtually nonexistent."

"This *must* be a trap, then." Serania's eye roved over every inch of the cavern but failed to find anything out of the ordinary. "I just can't tell how it'll wrap its jaws around us. One thing I know for certain, however, is something's wrong."

Thuradin stroked his beard, a hard look on his face. "It would have been easier ta defeat us when our forces were separated. Why wait for us ta reunite before springing the trap?"

"You might have a point," Serania said distractedly. "But it would be just as easy to have some of her servants hidden along the mountain pass you climbed with orders not to engage until you were well within the tunnel system. She could have the majority of her forces hidden deeper in the mountain, just waiting for the word to rush in. There could be more hidden in the hills surrounding the vale as well, waiting to come out and completely cut us off from escape."

"It would be an intricate plan," Felix said, though by his tone, he doubted its plausibility. "I do not believe, however, that she could pull that off."

"Her new commander might," Thuradin pointed out.

"Then where are they? We are already vulnerable, yet they do not take advantage. Why do they not swoop in and finish us?"

Serania and Thuradin glanced at each other, but there was no good answer to give.

"I say we should pull out," Serania's gaze finally settled on Felix, a hard look entering her eye. "We risk much by staying here unprepared as we are."

The elder viatari ran his fingers through his hair, a throbbing pain building up in his head. "I agree we have been duped in some way, but this battle, as small and easy as it was, is over and won as far as our original plan is concerned. We will continue with our search through this tunnel system until we find what we are looking for. We have come too far to give up now."

"I take it then that you have yet to find the Purity Scepter."

"It's possible they never moved it from its original location like The First One thought," Thuradin shrugged. "If it's still where I found it last time, that room isn't too far from here. I can take a few dwarves and have a look."

Felix nodded, though he suspected that the dwarf would return empty-handed.

"Go."

Thuradin brought his fist to his chest in a salute and marched off, calling several others to his side as he headed for the stone steps.

With a sharp sigh, Felix turned his attention to Serania. "As for the rest of our forces, you may take them back to camp. I do not believe we will meet any more of the enemy."

Serania saw right through him. "You're going to search for her by yourself, aren't you?" She bit her lip, concerned. "You should take a few others with you. Just in case."

But he was already shaking his head. "No, this is something I must do alone."

"What if you're wrong?" She persisted. "What if the enemy is here, just waiting for you to come to them?"

Felix drew his blade and walked off, heading for the stone steps.

"I have come too far," he called back. "No army will keep me from her."

Serania watched his back disappear from view, hoping it wasn't for the last time.

CHAPTER THIRTY-EIGHT

Victria remained as she was until her body could no longer bear it.

She stood up, blood flowing painfully back into her legs, looking around for something they could use to cover Natiari's body. There wasn't much to work with, but bundled in a forgotten corner of Gar'Gir's shelves was an old and tattered cloth. She pulled it out, revealing more jars full of exotic creatures whose sole purpose she would never discover. She turned away, disgusted.

The cloth wasn't large. They wouldn't be able to cover Natiari's body completely. It was, however, enough to wrap around her head. Victria tied a knot around the back to ensure it didn't slip out of place and then sat back, looking at her handiwork with unseeing eyes.

Tessa sniffled next to her, and Victria felt her head lean in. An arm wrapped around her shoulder. Madira joined them.

"We can't sit here forever," Tessa eventually said, her voice weak but resolute. "If you have a plan for us to escape, now's the time to share it."

"There is no plan," Victria shook her head. "But we won't stay here and wait for someone to find us. We leave this cavern and see if we can get lucky enough to find our way out. That's as much as I can think of doing right now."

"What if we get caught?" Madira shuddered. "We're in no shape to fight."

It was true. Now that she could focus on other things besides her captivity, Victria felt acutely how hungry and weak she really was. Her stomach throbbed with pain, as if it was trying to eat itself. Her limbs were thin, yet so heavy. Now that adrenaline, which had been fueling her during her fight with Gar'Gir, was gone, she doubted she could even throw a punch with much force.

"Doesn't matter," she answered. "We try our best to escape anyway. If we're fortunate enough to sneak up on any patrols, maybe we can take them out. If we get caught up in a fight," she hesitated. "Well, let's just say I don't intend on being taken prisoner again."

"Agreed," Tessa murmured.

Madira nodded.

"This is our last chance to take our lives back," Victria's gaze gravitated to the shadowy entrance that had brought their tormentor to them so many times. Now, that same portal would be their escape. "Let's do what we can."

"I'll carry her," Madira offered as they stood up. She bent down and, with some help from the others, lifted Natiari's limp body over her shoulder. She swayed from the extra weight but eventually found her footing. Putting on a brave face, she nodded. "I'm ready."

The three viatari made their way for the exit, Victria leading the way. She pushed cautiously against the door, unsure if she would find guards on the other side. Swinging it open fully, she saw that the next room was bare. It was a narrow stone quarter with an even narrower hall on the other end. They followed it.

Shortly after, they found themselves in a wide tunnel, torches flickering along the walls providing a dim light. Victria looked left, then right. There was no way of knowing which way led to their freedom, and which led deeper into the darkness.

"We move slowly," she whispered. "Stick to the shadows."

She turned left. They followed the tunnel wall, straining their ears to catch any hint that someone was approaching, but for a long time the only thing they heard was their own shuffling feet.

Eventually, heavy footsteps reverberated along the surrounding rocks ahead of them. The viatari stopped in their tracks. Madira gently put Natiari down on the ground, and they waited.

Shadows appeared against a curve in the wall as whoever they belonged to drew nearer. There were four of them; burrowers, Victria realized, by the way they moved. When they were close enough for her to see their black eyes, smell the stench of corruption in the air around them, she knew they were servants of The Turned One.

These burrowers were on patrol, but it quickly became apparent that they weren't too focused on their task. The viatari crouched against the wall, hoping the grime that had built up all along their skin, their hair, and their clothes would be enough for the shadows to hide them completely. They held their breaths.

The burrowers walked right past them.

Victria heard their receding footsteps and nearly doubled

over as another pang of hunger struck her. An idea came to her mind. A horrible one. But these were dire circumstances, and there was no telling what wildlife, if any, they might find in these tunnels.

Looking at her two companions, she pointed at her fangs, then her stomach, then behind her at the patrol that had just passed. Tessa and Madira both stared at her in horror, but their own hunger soon convinced them to see the option in another light. They rushed after the patrol.

Their attack was so swift and brutal, the burrowers didn't know what hit them. Victria jumped out of the shadows, leaping for the nearest one and with most of her remaining strength, grabbed his head and twisted it. As his limp body fell, Tessa and Madira made their move, jumping onto the backs of two other burrowers and burying their fangs into their necks. Victria grabbed the last one and did the same.

The burrowers tried to shake them off, but as the viatari consumed their life-energies, their movements weakened, their bodies grew brittle. They dropped to their knees, gasping for breath. The viatari bit down harder, their hunger driving them into an animalistic frenzy as they summoned every last drop of life-energy from their prey.

By the time they were finished, the burrowers had become mummified skeletons. They fell to the floor, faces etched in terror and confusion.

Victria stumbled back, wiping her mouth and spitting out the bitterness that lingered on her tongue. There was a reason why the viatari fed on animals and not more intelligent creatures. Despite the horror stories humans of the plains spread about them, the viatari had, long ago, decreed it forbidden for anyone to consume the life-energies of anyone with their own level of intelligence. Though these burrowers had been servants of The Turned One, there remained a vestige of remorse for what she had done.

A fresh wave of energy rushed through them, clearing their minds a little and taking away some of the pain they'd been feeling in their stomach. Even so, the viatari shared a look.

"This stays between us," Victria stated, spitting once more as the lingering taste that had come with the burrower's life-energies flared up again. "It was necessary to survive."

Tessa and Madira nodded, and together they ran back to where they had left Natiari. Once she was securely over Madira's shoulder again, they continued making their way through the tunnel.

As they walked, something lingered on the back of Victria's mind. A warning. An alarm. Something important she had forgotten about the burrowers and what they had just done. But for all her effort in trying to bring that thought to the fore-front, she couldn't do it, and it slipped away.

Felix ran as fast as he could afford to without taking the risk that he might miss some sign of Victria's presence. He kept his blade in hand, waiting for the moment when the enemy would jump out at him from the shadows, but that moment never came. As he ran, his eyes constantly scanned his surr-oundings.

He looked for crevices in the wall that might point to a secret passage. He checked as many rooms as he encoun-tered during his progress. All were empty, save one that housed a small group of humans rummaging through half-empty boxes of supplies. They heard him enter and stopped what they were doing. Felix took note of their black eyes.

He dealt with them quickly.

As the last corrupted human fell, falling face first into a

pool of his own blood, Felix wondered if he should rummage through these boxes himself and see if the Purity Scepter sat in one of them. It had looked like these humans had been about to move these supplies elsewhere.

But he shook his head. His thoughts were singularly focused on one goal. That was the only reason he was here. He couldn't bring himself to care about anything else. If Serania or Thuradin ended up following him by chance, they would find this room. They could search through these supplies then.

Moving on, he soon came upon a split in the tunnel system. He paused, breathing hard and debating internally which way he should go. There was no telling which route was better. Both could lead to traps, the enemy's whereabouts, a deeper section of the mountain, anything. And if there were more splits like this, he could easily lose his way and wander within these mountains forever.

Bringing his breath back under control, he focused. From his left, he could hear voices and the steady shuffling of dirt and breaking of rocks, as if a great many people were digging together. The voices were soft, barely perceptible, but commanding. He couldn't tell what they said, but there was definitely *something* waiting for him down that way. Accompanying the voices were a series of bestial growls that made him think of darimun.

That helped make his decision.

If he went down the left tunnel, it was almost guaranteed that he would run into the enemy. As much as he would have enjoyed the opportunity to thin their numbers, he couldn't afford the distraction. He couldn't afford being discovered. Yet.

The tunnel to his right was silent. It wasn't a guarantee that a threat wasn't there waiting for him, but the odds seemed better. He entered the gaping hole, giving it a chance. If he didn't find something promising quickly he could always go back and try the left side. But something felt right about the path he'd chosen. Some air of assurance wrapped itself around his shoulders like a protective cloak as he took his first step in, encouraging him onward.

She was close. He could feel it.

Silence accompanied their every step as Victria, Tessa, and Madira dragged their feet through the enveloping darkness.

They'd run into a few more patrols—burrowers and humans, no darimun yet—and while they'd been able to kill them quickly, their energy was running low again. This wasn't something they could continue all day. And none of them wanted to consume the life-energies of another burrower. Though, hunger could change minds if it got bad enough.

They had to find their way out quickly if they wanted to survive, but no matter how far they went, their surroundings remained the same. The same rock wall surrounded them, the same dim flames flickered from the sconces that held them. There seemed to be no end. At this point, they couldn't even tell if the tunnel was running straight or twisting and turning.

"Let's take a break," Victria panted, slowing down to a stop and leaning against the wall. "We need to rest."

Her companions agreed and dropped where they were, breathing deeply.

Victria put her hands to her knees and coughed harshly. Her chest burned. She shook her head, putting a hand to her cheek and realized with a start that she was burning up. She glanced at Tessa and Madira. They didn't look much better.

Their eyes drooped. Their skin sagged and was pale—no, it was gray. . . .

She'd seen this before.

The nagging thought from before returned. And as the first trails of steam drifted up from Madira's forehead, she finally remembered.

She'd seen these symptoms when Felix had fallen deathly ill after consuming water from a lake that The Turned One had corrupted with her essence. And then a shocking moment of clarity exploded in her mind like a bolt of lightning as she realized the terrible mistake they had made.

They had consumed the life-energies of burrowers under The Turned One's control, control she had gained by corrupting them with her essence. It ran thick through their bodies like blood in their veins. Being so thoroughly corrupted as they were, it would make sense that the corruption would be in their life-energies as well.

She cried out softly from the realization.

"Victria?" Tessa called out weakly. "What's wrong?"

"I've doomed us," was all she could utter. Then she laughed. And she kept laughing, even as tears pricked the corners of her eyes and trailed down her filth-caked cheeks. Above her, thin trails of steam rose up, fading after a short distance.

The viatari body couldn't handle corruption. Not even their natural regenerative abilities could do anything about it. Felix's bout with The Turned One's essence had incapacitated him for months, and that was when he had been in pristine health beforehand. Even so, it had nearly killed him. And they had infected themselves when they were at their weakest. There was no hope for them to recover, not even to hold the corrupting illness at bay long enough to find help. There was no help within these mountains, after all.

"Steam," Tessa said weakly, pointing at Victria. "But that means—"

"Don't say it," Victria coughed. Her throat felt raw from laughing. What she would give to feel the cool trickle of water at this moment. "There's no point in saying it."

"Then, we do nothing?"

"There's nothing to be done."

She observed her companions, each one trying hard to catch their breath, breath that was growing shallower by the minute. Her own weren't bringing in as much oxygen as they had before. Her mind pounded within the confines of her skull.

"I'm sorry, Tessa, that this is how our end comes. You too, Madira. I didn't mean for it all to go so wrong."

They kept silent, though Tessa reached out for Victria's hand. She took it, squeezing gently.

Leaning back against the tunnel wall, Victria let her thoughts wander. She thought of the forest surrounding her home. She tried to imagine the earthy scents that place held but couldn't quite remember them. All she knew now was this mountain. The darkness that surrounded them. The feeling of dirt and grime and blood. The thought of dipping into a cold river and letting its cleansing waters flow around her body was like a fantasy to her.

She closed her eyes and tried to picture Felix's face, if only to console herself. She remembered his steadfastness, his sense of calm. She tried to hold onto those feelings, but her head continued to pound, now with more intensity, as if it were being bashed against the wall. She had to let the image go.

She blinked and felt more tears fall. As much pain as she was feeling physically, it was nothing compared to what was in her chest. Felix hadn't come for her like she thought he would.

With a sigh, she realized she would never see him again.

The tunnel on the right proved rewarding.

Within a few minutes of entering it, Felix had come across a narrow passage leading into a narrow room with a door on the other side. The initial room was empty, but enough curiosity remained for him to check the subsequent one as well.

When he went through the door a surge of energy shot into his limbs, driving him forward. Before him was a large circular cavern. Three sets of chains hung loosely from the wall opposite him. In the center sat a metal table with a half-eaten burrower corpse lying on top, a fourth chain tying him in place. At least, Felix thought it was a burrower. It was difficult to be sure, as most of the body had been eaten away by fat wriggling worms that even now continued consuming whatever tissue they could find. Looking around, he saw that there were rows upon rows of jars with similarly grotesque creatures sitting on a series of shelves carved into the stone wall.

They were here—had been here. If they were the ones responsible for this burrower's death, he judged that it was only recently they had made their escape. He was close.

Running back the way he came, he fell back into the tunnel and turned left, running deeper into the mountains. They had to have come this way, not knowing that the other direction would have taken them to freedom. They had taken a chance, and had chosen poorly. But now he would find them, and he would lead them out.

As the minutes passed and Felix continued making his way deeper into the Three Spires, he ran into a patrol of burrowers—already dead—then another, and another. The first one had caught his eye because of the state of three of its members. If he didn't know any better, he would have said that they'd had their life-energies consumed, but he spent little time dwelling on it. Only one thought was prevalent in his mind.

He was close.

Perhaps close enough to be heard.

Desperately, drawing in as much breath as he could, he shouted her name.

"Victria!"

His voice echoed, bouncing off the tunnel wall and delving deeper and faster than he ever could.

He called again, "Victria!"

There was no answer. But he didn't need one. She could hear him, he was sure of it. And she would come to him. And he would lead her out of this place. And once they were back home, he would hold onto her, never letting go.

"Victria!"

Victria's eyes were nearly closed, a slumber that she didn't know if she would ever wake from only seconds away, when she heard her name bounce off the walls.

Her eyes snapped open. Her heart restarted. She recognized that voice.

"Victria!"

It came again. This time closer.

Felix.

He *had* come. Tears welled up again. She choked back a sob as she clawed her way back onto her feet. Strength flowed into her limbs, helping her take first one step, then another back the way they'd come. Back toward the voice of her beloved who was calling her to him.

Tessa and Madira heard the voice, too. They stirred, desperately reaching for one last chance at life as they pushed themselves up. Together, they stumbled, leaning heavily against the tunnel wall to keep them upright.

Victria hoped she would hear her name again, if only to hear his voice. Despite her newfound strength, each step was a struggle to take. Nails drove into her head. Bile burned her throat every time she coughed. Her thoughts were no longer cohesive, interrupted by a constant buzzing, like flies swarming her rotting mind from within.

She stumbled again, catching herself against the tunnel wall. Breathing hard, she pushed herself off and continued walking along. She whispered his name.

The flames along the wall blurred as her vision darkened. Still, there was enough light, enough focus within her to see the silhouette of someone running toward her.

Her heart soared weightlessly as if it had grown wings and taken flight. He was there, right in front of her. Almost within reach.

She had known he would come for her, had known he wouldn't abandon her. Just as he never had before in all the years they'd been together.

Just a few more steps and she would be in his arms, right where she belonged.

Another step, and her legs finally buckled. Weightlessness took hold. She felt herself fall forward, waited for her body to crash against the hard stone floor. But the pain never came. Strong arms hooked themselves under her own, holding her up, and she finally knew she was safe.

As soon as Felix saw them from a distance he knew something was wrong.

He ran as fast as he could, putting all of his strength into his legs. He was close enough now to see their disheveled state.

They were gaunt, their clothes no more than rags at this point. They leaned heavily on the tunnel wall, doing their best to walk toward him. Tessa and Madira collapsed behind Victria, their chests heaving with great difficulty. Victria took a few more steps, then her legs buckled and she fell as well.

Diving forward with outstretched arms, he caught her just before her face hit the ground. Gently, he turned her over as he pushed himself onto his knees where he then placed her head. He noticed steam drifting from her forehead and realized what was wrong. An image of the three burrowers who'd had their life-energies consumed flashed through his mind.

Victria, Tessa, and Madira were sick with corruption. In the weak state they were in, he knew they wouldn't last long. He needed to find help but didn't know how. He couldn't carry them all out of here by himself. He cursed himself now for choosing to carry out this search alone.

Not knowing what else to do, he caressed Victria's cheek, wiping away some of the grime that was caked onto it. His heart hurt to see her like this. She had been through horrors he couldn't imagine, all because she had believed he would come for her.

Heat radiated from her forehead, but still he continued to gently hold her, wanting to convey how sorry he was for taking so long, though he knew how insufficient this simple gesture was.

Moving on from her cheeks, his fingers found strands of dirty silver hair that he brushed to the side. Her breathing was shallow, but suddenly she took in a large gulp of air, her eyes fluttering open. They were panicked, disoriented, but they fixed onto his face and relaxed, the trace of a smile lifting her lips.

"I knew you'd come," she whispered weakly. "I knew you'd

save me." Victria's heavy eyelids slid shut and her head fell limply to the side.

CHAPTER THIRTY-NINE

The first thing Victria saw when she opened her eyes were rays of sunlight streaming through fluttering white curtains. She lay where she was for several minutes just taking it in, feeling the warmth of the sun on her face. It took her a moment to realize where she had seen such a scene before. She bolted up into a sitting position and gasped.

Aleganthia.

This was a room within its keep. In fact, this was *her* room. She looked away from the window and realized she was in her own bed. A sudden, terrifying thought crossed her mind as the most recent memories of her time in the Three Spires came back to her.

Was this a memory? Was her reality still on that metal table with Gar'Gir looming over her, peering into her suff-ering face? Had he led her to believe that she had made her escape in an attempt to lower her guard?

She brought her hands into view and saw that they were neatly bandaged. It was then that she registered the pain puls-ing through her entire body. It felt battered, like she had taken a beating. Her head throbbed and spun at the same time from her sudden change in position. Her stomach relentlessly stabbed into itself. A cage containing a few rabbits sat on the nightstand next to her and she quickly took one out, sinking her fangs into the critter's neck and viciously consuming its life-energies. The rabbit withered away with a squeal, and a small rush of energy coursed through her limbs, easing her stomach and clearing her mind.

She sighed with relief and fell back onto her pillows, gazing calmly at the ceiling. She could think of no time in her life where she had woken up in bed, bandaged, and with her whole body hurting. Not to mention the hunger. No, this was a first for her. Which meant this was no memory. This was the present.

Closing her eyes and basking in the peaceful silence that surrounded her, she tried to recall the last thing she could remember. Flashes of horror presented themselves, one following the next in quick succession. She saw Felix's hazy figure, remembered him catching her and then . . . nothing. No matter how hard she tried, no semblance of a recollection could be brought forth after that moment. For all she knew, she had been dead to the world.

The door to her room opened and a viatari woman entered, her silver hair tied up in a messy bun. She was dressed in simple garments, a belt bristling with cleaning equipment strapped around her waist. She carried a clean stack of towels in her hands, which she promptly dropped as soon as she saw Victria staring back at her.

The viatari gasped, her red eyes widening in shock. Before Victria could say anything, she backed out of the room, closing the door with one hand while the other covered her mouth, as if holding back a scream.

Blinking in confusion, Victria simply remained where she was. She tried to sit up again but found the position too painful for her to maintain, so she gave up and let the soft mattress mold itself around her body. She reached for another rabbit, this time taking her time in savoring the sweet life-energies that came from it.

As she finished off the critter, a loud commanding voice and the sound of stomping feet could be heard coming from the hallway leading to her room. The door burst open, and the stout figure of Thuradin Stonebeard marched in. Lines of worry that had riddled his face faded away when he saw her.

"Thank Nythirim ye're awake, lass," he clapped his hands, grinning broadly. He laughed as he approached, inspecting her face more closely. "I must say, I've never seen ye look so bad."

Victria cracked a smile. A strange weight pressed against her chest as she beheld her dwarven friend. "I can't describe how good it is to see you again, Thuradin. I didn't think I ever would."

Thuradin's face turned somber. "Aye, ye had us all worried, lass. I cannae imagine the brutality ye've survived. I'm only sorry we couldn't save ye from it sooner."

She nodded, not wanting to say more for fear that if she opened her mouth, she might finally crack and break down. Instead, she changed the topic.

"The others?"

"They're safe," Thuradin reassured her. "They remain asleep."

Victria nodded, tears threatening to make an appearance. "And Natiari?"

"Aye, we brought her back, too," the dwarf said in a soft voice. "I had ta see for myself when they told me. Hard ta believe . . . I'm told she's ta be buried tomorrow in the style of yer people."

Again, Victria nodded, letting the tears go and feeling their warmth crawl down the sides of her face and into her ears as she kept her gaze locked onto the ceiling.

"Ta be honest, lass, it's lucky that ye three aren't joining her. Ye were on the brink of death when Felix found ye."

Victria took in a deep breath, blinking away her remaining tears. She cleared her throat and winced. "What happened after he found me? I can't remember much."

Thuradin grabbed a chair from the other side of the room and brought it over to sit next to her. He stroked his beard as he gathered his thoughts.

"It's difficult ta say—there were so many moving pieces that it's hard ta keep track of everyone's accounts. From what I understand, Felix had gone ahead by himself ta find ye after we took the Three Spires from The Turned One. Serania tells me she didn't like the idea of him getting lost in those mountains, so she sent several of her viatari after him. Lucky she did, too, because if they hadn't found him, he would have been hard-pressed ta carry the four of ye out of there."

"You didn't see any of this happening?" Victria asked.

Thuradin grimaced. "As I said, there were many moving parts. I had taken a few dwarves with me ta look for the Purity Scepter where I remembered seeing it the day ye were captured. I was in a different part of the tunnel system entirely."

"What's the Purity Scepter?"

But Thuradin shook his head, saying, "I'll let others explain that ta ye in due time. Ye need nae worry about it right now." A scowl marked his face. "Needless ta say, it's an important piece of the puzzle in this war, according ta The First One. I couldn't find it. Which means The Turned One continues ta have the upper hand against us."

Victria nodded, her head flaring with pain, reminding her of the state she was in. "Then what happened?"

"With the help of the others, Felix carried ye and yer friends back ta where most of our forces were by the pools. He had the vashi liquefact ye lot out ta the hot springs where he was able ta grab hold of a few lyruun riders. With their help, he transported ye all back home.

"I was back in the vale by the time Felix came through with ye in hand. Ye looked terrible. Truthfully, I thought ye were already dead. But I knew by the frantic way in which Felix was giving orders and taking action that ye must still be alive."

"Yes," Victria murmured, memories of her escape coming with greater ease as Thuradin continued speaking. "During our escape we ended up getting infected by The Turned One's essence." She looked away, leaving out *how* they had been infected. "I thought we were close to death myself. We had hours, not days left. How did we get treated when the antidote for that corruption is all the way in Dalyr?"

A knowing smile crept across the dwarf's face. "Felix's sheer determination, that's how."

"What do you mean?"

"Before he sent ye back ta Aleganthia on a lyruun, he had a few vashi take some viatari ta Dalyr by liquefaction. There, they were ta get enough antidote for the three of ye, and then liquefact ta Aleganthia. His plan worked flawlessly. By the time the lyruuns landed in the keep's holding pens, the antidote was here and waiting ta be administered."

Victria whistled softly. "He really does think of everything, doesn't he."

Thuradin's face darkened briefly. "He's nae had an easy time of it, I'll tell ye that much. Yer capture affected him deeply."

Before Victria had a chance to ask him to elaborate, the door to her room burst open again with Felix hanging just beyond the threshold. Her heart jumped. She could feel its incessant rhythm in her fingers. Nervous energy flittered in her chest, seeping into her limbs, making her acutely aware of every single movement she made. Their eyes met, and time stood still. Thuradin turned in his chair.

"Ah, Felix," he said cheerily. "I was wondering how long it'd take for ye ta show up." He hopped to his feet and turned to leave. Felix stayed where he was, his face unreadable. Thuradin clapped him on the arm, jolting him out of whatever trance had taken hold.

"I'll give the two of ye some time, then." He looked back once more at Victria, winked, and then he was gone. Felix closed the door behind him and slowly approached the chair their dwarven friend had vacated. His gaze never left her.

"I'm—" Victria abruptly cleared her throat, despite the pain, taking control of the tremors she felt in her voice. "I'm happy to see you again, Felix."

The elder viatari sat down, a relieved grin easing onto his features. "As am I. You have no idea how I—we—all have been."

There was an awkward silence that followed as neither one knew what to say next, though both knew they had so much to say to each other.

"Thuradin was telling me how you got me out of those tunnels," Victria finally said, she pushed herself to sit up so she didn't appear so helpless. Pain gripped her, but she hated to think she might make him worry about her more than he already was, so she endured it.

Felix nodded. "Yes . . . I am only sorry I could not have taken you from that cursed place sooner."

She reached out for his hand and to her surprise, he took it. Warm ripples of electricity coursed through her fingers as their skin touched. This was real.

"He said that we took control of the Three Spires. Does that mean The Turned One—"

"No," Felix shook his head bitterly. "After I took you out of there, we had scouts go through the remaining tunnels we had left unexplored to search for clues as to our enemy's whereabouts. I only just got their report the other day."

"And?"

"It appears, in the time it took for us to gather ourselves for our final assault, The Turned One had her burrowers dig deeper into the Three Spires, deeper than we thought possible. She left only a small rear guard to distract us as she made her escape deeper into the Northern Mountains."

"But then, we could still catch up to her and pin her down," Victria suggested. "If she's digging into the mountains, there's nowhere for her to escape."

But Felix was already shaking his head. "It is too dangerous, and they have had too much of a head start as it is. In a confined space like that, a prolonged battle would be a nightmare scenario for our forces. The humans and vashi, not to mention our own people, are not well suited for that kind of fighting. No, our opportunity to defeat the enemy was when we could still draw them out into the open—and we failed."

"Then, we just let her escape?"

"We have no choice," Felix sighed. "We know where she will go. The First One has mentioned that she needs to take the Purity Scepter to the Temple in the Eastern Wald, so she will likely dig her way eastward after she has gone as far north as she desires. It will take time, but with her corrupted burrowers constantly digging, she will likely finish that extensive tunnel within the year."

"Again with this Purity Scepter," Victria muttered. "Someday someone will tell me about it, I'm sure."

Felix smiled, some humor returning. "As impatient as always. You will learn the fullness of our predicament, but not today."

Their hands were still clasped together. Victria glanced down at them, remembering all those times she had been in chains and wallowing in regret for having left so much unsaid. Now that she was free though, and not in a memory, she remembered how hard it was to bring these feelings out into the open. Still, she knew she couldn't keep this desire walled up for much longer. She just had to find the right time and—

"I nearly lost my head when I learned you were captured," Felix said, his words uncertain, hesitant. "There was a moment where I realized a possibility existed that I might never see you again."

Victria understood better than he probably realized. She'd had the same fear constantly gnawing at her in the darkness of her prison.

"Which is why," his gaze fixed onto her, steadfast and rich with feeling. He moved from the chair onto the side of her bed, his face coming in close to hers. He grasped her hand now with both of his. "I cannot risk losing you again. I never want us to be apart, to risk not seeing your beauty with each passing day."

Victria, stunned, yet thrilled at the same time, could barely bring together enough coherent thought to ask, "Felix, what are you saying?"

He looked down at their hands, squeezing gently, a hint of heat visible on his cheeks. "I think you know."

Tears burned their way into existence once more, but this

time Victria let them flow freely.

"I knew you would rescue me," she said, trying but failing to keep her voice steady. "But there were still parts of me that felt it was a hopeless fantasy. Even so, it was your face, and only your face, that kept me alive each day I was stuck in those mountains."

She delved deeply into his ancient eyes, soft with an emotion she only now recognized. She was sure he could see the same in hers.

"I love you, Felix," she confessed. Heat thrust its way into her head, but she ignored it, letting her feelings rip out of her like they'd been wanting to for so long. "I love you. I've loved you for so long. I never want to part from you. The thought of it . . . well, I would rather die than have to endure such a scenario."

The two viatari brought their heads together, Victria crying from a mixture of pain and sadness for what she'd endured and now happiness for what was to come. Felix wrapped his arms around her, holding her close, a bulwark of solid stone against waves of emotion now crashing around them like a stormy sea.

"Then," he said softly, tenderly. "Let our hearts be one, forever."

Still with tears, Victria nodded happily and leaned into his embrace, diving headfirst into a future where there was nothing but possibilities.

Despite her body's protests, Victria forced herself out of the comforts of her bed when the sun rose the next day. She limped across her room, pulling on a soft tunic which she secured around her body with a simple leather belt. After struggling with some leather pants and a pair of boots, she made her way out into the keep, taking her time as she tread through hallways and down the numerous staircases that populated the building.

Approaching the keep's exit, leaning against the wall for support, her heart fluttered when she recognized two figures, just as bandaged as she was, waiting for her. Tessa and Madira's faces lit up when they saw her. They ran to each other, falling into each other's arms where they stood, sharing in the trauma of their recent past but also basking in the comfort that each one offered the other.

After some time, they separated and made their way out of Aleganthia's keep together. The city's plaza was packed with members from all races of Azar. In the center stood a troop of six viatari, with a litter on their shoulders. On it was the outline of a body, draped with the banner of Aleganthia, a black flag with a single, white pine tree in the center.

Felix saw them coming, briefly taking Victria's hand and squeezing it before letting her continue on with her friends.

Once they situated themselves behind the litter, its bearers began marching forward at a slow pace. All eyes followed their progress through Aleganthia's streets. The procession was utterly silent as the bearers turned toward the city's western gate. They traversed the long, wooden bridge spanning the ravine that separated the mesa Aleganthia sat on from the surrounding forest.

As they entered the forest, Victria took in the smells. A comforting earthy aroma filled her nose, and she let out a wistful sigh. A soft breeze wound its way around the trees, caressing those in the procession with its comforting touch as they spread out into a wide clearing.

Within this clearing stood a tall, wooden pyre. The procession filed into the meadow and surrounded the structure.

All eyes were glued to the litter bearers as they brought their charge up a steep set of steps leading them to the top of the platform. There, they lay Natiari's body in its final resting place.

Once the litter bearers completed their job and descended the stairs to rejoin the crowd, Victria, Tessa, and Madira took charge and climbed up. Their legs ached with each step they took but they forced themselves to continue. Their thoughts were focused on one thing, reaching their fallen friend. No amount of pain could stop them from giving Natiari this last honor.

They reached the platform and took a moment to catch their breaths, holding onto each other for support. Though all eyes were on them, Victria hardly noticed. Her own fell on the still body before her, thankfully still covered by the Aleganthian banner. She stumbled forward, taking the last few steps required to stand next to the wooden bed where Natiari lay.

The three viatari stood there, looking down at Natiari without really seeing her. No one could think of anything to say. There were no heroic speeches of her bravery during the last few days she lived, no final conversations to be had. Though tears stung their eyes they held them in, doing what they could to maintain a brave front.

Only one sentiment could be expressed here. Victria said it in a voice so soft the gentle breeze dancing around their shoulders carried it away immediately for no one else to hear. It was all she could muster.

"I'm sorry."

With one final look, the three viatari went back down and rejoined the crowd of friends, grievers, and allies who had all come to see Natiari's send off.

The litter bearers stepped forward again, this time with torches in hand. Together, they threw them into the hollow center of the pyre, where enough kindling and dry wood had been placed for flames to catch easily. Smoke soon drifted skyward. Flames made their presence known, licking along the edges of the wooden stack as they crept up, eventually spreading out onto the platform to join Natiari.

Standing next to Felix, her hand in his, Victria kept her gaze locked onto a small corner of black fabric, the only part of her friend that she could see. As the flames approached, it fluttered from the surrounding heat, pulling back and revealing the sole of a leather boot. Eventually, the flames grew so dense that even that small thing disappeared.

Fire consumed, and all that was left was smoke.

While most of those who had followed the procession out to the meadow began shuffling their way back to the city, Victria, Tessa, and Madira stayed where they were. Their eyes never left the pyre. Even as friends approached to offer condolences, their gazes never wavered.

They stood there all day as the fire consumed. Only after the last flame had snuffed out, leaving behind a mound of burning embers and ash that was already being swept away by the wind, did they finally turn away.

CHAPTER FORTY

Days after Natiari's funeral, Victria and Felix announced their intention to be wed. The city went into an uproar at the joyous news, and for the next month, a frenzy fell upon its inhabitants as they did anything and everything they could to ensure that the coming ceremony would be the grandest event in living memory.

Hunters worked hard capturing wildlife and bringing them to the city's caretakers for storage so that everyone could be fed several times over during the feast. Allocations were made for barrels of wine to be set aside for the festivities. Large orders of ale were to be brought from the Dwarven Kingdom. The viatari went about their day purging the city of whatever blemishes they could find, decorating the surrounding buildings with pretty white banners that fluttered in the wind.

Among all these preparations remained a nagging sense of urgency that they should instead be preparing for an expedition to the Eastern Wald. As The First One reminded them on a regular basis, they had spent too much time idle within the city as it was, and the threat of The Turned One remained prevalent. The war would not wait for them.

And while Felix agreed with the acolyte to a certain extent, he knew his people. He and Victria, everyone who had been fighting for so long against the corrupted acolytes, needed this small semblance of normalcy. The wedding would go on as planned. They would spend this time recuperating from a draining siege, from countless battles that had led to terrible losses . . . Losses that had touched everyone. That way, when they did finally depart Aleganthia to rejoin the fight, they would be all the more willing to participate in the struggle to preserve the world they knew and loved. Eventually, The First One acquiesced, though not happily.

As the days passed, word came of Salevari's success in Donsea and Halding Port and soon she returned with her companions, a retinue of humans on horseback following her. They were brought to the city's keep, where Felix waited eagerly to greet them, Victria standing at his side.

"Hello, brother," Salevari greeted him with a warm smile, raising her arms and taking Felix into an embrace. She nodded her head at Victria. "I thought I had good news to share when I returned but it seems you have me beat in that regard."

All but one of Salevari's party dismounted, the last of them sitting on her horse in a daze. Tera's eyes were expanded to their limits as she took in Victria in the flesh, smiling up at her. In one swift movement, she leapt off her horse and rushed to the viatari, tackling her into an embrace. The human wanderer's shoulders trembled as she unleashed all of her pent-up feelings with one breath, "You're alive! You're safe. I can't believe—I can't tell you how sorry I am for my failure. I know it's not enough to just apologize but—"

Her words were cut short as Victria wrapped her own arms around Tera. A gentle smile marked her features. Her eyes were soft as she said, "I never blamed you. Not once. What happened in those mountains wasn't your fault."

An unfamiliar whimper came from the human wanderer as she buried her head into the viatari's shoulder.

Felix smiled warmly at the scene before him before responding to Salevari. "We need not measure which news is better. Good news is good news. I am happy to see you again, sister." His eyes moved past her, taking in the two new faces standing only a few feet away. They both regarded him with interest, yet they couldn't have been more different. One was a bulking figure of a man, with a bristled mustache that hung heavily on his lips. The other was as dark as the night sky, well built, and clearly not afraid to show off his physique as he wore a linen shirt cut down the middle that exposed his chest.

Salevari pointed to each of them. "This is Hadreen, Boss of Donsea, and this is Fradrick, Grand Admiral of Halding Port. They have both pledged their support to our cause."

Hadreen stepped forward, his calculating eyes studying the two viatari before him as if he could see straight through them. A crooked smile broke out.

"It be a pleasah meetin' da two of ya. Salevari done impressed me wit' her resilience. If da rest of ya be like her, we be alright. Donsea be honored to join dis fight."

He took both of their hands, gripping them firmly before stepping back. As Victria rejoined them after having extracted Tera from her shoulder and sending her on her way, Fradrick came forward.

The large man cleared his throat, taking Victria's hand and planting a scratchy kiss on it. "I must say, beauty must be a common trait among the viatari. Your eyes are enchanting, my lady." He glanced at Felix. "You're a lucky man to be marrying this one."

Victria blushed but did not pull her hand away. Felix smiled, though the humor behind it did not reach his eyes.

Releasing her hand, the Grand Admiral moved to shake Felix's. "As the lady said, the name's Fradrick. I lead Halding Port. I've come to appreciate the talents your people offer. Your sister has proven a valuable asset for me city and I look forward to repaying the favor."

Felix raised an eyebrow. "Even if it means fighting with the vashi?"

Fradrick's face darkened, but only slightly. "According to Salevari, the foe we'll be fighting, these darinsha, will be a far greater enemy to contend with if we leave this matter to itself. I've come to trust her word."

The elder viatari nodded, accepting the answer. "I thank you both for coming so far from your homes. We welcome your strength. My sister wrote, telling me that part of our deal for your aid was giving you dwarven cannons for your city, installing them into your fleet and defensive walls, is that true?"

The Grand Admiral nodded. "Aye. If they work half as well as Salevari boasts, then they'll be a boon to us. Halding Port's defenses have already shown their inferiority once, I wish not to repeat that mistake."

"And you, Hadreen, does Donsea have a need to incurporate cannons into your town's defenses."

The Donsea Boss shook his head, picking at his teeth. "We not be needin' such tings. We can protect ourselves our own way."

"Well, you are in luck then, Grand Admiral," Felix said. "I hear the dwarven king, Dunkell, will be arriving here within the week."

"That's good news indeed," Fradrick boomed. "I look forward to meeting him and seeing this dwarven technology in action."

"Yes," Felix said. "I have a feeling you two will get along quite well. Now, if you will excuse us, we have a great many things to take care of for the coming days."

Just as Felix had promised, within the week King Dunkell, Gruk-Gruk, the High Chieftain of the burrowers, and a large retinue of their combined peoples approached Aleganthia from the east with a great amount of fanfare. A long wagon train followed their rams into the city, each one laden with stacks upon stacks of barrels that could only contain the dwarves' favored drink. It wasn't long before the dwarven king could be seen in the company of the Grand Admiral, both leaders talking animatedly with their hands, discussing their new partnership.

A few days before the wedding was to take place, another slew of guests entered the city, this time comprising of vashi. At their head was their young Supreme Overseer, Avmoshir. Felix and Victria met him at the southern gate, Victria happily taking the young vashi into her arms.

Surprised, Avmoshir returned the embrace. "I am happy to see you alive and well," he said. "I feared for you when I was told the news."

Victria pulled away, a bright smile on her face. "It's good to see you again, Avmoshir."

"I must say," Felix stepped to the side as the other vashi passed by to enter the city. "I am surprised to see you here yourself. I did not think you would be able to make a personal appearance."

The young vashi shrugged. "The threat of invasion still looms within our waters, but it has been allayed. It does not feel so imminent anymore. I suspect Salevari's success with The Turned One's plot in Halding Port has something to do with it."

"Will your people accept the aid of the humans in this coming fight?" Victria asked. "I heard you made a pact with their Grand Admiral after your people saved their city."

Avmoshir groaned, raising his eyes to the sky. "I only just told the Assembly about that and the reason for it. Now, the matter is being discussed in committee. Who knows how long that will take. If we're lucky, it'll only takes weeks to have this alliance made official—or it could take months. But the Assembly knows I want this matter passed. I have advisors and representatives on my side who will help me get it done. So, despite the political theater I'm going to have to endure, when the time comes, I know we'll fight for our waters together. It's our only hope if we wish to survive as a people. What comes after . . . only time will tell."

"Who knows," Felix shrugged, leading Avmoshir along so that they could all enter Aleganthia together. "Perhaps fighting together will draw your two peoples closer."

"One can hope."

Finally, the day for the ceremony arrived.

The streets of Aleganthia were packed, starting from the city's main plaza and reaching all the way to the surrounding walls. Many spectators took to the walls themselves to have a better chance at viewing the spectacle. Some even climbed buildings, perching on roofs throughout the city to do the same.

The sun shone brightly overhead in a spectacularly clear, blue sky. A cool breeze came down from the mountains, winding its way through the crowd and bringing with it a comforting relief. A buzz of excitement filled the air as the whole city held its breath.

Everyone wore their best. The dwarves' armor was well polished, gleaming in the sun's light. Humans from the plains were laden with heavy fur coats and fine leathers, while their cousins from the coast wore leather jackets over pristine uniforms. Even those from Donsea kept their exposed skin to a minimum. The vashi wore a varied combination of coral and scale armor, with soft fabrics of seaweed cloth covering the gaps in between. The burrowers too, known for wearing only loincloths, now covered much of their bodies with a vibrant set of orange leathers.

Felix came out of Aleganthia's keep, taking his place at the top of the stone steps leading up to it. He wore a green tunic inlaid with a variety of intricate shapes and images made in white thread with black trousers on underneath. His eyes scanned the crowd as he stood there expectantly, his hands folded in front of him.

Coming out behind him was Salevari and Serania, both wearing simple red dresses made of silk. They stood to Felix's side a step below him, their own eyes scanning the crowd.

As if on cue, music began to play from a small group of musicians who had taken their place to the side of the keep's stone steps. It was a soft tune they played. The notes from their woodwind instruments were taken by the wind and scattered across the city for all to hear.

The crowd within the plaza parted down the center, creating a path that led to the keep's steps, that led to Felix. And on the other end of that path stood Victria in a flowing white dress made of satin. Lace wrapped around her arms, running from her elbows to the gloves she wore. Sky-blue drapes of silk fell from her hips, dragging behind her on the cobblestones even as a pair of dwarves jumped out from the crowd to try and keep the delicate fabrics from getting dirty by holding the edges out. On her head, sitting atop a tightly woven bun of silver hair, sat a delicate tiara that sparkled brilliantly. Given to her as a gift by King Dunkell, at its centerpiece was a small cluster of Ernen diamonds which glowed a fiery yellow as the sun's rays hit it.

Flanking her were Tessa and Madira, both in green silk dresses with a single cut along one side that reached up to their thigh. They each held a bouquet of red and white flowers before them as they slowly followed their friend, step by step, through the makeshift path.

Many in the crowd caught their breath as Victria passed, the radiance from her vestments overwhelming, but nothing was as radiant as the smile that adorned her face or the excitement that burned in her red eyes, as if a living fire was lit behind them.

Though a crowd of thousands surrounded them, watching their every move, Victria's gaze stayed locked onto the elder viatari. He gazed back, his mouth hanging open slightly as he took in her beauty. The disbelief on his face was apparent for all to see.

For a brief instant, as Victria passed the second to last row of guests, her eyes shifted to the side and she caught sight of Thuradin, who beamed back at her. He nodded encouragement. She winked his way before turning back to Felix and slowly climbing the stone steps that led to her future.

Once she was level with him, they turned to face each other and the music stopped. From the crowd of dwarves, King Dunkell stepped forward, placing himself between them, facing the crowd. His voice boomed through the open area as he addressed everyone present.

"I, King Dunkell of the Dwarven Kingdom, will preside over this ceremony. By my authority as King, I shall wed this couple we see before us today. Will the ring bearer please come forth?"

Thuradin stepped out from the crowd, carrying a small, plump cushion with two small rings placed atop it. Both were golden bands, one with a ruby inlaid in the center and the other with an emerald. The dwarf huffed nervously as he made his way up the stone steps, careful not to slip and accidentally spill the precious trinkets he held.

As he reached the second to last step, he knelt and raised the cushion high over his head, presenting the two rings to the viatari.

"Felix, Victria," Dunkell's voice rang out. "Take the rings and present them ta each other."

The viatari did just that, Felix taking the band with the ruby and sliding it onto Victria's finger, while Victria did the same with the emerald. Once their rings were in place, Salevari presented a golden goblet to Dunkell, who took it and raised it over his head.

"Take this goblet," he said. "And each of ye drink from it. This wine represents yer mutual agreement ta love each other, hold each other, and support each other throughout the ages."

Felix took the goblet and drank first, then passed it to Victria. Their eyes never left each other as they went through each motion. Their smiles never faltered.

With a sign from Dunkell, they stepped closer to each other, placing a hand over the heart of the other.

"Now, if ye will," the dwarven king instructed. "State yer vows."

"I, Felix, will love you forever, Victria. You are the fire that burns in my soul. You are the tree under whose shade I can rest forever. For as long as I live, I will keep you safe and never apart from me. Let our hearts be one."

Sighs came from the crowd as Felix fell silent. A few guests dabbed at their eyes. Fradrick blew his nose loudly into a white cloth. A moment was given for the crowd to settle back down, then Victria spoke.

"I, Victria, will love you forever, Felix. You are my home, my shield. You give me peace and laughter and light. Your face is all I wish to see every morning when I wake up and every night before I close my eyes. For as long as we live, our hearts will be as one."

A broad smile cracked through Dunkell's face as he happily exclaimed, "Felix, ye may now kiss yer bride, and may this kiss seal the lifelong pact the two of ye have made."

The crowd roared its approval as Felix and Victria came together, their arms holding each other close as their lips met. Thuradin took his place back among the crowd and couldn't help but join in with the raucous cheering. The two viatari remained as they were for a long time, leading the crowd to cheer even louder with every second that passed.

Finally, they parted, their eyes staring deep into each other. Victria laughed as she turned to the crowd and waved. The chorus of voices intensified. Dunkell stepped forward and raised his hands, eventually achieving silence.

The crowd watched the dwarven king eagerly as he cleared his throat.

"With the ceremony now complete, I declare that the festivities begin. Let us feast!"

Another roar of approval.

Workers poured out of the keep, bringing out long tables piled high with cooked foods for all to enjoy. The city's livestock caretakers released their charges, letting rabbits, squirrels, deer, and many other wildlife roam freely for the viatari to consume as they desired. Long lines formed for wine and beer.

A few guests sipped from their own secret staches. The small band resumed playing their instruments and the mood grew festive.

A circle formed within the center of the plaza where everybody danced. Hours passed and the intensity of the festivities never lessened, even as the sun kissed the horizon, producing long, dark shadows.

The feast continued into the night. Torches and braziers were lit. Music bounced off the stone walls for all to enjoy.

Thuradin couldn't tell if it was the ale or the jubilant atmosphere, but he laughed and danced with abandon, pulling first Myrna out with him, then Lyrie. The three dwarves jumped around in a close circle, feeling the music move their limbs, their tankards spilling as they went.

As they danced, Thuradin's eyes wandered, taking in the merriment surrounding them. Many dwarves lay against the side of buildings, their love of ale finally catching up to them. Burrowers danced with vashi without any sense of rhythm. Humans and viatari formed a circle and jumped together, spinning from one end to the other. A few couples danced by themselves, spinning around the open plaza as if they'd been doing it their whole lives.

And in the center of all this swayed Victria and Felix. Her head lay against his chest, eyes half-closed. Felix held her tightly. As the music swelled, they looked into each other again. Victria lifted herself onto her toes, joining her lips to his, stealing the moment away as if no one was watching.

Thuradin turned away, warmth seeping through his body all the way down to his toes. He left the frenzy of movement in Aleganthia's plaza for a moment to refill his empty tankard. Standing in line, he sighed happily. Just for tonight, everything felt right with the world.

Thank you for reading this book, dear reader! As an indie author, I appreciate each and every one of you for supporting me. The best way to support an indie author, aside from buying and reading their book, is by leaving a review on Amazon and/or Goodreads! If you liked this book, I would appreciate it so much if you took the time to do so. Thanks!

WAR RAGES. . .

With Daniel Fansler's fifth book in the Chronicles of the First Gods, *The Purity Scepter*. . .

THE PURITY SCEPTER

Dawn's soft light gently illuminated the six warships out at sea. Their sails were unfurled, catching the early morning wind and sending them bobbing up and down in regular intervals as they glided over the constantly forming waves. Sea spray burst into the air as each ship sped its way westward.

Four of these frigates, middle-class ships from Halding Port, formed a staggered diamond formation while the two remaining smaller-class corvettes acted as both a vanguard and rearguard.

Aboard the flagship of this small fleet group, *The Justice*, Captain Arlan leaned against the portside railing and watched the distant shoreline. A thin blanket of mist rolled over and through the jagged mountains in the distance, spilling out into the sea where it eventually dissipated. He inhaled deeply, enjoying the salty tinge in the air. No storms nearby, as far as he could tell, and he should know. He'd been a sailor all his life.

Turning his gaze toward his own ship, he observed his

crew going about their daily routines. Sailors crawled up and down the ships various ratlines, performing maintenance work on the rigging or checking for any small tears along the length of the ships many sails. Captain Arlan nodded his approval. Every man here knew their job and knew how to do it well. Which was why his gaze inevitably followed the newer crewmembers he had onboard. Hands unlike any he had ever had.

The tallest one among them, he remembered, was called Vandaar Lumeward. He might have looked at home among his regular crew, with his vigilant gaze and confident air—that of an experienced fighter—were it not for his striking red eyes and silver hair—marks that he was not like the rest of the human crew onboard. He was viatari.

As Captain Arlan understood it, the viatari were a race somewhere far north from Halding Port. They were extraordinarily strong and fast and could, if they so desired, bend the light around them to change their form and disguise themselves as humans. In times past, the humans of the plains had pursued a centuries-long war of fear and hatred against them, and the viatari had fought back. But those old feuds were now a thing of the past.

Being born and raised along the coast, and thus never having interacted with a viatari before being put on his current assignment, Captain Arlan wasn't particularly prejudiced against them—nor were most humans of Halding Port, for that matter. Still, watching Vandaar speak with his smaller companions, he couldn't help but feel unnerved by the knowledge that this was a being completely different from what he was used to dealing with.

His eyes fell to Vandaar's companions, several of whom were half the viatari's height. Dwarves. The primary reason why these new, strange peoples were on his ship.

Captain Arlan wasn't into politics and didn't keep up with the goings-on of Halding Port's elite class. He was a simple sailor. His focus was primarily for the ships in his command and their crews. But even he knew about the new alliance Halding Port had forged with the viatari, and by extension, the dwarves, and recognized what such a treaty meant. He and his men were now involved in some war against evil—at least, that's how the Grand Admiral had put it when he had announced their new allegiance to these foreign peoples. And with that war, new weapons were brought along and installed first all along Halding Port's massive wall and towers, and then to her fleet.

Ships that once made do with the primitive ballistae now boasted an incredible boost in firepower with the dwarven cannon, a weapon Captain Arlan was eager to put to the test against a real enemy.

Of course, he had already seen the potential of this explosive weapon, having watched the dwarves demonstrate its effectiveness and then his crew practice loading, firing, then reloading it right after. And training continued on a daily basis, under the watchful eyes of the dwarves onboard who, for being dwellers of the mountains, had adapted quite well to a seafaring life.

Following the railing toward the bow of the ship, Captain Arlan stopped in his tracks as a humanoid figure climbed over the railing and landed in front of him. One of his men noticed the scaled being as well and stepped back in alarm.

"Vashi onboard!"

Captain Arlan eyed the vashi, the fish-man meeting his eyes with an equal amount of distaste. Not too long ago, the Captain wouldn't have hesitated to kill this vashi, but, he reminded himself, many things had changed. Along with their new alliance with the viatari, Halding Port was now obligated to protect the entirety of the Southern Seas *with* the vashi, a race that had been their mortal enemy for the past few centuries. In fact, that was the entire reason why he and his fleet group were now here, so far from Halding Port's normal maritime borders.

"Anything to report?" the Captain asked briskly as he resumed making his way toward the ship's bow. The vashi quickly fell into step.

"We are approaching the area we ssspoke of," the vashi replied, his sharp tongue and teeth creating a slight impediment as he spoke the common human tongue. "My ssscouts dare not give away our position by getting too clossse, but we can feel the water churning along the strait. There isss definitely sssomething happening there."

Captain Arlan nodded his understanding. His fleet group had been assigned to scout the straits to the far west, which connected the Northern Seas to their own. As much as his people hated the vashi, rumor had it that the Southern Seas were under threat of invasion by a race even worse than them, the darinsha, hence this newfound partnership.

Reports had come in a few weeks ago of unusual activity within the Passing Straits. Sightings of strange creatures. Distant and isolated towns along the strait suddenly going silent, despite their usual activity along the trade routes. It was enough to raise alarm among the vashi and Halding Port.

And so here he was to determine whether these rumors had any merit, or if it was another ghost they were chasing.

Reaching the bow of the ship, Captain Arlan took out his spyglass and looked toward the horizon, where the mass of mountains and high cliffs to his right abruptly ended. They were approaching the Passing Straits, but there was still too much mist and distance between them to make anything out with the naked eye.

Even with his spyglass, the Captain had a hard time distinguishing shapes, but shapes and figures he could see. And plenty of them. This was certainly unusual, and perhaps merited a more cautious approach.

"Private!" he barked.

A scrawny sailor dropped what he was doing near the main mast and quickly made his way to the Captain, saluting once he was by his side.

"Captain, sir!"

Arlan spared him a glance. "Signal the other ships. Approach Straits with wide berth. One thousand yards. Straight line formation. Have cannons at the ready."

The sailor saluted again and left to do the Captain's bidding. Moments later, large and variously colored banners began making their way up the flag halyard, loosely connected between the foremast and the bowsprit. The breeze caught the long banners, stretching the halyard outward so each color could be seen plainly by both the ships in front and those behind.

Movement could be seen coming from the ships in front of the formation as their crews scurried to send a reply. Once acknowledgement was received, each ship changed course a few dozen degrees starboard to make their wide approach on the straights. The staggered diamond formation, smoothed out into a single line, with *The Justice* in the middle. Captain Arlan kept his magnified eye on the Passing Straits the entire time, wishing the breeze would do something about the prevailing mist.

He got his wish just as his fleet group reached a position nearly perpendicular to the Straits. The mist cleared with a sudden urgency and Captain Arlan felt the blood drain from him.

One thousand yards ahead, the water churned with movement. Thousands upon thousands of serpent-like humanoids, clad in shining scale armor and bearing a multitude of harpoons, spears, and tridents, made their way through the shallow Straits toward the Southern Seas. Interspersed between the columns of deadly darinsha were several enormous crabs, each one the size of a small house. These slow-moving creatures were laden with supplies; racks of additional weaponry, foodstuffs, and a metallic building material which the Captain suspected might be used to construct some sort of siege engine.

He shook his head. There was a lot to see here, but what each individual thing was didn't matter. The fact was the darinsha had begun their invasion of the Southern Seas, and he was right in the middle of their crossing. And if he could see them, now that the mist was almost completely cleared as the bright sun broke through its shield with its rays, then they could see his ships.

"Any chance we can outrun them?" he asked the vashi, passing him the spyglass.

The vashi took a moment to observe what was before them, a soft hiss escaping his lips. "I do not believe ssso. The darinsha will have sssmall transport shipsss of their own, capable of traveling quickly underwater with the power of their waterseersss. They will ussse thessse to board your shipsss and defeat you. If they don't sssimply sssink you altogether."

The Captain grunted. "Then we need a distraction, while

a small part of the crew makes their escape on a smaller vessel. I will need you and your vashi to speed them on their way. Word must reach our peoples of this danger. We cannot be caught off-guard with such a dangerous force on our doorstep." He turned back to his crew and ordered for the dinghies to be prepared.

"Our task isss to protect your shipsss from any forcesss attacking beneath the wavesss," the vashi countered.

But the Captain was already shaking his head. "You've seen what we're up against. Your vashi will serve no purpose here except to tint the water red. Guide our survivors to Donsea. They'll be the nearest town that can do anything about this information. Then, make your way back to Zessarix. I'm sure your Supreme Overseer will need every warrior he can get his hands on before long."

"What of your men?"

After a brief hesitation, the Captain said, "Most won't get away. When the fighting reaches the deck, I'll order for everyone to abandon ship. Some of the dinghies will make it back, some will be destroyed by the enemy. Their fates will be their own after that. But you and your people must ensure that at least one of the dinghies makes it."

The vashi regarded the human with a begrudging respect and nodded. "There is no coming back from this course of action."

Now it was Captain Arlan's turn to nod. "It is often said that the sea is a treacherous maiden. Yet, we sailors brave her waters day in and day out because it is what we were born to do. Sometimes we die in her waves. It's part of the job." He turned toward the vashi and held out his hand, which the vashi took. "Today is that day for us. We will hold them back for as long as we can. Just make sure we aren't doing it for nothing."

A frenzy took hold of the crew as orders were passed down to prepare for battle. A new pattern of colorful flags were raised, relaying the same orders to the other nearby ships. In the distance, the darinsha continued crossing the Strait with a steady pace. If they saw the small fleet group from Halding Port ahead of them, they made no indication that they did.

Back at the helm, Captain Arlan was approached by his First Mate.

"The men are ready, sir."

Captain Arlan nodded and turned back to face the enemy. He would see their destruction first hand.

"Time to ring in the first shots of this war, then." He muttered. He gave the order, the sailors near him looking out toward the enemy in anticipation of the destruction they might see.

There was a chorus of yelling below deck, then the first explosion of cannon fire, followed by fifteen more guns sounding off. Then the other ships joined, a cacophony of deadly noise as each ship rocked from the recoil.

From his peripherals, flashes of fire could be seen shooting out of each ship's gunports, followed by a gush of smoke that drifted lazily with the breeze. The scent of *dynath* was heavy in the air. The Captain breathed it in deeply as he observed the effect of the first volley.

The waters around the darinsha erupted into chaos. Warriors were tossed into the air as cannonballs ripped through them, creating huge walls of water wherever they hit. A few rounds managed to find the giant crabs, obliterating the poor creatures and scattering the supplies they had been carrying into the wind. Seeing their vital supplies being lost, several darinsha went to work trying to coax the remaining supply crabs out of the open water or to bury themselves into the sand until the threat was gone. The waters churned violently as a majority of the invading host began rushing across the Strait in a frenzy to meet the small fleet group attacking them.

It looked as if someone had stepped on an ant bed, the Captain thought, as another volley of explosive fire rang out around him tearing new holes into the darinsha columns. He breathed in again, exhilarated. He felt it was a great pity that this would be the only time he would be able to bear witness to such raw power. But, shaking the morose thought aside, if the rest of Halding Port's ships were as equipped as his own, they would certainly cause many problems for these darinsha, and that was a comforting thought.

As a third volley burst forth, Captain Arlan noticed a strange surge-like movement beneath the waves. If he didn't know any better, he would have thought that a pod of large whales were making their way toward his ships. But whales never swam in such straight lines like these. These, then, must be the small boarding ships the vashi had told him about.

The ship to his right shuddered violently as the shadows just under the water rammed into its hull, where they stayed as if lodged in. His own ship shuddered upon impact. Even so, the devastating sound of cannon fire continued down the line.

"Swords!" Captain Arlan ordered. The sound of metal sliding out of their protective sheaths rang through the air as the crew around him waited eagerly for the fight to come to them.

The first darinsha climbed over the railing with a

challenging hiss, her serpentine face sharp with hostility. They were certainly ugly creatures, the Captain thought, as two of his crewmen charged forward to fight off the intruder.

While the top half of the darinsha resembled a more humanoid shape, her bottom half was more snake-like, morphing from the waist down into one long, thick tail. Using this tail, which she had coiled up beneath her, she launched herself at the two sailors, ripping through the chainmail of one with her trident easily. The sailor sputtered briefly in disbelief before going limp. His companion yelled with renewed fury and swung his cutlass but the darinsha caught the blow with one of the numerous bony spikes protruding from her back, deflecting the blade away. Ripping out her trident, she swung it over her head expertly, bringing the butt of the weapon around with a sharp crack to the side of the other sailor's head, rendering him instantly unconscious.

All of this happened within a minute as more darinsha climbed over the railing of *The Justice*.

Despite the impressive display of arms, the remaining crew of *The Justice* did not hesitate to join the fray and try to push the enemy overboard. Captain Arlan, too, joined the fight, swinging his razor-sharp rapier in dazzling arcs that cut its way through his foe's defenses, despite the darinsha's superior strength.

As he cut through his third opponent, he reeled back, nursing a shallow cut he had received on his shoulder close to his neck. He shrugged off the sailor who ran to his aid, directing him back to the fight while taking a moment himself to observe his surroundings.

There was no question in his mind that the darinsha were winning this battle. He had known they would. This small fleet group had no chance at stopping such a massive invasion by itself. Several of his crew lay dead, scattered across the deck. Those who remained fought desperately, even as more darinsha climbed onboard. Looking out to sea, Captain Arlan saw that two of his ships were already aflame, their crews dead or abandoning ship. It was time for the crew of *The Justice* to do the same, if he wanted anyone to have a chance at escaping to spread news of the darinsha's movements.

"Lower the dinghies!" Captain Arlan yelled, pointing to a group of five sailors who hadn't joined the battle yet. "Abandon ship!"

He stumbled backwards as someone ran into him. He held his rapier out in front of him, ready to block any incoming attacks but then realized it was only the viatari named Vandaar and a dwarf standing before him, both with their weapons out and bloodied. The viatari regarded him curiously.

"You are abandoning the battle?"

The Captain grunted. "There was never any hope of winning it in the first place. We who remain will hold them off while some escape to spread word of this invasion. I want you to be one of them, viatari. Get on a dinghy and the vashi should get you away from this battle and back to Donsea in a hurry. That's an order."

Fighting continued to rage around them as the viatari considered the Captain's words. Finally he nodded, laying a hand on his dwarven companion's shoulder. "Come, Murad, let us make our escape." They turned to leave, but had only gone a few paces before the viatari turned back. "What of yourself, captain?"

Captain Arlan grinned, his eyes set with determination.

"A captain goes down with his ship, viatari. But I'll be taking as many of these bastards off your tail as I can in the meantime. Now, get going!"

Vandaar nodded his understanding and, after a few words of farewell in his own language, finally turned and made his way to the dinghies being lowered on the starboard side of the ship.

A few moments passed where Captain Arlan stood where he was, taking it all in. Half of his men had disengaged to make their escape while the other half stayed in the fight, holding back the darinsha as best they could, but he knew they wouldn't last long. Within a few minutes, the dinghies were loaded up with as many sailors as could fit and were lowered down to the meet the waves. With that accomplished, Captain Arlan turned his focus back to the task at hand.

It was a given that his ship would go down—he would never let it fall into enemy hands. And he had a plan to make this happen. He just needed to make sure he could lure as many darinsha as he could on board before pulling it off.

The last of his crew fell limply onto the deck, now sticky and red with blood and all serpentine eyes turned toward Captain Arlan. He held his rapier aloft as he challenged the enemy.

"Chase me, if you dare."

And with that he ran. He bolted through a hatch and took the stairs three at a time down below deck, a chorus of jeering hisses following his every step.

As he continued down the stairs, he grabbed an oil lamp that was sitting by the wall, grateful that whoever had used it last had neglected to put out the flame before putting it down. He ran with it ahead as his feet finally hit the thick planks of the lower hold.

Thunks could be heard coming behind him as the darinsha awkwardly made their own way down the stairs. There wasn't much time for him to do what he intended, but thankfully, not much thought or effort would be required to pull off this plan.

He ran for the magazine room, bursting through the door and closing it behind him. He stomped toward the nearest barrel full of dwarven dynath and tore open its lid. The explosive black rock glistened under the light of the small flame in his hand and he hesitated. He could not help but reflect briefly on all the choices of his life that had led him to this very moment.

The door crashed open behind him and three darinsha poured into the small room, their weapons thrusting forward. Captain Arlan turned quickly and managed to parry the tip of one spear, but the other two blades found their mark and he coughed up blood as the darinsha tore through his light armor, flesh, and bone. His body shuddered as the pain quickly numbed.

With a great effort, he swiped his rapier in one final show of defiance, catching one of the darinsha across the face. The serpentine being hissed in fury and released the hold on her weapon. Before she could regain it and hold him in place, and with the last of his strength, Captain Arlan twisted himself around and smashed the lantern in his hand against the barrel of dynath.

Oil splashed along the barrel and floor and quickly ignited from the small flame the lantern had been containing. The darinsha, seeing what the Captain had done but not realizing what was stored in this room, took their time pulling out their blades from their vanquished foe.

Captain Arlan coughed and fell backwards against a separate stack of barrels. He looked at his looming foes with bleary eyes, his thoughts weak, his vision blurring. Four figures stood before him. But, he thought briefly, there had only been three vashi that had attacked him. He focused on the fourth figure and saw a beautiful maiden from years long forgotten with wavy black hair and piercing green eyes.

The Captain caught his breath, a shadow of a smile curving his lips even as blood trickled out of them.

"Diane," he mumbled. Then everything went dark.

About the Author

Daniel has known he's wanted to be a writer since he was thirteen. His debut novel, *The Lost King*, was written and the world and peoples of Azar born during his senior year in high school. He graduated from Stephen F. Austin State University with a BFA in Creative Writing, which helped him hone his writing into what it is today. He lives in Fort Worth with his wife and children.

www.ingramcontent.com/pod-product-compliance
Lightning Source LLC
LaVergne TN
LVHW100459110826
845146LV00002B/459